QUAKER AUTHOR

MY SHANGHAI, 1942–1946

My Shanghai, 1942–1946

A NOVEL

by

Keiko Itoh

RENAISSANCE BOOKS

MY SHANGHAI, 1942-1946
A NOVEL

First published 2016 by
RENNAISANCE BOOKS
PO Box 219
Folkestone
Kent CT20 2WP

Renaissance Books is an imprint of Global Books Ltd

Reprinted 2016

© Keiko Itoh 2016

978-1-898823-23-0 (Hardback)
978-1-898823-41-4 (e-Book)

British Library Cataloguing in Publication Data
A CIP catalogue entry for this book is available
from the British Library

Set in Adobe Garamond Pro 11.5 on 13 pt by Dataworks
Printed in England by CPI Antony Rowe, Chippenham, Wilts

*In memory of
my Mother and my Aunt*

Contents

Names of Main Characters

Family

EIKO KISHIMOTO, the diarist
HIROSHI (HIRO), her businessman husband
KAZUO (KAZU), their first son
TAKAO (TAKA), their second son
MIYO, their Japanese nurse
CHOKUGETSU-KEN AND AMAH, their Chinese cook and his wife

TAMIKO YAMANAKA, Eiko's older sister
ROKURO (ROKKI), Tamiko's banker husband
SACHI, their first daughter
ASAKO, their second daughter

HISAO KANDA (DADDY), Eiko's father
FATHER AND MOTHER KISHIMOTO, Hiroshi's parents in Japan

Friends and Acquaintances

IRMA CZESKA, a Jewish refugee
AGNES FLYNN, an Irish Quaker
KEITH AND JOYCE LEIGH, a British Quaker couple
WEN-TSU MAO, a Chinese businessman
MIDORI, WEN-TSU's third wife, a Japanese national
SHIN-TSU, WEN-TSU's son by his first wife
JIRO AND SAYAKO SEKINE, Rokuro's bank colleague and his wife
MASAYA SEKINE, Jiro's older brother
DAISUKE AND CHEEKO OTSUKA, Japanese businessman and his wife
AKIRA IKEMOTO, a Japanese YMCA lay missionary
KIMMY (KIMIYO) NOGUCHI, daughter of Kishimoto business acquaintances
S.P. CHEN AND MONA TONG, a Chinese academic and his wife

Historical Names

CHIANG KAI-SHEK, Leader of the Chinese Nationalist Party, the Kuomintang
WANG CHING-WEI, Leader of the pro-Japanese Nationalist Government in Nanking
LU HSUN, leading figure of modern Chinese literature
MR AND MRS UCHIYAMA, owners of the Uchiyama Bookshop
LI KORAN, Manchurian singer and actress

Brief Historical Timeline

September 1931	Japanese invasion of Manchuria
July 1937	Outbreak of the Sino-Japanese war
November 1938	Kristallnacht, ransacking of Jewish property throughout Germany
September 1939	German invasion of Poland. Outbreak of European War
September 1940	Signing of the Tripartite Pact between Germany, Italy and Japan
December 1941	Japanese bombing of Pearl Harbor. Outbreak of Pacific war
May 1945	German surrender
August 1945	Atomic bombs on Hiroshima and Nagasaki. Japanese surrender
1946	Resumption of the Chinese civil war between the Kuomintang and the Chinese Communist Party

Japanese Honorifics

A broad range of honorific suffixes is used in Japanese etiquette for addressing or referring to people, as follows:

san, the most commonplace honorific, a title of respect almost universally added to a person's name
sama, a more respectful version of *san*, used mainly to refer to people of higher rank than oneself
chan, a diminutive suffix, denoting a sense of endearment, most often used for children or persons close to oneself
kun, used by persons of senior status towards persons of junior status. Also a diminutive suffix used for boys
sensei, an honorific of respect used for teachers, doctors and other authority figures. (*hsien-sheng*, is the Chinese language version of *sensei*, used more broadly as 'Mr')

Dropping an honorific implies a high degree of intimacy and is generally reserved for one's spouse and children

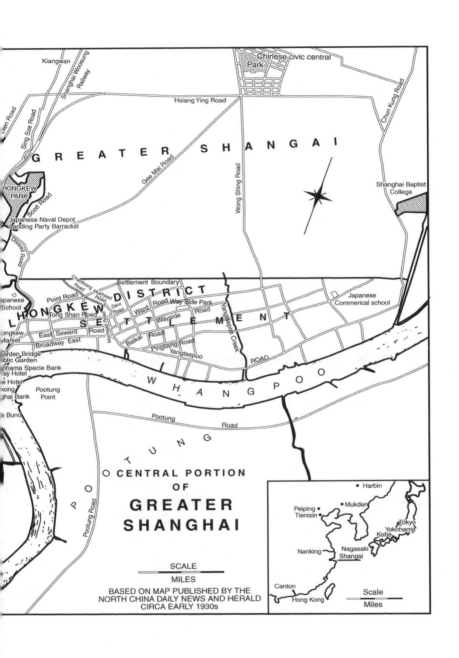

Kiangwan

Shanghai Woosung Railway

Kien Road

Sing Sze Road

HONGKEW PARK

Scott Road

Japanese Naval Depot (Landing Party Barracks)

Daxiba Road

GREATER SHANGHAI

Hsiang Ying Road

Gee Mai Road

Wong Shing Road

Chinese civic central Park

Chun Kung Road

Shanghai Baptist College

Chapoong Road

Muirhead Road

Settlement Boundary

DISTRICT

Point Road

Tong Shan Road

Dent Road

Ward Road

Road Way Side Park

Wayside Road

Japanese Commerical school

apanese School

HONGKEW

Muirhead Road

SE T T L E M E N T

ongkew Market

East Seward Road

Broadway East

Baikal Road

Pingliang Road

Yangtsepoo

Yangtsepoo Creek

ROAD

arden Bridge ublic Garden ohama Specie Bank ay Hotel kong ghai Bank

Point Road

Pootung Point

W H A N G P O O

e Bund

Pootung Road

Pootung Road

P O O T U N G

O CENTRAL PORTION
OF
GREATER
SHANGHAI

SCALE
_____
MILES

BASED ON MAP PUBLISHED BY THE
NORTH CHINA DAILY NEWS AND HERALD
CIRCA EARLY 1930s

Harbin

Peiping • Tienisin •

• Mukden

Tokyo Yokohama Kobe

Nanking

Nagasaki Shangai

Canton

Hong Kong

Scale
_____
Miles

Part I

1

Thursday, 15 January 1942, Cathay Hotel, Shanghai

Is this uncontainable sense of liberation improper? But how could I not bask in my good fortune to be in this luxurious hotel, far away from stifling Japan – a country engulfed in a sense of moral superiority ever since Pearl Harbor.

Shortly, I will be dressing up and applying make-up to my heart's content, in preparation for our second wedding anniversary dinner. It can't be like the sad send-off party for Hiroshi-sama's promotion and transfer to Shanghai, with little to eat and drink even though it was supposedly a celebration – austerity now a Japanese virtue, to feed the samurai spirit that will bring victory to Japan. No, I will be gliding into the grand Palace Hotel, just as I used to go to Claridge's in my London debutante days, and will be seated in the glittering dining room as if in a Hollywood film.

Was our wedding only two years ago? How desperate I was to appear the perfect bride, trying to suppress my jittery nerves and discomfort, clad in a heavy silk bridal kimono, head weighed down by the wig and head-dress – quite an ordeal for a Western-educated bride unaccustomed to traditional Japanese ways, moving from London to Japan to marry the heir of an Osaka merchant house!

If it hadn't been for the warm acceptance of Father and Mother Kishimoto, treating me with such respect as the bride of their precious first-born son, I would have been completely overwhelmed by my life change. I couldn't believe it when Father Kishimoto even cancelled a business meeting to attend Benji's birthday party – a tea party for his daughter-in-law's dog! Even so, it certainly felt like a marriage into the Kishimoto clan rather than to Hiroshi-sama himself. I must surely have spent more time with Mother Kishimoto than with my husband.

Here, it is just the two of us, living in this beautiful room with rose-coloured curtains and crystal lights, on the seventh floor of the Cathay Hotel, overlooking the Bund and the Whangpoo. Spread before me is a whole new world and lots of free time – a golden opportunity to keep a diary. I want to record my impressions and remember all that happens in the life ahead of me, and perhaps one day, when I'm an old woman, I will pick it up and recall my twenty-year old self. Or perhaps my grandchildren or great grandchildren will stumble upon it sometime. Oh the joy of scribbling in English!

I still feel the anticipation of approaching Shanghai. Everyone in Japan had said how wonderful it would be, to live in the Paris of the Orient now governed by the Japanese. The excitement mounted on the fourth morning at sea, noticing the water turn murky and sensing we were finally close to shore. But the muddy waters never seemed to end, until suddenly, the ship made a left turn, and spread before us was the Bund, with its imposing Western buildings lining the waterfront magnificently. It reminded me of London, and I felt quite a pang of nostalgia.

One foot on shore, however, threw me back to Asia. Not even the noisiest market in Osaka could have made half the sounds of the docks of Shanghai. The honking cars, bicycle bells, shouting pedlars, Sikh policemen's whistles – everything adding to the general cacophony. Even more overwhelming was the smell. I nearly gagged on the rotting fishy smells, mixed with exhaust fumes and sweat, but felt enticed by the waft of sizzling garlic and fried food. Such vibrancy of human activity – a vibrancy so different from dark, war-mongering Japan.

I know that Hiro (no longer Hiroshi-sama in this diary, in a spirit of liberation!) also feels happier and freer being here just from the way he prepares to go to work in the mornings – the extra care he takes in choosing his suits and ties, the spring in his walk.

My diary, I know, will be my friend with whom I can share also my heartaches – the two dark clouds hanging over me. How I miss my little Kazu, always by my side since his birth until now. I still wonder whether it really was the right decision to leave a fourteen-month-old baby behind in Kobe. But Mother Kishimoto was insistent that he was too sickly to travel, and she's probably right. And there is Daddy, under house arrest in London, in a state of limbo with no bank to manage. I can see him in my mind's eye, dressed in his three-piece suit, the gold chain of his pocket watch glimmering as he set off every morning to catch the Number 9 bus to the City. I can't imagine how dejected he must feel.

But even these pangs of sadness, once put on paper, seem bearable, at least during this particular evening of our wedding anniversary.

Saturday, 17 January

I certainly didn't expect a dinner invitation from a business acquaintance of Hiro's father to result in revisiting the circumstances of my marriage. But that's how it ended, this dinner at the Noguchi's home in the Japanese section of town. Pleased by having a social engagement so soon, I put on my tight-fitting charcoal grey suit and a pink silk blouse to make a good impression. Hiro said Mr Noguchi was head of one of the biggest cotton mills in Shanghai.

We set off early to explore the neighbourhood in daylight, and I enjoyed the stroll along the Bund, passing the Bank of China and then the Yokohama Specie Bank, Daddy's bank, as we headed towards Garden Bridge – its double camelback steel structure looking particularly picturesque against the clear blue winter sky. We had to show our papers to Japanese sentries before crossing the Bridge, which surprised me somewhat, but in a way it felt reassuring too, reminding me of passing London Bobbies on the street.

Across the Bridge on the Hongkew side, we picked up rickshaws and whizzed through 'Little Tokyo' and on to North Szechuan Road, the major shopping thoroughfare. Over the hunched head and shoulders of my trotting coolie, I saw Japanese shop after Japanese shop – the Morinaga Confectionery and other familiar names, inns and cafes and even a pawnshop. I hadn't realized that just across the Bridge existed a completely Japanese Shanghai, so different from where we are in the International Settlement.

After turning a couple of corners, we were on Dixwell Road, the Noguchi's street, which looked like suburban London, lined with three-storey Victorian brick terraced houses. My cheeks felt red from the cold air and the excitement of meeting new people.

The moment I met Mrs Noguchi, however, I felt ill at ease. A sharp-featured middle-aged lady with a superior air, she seemed to be assessing me throughout the evening. 'Tell us a little about yourselves. Have you been married long?' she asked, taking me aback with her forthright approach. Perhaps she decided I was young enough for her to be personal without overstepping social etiquette.

'As a young housewife, you're lucky to be here when life has become so convenient for Japanese,' she went on. 'When we first arrived, everything was focussed on catering for Westerners. Now, with over 100,000 Japanese living in Shanghai, you can get anything. Even the rarest Japanese fish is available, not to mention all the services, ranging from shiatsu massages to specialized bonsai gardeners.'

As I reflected on whether I might have found the old Western days more comfortable, their bright-eyed daughter, Kimiyo, about eighteen years old, suddenly piped up: 'Some Japanese think we are actually in Japan. I heard of a family who decided to replace their wooden floors with tatami mats, and had a huge row with their Chinese landlord!' Mr Noguchi, genial and relaxed, emitted a soft chuckle, but Mrs Noguchi gave her daughter a dismissive glance and steered the conversation back to where it was.

'I heard about your grand wedding in Osaka. Tell me, how did your marriage come about?'

Feeling blood rise to my cheeks, I muttered that we had met in London, when Hiro was at Cambridge. It was as if I was being formally interviewed, and I rattled on. 'Yoshihisa Kanda, my banker father, was an adviser to the Kishimoto Company and became

Hiroshi's guardian during his studies. When we met in 1934, Hiroshi was twenty-three, having graduated from university in Japan and spending one year on a tennis tour. I was thirteen at the time.' As I spoke, I worried whether I sounded formal enough to her.

'Oh, so it wasn't an arranged marriage then,' Mrs Noguchi said, rather disapprovingly.

Perhaps to prevent his wife from prying further, Mr Noguchi swiftly picked up on Hiro's tennis career.

'I remember your father mentioning you played at Wimbledon and on the Japan Davis Cup team,' he said. 'There are many tennis players within the community of Japanese trading firms and cotton mills, and they would certainly want to play with you.'

Mrs Noguchi continued to stare at me with a frown. I had probably shattered all her preconceptions, turning out to be, in her mind, a Westernized bride somehow managing to capture a promising tennis player from a prominent family.

Had she been more sympathetic, I would have told her how it really was. How Hiro's existence barely registered in my mind, only mildly curious that Mummy was so nice to him on his occasional visits to our London flat.

What a surprise when, four years later, after Mummy had died and my world had changed completely, a go-between contacted Daddy to say that the Kishimoto family wanted my hand for Hiro. They were willing to wait until I turned eighteen.

I will never forget the day Daddy broke the news to me – resting on a bench in Hyde Park during a walk with Benji. 'Eiko, you are approaching marriageable age, and I owe it to your mother to ensure a good match for you,' he said solemnly. 'Although our backgrounds are different, there is nothing we can fault with the Kishimoto family, they are affluent, and Hiroshi is known to us. This proposal gives me great pleasure and relief.' I remember his exact words because they were so unexpected.

Marriage hadn't entered my mind till then. There was never any doubt that I would marry whomsoever Daddy thought was appropriate, but Hiroshi Kishimoto, rather than a mysterious groom through an arranged marriage? It was flattering that Hiro was specifically asking for me as his bride, but still, my only impression of him was as a rather pampered rich, aloof man. Yes, he seemed very grown up to my thirteen-year old eyes. Even now, after two years of marriage, he still seems so much older and only marginally less aloof.

Mrs Noguchi wasn't to know this, and throughout the evening, I felt her critical glances. I doubt I'll be seeing any more of them, now that they have done their duty of entertaining their business acquaintance's son. I'm sorry it wasn't an evening that might have expanded my social circle. I was particularly interested in getting to know the daughter.

Sunday, 18 January

Hiro abandoned me and set off for a round of golf with work colleagues, leaving me to find ways to amuse myself. I couldn't help thinking, if only little Kazu were with me now, healthy and bubbling… And better still, if Tamiko hadn't accompanied her husband on his business trip to Nanking, we sisters could be getting together with our babies and having a jolly good time. I couldn't believe I'd been in Shanghai for over a week and hadn't yet managed to see Tamiko – my biggest reason for wanting to be here, to be close to her for the first time in eight years! Even though much older than me, it was always so much fun to be with her and how it felt like losing a soul-mate when I left for London with Mummy and Daddy! Not that going to London wasn't exciting. But being the baby of the family meant becoming suddenly an only child, separated from married Tamiko and our brothers at university.

After wallowing in my thoughts for a while, I decided to do something positive and went down to the Lobby to explore this grand hotel that is our temporary home.

'Sir Victor Sassoon build in 1929, best hotel in Far East,' said the elderly Chinese concierge when I approached the front desk.

'Madam speak beautiful English. Too bad you not here few years earlier. So many elegant people come through revolving doors, so many parties take place here! Movie stars, playwrights, business tycoons, anyone who anybody sooner or later come. Charlie Chaplin, Noel Coward both stay.'

He – Mr Hsu, according to his nametag – spoke in a voice belying British training but with charming Chinese intonations. Slight, and with thinning hair, he might have been any Chinese man on the street except for his exceptionally erect stature and impeccable grooming. I instantly took a liking to him.

'Sassoon House right behind, and here also Shanghai's best shopping arcade. Sir Victor live up in penthouse suite, view of all Shanghai. He give much lustre. When hotel first open, big sensation. Air condition, clean water pipe from Bubbling Well Spring, every room have mahogany wardrobe!'

I became dreamy imagining the early days of the hotel, until suddenly, Mr Hsu's tone changed and he said, 'Everything change when Japanese come.'

My body stiffened. Surely he knew that I was Japanese but that didn't stop him from telling me that once the Japanese took over the International Settlement, Sir Victor tidied up his business and went to Bombay. 'With no Sir Victor, light go out. Hotel not like before,' he said.

I didn't know how to react and cast my eyes down on the shining mahogany counter staring at the reflection from the chandelier above. Seemingly oblivious, Mr Hsu went on.

'Madam, if Sir Victor still here, he like you, I know. Sir Victor very debonair, dashing figure. Hurt in First World War, and now walk with two stick. Stick have silver handle. Very much ladies' man. Shame you no meet him!'

Was it just me, being overly sensitive about my nationality? How strange it is, to be in a city where presumably the Japanese are masters, and yet, why do I prickle with tension at the mention of 'Japanese'? Most likely, Mr Hsu was simply stating facts, making no judgments. He certainly seemed to warm to me, as I had to him.

Monday, 19 January

Having seen Hiro off to work, I ventured out for a walk, and the minute I stepped out of the tranquil lobby, I was struck by the bustle and noise. Lingering at the corner of the Bund and Nanking Road to get my bearings, I stood behind a couple of well-groomed Western gentlemen for protection. A coolie pulling his rickshaw nearly ran into a maimed beggar at the edge of the kerb, making me jump. Only after watching a blondish, middle-aged lady -dressed rather shabbily for a foreigner – rush along the pavement and over-take an elderly Chinese matron tottering on her unstable feet, did I feel courageous enough to start walking.

Immediately, I was approached by a couple of dirty street chil-dren, their thin, soiled arms reaching out at me. A shiver ran through my spine, and I'm ashamed to say, I turned around and fled back into the hotel.

In my mind's eye, the smudged faces of those children overlap with Kazu's delicate features, his big round eyes and sweet little mouth. Even in his weakened state from autotoxemia, his cheeks never sunk like those children. Where is my compassion? I want to feel for them, yet all I can think of is the filth and the germs and how I must do my best to protect Kazu from all of it once he gets here. Mother Kishimoto was wise, after all, to insist on keeping him in Japan until he is stronger.

Tuesday, 20 January

Finally, I managed to have a day with Tamiko. I don't know why she chose to live out in Hungjao. Despite being called the Western sub-urbs, it took a good hour trundling through field after field of rice paddies on a rickety open-top train, giving me the feeling that I was heading deep into the countryside. But the long journey allowed me time to remember how I looked up to my older sister when I was little, wanting to do everything like her – down to tucking a handkerchief in a cardigan sleeve, the ultimate of sophistication in my mind! My heart raced in anticipation as the train finally approached the station.

There she was, sticking out her scarf-clad head beyond the ticket barrier. She pulled me towards her the instant we were close enough, and welcomed me with a simple, familiar 'Hello', as if I was always part of her everyday life. I slipped my arm into hers as she led me home.

Their suburban red brick flat seemed modest compared to the Cathay Hotel, but I revelled in the homely atmosphere. 'Not as convenient as being in town, but Rokki has colleagues out here, and it suits us,' Tamiko said with a contented smile. I was amused that she referred to her husband as Rokki instead of Rokuro, making the brother-in-law I hardly know seem closer.

Seeing me stare at little Sachi banging her fists on the table as their amah tried to feed her, Tamiko immediately picked up on my longing for Kazu. 'Good thing Kazuo is being fortified in Japan before he encounters cousin Sachi!' she said. 'This one is quite a madam, and she'll certainly make the most of her six-month age advantage over him. And she is big for her age.' I laughed in spite of myself, looking forward to the day we could all be together.

We spent most of the day in the kitchen. 'Too bad you won't be staying for dinner after all the work I'm making you do!' she said, as I chopped garlic and ginger for the *ha-fun mu-du* dumplings. She skirted around me mixing sauces and spices, impressing me with her Chinese cookery skills she must have acquired in the seven months she's been here.

She was busy with the live crabs she would later steam, when she suddenly said, 'I'm so happy that Daddy remarried. What a comfort it must be to have a wife with him in these difficult times. Can you imagine how lonely he would have been otherwise, with you gone?'

'Hmmm,' I said, recalling the suddenness of the woman's appearance and how quickly Daddy ended up marrying her.

'I don't know why she came to London at a time when most Japanese families were leaving, just two months before Britain declared war on Germany. She came on the same boat that I then took back to Japan – as if she knew Daddy was soon to be on his own.' I said, with my eyes fixed on Tamiko's, willing her to agree with my disapproval.

'Eiko, perhaps you should refer to her by name and call her Sachiko. A rather nice name, as it happens to be the same *kanji* character as our Sachi's,' Tamiko said, with an amused smile.

'I know our naughty older brothers joked about her being a spy, sent by the Japanese military to change Daddy's pro-Western stance. But you know they were just being silly, and that she'd been working at the Japanese Embassy in London.'

I'd wished the spy story were true, even though she hardly looked like a military agent – a rather small, but voluptuous woman, with beautiful skin is what I saw the one time I met her at an Embassy party. But she had a hungry, aggressive look when she met Daddy.

'You're just imagining that from what happened afterwards,' Tamiko said. 'I've heard that she's attractive and stylish, and Daddy must have been impressed. If he's happy, that's all that matters, isn't it?'

Put like that, I couldn't argue, even if I could never bring myself to like the woman. Tamiko must have sensed my petulance.

'Just think, Eiko, maybe she was a spy, and despite all her efforts, Daddy's love quelled her military machinations!' Tamiko said, her eyes dancing mischievously. Imagining Daddy – balding with a loveable pug nose – as a romantic hero set me off immediately. The two of us laughed so much tears came rolling down our cheeks.

Being with Tamiko reminded me of why I had missed her so much. She has a way of lightening one's mood, while being sensitive to one's deepest concerns.

Friday, 23 January

The joy of hotel life is starting to wear off. When I look out onto the streets and see the mass of humanity – hawkers offering wares I wouldn't even want to touch let alone buy, rickshaw coolies fighting the ongoing traffic, beggars hunched in doorways – I feel guilty being dissatisfied in my luxurious surroundings. Yet, I can't help being a bit envious – all those people out there having something to do.

Perhaps it's the isolation that makes me feel this way. Having Tamiko in the same city is a great comfort, but it's not as if she's right next door, as Hiro's parents had been back in Japan. Even though uprooted from my London upbringing, I don't remember ever feeling lonely marrying into the Kishimoto family. Could it have been the sheer effort of trying to get accustomed to a different way of life?

Unlike the cosy father-daughter household in London, in Kobe, Hiro's relatives seemed to live in each other's pockets. So many new people to get to know, when I hardly yet knew my husband! But what a novelty it was, having a position within a family institution at the age of eighteen, being treated with due respect as bride of the heir.

Sitting alone now in the hotel room, I look back in wonder at those shopping days with Mother Kishimoto. There were elaborate lunches at relatives' homes, followed by merchants arriving to show their wares: one day it would be kimonos, another day jewellery, another day furniture; Mother, grandee within the clan and taste arbiter, selecting what should go into the marriage chests of the unmarried female Kishimoto cousins, always choosing the most exquisite for me.

With Kazu's birth, traffic between the Kishimoto main residence and ours became even heavier – people, food, gifts, going backwards and forwards constantly. No time for boredom or loneliness.

Perhaps my wistfulness will pass when we have a home. Hiro says we will start looking for permanent accommodation soon. I cannot wait – to potter about, rearranging furniture, making a cup of tea, checking up on little Kazu to see if he is awake from his nap…

Sunday, 25 January

Dinner at Tamiko and Rokki's today made me realize how unaware I've been of what's been happening in Shanghai.

It all started with Rokki and his bank colleague, Jiro Sekine, reminiscing over what happened on 8 December. 'It's amazing to think how normal everything seemed on the Friday before,'

Rokki said. He and Jiro had been at the Japanese Club looking over the Whangpoo and saw as usual the *Idzumo*, anchored on the Hongkew side, and a few British and American gunboats moored in the middle of the river.

Jiro, a man of small frame exuding an air of sincerity, nodded and recalled how calm the weekend had been too. 'What a shock to be awoken on Monday morning with sounds of explosions all over Shanghai,' he said, suddenly becoming animated.

'We hadn't heard the explosions out here in Hungjao, but I had a strange feeling that something wasn't right,' Rokki said. When he arrived at the Bund, Japanese armed soldiers were stationed at every intersection making it difficult for him to make it to the office. The way he described the scene, I could almost smell the gun-smoke and feel as if I were one of the panicked people on the streets in the drizzle. When Rokki finally arrived at the office, everyone was glued to the windows looking outside.

'We knew by then that Japan had attacked Pearl Harbor about four hours earlier, and that war had been declared on the US and Britain,' Jiro said. The explosions they had heard came from the *Idzumo* firing cannons at the British gunboat, the HMS *Peterel*.

Rokki frowned and said, 'The river scene wasn't pleasant.' He looked at me and Sayako, Jiro's wife, to check on our expressions before saying more. Sayako's calm composure seemed to have reassured him.

'There were still some fires on the water, and things bobbing on the surface – could well have been bodies,' he said.

Hiro and I listened in horror as we munched through the many courses of the Chinese dinner. Back in Japan, for all the talk and excitement over Pearl Harbor, it was something that occurred physically far away. I had no idea that the impact on Shanghai had been so real – the war brought close to home.

'With war declared, the Japanese military moved swiftly to take over the International Settlement,' Jiro said. The Navy requisitioned the Shanghai Club, famous for having the longest bar in the world, and the Army took over the British Country Club and Race Course.

Rokki grimaced and muttered, 'Rivalry between the Army and Navy even in what they confiscate.'

Tamiko had until then been busily ensuring that our plates were constantly filled, but suddenly looked up with a clouded expression. 'It's the changes that are yet to come that worry me most,' she said. Having been in Shanghai for nearly a year, she has a wide circle of friends, and it was their fate that she was talking about. Apparently, just last week the order came that all 'enemy nationals' have to register with the Japanese authorities.

What does it mean to have to register? I'd like to think that it's just a matter of giving one's name and address, but somehow, hearing what I have of the events of 8 December, I'm filled with unease. How naïve I'd been, to expect Shanghai to be the cosmopolitan metropolis of a bygone past. Even Daddy's fate – being an 'enemy national' in Britain – feels suddenly cast in shadow.

Tuesday, 27 January

And now I've just witnessed for myself Japan's actions. Walking down the Bund, I was looking up at Big Ching, the Big Ben replica above the Maritime Customs Building, and on to the huge white dome of the Hongkong and Shanghai Bank. Only when I stopped in front of the imposing bank entranceway did I notice the commotion – Chinese coolies, surrounded by Japanese soldiers, pulling ropes with all their might, while two Japanese military officers barked orders. Sweat was dripping down the coolies' faces, and some had bloody hands from the tight grip on the rope.

I couldn't believe it when I saw what the ropes were attached to: the magnificent pair of bronze lions, crouching between the bank's Corinthian columns. It seemed they were trying to remove the lions.

I must have been standing open-mouthed, for eventually, a Japanese soldier came to shoo me away. But I was too curious to obey immediately, and I timidly, but respectfully, asked what was going on. He seemed surprised to hear me speak Japanese, and his disapproving look swiftly disappeared. He puffed out his chest and said, 'You should be proud that these lions now belong to Japan and are going to contribute to our war effort! We're shipping them home, where they'll be melted down and made into weapons.'

I bowed quickly and made a hasty getaway from the scene. I didn't want him to see my look of dismay. His sudden change of attitude when he saw that I was Japanese was unsettling. If I were Chinese, I'm sure he would have continued with his intimidating manner. Besides, I couldn't believe Japan would be so desperately in need of the metal the lions would provide. Surely, it must be just a display of Japanese might.

Mr Hsu caught sight of me panting back into the hotel. 'Good afternoon, Madam. You have good, vigorous walk?'

His friendly face made me blurt out, 'Mr Hsu, the lions – the Hongkong and Shanghai Bank lions! They're being removed to become scrap metal!'

I noticed a quick astonished blink, but being the proper professional, Mr Hsu simply cocked his head and said, 'Madam, you been down Bund? Too many changes, difficult keep up.'

'Those lions, people rub feet bring good luck, and paws always gleaming shine,' he said with a smile, I think to cheer me up.

'Lions have another story, too,' he added, with a mischievous glance. 'They male lions, you see. They suppose to roar when virgin passes. But in Shanghai, no virgins, so lions always silent.'

It took me a while to understand, and then I burst out laughing. He certainly managed to distract me from the unease of witnessing Japanese insolence first hand.

Friday, 30 January

At breakfast this morning, as Hiro and I were about to be seated at our usual table in the dining room, a party of three Japanese Army officers was ushered in, causing us to remain standing until they passed by. I recognized the oldest officer as a regular in the breakfast room, and gave him a light bow. One of the younger officers, a man with close-cropped hair and a noticeably short thick neck, suddenly stopped, barely two feet from Hiro, and eyed him from head to toe. He then turned away, mouthing in a most contemptuous voice, 'Westernized dandy. Breakfasting with dolled up wife. It's people like them that make Japan weak and corrupt.'

I was stunned by the rudeness and arrogance, and could feel my cheeks flush. Apart from anger, I was hurt for Hiro, scion of the Kishimoto conglomerate, who would never have been spoken to in such a way. I could barely look up to see his expression. But Hiro acted as if he had not heard the man, respectfully lowering his head to the older officer – who was trying to hide his embarrassment – and sat down and picked up the menu. It was only when studying the menu that I sensed a flash of annoyance in Hiro's expression. But once the order was placed, it was as if nothing had happened.

Thinking back on it, I'm even more disturbed by the incident. Why should Japanese officers, staying at this luxurious hotel, be so contemptuous towards us! Daddy had military officer friends in London, and they were such gentlemen. I remember they talked of how Japan, being such a small island nation, needed more markets and access to resources, just like the Western countries that already had an overseas presence. How devastated Daddy was that the pursuit of that goal had ended in war! Once at war, though, I know his hope was for a quick end, and for Japan to act honourably and settle for a few gains. I want to hope and believe so, too – which is perhaps why the attitude of this morning's officer fills me with unease.

2

Tuesday, 3 February 1942

Kazuo set sail for Shanghai with nurse Miyo on Taiyo-Maru stop

I've read the cable from Hiro's father over and over, the words etched in my mind. I can hardly believe that Kazu will be with me in a few days' time.

But with the longing comes the anxiety. Just last week, there was news of increased US submarine activity in the East China Sea. Kazu is so small and delicate. What if something happens to the boat and he's thrown overboard into the deep cold sea? No, no, I must not think such things.

Wednesday, 4 February

Feeling too restless be remain on my own, I took the train to Tamiko's. With sisterly bossiness, she admonished me for fretting when I should be happy that Kazu was on his way. But her eyes were filled with tenderness and she launched straight in to telling me about her strict convent school days in Japan, so different from mine at the Glendower School in London where we spent most of our afternoons at nearby museums or in Hyde Park for games.

'Did I tell you about the "exemption" ritual at school? We had to receive our weekly behaviour cards from the Reverend Mother every Monday morning. The girls' names were called out to the whole school, with ratings of very good, good, fair, or, if one was really naughty, "no note". And we had to curtsey to Reverend Mother when receiving the card.'

Tamiko suddenly pulled me up with both hands. 'Like this,' she said, demonstrating a curtsey and making me do the same. We took turns, being Reverend Mother, acting sillier and sillier, until finally, Tamiko went too deep and collapsed on the floor. Little Sachi, watching from Amah's knee, squealed with delight, her arms and legs splaying in the air, while we were helpless with laughter. It was such spontaneous fun. But as I was leaving, Tamiko said she wanted to take me to meet her Quaker friends, Joyce and Keith Leigh, on Friday. And I realized she was thinking of ways to keep me occupied so as not to wallow in anxiety.

Thursday, 5 February

The day passed with no news of incidents in the waters between Kobe and Shanghai. One day less to worry …

Friday, 6 February

'What are Quakers like, Tamiko, teetotal, homely and very serious?' I asked, poking my elbow into her arm, as the tram headed to the French Concession. I noticed the neighbourhood had become more residential, the avenue lined with London plane trees, still leafless, making it easy to catch glimpses of elegant Western apartment buildings and solid chimneys on tiled rooftops.

She cast me a wicked glance and said, 'Of course. They're here to do good works and lead a very austere life. I'm taking you to meet them so you'll learn to behave.'

The Leighs' home was at the end of a row of neat two-storey brick terraces, and we were greeted by a couple in their late twenties, so thoroughly English – tall and solid, both with chestnut brown hair and an air of comforting reassurance. I felt immediately at home, and slightly ashamed of having been rude about Quakers.

Tea was laid out in the living room, a woolly tea cosy covering the pot. 'Our home is a Quaker gathering place. People from different nationalities come for study and discussion every week,' Keith said. Maybe it's not so bad, being a missionary, to arrive from England to this comfy abode, I thought, as I sunk deep into the soft sofa.

'Our first home, in the summer of 1940, was a children's orphanage,' Joyce said cheerfully. 'The Friends had just opened a home for children picked up by social workers, and we became the first live-in "mother" and "father". That was quite an experience, wasn't it Keith.'

'Indeed,' Keith said, with a soft laugh. 'Those damaged walls from the earlier battles in Shanghai, and that garage, which we called the "cleansing station" where the children were hosed after being dropped off by the police car!' Keith's blue eyes twinkled at the memory, but I was horrified by the thought of living in a run-down home filled with dirty children. I must have visibly flinched, because Tamiko flashed me her knowing sideways glance and a suppressed smile. She's always been dismissive of my fastidiousness.

Joyce quickly caught on to the sisterly exchange. 'We dressed the children in clean clothes, disinfecting and saving their old clothes for when they leave. Once the sores and skin troubles were treated, they became part of the family!' I noticed her flash a playful glance at Tamiko which made me smile in spite of my queasiness.

'We miss the children,' Keith said. 'Some were pretty feisty characters, but they looked after each other and one or two always pulled the group together, making it feel like a real family. Remarkable, considering the tough lives those kids had. Some were dismissed from factories being too weak from illness, and a good many spent time in juvenile prison. Shanghai has many "wild uncles", as they're called, modern Fagins who make a living by training waifs and strays in criminal practices.'

I was amazed how the Leighs could be so affectionate towards these children, who I would most likely try to avoid. Would I ever be able to see the humanity in those street children who cluster around me every time I step out on to the street, pestering people and begging?

And there's Kazu, living in a different privileged world, occupying my thoughts all the time. Meeting the Leighs hasn't lessened my concern over him, but I realize how caught up I have been in my narrow world.

On our way home, as we were walking by a well-established Jewish delicatessen on Avenue Joffre, Tamiko mentioned that the Leighs were now helping Jewish refugees who had poured into

Shanghai from Germany in 1939. I looked curiously into the delicatessen thinking it was run by those refugees.

'No, Eiko. These Jewish shops along here are run by Russian Jews who fled the Russian Revolution – much earlier arrivals and a different community from the German Jews,' Tamiko said, having read my mind. There's still so much to learn about Shanghai.

Saturday, 7 February

Hiro out playing tennis. He's doing what he has always done since we were married, and it shouldn't bother me; but it does. Couldn't he have stayed home this one time, while our son still has another day on the perilous waters? Hiro's acceptance of life as it comes is what makes him special. But still...

Something Tamiko said yesterday – that it was Rokki who wanted to contact the Quakers – made me think about their marriage. I hadn't known that Rokki was a Christian, let alone religious. 'Not a Christian, although he's interested, and not really religious,' she said, smiling.

'Rokki is torn by the war – he loves China and he is deeply saddened by the state of things now. When he learned that the Friends' Centre was created to bring together people of different nationalities to understand each other, he became very excited.'

I knew little of Rokki, only that he came down with some chronic illness shortly after marrying, and that Tamiko had a difficult time for many years. I'd never thought about their relationship, but obviously they discuss their deepest thoughts and understand each other. But then, I suppose they have been married nearly ten years now. Will Hiro and I come to share more as the years pass?

Sunday, 8 February

I can't help constantly peering into to Kazu's cot to make sure he is breathing. He is here, asleep beside me!

How long it seemed for the boat to make its final approach. Then the even longer wait while the queue of passengers disembarked. My eyes desperately searched for a woman with a baby, without a clue about the face I was looking for. In the meantime, the awaiting crowd pushed and shoved, and hawkers and loiterers fought for space. My heart thumped against my chest as I tiptoed to see over the heads.

Eventually, a grey-clad woman of indeterminate age appeared, pushing a pram, escorted by a steward. We spotted each other simultaneously, and after a quick exchange of bows, she efficiently picked up Kazu and placed him in my arms. The moment I so longed for!

Kazu looked bewildered and didn't seem to recognize me. But I was too overjoyed to care, wanting just to hold him tight against me. I gently rocked left and right, bending over him to take in the sweet scent of baby hair. I must have tickled him, for he wriggled and looked up, and broke into a most beautiful smile. He remembered me after all!

Looking over to Hiro, and back to me, he made gurgling sounds as if talking to us. I wanted to bottle my happiness and save it forever. Yes, keeping him in Japan until his bout of autotoxemia disappeared had been the right thing to do.

I look at his angelic sleeping face, and pray to God that he will thrive here. He's always been a sickly child, and now that I have him safely with me, I must make sure he's protected against the germs in this unhygienic city. We will have to be vigilant – I must make sure Miyo disinfects everything.

Tuesday, 18 February

We've found a flat to move into! All thanks to Jiro Sekine, Rokki's kind colleague, who arrived at the hotel with Mr Wong, a bespectacled Chinese estate agent. Jiro said that Westerners were leaving Shanghai in droves because of the war, and there were many attractive vacant places. 'There's one in particular that sounds most suitable, not far from where we live. It's currently occupied by a Mr and Mrs Baker, an American couple, and I've stressed to Wong that that's the one he should show you before anything else.'

I was reminded of our London flat at Prince's Gate the minute I entered the tall art deco Grosvenor House, through the heavy glass and brass doors into the marbled hallway. The more I saw of the place, the more I fell in love with it – an eleventh floor two-bedroom flat, the main rooms facing the large courtyard. Hiro too seemed impressed as we walked through the elegant living room, the separate dining room and into the kitchen, beyond which was a small servants' room. The huge master bathroom took my breath away – all in black marble, with golden taps, and a turquoise bathtub.

The smiling Mr Wong, who hadn't said a word till then, proudly announced, 'Busloom best. Other floor difflen colour, pink, yellow, mauve.' I was happy with the turquoise.

It was only when we finished our tour that the current tenants, a handsome couple in their early thirties, appeared in the hallway. Instead of coming towards us, the Bakers eyed us with suspicion, hands dangling by their sides. It seemed strange, especially as they were almost like an American version of us, dressed similarly, the men in navy blue blazers, us women in prim woollen suits. And then it suddenly dawned on me. We were Japanese.

These people were being forced to move because Japan has taken over Shanghai, and we were taking over their home as nationals of the occupying power.

After what seemed a long awkward silence, I mustered up my courage and, offering my hand to Mrs Baker, said, 'You have such a beautiful place.'

The Bakers looked at each other, seeming confused. Finally, Mr Baker said, 'Excuse us, we weren't expecting to meet an attractive Japanese lady who speaks perfect British English.'

As if making an effort to further break the ice, he said, 'We plan to return to New Jersey, my home state in America.'

'Oh, my parents and siblings lived in New Jersey before I was born, and my father still has friends there' I said, pleased with the common thread. The Bakers visibly relaxed.

'We hope to return when the hostilities are over,' Mrs Baker said. 'We've loved it here, and Ted is eager to resume his business in this part of the world.'

'I have an idea!' Mr Baker suddenly said. 'We see our departure from Shanghai as a temporary move, and can't really take all our furniture back to New Jersey with us. Do you think you could make use of it, if you wish, that is?'

Hiro's eyes lit up. 'You have good quality furniture. We are happy with your kind offer,' he said, and showed the business side of him that I rarely see. 'We must sign a contract for borrowing your furniture. These are uncertain times, and it's better to have proper paperwork.'

After Hiro and Mr Baker exchanged signatures and papers, we made our departure, offering best wishes for the future and hopes of meeting again in peaceful times. The smiling Mr Wong was lost on the details, but happily followed after us, knowing he had a successful deal.

'I guess the Bakers didn't expect Japanese civilians moving into their flat. They were probably expecting military officers,' Hiro said.

How peculiar this war situation is. Meeting lovely Americans, concluding a friendly housing transaction, feeling that we could be friends. Had they been forced to be charming to us because they didn't think it wise to offend Japanese people? No, they must have felt favourable towards us, otherwise why would they have entrusted us with their furniture?

I hope it won't be too long before they can return to Shanghai, and in the meantime, I shall treat their furniture with utmost care, even more so than I would our own.

Friday, 20 February

Kazu is with Miyo for his afternoon stroll in the Public Gardens. It's been strange having Kazu with an additional person involved. When I longed for him, I had imagined a close mother-son bond that nobody could intrude upon, not even Hiro. But now, there is Miyo. She is a professional, and is very matter-of-fact with him, not showing any overt affection. But the boat journey has made him

24

dependent on her, and it is to her that he turns whenever he wants anything, not to me. He knows I'm his mother, and seeks my attention, too, but not for comfort. He performs for me. I'm becoming over sensitive, watching them like a hawk. Miyo happily hands Kazu toys that have been on the floor. Does she not realize how filthy the streets of Shanghai are, how people come into the hotel in their street shoes? The thought of all the germs around us makes me shudder.

Apart from that, I can find no fault with Miyo, but she isn't what I had imagined. What had I expected? Someone older and motherly, perhaps like old Winifred from London? Winnie, who was so devoted to Mummy, and after Mummy died, she provided stability to the household and made daily life go on as usual, just what Daddy and I most needed at the time.

But when Daddy put me in charge of his dinner parties, Winnie treated me as the mistress even though I was only fifteen, never questioning my authority, always supportive. I suppose Winnie would have had to leave Daddy's employ – she couldn't be working for a Japanese under house arrest. What could Daddy's everyday life be like now? Not at all the way I remember it, most certainly. He has a new wife for a start. Perhaps Tamiko is right, that it is a good thing that he has a companion in these difficult times, even if, from my impression, she could be the type to give him more challenges than comfort. At least he is at home, thanks to his close contacts with people in the Foreign Office, unlike many of the other Japanese businessmen who were interned immediately after Pearl Harbor.

I digress. Miyo, somewhat distant, nearly thirty with professional qualifications, is a far cry from sweet Winnie. It would be dishonest to say that I am completely comfortable with her. Maybe things will be different when we move into the flat and have a normal family life.

Saturday, 28 February

With the boxes and suitcases packed, I went to say farewell to Mr Hsu, my first friend in Shanghai. He knew why I'd come, and in typical Hsu fashion, he launched into one of his stories.

'I ever tell you of shooting on Hotel doorstep? Chinese businessman go down right outside, stumble almost into lobby. I rush to door but big White Russian bodyguard protect him and start shooting back. Chinese man hurt only in shoulder. Shanghai in 1930s have lots of terror – shooting, mail bomb, kidnap. Often finger and ear come in post demand ransom.'

'Who was shooting who?' I asked, forgetting about the envelope in hand.

'Very difficult to say, Madam. Very complicated. Much underground activity – secret police, Chinese patriot, gangster, foreign country spy. Sometime people don't know who side they on. Terror everywhere those days. Japanese take over and much stop.'

He looked at me with his sly smile, satisfied that he managed to distract me. He then deftly manoeuvred a simple farewell by a glance towards the lifts and his watch, giving me just enough time to hand him my envelope with a brisk thank you and goodbye.

3

Sunday, 8 March 1942, The Grosvenor House

Spring has arrived. It is particularly beautiful here in the French Concession, with the leaves of the plane trees just starting to unfurl, giving the whole area a light-green sheen. I see the children from the compound, Kazu among them, playing in the courtyard, watched over by their nannies and amahs. It's still so international here, just how I imagined Shanghai would be.

Life in the Cathay Hotel now seems another world, as if it was just a passing visit to Shanghai in the dim distant past. Being in the flat gives a sense of permanence; that Shanghai is home.

And how I love the flat! The high ceilings give the place an open airy feel, while the dark, highly polished wooden parquet floors add weight and warmth. The Bakers' furniture was obviously carefully chosen – solid and angular, each piece different from the other, but all fitting in together perfectly. The sofa is my favourite, a boxed-in walnut frame with firm, but very comfortable cushions. It gives the living room a homely feeling while still being stylish. Kazu's room, which he shares with Miyo, is a proper little boy's room, with blue curtains and cuddly toys. Also, a blue carpet so he won't slip, and pale enough so that any dirt would be instantly noticeable.

Boy and Amah have joined the household, a discreet couple, never in the way. Boy says we are to call him Chokugetsu-ken, the Japanese pronunciation of a Chinese name, perhaps because that's what his previous Japanese employers called him. He has a wide round face, and a big mouth that stretches almost to his ears when he smiles. Amah is small and quiet, but with a presence that exudes goodness. Amah is happy to yield to Miyo where their duties overlap, and Miyo, to her credit, is reasonable and cordial with Amah.

Miyo still remains an enigma. At first I thought her detached manner was because she wasn't yet comfortable with us or with Shanghai. It's been a full month now, and I believe we treat her as part of the family, yet she still seems rather distant. Could she be dissatisfied with something? Or is it just the way she is?

Wednesday, 11 March

The flat, on the Rue Cardinal Mercier, is diagonally across the street from the French Club, so easy for Hiro to pop over to the beautiful lawn tennis courts. Tamiko decided that we should have lunch there so she could introduce me to her friend Midori Mao. 'Now that you're settled in your new home, I want you to get to know people,' she said as we headed towards the white clubhouse dazzling in the sunshine.

She contentedly breathed in the fresh air and explained that Frenchtown seemed more relaxed because there were fewer Japanese sentries around. 'Because the French are now a Japanese ally,' she said.

Shortly, Midori appeared – a stunning lady, dressed in a tight-fitting *cheongsam* that accentuated her height and curves. Had I not known that she was Japanese, I would have taken her for a Chinese lady, not only because of her outfit, but by the way she carried herself, tall and erect. I noticed several heads turn, especially from tables occupied by Japanese businessmen, as she took her seat. '*Ni hao,*' she said, offering me her hand after she gave Tamiko a friendly pat on the shoulder.

'I'm Mao *tai-tai*, but please call me Midori. As you may have gathered, my husband is Chinese. He's much older than me. In fact I am his third wife,' she said by way of introduction.

Her Japanese conversation was laced with Chinese expressions adding an exotic touch. 'Eiko-san, *due bu chi*, can you pass me the salt;' 'This *beouf bourguignon* is absolutely delicious, *hen hao!*' she would say, in between relating entertaining anecdotes ranging from Chinese ladies' bound feet to the eating of monkey brains – apparently a delicacy. Sometimes she rattled off several phrases in Chinese, making Tamiko laugh, but keeping me in the dark.

'How I would like to learn Chinese,' I sighed out loud. Much to my surprise, Midori immediately offered her stepson as a tutor for me, saying that he was a university student wanting to polish up his English.

'He can teach you Chinese and you can teach him English,' she declared. She indicated a done deal with hand gestures and said that Shin-tsu, her stepson, would be in touch with me shortly.

On that note, she looked at her watch and said she had to be on her way, leaving Tamiko and me rather breathless.

'How do you know her?' I asked Tamiko as soon as she was gone.

'Her husband, Mr Mao, has bank dealings with Rokki. We met at a party. Interesting lady, no? There's more depth to her than appears,' Tamiko said.

I feel my world expanding!

Monday, 16 March

Tamiko rang midday. 'Guess what, we are moving to Frenchtown, to the Grosvenor Gardens right next to you! We've decided Hungjao is too inconvenient.'

She hadn't mentioned anything the other day, perhaps wanting to keep it a surprise until definite. I nearly screamed with joy.

Wednesday, 18 March

Another call from Tamiko, about their move, I thought. But it wasn't.

'Eiko, Daddy's been interned on the Isle of Man – on 12 March,' she said, sounding unusually agitated.

She rushed over from Hungjao, and once we embraced we both felt better.

I could see in my mind's eye Daddy coming home exhausted after extensive meetings at the Foreign Office. And how he would stay up late into the night to write letters to Japanese officials close to the Emperor, desperate to persuade Japan to think rationally, prevent military hotheads from leading the country into war. I always believed his involvement in maintaining peace was why he wasn't interned.

'What could have happened for the situation to suddenly change, I wonder,' Tamiko said, staring into my eyes.

I couldn't imagine what life in internment would be like for Daddy. At least the British are civilized and would treat him decently, I told myself.

'It must be hard to be parted from Sachiko-san and even worse for her,' Tamiko said. I hadn't even thought of Daddy's new wife. Unlike Tamiko, I couldn't help feeling a tinge of pleasure that they were now separated.

But Tamiko is right, it must be a big blow for Daddy. When Mummy died, Daddy had me around, as well as all his work responsibilities. Even so, I could sense the deep loneliness he felt, and knew he poured even more into his work to keep himself going. With internment, he wouldn't have his work nor his wife. I know he will cope, but how difficult it must be for him. I do hope that his wife will have the decency to keep us informed of whatever news she receives.

Monday, 23 March

In the morning, I saw a lady with limp brown hair, I think English, walking her Scotch terrier. The dog rushed over to me wagging her tail, and I stooped down for a pat. Immediately, the English woman pulled on her lead with a big frown, calling 'Jane! Jane!' But the dog refused to leave my side. Finally, the woman came over and picked the dog up with a furtive 'Sorry', barely looking at me, and swiftly walked away. I felt crushed. I think her being English was what made me want to get to know her, to talk about London, to exchange dog stories. Her suspicious attitude suddenly brought home Daddy's situation. We couldn't escape being from enemy countries.

Shortly after, in the lift, I met a handsome older German couple, who introduced themselves as Herr and Frau Schmidt. 'Guten morgen,' the gentleman said, giving me a slight bow, and the lady a rather stiff handshake. 'Ve live above you,' she said, with a heavy German accent. As I was getting off, Herr Schmidt, with another bow, said 'Auf wiedersehen. We must get together some time.'

At least the second encounter lessened the bitter aftertaste of the first, although I suppose it isn't surprising, Japan and Germany being allies.

Wednesday, 25 March

Kazu and I spent most of the afternoon in the courtyard, where a pretty girl named Betty, about seven years old, took charge of playing with him. She patiently held his hand and walked him round and round the garden. At one point, when Kazu stumbled over a stray ball, Betty swiftly picked him up and distracted him with a toy in her hand. Kazu beamed at her, forgetting to cry. I was impressed.

Shortly, a Japanese lady came over and introduced herself as Betty's mother. It explained Betty's exotic looks – fair complexion and chestnut brown curly hair, but with distinctly Oriental features. 'I hope Betty hasn't been any trouble to you. I am Ayako Ringhausen, my husband is German, and we live in Grosvenor Gardens,' she said, with a gracious bow.

I am getting to know more neighbours, and how wonderfully international it all is! It will be even better when Tamiko and family move here, in less than a week's time.

Thursday, 26 March

I was at Tamiko's going through her clothes on the pretext of helping her pack. Not impressed with some of her dull outfits, I was in the middle of saying, 'We must go out and get more interesting outfits for you once you move to Grosvenor Gardens,' when Rokki poked his head around the door.

His stern expression instantly stopped our light chatter. 'This just came to the bank today,' he said, handing a piece of paper to Tamiko. Tamiko read through it quickly with a frown, and passed it to me, saying, 'I'm surprised it got through the mail censors.'

It was a clipping from the *Daily Express*, dated 11 March. What first caught my eye was the photo of Daddy – in his formal three-piece suit, in the familiar pose of hands slightly parted with a soft smile – filling me with nostalgia. The headline read:

But A Viscount Is Unmoved: Japanese, lives in a London flat, does not believe Eden.

Beside the headline was a photo of a Japanese solider sticking a bayonet into a man crouched on the ground. My hand started shaking, and I pushed the paper back to Tamiko, unable to read any further.

'Eiko, this explains why Daddy was interned,' Tamiko said, reading out some bits:

> *He is still at liberty and living an almost normal life. He had heard Mr Eden's terrible indictment of his army. But it did not move Viscount Kanda. Eden's statement about Japanese atrocities is so much propaganda, he said.*

Scanning the paper further, Tamiko said, 'There's more. It quotes Daddy as saying:

> *Atrocities? Japanese do not behave like that. It is not in us. Probably the report was inspired by Chinese propagandists – they have told dreadful untruths about us.*

Tamiko and I sat across the kitchen table staring at each other. The story made Daddy sound so nationalistic, and the tone of voice hardly sounded like him. 'I can't believe he actually said those words,' I said, shaking my head and biting my lips. Tamiko was taking a closer look at the piece.

'It's cleverly written. They refer to Daddy's earlier pronouncements that he didn't believe Japan would be engaged in war, to show how wrong he was or perhaps that he's a liar, and mention the expensive furnishings of his flat. And then it poses the question, why is Viscount Kanda not interned?' Tamiko let out a big sigh.

'No wonder he was sent to the Isle of Man,' she muttered. 'The newspapers want to paint everything in black and white. Daddy had no chance – a Japanese man in London had to be portrayed as the enemy, no matter what the real truth is.'

I glared at Tamiko. 'It's so unfair! Daddy was horrified when Japan started the war against China. I know! I'll never forget the date, 7 July 1937. Daddy and I were on a boat to Scandinavia, and we'd just arrived in Norway when Daddy learned of the invasion. He went straight to the booking office and we took the next boat back to London, without a single night in Norway. The *Daily Express* has it all wrong!'

As I was wailing, a dreadful thought crossed my mind. 'Tamiko, do you think that Daddy will be ill-treated in the internment camp? I'm not sure how civilized the British are, seeing how they can twist newspaper stories,' I blurted.

She remained silent for a minute, looking out of the window, and then gave me a soft smile. 'I'm sure Daddy will be all right. Let's hope so.' I want to believe Tamiko.

Saturday, 28 March

The day started inauspiciously – a heavy heart over Daddy's situation, nothing special to do – Hiro setting off to play tennis, leaving Kazu and me behind. Perhaps my annoyance showed while I was helping Hiro prepare his tennis bag. He suddenly suggested that Kazu and I come along to watch him play, as it was a beautiful spring day.

We set off to the tennis courts at Saint John's University, a large campus at the west end of the International Settlement where the Soochow Creek bends. The beautiful grounds were a curious of mix of East and West, the lower buildings cloister-like with long corridors, arches and pillars, and Western-style buildings with roofs curling up at the ends like pagodas.

The tennis courts were in a park-like setting, and I sat on a bench, Kazu on my knee, watching the ball go left, right, left, right – feeling Kazu's hair tickle my chin as his head, too, followed the movement of the ball.

As the tennis heated up, I became absorbed watching Hiro: movements so graceful and seemingly effortless, yet all of a sudden a powerful stroke landing in a perfect position, defeating the opponent. Even Kazu seemed to appreciate those moments, bouncing on my knee and clapping his little hands, probably imitating the other spectators, for surely he can't yet understand tennis, or could he possibly? I sometimes wonder whether he understands more than one expects.

During a pause between sets, an attractive lady dressed in a pretty cotton frock approached and said, 'May I join you? The two of you seem to be enjoying the tennis so much, it would be lovely to watch together.' She spoke perfect English with a hint of a Chinese lilt.

She took Kazu's hand and shook it properly, making him beam and gurgle, 'na-na, na-na!' – his version of a greeting.

'How clever, you seem to already know my name,' she smiled. To me, she said, 'I am Mona – not quite Nana. I'm the wife of S.P. Chen, who is playing tennis against your husband just now.'

The man she indicated was the one I had been admiring, not only a good tennis player, but good-looking too, deeply tanned with exotic Southeast Asian looks. I hadn't realized that Hiro's group included Chinese players and had assumed he was Japanese.

'S.P. and his double's partner, Allan Chang, teach here at the University,' she said. 'This is an old Christian university, founded by an American Anglican bishop and is renowned for its arts and sciences faculties. S.P. teaches law.'

Conversation with Mona came easily, as if by instinct we sensed common ground despite coming from different countries. She's from a wealthy, Westernized Christian Chinese family, her grandfather having held an important position in the China Merchants Steam Navigation Company. She seemed interested to hear about Grandfather Kanda, a progressive governor of a prefecture in Kyushu, who sent his children, including Daddy, to Western missionaries for English and Bible lessons.

We stopped paying attention to the tennis, chatting away about our childhoods and upbringing. I was particularly impressed that she had gone to Smith College in America.

'But I did not graduate,' she said. 'It's not that I was actually failing, but my parents thought it better that I return to Shanghai before I became an old maid!' She said this light-heartedly, and before I had a chance to inquire further, quickly asked me what I had been doing before I married Hiro.

'I was in my last year of school in London and preparing to come out as a debutante. Ours was the last group to be presented at court, before war broke out in Europe in 1939,' I said, and in that instant, I realized she must have had to cut short her American education because of the war in Asia – of course caused by Japan. She'd deliberately switched the subject out of concern for me.

'How exciting! You must tell me what it was like to be a debutante,' Mona said, with genuine curiosity. It had indeed been exciting at the time – the dressing up, the parties, the newspaper society pages – but upon reflection now, it was a bitter-sweet memory, the end of a happy era. By then, the Japanese community in London was consumed by the European situation and by mounting British criticism towards Japan over her policies in China.

'It was a wonderful cultural experience, being part of a very British tradition. But as a foreigner, it really had no social consequence and I just rushed back to Japan to marry Hiroshi,' I said.

'And your wedding, what was it like?' she asked. As soon as I told her that it lasted three days, she exclaimed, 'Mine, too! Quite exhausting! The only part I enjoyed was the food. So many of my favourite delicacies – thousand-year eggs, abalone, jellyfish!'

She laughed mischievously, giving me the impression that she had truly enjoyed her wedding parties – unlike me, having been much too nervous.

So pleased at having met Mona and excited about making a Chinese friend, I bubbled my thanks to Hiro for taking me to the tennis courts. I was taken aback by the frown that appeared on his forehead. 'I don't know S.P. that well, so be careful about getting too close. We have to be circumspect when we are mingling with non-Japanese in a place like Shanghai,' he said. I wasn't quite sure what he meant, but felt deflated.

Tuesday, 31 March

When Chokugetsu-ken said there was a phone call from Kimiyo, I thought it was someone I didn't know until I remembered the Noguchi daughter from that uncomfortable dinner. She was ringing to invite me to explore the western part of Shanghai. At least she's Japanese, I thought, still somewhat piqued by Hiro's unexpected caution over Mona.

Kimiyo came to pick me up, looking fashionable in her brimless blue hat, neatly pinned with a feathered hatpin to her permed black hair. She was going to show me around the Western part of Shanghai.

'Let us take a *se rin tsu*,' she said, pointing to one of the pedicabs lined up at the kerb. 'These are relatively new in Shanghai now that taxis are disappearing – shortage of gasoline,' she explained, impressing me with her knowledge and Chinese language skills.

We trundled west along Avenue Joffre and then southwest along Avenue Petain. 'We're heading towards an area that was given to the Catholics by the Hsu family, early converts of Matteo Ricci in the sixteenth century.' Kimiyo spoke in a formal Japanese voice, as if she were a tour guide. Was she showing deference because I'm older and married? I wondered. Then it occurred to me that perhaps it was her mother who told her to show me around. I tensed a bit at the thought.

At that moment, the pedicab hit a bump on the road, and my handbag slid from my knee, about to fall to the street. 'Whoopsy-daisy!' I shouted, as I grabbed onto the bag. Kimiyo also held on to the bag and squealed, 'That was a close one!' We looked at each other, realizing we'd switched from Japanese to English, and fell into a giggle. That broke the ice. Suddenly, all formalities were dropped, age differences forgotten.

'You must call me Kimmy, which is what my close friends call me,' she said. 'We're nearly there, you see that big, red building with the two spires, that's St Ignatius Cathedral. We'll skirt around the church, and go to the shops run by the Jesuit orphanages. The nuns train the orphans in French embroidery, and they sell lovely pieces costing next to nothing! You'll love it.'

While we meandered around the area, dipping into one shop and another, Kimmy told me she had attended the British-run Public School for Girls, and sat for the Cambridge matriculation exams. 'I had a chance to live in Japan twice, because of fighting in Shanghai in 1932 and 1937, and it was too dangerous to stay. But both times, I went to an international school, so my Japanese isn't that great,' she said, shrugging her shoulders. I smiled, thinking we're in the same boat although she's better educated than I am.

'Having a Western education is frowned upon in Japanese Shanghai these days,' she said, fingering some of the fine embroidery. 'So many Japanese are "frogs living in a well" – no idea of the bigger world – and it's very annoying. One of my mother's Japanese friends brought her daughter over, and this girl berates me for going to what she calls a "foreigners'" school. "It's unpatriotic to be mixing with people who are enemies of Japan," says this little Miss know-it-all.' Kimmy's little blue hat bopped up and down as she shook her head in fury.

'Japanese ignorance is one thing, but the Chinese situation can be hurtful,' Kimmy went on. 'We had two Chinese girls in my year, one quiet, and the other outgoing. The outgoing one was always nasty to me, but one day, when I was asked to read an essay, she heckled in such a rude way that finally the teacher told her to leave the room.' I stared in disbelief that such a thing could happen at the British Public School.

'I'd wondered why the teachers hadn't intervened sooner, and realized things were more complicated,' Kimmy said. She explained that the quiet girl was the daughter of an official in the Wang Ching-wei government, and the rude girl's father was the daughter of someone on the Chiang Kai-shek side.

'I think the rude one wanted to embarrass the other Chinese girl by showing overt anti-Japanese feelings, and I just happened to be the target. Real life hostilities played out in a British classroom!'

Kimmy's description of her Chinese classmates softened my annoyance with Hiro – the complexity of Shanghai is something I have yet to grasp. As for Mona though, I know my instincts are right and given a chance, we could be good friends.

4

Wednesday, 1 April 1942

Tamiko and family are now practically our next-door neighbours.
They left Sachi with us during the move, and Kazu ended up
being bossed around all day long. What a pair they are! Sachi walking and talking much better than Kazu, treating him as a wonderful
plaything, Kazu, for his part, loving the attention and following
her around everywhere. At one point, there was a big wail – Sachi
grabbing a toy from him. I almost jumped up to Kazu's rescue,
but checked myself. Miyo was looking after them after all. Miyo
watched, smiling calmly, and it did occur to me that I might be
overprotective.

Tamiko and Rokki arrived for dinner – a merry gathering of
extended family, with Hiro and I at each end of the table, Kazu in his
highchair, Miyo by his side, and Sachi, propped up on cushions next
to her. Chokugetsu-ken made something called *suzutou* – four meat
patties arranged over some greens, which turned out to be Tamiko's
favourite Shanghai dish. We tucked in and talked, all at the same
time, the children making as much noise as the adults. Miyo seemed
relaxed for once, surrounded by the happy clatter. I am content.

Sunday, 5 April

Easter Sunday. Ayako Ringhausen, Betty's mother, organized an
egg hunt in the courtyard for the children of the compound, and
Kazu managed to find an egg, all on his own. He looked so pleased
with himself, cuddling the brightly painted blue and yellow egg
preciously in both hands. He seems to have developed so much
in the month we've been here. I suppose it's the stimulation from
being with other children.

In the afternoon, I left Kazu with Miyo and accompanied Tamiko and Rokki to a Quaker Meeting. I wanted to be in the solemn surroundings of a church, to pray for Daddy in internment, to express gratitude to God for all the blessings of our comfortable life here in Shanghai. It was a long time since I had set foot in a church, the last time probably being Mummy's funeral. There hadn't been any opportunity in Kobe, the Kishimotos being Buddhists, but I suppose it didn't matter too much as the Kanda family followed the non-church form of Christianity which called for bible readings and hymns within the home. I think Tamiko mentioned her association with the Quakers dated back to when the family lived in New Jersey before I was born and Daddy had some Quaker friends. I looked forward to this Easter service in a proper church.

Unexpectedly, Tamiko walked up to a pretty little brick house further west in the French Concession and said, 'Here we are!' It turned out that the Quaker Meeting was being held in the home of an elderly Irish lady named Agnes Flynn, a silver-haired petite lady with remarkable grace. Her home was equally graceful, a vase of Easter lilies arranged in the entrance hall, but hardly a church-like atmosphere. We were led to the sitting room, where several people were already assembled, including the Leighs.

Calm permeated the bright room, as we sat waiting for the Meeting to begin. Nobody else arrived after us, so I was sure it would start soon, and waited and waited, and nothing happened. It must have been a good thirty minutes of total silence, when finally, Agnes, in a clear voice, spoke of her gratitude at being able to celebrate Easter with people from different countries, including from Japan and China. Then total silence again for another ten minutes or so, and Rokki said something about sensing a greater presence among us. And then silence again. And finally, Agnes, Keith, Joyce and a couple of other people shook hands, and all stood up marking the end of the Meeting.

What a strange Easter service! I was expecting hymns and Bible readings, an Easter that would remind me of Daddy. As soon as I had a chance, I rushed over to Tamiko and quietly berated her for not having warned me about Quaker Meetings beforehand. She was expecting this, I could tell, and seeing her gleeful smile, I knew she deliberately kept me in the dark just to enjoy my reaction.

'But you see, Eiko, you were doing exactly what you're supposed to do in Quaker Meetings – wait in silent expectancy!'

I can't deny that the Meeting created a sense of peaceful fulfilment, which spilled over to the following tea. Everyone smiling, greetings and conversation conducted in joyful tones. I was introduced to Agnes, who gave me a warm handshake. 'I was so pleased when Tamiko and Rokki arrived in Shanghai, and now we have you! It is a true blessing to have so many nationalities present here at a time of war,' she said, with a charming Irish lilt.

Keith, who was standing by, said 'Ah, Eiko, I see you have now met Agnes, the "mother" of our Meetings here in Shanghai. Agnes really is like a mother and showers her love on all of us. But,' he added mischievously, 'she isn't exactly an impartial mother and has her favourites. Isn't that right, Agnes? Many a refugee in need has been welcomed in her home, and Irma Czeska now lives with her permanently after her husband passed away.'

As he said this, he gently pulled over a motherly middle-aged lady with greying ginger curls. 'Eiko, meet Irma from Germany. In the days when the Meetings were still held at the Friends Centre over in Hongkew, she started accompanying Agnes there, and now she has become a regular participant.'

I was surprised to learn that Jewish people also attended Quaker Meetings.

Irma took my hands into hers, which had a comforting roughness. 'I adore Tamiko, and it's *wunderbar* to meet you!' Her wild curls and ample body reverberated as she vigorously shook my hands.

'Irma runs the Friends clothing centre, which distributes clothes to refugees. She's the ideal person for the job,' Keith said, affectionately placing an arm around Irma's shoulders.

Irma laughed. 'That's because Keith thinks I am *herrisch*, bossy, you say in English. I help interview refugees in camps to find what they need, and Keith is saying, "There goes another one who couldn't hoodwink you!"'

Casting a little wink towards Keith, she chuckled, 'I am also refugee, so I know you need to push to get by, but I know when people push too far!'

On our walk home, I huddled up to Tamiko. 'It wasn't the kind of Easter I expected, but it's amazing how the Quakers create an atmosphere of peace and joy in difficult times.'

'They really are remarkable,' Tamiko said. 'Did you notice that Joyce is looking a bit heavier? They're expecting a baby, due in July. They're so happy, and I'm happy for them, too. But Eiko, things are getting tougher for Westerners. They will be made to wear armbands as "enemy" nationals soon. Japanese control is tightening.'

What did Tamiko mean? Would Westerners' movements be restricted, and does that mean we wouldn't be able to easily see our friends anymore?

Wednesday, 8 April

As it was too wet for the courtyard, Ayako had a small mother-and-child tea party at her place. The Ringhausen home, filled with books and knick-knacks, seemed less elegant than our flat, but had acquired a cosy lived-in atmosphere, perfect for a gloomy, rainy day. Apart from Sachi and Tamiko and Kazu and me, there was another Japanese mother, Junko, with Wolfie, her four-year old son, whose father is also German. Betty was in charge looking after the little ones, with their Amah close at hand.

'There's a sprinkling of Germans here in the Grosvenor complex. Your upstairs neighbours are the Schmidts, right?' Ayako said. 'He is an important businessman. They've been here for over ten years, and Mrs Schmidt is active in the women's group at the German Club.'

'I just met another German lady,' I said, eager to talk about the resourceful Irma. 'She's full of energy, although not young, and is actively involved with the Quakers' relief work.'

All of a sudden, there was this cold pause, and Junko looked as if she'd swallowed something unpleasant. Ayako and Tamiko, at exactly the same moment, focussed on the children, Ayako asking if the children wanted more biscuits, and Tamiko leaping up to see if Sachi was behaving.

Obviously I had committed some social faux pas, but what had I done? Fortunately, the children came rushing in, and our attention distracted, things seemed back to normal. Very shortly after, Junko said she must be getting home and swiftly collected Wolfie. After a quick thank you to Ayako, and barely a nod to Tamiko and me, off she went.

I felt terrible, but still didn't know what I had done. Ayako shifted uncomfortably for a while, and finally said, 'Eiko-san, I know you meant well, but you have to be careful among Germans. There are a lot of sensitivities.'

She stared at me, and seeing my perplexed expression, sighed. 'You see, Junko's husband works at the German Embassy, and is very loyal to Hitler, and they do not look kindly to the Jewish refugees. I hadn't realized that Junko identifies so strongly with her husband – that was a surprise to me, too.'

She frowned, and I sensed her annoyance with me.

'The truth is, even Germans like my husband, Frederick, are finding it very uncomfortable these days,' Ayako said, in a resigned tone. She explained that Fred was a professor at one of the universities originally founded by German Christians, and was totally opposed to Hitler, but had to be discreet about where his sympathies lay because there was a high proportion of Nazi party members within the German community who wielded power. One's career could be crushed if one was deemed disloyal to the Nazis.

Offending Junko was one thing, but I finally realized I had also jeopardized Ayako and Fred's standing within the German community. What if Junko rushed back to tell her husband that the Ringhausens had friends who sympathized with the refugees? Would the Nazis now view Frederick with suspicion? Blood rose to my head, and I felt my cheeks burning from shame.

'The Germans being a small, closed community here makes it all the more difficult, I imagine,' Tamiko muttered. 'I suppose it's not too different from the Japanese – the *kempei-tai* military police and the special police trying to weed out dissent. Only in Japan's case, they have to control a huge population – the "enemies" as well as Japanese citizens, so maybe we are let off the hook a bit.'

Ayako seemed to soften by Tamiko's intervention, knowing she was understood.

The rest of the visit was a blur, my mind filled with worry of what I had done. After we left, Tamiko huddled close to me and said, 'It's not as if you did anything wrong deliberately. You learned a good lesson to watch your mouth.' She gave me a soothing rub on my arm, and only then did I feel a little better.

Saturday, 11 April

We were invited to Jiro and Sayako Sekine's for dinner to meet Jiro's older brother, Masaya, who recently arrived in Shanghai.

As soon as Masaya saw Tamiko, an expression of pure delight spread across his face. 'Tamiko-san, my decision to come to Shanghai was made easier knowing that you are here!' he said, shaking her hand tightly. Tamiko responded by wrapping her other hand over his, and returning an affectionate smile. Rokki looked pleased, not appearing at all surprised by the un-Japanese greeting. I wondered why Tamiko knew Masaya so well.

Masaya then turned to me and said, 'Eiko-san, you do remember me, don't you? We met in the winter of 1937, when I was on a special mission to meet the Archbishop of Canterbury.' I stared into his face. Did I know him, too?

Taller and broader than Jiro, he had a charismatic air. Suddenly, I remembered the occasion. We had met at a reception at the Japanese Embassy in London, when I was still a schoolgirl. He looked different now because back in London, he was wearing a clerical collar.

'I'm no longer a priest,' he said, reading my mind and making me blush. 'I'm here to work for the Imperial Navy, in the Jewish Affairs Bureau. And this lady here, Laura, will be keeping me on my toes, telling me what the refugees' needs are.' Masaya led me to a petite American woman, with intense dark eyes, who worked for a Jewish relief organization.

'Yes, Masaya. I am counting on you to smooth out administrative problems to get the money and food flowing!' Laura said, in an unexpectedly deep, husky voice. 'Your boss's predecessor was good at working the bureaucracy, and I trust Captain Saneyoshi and you will be equally effective.' For a small woman, she was very forceful, her words sounding almost like a command.

'I'm devoting my life to serve this humanitarian cause, so I certainly hope I'll do a good job,' Masaya responded. 'I can't say I had any regrets leaving the priesthood given how the Japanese Anglican Church is increasingly bowing to Japanese government demands. But joining the military was a much tougher decision, even if it came as a personal request from Captain Saneyoshi, a fine, rare Christian in the Navy.'

Masaya said that in the end, he took up the assignment because he believed he would be serving God through serving the refugees.

I hadn't known that the Japanese military had an office to help Jewish refugees. How confusing it is, that Germany is persecuting the Jews and they escape to Shanghai, and the Japanese help look after them, even though Germany and Japan are allies. It's good news for Irma and the refugees that people like Masaya and Captain Saneyoshi are in charge, and I certainly hope the German authorities here never find out. Given what Ayako said the other day, I can't imagine the Nazis would be accepting of a Japanese Jewish Affairs Bureau that was overly sympathetic to the refugees.

Monday, 13 April

Kazu seems to be coming down with something. I've been dreading this ever since his arrival in Shanghai. What will I do if it is another case of autotoxemia, keeping him in bed for weeks on end? Thankfully, Miyo is being very calm and professional, making sure he takes liquids. She spent a lot of time in the kitchen boiling water and sterilizing his bottles. I must take him to the doctor if his fever is not gone by tomorrow.

Tuesday, 14 April

Kazu's condition worsened overnight, and I rushed him to St Marie Hospital with Miyo, cursing unhygienic Shanghai and all its germs along the way.

A rather intimidating Japanese head nurse took our registration, but the doctor – Dr Epstein – was a Westerner, who reminded me of my old GP in London. I was relieved to be able to explain in English Kazu's symptoms and medical history, especially of his fevers and vomiting despite our added care regarding hygiene.

The doctor looked into Kazu's eyes, listened through a stethoscope front and back, gave his knee a few pokes, and then gave him a pat on the head and a smile. 'You'll be fine by tomorrow, young man,' he pronounced.

'Make sure he gets lots of clear liquids, and take this just in case. Your son won't need them, but they'd be good to have around as medicines are harder to come by these days,' he said, handing me a packet of aspirins.

Looking intently into my face, he softly added, 'Mrs Kishimoto, I think you should relax a bit. Babies are very sensitive and react to their mother's emotions. If you are constantly worried that he will get ill, then he is more likely to do so.'

I was stunned, and relieved that Miyo didn't understand English well.

I wasn't entirely convinced by Dr Epstein's admonishment, but being told that Kazu would be fine helped me relax. By this evening, Kazu was able to keep down his food and started looking visibly better. In retrospect, I might have over-reacted this morning – demanding that Hiro order a car despite the hospital being around the corner, and raising my voice at Miyo for being slow at getting Kazu ready. With the worry now gone, I am exhausted and ready for an early night.

Thursday, 16 April

With Kazu back to normal, Tamiko and I took a stroll along the Bund, dropping in at the Cathay. It seemed so much longer than just a month and a half ago that the hotel was our home. Mr Hsu greeted me as if I had just gone out for a stroll. 'You come back with sister, today, Madam. Very beautiful and big sister very wise, I see.' Tamiko laughed and said something to him in Chinese, and then they both laughed, as he waved us towards the dining room.

'What was that about?' I asked.

'A little joke about how wise people can always spot each other.' I was amazed by Tamiko's fluency in Chinese.

After lunch, we walked towards Garden Bridge and moored on the river was a looming white luxury liner that shone brightly in the sun. The single green line all around the middle of the body accentuated her elegance. 'That's the *Conte Verde*, the boat that carried many a Jewish refugee to Shanghai, sailing from Genoa to the Far East,' Tamiko said, shading her eyes with her hand as she looked up at the Italian national flag waving atop the mast.

Irma had told her that only the lucky ones with tickets could travel on the boat, but even they had to endure enormous hardship getting out of Germany, losing most of their possessions by the time they reached Italy through Austria. 'Can you imagine, Eiko, their solace, boarding the *Conte Verde*, with all its European luxury?' Tamiko sighed.

I felt I could physically share the sense of relief just by looking at the magnificent boat. How soothing a sight, a welcome break from the black and grey battleships and gunboats, scattered in the Whangpoo.

Sunday, 19 April

Tamiko and I were approaching Café Vienna on Avenue Joffre when Masaya and an older, distinguished-looking moustachioed Naval Officer in uniform came out of the door. Masaya beamed as he spotted us.

'Tamiko-san, Eiko-san, what a pleasant surprise! Let me introduce you to Captain Saneyoshi, my boss,' he said. Tamiko and I bowed deeply, and I noticed how well polished the Captain's shoes were. When we looked up, the Captain was smiling benignly in a grandfatherly way.

'Sekine-kun and I dropped by for a cup of coffee after the Sunday Church service to discuss some office matters. I find it easier to deal with them after attending Church,' he said, with a soft chuckle. 'We've done enough work today, and I'm ready for my constitutional, Sekine-kun, are you coming?'

Masaya hesitated, casting a pleading look towards Tamiko. She didn't seem to notice, her attention was focussed on the captain. 'It is a lovely day for a walk. I love this neighbourhood with so many grand villas. Captain Saneyoshi, would it be all right to detain Sekine-sama for a short while here? I have some messages from the Quakers I'm meant to pass on,' she said.

'By all means. I am sure Sekine-kun would be happier spending time with you ladies than accompanying an old codger like me. In any event, I was intending to have a solitary, contemplative stroll.' He bowed lightly with a warm smile before turning around, placing his naval cap on his head and walking away.

He seemed like a very nice man and reminded me of some of the Naval Officers Daddy used to know in London. If only all Japanese soldiers were like him, I thought.

'What is this about a message from the Quakers?' Masaya asked Tamiko, as we were being seated at a table.

'Nothing. I just made it up, thinking it would be nice to have an excuse to spend some time with you,' Tamiko said. Masaya beamed and I couldn't help being curious about their relationship.

'Good, I wanted to talk to you,' Masaya said. 'Or rather, I want you to hear me out about my woes. As fine a person as Captain Saneyoshi is, as far as military politics go, I am afraid he is out of his depth. He's just too decent a person to know how to operate in power struggles. The Army knows this, and is swiftly moving in, taking much of Captain Saneyoshi's responsibilities away from him, right under his nose.'

Masaya slowly twirled the half-empty coffee cup in his palm, telling us how the Army always wanted to strip the Navy's authority, from before Saneyoshi's time, but that Captain Inuzuka, his predecessor, was seen as Japan's foremost Jewish expert and managed to keep his grip.

'The Japanese are incredibly ignorant when it comes to foreign religions and cultures,' Masaya said. 'The only thing the Japanese know about Jews is that Jewish money financed the Russo-Japanese War in 1904, enabling Japan to achieve a spectacular victory over a white, advanced nation. After all efforts to raise money on the London markets failed, this American Jewish financier, Jacob Schiff, came up with 200 million dollars, and immediately became a hero in Japan.'

It's true, I thought, about myself being ignorant of Jews. I hadn't even heard of Jacob Schiff! During all my years in London, I had never thought of people being Jewish or not, although subconsciously I was aware that Rebecca at Glendower was Jewish because she often missed school church assemblies. But it made no difference; all my British friends were British as far as I was concerned. Suddenly, here in Shanghai, I realize being Jewish has huge negative significance, and knowing Irma and the Quakers makes the Jewish question seem so much closer. I couldn't help being drawn into what Masaya was saying.

'Because of what Schiff did for Japan, Inuzuka believed that American Jewish financiers were highly influential,' he said. 'Inuzuka thought that if Japan treated the Jews in China well, they would put pressure on the American government to allow Japan to have access to funds and materials for the war effort. He really thought they would help Japan.'

Tamiko was wide-eyed. 'Did the Japanese military really go along with that view?' she asked.

Tinkering still with his coffee cup, Masaya said that this blind faith in Jewish financial influence gave Captain Inuzuka the green light to pursue his plan, all operated from what was now his office, the Navy Jewish Affairs Bureau.

'But it didn't work!' I exclaimed.

'You're right,' Masaya said, giving me an approving nod. 'Despite all the secret correspondence between Inuzuka and various middlemen with access to Jewish financiers, nothing came of it. And with Pearl Harbor, the plan was completely dead. In fact, that's why Captain Inuzuka was removed from his post, and why the Army hate the Bureau being under the Navy.'

Tamiko matter-of-factly said, 'But still, if it made Japanese treatment of Jewish refugees more humane, that's what counts, whatever Captain Inuzuka's motives were.'

Masaya looked admiringly at Tamiko. 'You're right. Without Captain Inuzuka, the Jewish refugees would be in more difficulty. To his credit, even after Pearl Harbor, Inuzuka arranged to have funds unfrozen, and thousands of sacks of cracked wheat released for the refugees. He was certainly better at getting things done than my Captain Saneyoshi.' Masaya heaved a big sigh.

Tamiko gave Masaya's arm a light pat, and with an appreciative smile, he squeezed her arm in return.

Monday, 20 April

Kimmy Noguchi rang to say she's now working for some Japanese company, in the same building as Rokki's bank, and suggested lunch in a little Japanese noodle shop across the bridge in Hongkew.

She appeared in a tight-skirted navy-blue suit and white blouse, looking very business-like, making me self-conscious of my matronly frilly beige outfit. In Hongkew, though, we both stood out: most of the Japanese women around were in kimonos, scurrying about in their wooden *geta* sandals, just like going to market in Japan.

Once in the noodle shop, I could almost believe I was in Japan, for the smell was distinctly of Japanese noodles, not the rich oily smell of Chinese noodles, but the aroma of dry bonito stock permeating the busy place. We sat in a cramped corner, our elbows practically bumping into the wall.

'I'm so glad we can speak in English,' Kimmy said. 'This place is full of Japanese people, seated so closely together. I wouldn't want them to know what we are saying.'

In the month since seeing her last, Kimmy seemed more grown up, perhaps it is the confidence that comes from having a job, an experience I've never had. I couldn't help wondering how exciting it must be, having an existence of one's own outside the home.

'It might sound impressive, working in the research department of this government-related company, but all I do is run around getting things for the researchers: "Noguchi-san, a cup of tea, please; Noguchi-san, please pass this report on to Mr so-and-so; Noguchi-san, keep this book in your desk for me", etc. etc.' she giggled. 'But it is good to be out of mother's reach, doing something useful and earning a bit of pocket money.'

'The other good thing,' she continued, 'is to be among these brainy, young men, all graduates of elite Japanese universities. Fortunately, because my English is better than most of them, they treat me with some respect and not just as a tea-pourer. They sometimes even ask me to decipher an English sentence for them. The trouble with that, though, is the material they read is usually far above my head and I haven't a clue what it is about!'

I had a feeling she was being modest, but then she produced a book from her bag with a dull cover and small lettering and said, 'Eiko, this is one of the books they asked me to help with. I'm supposed to keep it till they need it back. But I have about five such books at home, so I brought this one for you. I was hoping you might help me with the English.'

I was flattered that Kimmy would even think that I could understand what she couldn't, and was happy to keep the book till my help might be needed. Putting it in my bag gave me a sense of importance, a direct connection to the working world through Kimmy.

We couldn't linger very long because the place was teeming with people, and besides, Kimmy's lunch hour was running out. We said our goodbyes and I let Kimmy hurry on without me. She looked very professional, charging straight back towards the office in a brisk walk.

Friday, 24 April

I was sitting in the courtyard with Kazu and Miyo, soaking in the warm sunshine, when I noticed the Englishwoman with little Jane on a lead. I hadn't seen them for a couple of weeks, and was taken aback by the woman's appearance – so much thinner and weary looking. The Scotch terrier, as usual, pulled her towards me, and perhaps she didn't have the energy to resist, she nervously looked around as she came closer.

I stooped to pat the dog and looked up with as friendly a smile as I could manage. 'This is Jane, isn't she? She reminds me of my dog Benji. We used to take walks in Hyde Park all the time when I lived on Exhibition Road,' I said.

The lady stared at me, and moved a few steps towards the hedge. I realized she was trying to block the view so people wouldn't see her talking to me.

'I hadn't realized you speak such perfect English,' she said, hesitantly. 'I am sorry for having been aloof, it's not easy being British in Shanghai now, and I confess to being wary of Japanese people. My name is Anne, by the way. Although I don't know whether there'll be a chance to run into each other again. Life is getting pretty fraught for us Brits and Americans. All everyone thinks about now is how to get out of China.'

I didn't know what to say. I felt ashamed for not noticing the plight of some people living in our own compound. I continued to pat Jane, thinking that even she seemed thinner under her fur.

'My father is still in Britain, interned on the Isle of Man,' I said. The words came out of my mouth without much thought – I just wanted to show Anne some sympathy, let her know that things weren't all rosy for us Japanese, how little I knew what was happening to Daddy. And I realized then that he had been in internment for a month now.

Was he getting proper meals? Daddy, who liked butter so much it was difficult to tell which was thicker, his toast or the butter. But very strict about table manners – to him, behaving properly was a sign of self-respect and respect for others. So difficult to picture noble and amiable Daddy in internment. How I wished for any bit of news on how he was.

Anne, too, seemed to have been lost in thought. Suddenly, as if waking from a dream, she gave me a wan smile and walked away, into the mottled shadows cast by the unfurling spring leaves of the London plane trees.

5

Sunday, 3 May 1942

Although it was night time, Hiro and S.P.'s faces glowed from the reflection of the neon lights along Nanking Road – a healthy, post-tennis glow, ready for a big Chinese meal. We were approaching Sun Ya, a well-known Cantonese restaurant for dinner. Despite having told me to be cautious about socializing with non-Japanese people, it was Hiro who took the initiative for the get together. Perhaps, he came to know S.P. better, and wanted to please me, knowing how fond I was of Mona.

'The restaurant has four floors, and the higher you go, the more elaborate the menu becomes,' S.P. said, as we entered the lift. I expected him to press the button for the third or fourth floor, but his strong brown finger was firmly on 1. He must have seen my expression.

'You wouldn't want to eat in the banquet rooms, Eiko. They are for large groups, like wedding parties,' he laughed, making me blush. 'The first floor is only slightly fancier than the ground floor, where people casually walk in from the street. But you won't be disappointed with the food.'

The vast dining room was packed with Chinese families eating and talking all at once, creating an overwhelming din. We were led to a large round table, which was already half occupied by two elderly Chinese couples, the women dressed in plain *cheongsam* and the men in grey gowns. They stared at us as we approached – we did stand out, S.P. and Hiro looking rather dashing in their sports blazers, and Mona and I colourful in our cotton frocks. I noticed one of the men raise his eyebrows as we were taking our seats, and suddenly felt self-conscious. Perhaps they didn't want any Japanese at the same table.

I don't know if Mona noticed, but she beamed a warm smile and said something, which made the man with the raised eyebrows break into a soft chuckle. I understood nothing, but couldn't but admire how she spoke to them light heartedly, and respectfully at the same time. The older couples went back to their eating and talking, seemingly forgetting about our presence.

Mona and S.P. did the ordering, and we had one wonderful dish after another, including an abalone appetiser and something I found particularly delicious – very delicate white meat, not quite fish and not quite chicken. Mona watched amusedly as I savoured each bite. 'That's snake meat. You have extravagant taste, Eiko!' I wished I hadn't been told. She started to giggle, and we all had a good laugh over how Hiro and I enjoyed the particularly exotic dishes.

'Hiroshi, your volleys are spectacular. I'll have to practise more if I'm ever going to win against you at tennis. Maybe I'd have better luck with golf,' S.P. boomed. His tanned face glowed from the warm Chinese rice wine, as he swung his arms above the table. Mona winced.

'Your manners, S.P.! Don't start practising your golf swings now!' she admonished. Turning to us she chuckled, 'We've recently joined the golf club here. S.P. is pleased he can show off his skills acquired in England.' S.P. and Hiro discovered they had been at Cambridge only years apart, and launched into talk of the various golf courses they knew in England, getting into friendly arguments over which holes had water hazards or where the bunkers were. Mona rolled her eyes and leaned towards me.

'Eiko, you don't mind if I'm frank about things, do you? I can tell you are thoughtful of Chinese sensitivities just seeing your face as we approached to sit at this table,' Mona said with a smile.

'You see, as Chinese – even as Western-educated, relatively well-off Chinese – we were not able to join the golf club reserved for Westerners. That changed after the Japanese took over the International Settlement. But some of our acquaintances criticized us for becoming members, saying we've sold out to the enemy and are playing into their hands,' Mona said. I looked into her face, trying to grasp her meaning.

54

'It's the same at St John's. Some people are critical of S.P. for teaching at a university that is now taken over by the Japanese.' She proceeded to explain that there were two devout Christian Japanese professors who prevented the military from appointing hard-line faculty. Thanks to them, St John's remained a Christian, liberal institution, enabling S.P. to teach with a clear conscience. I was reminded of Masaya and his Jewish refugee work – Japanese Christians attempting to soften the harshness of Japanese occupation.

'But you see, Eiko, it's a bit like walking a tight-rope for us Chinese. Unless we're staunch nationalists moving to Chungking, we have to accept the Japanese if we want to earn a living. But some Chinese see any involvement with the Japanese as giving in. Even well intentioned humanitarian Japanese acts are interpreted as part of Japanese propaganda, a ploy to make the Chinese like them. They don't seem to realize that co-existence is all part of Shanghai life today.'

Having said so much, Mona stared into my eyes, perhaps thinking she had said too much. But I was grateful – how else could I comprehend such complexities? I sighed and gave her hand a light squeeze.

'Sorry Eiko, I feel so comfortable with you, I forget you're Japanese!' Mona said, returning the squeeze with an impish shrug of her shoulders and an apologetic smile.

Thursday, 7 May

I saw Anne, the English woman, walking with Jane on a lead again today in the courtyard. Jane, as usual, tried to pull towards me, and this time, Anne showed no resistance. As the dog sniffed at my legs, Anne quickly said to me in a low voice, 'I'll go and sit on the bench behind that shrub. Would you mind joining me for a chat?'

My heart started to pound, as if I'd been called into the Headmistress's office at school.

As soon as I sat beside her, Anne said, 'Eiko, didn't you say that your father is interned on the Isle of Man? I wanted to tell you that exchange repatriation is being worked out now. Meaning, as we

Brits in the Far East are shipped back to England, the Japanese in England will be shipped back to Japan. Your father could well be on the boat.'

It took me a while for her words to sink in. 'Does that mean he would be released from internment and returned home?' I asked timidly. I held my breath, hoping she could tell me more.

'Repatriation negotiations are complicated, it will take some time to organize – they need separate boats for Europe and America, they'll have to sort out who will be repatriated, given the limited available space,' Anne said. I was disappointed that she didn't seem to have specific information.

'My husband is a British diplomat and is involved in the negotiations – a total nightmare, especially for lower-ranking people. Your father held an important post so he should be high on the list. The boats are leaving sometime in the summer,' she said.

The sun moved, taking us momentarily out of the shade, and I noticed how lined Anne's face was, accentuated perhaps from weight loss.

'We are among the lucky ones because we can continue to live here until repatriation, unlike so many who can no longer afford expensive flats. You can't imagine the scrambling and manoeuvring that is going on to secure a place on the boat. My days are spent trying to soothe the nerves of those around me, and my own nerves are nearly gone now!' She gave me a wan smile.

If Anne could be so fraught, what was it like for those in internment? I shuddered at the thought of Daddy's face becoming gaunt, like Anne's.

'When it comes time for us to leave, or possibly even before that, Eiko, could I ask you a big favour?' Anne said, looking out in the distance.

My body stiffened. Perhaps she wanted Japanese information from me in exchange for telling me about Daddy. But what would I possibly know?

Anne turned and looked straight into my eyes. 'Do you think you could look after Jane for us until the time comes when we can

take her back? As a childless couple, Jane has been our pride and
joy, and if she can't be with us, being with you is what Jane would
most like, I am sure.'

I was so overwhelmed I averted my gaze and stooped to ruffle
Jane's head. As the familiar doggy smells wafted into my nostrils, I
regained my composure enough to say, 'Thank you, Anne.'

Our eyes locked for a few seconds, and without any further
words, Anne stood up and disappeared into the shadows, Jane following behind her.

Saturday, 9 May

The wireless announced the sinking of the *Taiyo-Maru*, torpedoed
by a US submarine in the East China Sea. It was the boat that
brought Kazu and Miyo to Shanghai, and I felt my knees go wobbly. To think that Kazu missed the incident by a mere two months!
Then I thought of Daddy, likely to be on the seas soon, and felt
a rush of true panic. Just when I was getting my hopes up for his
repatriation. How wretched this war is.

Tuesday, 12 May

Would Daddy be thinking of Mummy, too, on this anniversary
of her death, eight years ago? To mark the day, Tamiko suggested
an outing for just the two of us, and took me to the Uchiyama
Bookshop – 'a famous Shanghai institution for Chinese and
Japanese intellectuals,' she said. We sat on the upper deck of the
Number One bus that runs from Jessfield Park on the western
edge of the International Settlement through to Hongkew, giddy
as schools girls, as we watched the Shanghai hustle-bustle pass
beneath us.

Being with Tamiko awakens a childlike spirit within me, suppressed since the death of Mummy at the age of fourteen. Daddy
thrust me into adulthood, treating me as a grown-up, and I loved
the challenge, being complimented on my poise and maturity at
social functions. But I could never let my guard down, as I can now
with Tamiko, as when Mummy was alive, carefree in the knowledge

that I am loved and accepted however I behave. In Tamiko, I have a reminder of Mummy and also someone to share my loss with.

I had never had a chance to tell Tamiko of Mummy's last hours, details that didn't fit in a letter: how Mummy had been in perfect health, having her usual Saturday morning riding lesson in Hyde Park just the day before; Daddy, away in Basel for a monthly Bank meeting; Mummy and I reading the bible and singing hymns on that fateful Sunday; Mummy knitting, lifting the jumper bodice against my back to check for size; and then the sudden dizzy spell, falling to the floor, and never coming to again.

I leaned over and cradled my head against Tamiko's shoulder. Sharing those memories didn't bring sadness, but enhanced appreciation of each other and of Mummy.

After a short silence, Tamiko said: 'I suppose Hiroshi was still at Cambridge when Mummy died.'

I raised my eyebrows. Hiro hadn't entered my mind during those confusing times. Had he come to see Daddy shortly after Mummy's death before returning to Japan? We had so many visitors coming to express their condolences, I couldn't recall.

'Ah, but I bet he remembers seeing you in those difficult times, and your composure probably made a big impression on him!' she said, with a soft, teasing poke. It hadn't occurred to me, but it rang true, given the surprise approach from the marriage go-between three years later. How little I know of my husband.

The bus inched along busy Nanking Road, crossed the Garden Bridge and then on to North Szechuan Road. Women in kimonos rushed in and out of the Japanese shops lining the neighbourhood.

We alighted at the last stop and walked a short distance to the Uchiyama Bookshop. Coming in from the sunshine, the place seemed dark, even more so because of the tall bookshelves crammed in the space. Beyond the musty smell of paper, leather and dust, there was an aromatic scent of green tea wafting from the back, enticing us towards that direction.

An older couple sat at a table, hands cupped around Japanese tea mugs. As soon as the man saw Tamiko, he waved his hand beckoning us to join. 'Yah, Tamiko-san! Come, come, you must have some tea.'

His movements and demeanour reminded me of Humpty Dumpty, chunky with a meaty oval face and very little hair. His eyes crinkled with his broad smile, cutting an endearing figure. His equally chunky wife was busy preparing tea for us, and said, '*Saa, saa, osuwari!*' telling us to sit down and make ourselves comfortable.

'We don't get many people in the shop during the day,' Mr Uchiyama said. 'And the only ones who come in the evenings are Japanese businessmen and a sprinkling of military men. Not like it used to be. But people we care about still visit us, like you, Tamiko-san.' He flashed her a warm smile.

'But you've been keeping well, Uncle?' Tamiko asked.

He said he was busier than ever since the Japanese military made the American Publishing Company on Nanking Road come under his management. He tried to refuse, not wanting to take over a confiscated enemy property.

'But they said I was being unpatriotic. "Don't you want your business to expand? It would be good for you," they said, as if I would want to profit from this sad war.'

'As you can see though, I still have time to loll at the back of the shop with my missus and enjoy good company!' he said with a hearty chuckle.

I found the Uchiyamas delightful, but it was hard to believe that the shop was a famous Shanghai institution given their unassuming presence.

'You mustn't be deceived by appearances, Eiko,' Tamiko said. She told me that Uncle came to China in 1912 as a travelling salesman for some Japanese eye medication, and because he had to travel so much, he encouraged Auntie to start a business. So she set up shop on empty wooden beer crates in the entranceway of their home selling hymnbooks and Christian publications.

'And by the 1920s and 30s, the shop had become a literary salon for left-leaning Chinese and Japanese intellectuals. Uncle's the first to admit that he himself isn't an intellectual. But his knowledge of China and Chinese culture is phenomenal. Rokki worships him,' Tamiko said.

'I wish Daddy were here with us. He would get along so well with Uncle Uchiyama,' I said, when Tamiko told me how Uncle's keen sense of justice made him protect Chinese intellectuals who were sought after by Chiang Kai-shek's anti-leftist purges, including those marked as instigators of anti-Japanese movements.

The more I think of it, the more I see similarities between Daddy and Uncle Uchiyama. It's so hard to imagine such a man of principle behind the Humpty Dumpty-like figure, just as Daddy's amiable round face and pug nose belie his steely uprightness.

Friday, 15 May

Hiro gave me a curious look after dinner and said, 'Eiko, that English language book on the shelf in the living room, is that something you picked up from the Uchiyama Bookshop the other day?'

I hadn't bought any book from the Uchiyamas. Suddenly, I realized he was referring to the book Kimmy had handed me, in case she needed my help with the English.

Hiro carefully examined the cover with uncharacteristic interest. 'This is one of the Special Police's black-listed books,' he said. I stared back in astonishment, my heart skipping a beat.

'Nobody's going to be searching here, but perhaps you should leave the book somewhere less visible' Hiro said, fingering the pages. 'Gunther's *Inside Asia* – it's the kind of book Rokki would read. I wondered if he left it here. It's supposed to contain a good political analysis of Asia leading to the war. The Special Police probably should be reading it rather than banning it.'

Having said so much, Hiro casually placed the book before me, sank into the sofa and went back to his newspaper.

It never occurred to me that having a book in one's own home could be dangerous. I wasn't sure whether Hiro's nonchalance was his way of trying to put me at ease, but his mention of a search made my knees go wobbly. Could even someone like me become suspect in the eyes of the Japanese authorities?

Had Kimmy known about the book before handing it to me, and deliberately thrust it upon me? And what of the other books she said were at her home? I didn't know whether to feel hurt and angry, or whether I should be worrying about her safety. I didn't have the courage to ring and ask.

I put the book under shoeboxes at the bottom of my wardrobe in the hope that I could forget about it altogether.

Monday, 19 May

'Missy, you have phone call from man,' Chokugetsu-ken announced this morning, making me freeze on the spot. Hiro had gone to the office, and I didn't know how to respond to the Special Police. I picked up the receiver with shaking hands and timidly said, '*Moshi moshi*,' certain of a Japanese on the other end.

'Halo? I speak to Mrs Eiko Kishimoto?' was the response, a mellifluous young male voice, which relieved and puzzled me in equal measure.

'My name Shin-tsu Mao, Midori Mama say to call you to arrange Chinese lesson.' Goodness! I had completely forgotten about Midori Mao's promise to have her stepson contact me for Chinese and English language lessons. My lunch with her at the French Club was months ago.

'Midori Mama suggest we meet at family outing to races coming weekend. We come pick you and Mr Kishimoto up Sunday morning. Look forward to meet you,' Shin-tsu said, making me twirl with delight as I hung up. I've never been to the horse races.

Monday, 26 May

Just as promised, the Maos came to fetch us in two chauffeur-driven cars yesterday, and off we went to the races. Tamiko, Rokki and Sachi went in the Packard with Mr Mao and Midori – how could Tamiko even think of taking Sachi to the racecourse! Hiro and I joined Shin-tsu in the Buick. Kazu of course remained happily at home with Miyo, safe in a clean environment.

Just one glance said much about Shin-tsu – a well brought up scion of Chinese wealth, delicately good-looking, confident and gentlemanly. He was dressed in a well-cut blazer, his gentle demeanour avoiding any hint of dashing arrogance. I had been expecting a youth less refined. My confidence drained: how much easier it would be to learn Chinese from and teach English to just a simple student!

'Are we heading to the Shanghai Race Club in the middle of town?' I asked, wanting to break the ice. Hiro raised his eyebrows, and gently reminded me in Japanese that the racecourse had been requisitioned by the Imperial Japanese Army and turned into barracks. Of course I had known that! I felt blood rush to my cheeks. But Shin-tsu responded as if I'd asked a most normal question.

'We go little further out of town to International Race Club in Kiangwan, founded by wealthy Chinese when they cannot be member at Shanghai Race Club. Chinese always more comfortable at International Race Club,' he said, with a sweet smile.

He seemed mature and composed, with little need of English lessons. I wanted to get to know him, and suddenly felt excited by the prospect of regular Chinese lessons from him.

The sky was slightly hazy, the humidity already high enough to make it feel like stifling mid- summer. But being out in the open was liberating. Mr Mao, tall and solidly built, with thin smiling but shrewd eyes, generously handed us money to bet on any horse we wanted. Hiro and Rokki decided to be spectators, not really comfortable with the betting, and Rokki busied himself looking after Sachi. Tamiko and I were left to wander freely.

We rushed to the paddocks to check out the horses: they all seemed frisky, blowing air from their noses and lightly stamping their hoofs. Tamiko poked me. 'Look at that one,' she said, pointing to a horse in the corner, with a forlorn expression, limp and out of place among the others. We felt sorry for it, and decided to put our money on her. 'At least she'll have the two of us cheering her on,' Tamiko said.

Under the marquee, the Maos stood out among fellow spectators, Mr Mao looking most distinguished, Midori ravishing in her cream-coloured linen suit, and Shin-tsu, totally at ease mingling with his parents' social set. Midori being close enough in age to Shin-tsu to be his sister, I wondered what I would have made of this attractive threesome had I not known their relationship.

Once the races started, I was completely captivated. From the minute the gates opened, we were on our feet, mesmerized by the sight of those beautiful beasts pushed by their jockeys to give their best. The speed, the sound of dozens of hoofs pounding the ground, and the cries of the crowds raised my blood level and I could feel my beating heart. In the close melee of horses, I couldn't tell which one was ahead, but after the last bend, one horse started to spring out, extending the distance between those behind her.

'It's ours!' I shouted, and Tamiko and I clasped our hands together and jumped up and down as our horse passed the finishing post.

Mr Mao laughed heartily at our excitement, and seemed very pleased with our winnings. 'That is all yours, ladies, we now go to Sincere's for some shopping!' Amazingly, he really meant it, for on the way home, we were taken to the department store on Nanking Road, where Tamiko and I bought lovely raincoats and lacy handkerchiefs, all thanks to Mr Mao.

6

Wednesday, 3 June 1942

When Chokugetsu-ken announced Kimmy on the phone, I hesitated. What was I to say to her? All I could think of was the book hidden in my wardrobe and the anxiety she'd thrust upon me.

'Could you come to the Public Gardens? We could pick up some street food and eat on the benches. I need to see you,' she said. Her voice sounded faint and timid, and my annoyance was quickly replaced by concern.

I asked Chokugetsu-ken to prepare two Japanese *bento* lunch boxes and a thermos flask of cold buckwheat tea. I would certainly not touch street food, and a homemade picnic seemed comforting. I thought briefly of giving the book back to her, but what if I were caught with it on the way? It seemed too risky. I set out on the tram towards the Bund with trepidation, gazing out of the window without taking in any of the street scenes.

Kimmy was standing at the gates of the park looking pale and shaken – quite a contrast from the confident girl of our last meeting. We sat on a bench well shaded by a large tree, overlooking the Whangpoo. Fortunately, the breeze blew the other way, taking with it the murky smells of the waters, and giving us a clear view. The river looked bare despite the usual throng of sampans and junks and tugs, and I realized it was because the *Conte Verde* was no longer there.

Once we settled, Kimmy blurted, 'Eiko, it was just terrifying, I was so frightened!' She looked ready to burst into tears. I suggested we eat first, to calm her down.

After a few bites, she said, 'I was the first to arrive at the office. It's part of my job to open the place up, let some fresh air into the stuffy room – we're all in one big room and the researchers are heavy smokers. I heard footsteps, and thought it was rather early for the researchers to show up, but didn't bother to look up and continued opening the windows. When I turned around, I nearly jumped seeing two unknown men standing there.' She put down her chopsticks and sought my eyes.

'They came up to me and asked who I was and what I was doing, as if they owned the place. It should have been me asking them the question! Once they realized I belonged there, they started asking about the researchers, which desk belonged to who, that kind of thing. I hesitated because I didn't know if I should be telling them anything, and then one of them said they were policemen and it was my duty to answer their questions.'

If they were after Kimmy, they would come after me, too, I thought, starting to feel resentful.

.'Kimmy, do you have any idea why the police came?' I asked, more sharply than I intended. She looked at me somewhat sheepishly.

'There've been rumours of a crackdown against groups with 'undesirable thoughts'. Recently, a division of the Manchurian Railways was raided because the researchers there were suspected of becoming too left leaning. The fellows in my office sensed it might happen to our office, too, and started getting rid of documents and books.'

'That's why you gave me that book, isn't it,' I said, feeling increasingly put upon.

'No, no, Eiko. Please believe me, I had no idea what was happening back then.' She peered at me with tearful eyes. 'It is only recently that the researchers started destroying documents, and I demanded to know what was happening. To tell you the truth, I didn't even know what kind of research my office does.'

I knew she was telling the truth – put in her situation, I would have been equally, or perhaps even more, naïve. But I still felt annoyed.

'You should have told me as soon as you knew,' I said.

'I didn't have the courage to, and then this thing happened today, and I had to let you know immediately. I am so, so sorry, Eiko, please forgive me.'

Seeing the tears roll down her cheeks, I couldn't hold the matter against her any longer. At least Hiro didn't seem too bothered about the book in our flat. How did her parents react? I asked.

'My father was relatively relaxed – a respectable private Japanese home wouldn't be raided, he said - but my mother was in a panic. She wanted to get rid of the books immediately but didn't know how. Then she remembered a friend with a proper Japanese bath installed in their house – the kind with the outside wood-burning furnace to heat the water. After she rang her friend, she bundled all the books in a *furoshiki* kerchief and disappeared. She came home later smelling of smoke, but looking very pleased with herself.'

With the air between us cleared, the description of Mrs Noguchi and her book-burning mission caused us to collapse into uncontrollable hilarity. It bothered me though, that she had managed to get rid of the suspect books in her house, but I still had mine.

Before parting, I asked what her office did. 'As far as I can tell, the researchers monitor Chinese students suspected of having communist tendencies and spreading anti-Japanese sentiment,' she said.

'If they're following government orders, why a raid on them?' I asked, getting confused.

'I know. It's strange. One researcher told me they read lots of communist literature and try to mingle with the radical students to gather intelligence. So the special police became suspicious. It's crazy – ours is a government office and the researchers are supposed to find out about anti-Japanese elements, and by doing so, another part of the government decides that they are suspect for harbouring dangerous thoughts.'

I'm too tired to think about this convoluted logic.

Tuesday, 9 June

Shin-tsu appeared at 4 o'clock sharp, looking cool and fresh, despite the outside heat – a bright white shirt over nicely pressed navy blue trousers. He confidently shook my hand - no teenage awkwardness, no pushiness, just the ease of a well brought up young man.

Over tea, we started with English conversation. It was an opportunity to find out more about him and his family. 'We live in big house in French Concession, many people in house – Baba's three wives and cook, gardener, other servants. Number one wife my mother, Midori number three, she arrive when I am ten years old.' I was fascinated – and didn't interrupt, even to confirm that *baba* was father in Chinese.

'Midori same age as me now when she marry Baba. Very beautiful. She talk to me and make me feel happy. I no longer lonely. Before she come, Baba and *I*-Mama and *Er*-Mama always out or busy.' Knowing Chinese numbers – *i, er, san, su* – I was amused how he referred to his father's wives. The English lesson ended with just a few grammatical corrections, no need to rush to work on his mild Pidgin.

The Chinese lesson was a struggle. Despite his mild manners, Shin-tsu was a tough teacher. He made me repeat the same sound – 'ma' – over and over, sometimes the tone going up, or stretching, or falling and rising. 'Four tones, very important, changes meaning of word,' he said, in all seriousness. A half hour went by just making funny sounds without learning a single word or phrase. But being the first day, I was happy to stare into his handsome face and listen to his beautiful tones as he kept on trying, unsuccessfully, to make me reproduce the same sounds. 'No Eiko-san, my 'ma' mean horse, but your 'ma' is hemp. I want you to repeat horse!'

By the time we finished, it was close to when Hiro would be home, and I invited Shin-tsu to stay for dinner. But he politely declined, saying he had to go out to meet friends. Of course, university students would have their own activities – silly of me to think he would want to stay.

Wednesday, 17 June

Amah appeared yesterday morning looking pale and unwell, and I sent her to bed immediately. As she turned towards the kitchen, she let out a big groan, bent in half and nearly collapsing on the floor. 'Missy, I sorry, sorry,' she repeated.

Chokugetsu-ken, so efficient with food shopping and cooking, stood looking bewildered, not even thinking of helping his wife to their quarters. My mind raced – what was I to do? For a family member or a Japanese visitor, I would ring the doctor or hospital, but would Amah be comfortable with a Japanese or Western doctor?

While I was at a loss, Miyo quietly helped Amah onto a kitchen chair, took her pulse and gently questioned her on her symptoms. I had never paid much attention to how Miyo and Amah communicated, and was fascinated by their mixture of hand gestures and English and Japanese words.

'Where hurt?' Miyo asked, and Amah returned a blank look. Switching to Japanese, Miyo asked, '*itai?*' pointing to the abdomen and received a positive nod. Amah also pointed to her shoulder, indicating pain there. After a light prod to determine the spot, Miyo turned to me and said, 'Oku-sama, I think she has an ectopic pregnancy and needs a doctor.'

Miyo further amazed me by suggesting a Chinese herbal doctor she knows over in Hongkew. I immediately told Chokugetsu-ken to take Amah there by pedicab. Upon their return at nightfall, I learned that Miyo's diagnosis had been correct. The Chinese doctor had given her special herbs to induce a miscarriage, and the naturally robust Amah recovered remarkably quickly.

Although still pale, she seemed a different person by morning. 'Missy, Meeyo, savey life, tank you, tank you,' she repeated, with tears in her eyes. Miyo simply smiled, and helped Amah brew the herbal medication given by the doctor.

'Oku-sama, with the brew and a few days' rest, I think she will soon be back to normal,' Miyo said.

My eyes were opened to Miyo's professionalism and resourcefulness. Her reticence, which I thought was from her discomfort with us, I now see as her natural thoughtfulness. She said she came to know of this Chinese herbal doctor through her visits to the

Uchiyama Bookshop on her days off. I'm glad she has her own social circle among old Hongkew hands.

Tuesday, 23 June

Had my second session with Shin-tsu today. We started with Chinese, and we sat across each other at the table, making it easier for me to focus on the movement of Shin-tsu's lips as he embarked on the endless repetition of 'ma' 'ma' 'ma's to get the tones right.

During English conversation, I asked him about his friends. 'Friends, my *tomodachi*, many from different places, not easy to describe.' I was surprised that the Japanese word for friend popped out of his mouth.

'Eiko-san, I speak Japanese *sukoshi*. Picked up when spend time with Midori Mama, who take me to Uchiyama Bookshop many time. Mrs Uchiyama give Japanese sweets, and Mr Uchiyama read me Japanese folk tale,' he said. It surprised me that Midori, flashy and glamorous, had been a frequent visitor to the Uchiyama Bookshop.

'When Midori Mama arrive, she not very happy at home. *I*-Mama and *Er*-Mama not nice to her. Say mean things, that she don't belong because she Japanese, things like that. Baba never home during day to see this. So Midori go to Bookshop to see her friend, Mrs Uchiyama. She say Mrs Uchiyama most understand her because of same background. Don't know what she mean, but she always take me with her, and I love them.' Shin-tsu's eyes glowed as he spoke.

'Mr Uchiyama use to have Japanese children group, and he tell them Chinese stories. He include me, and when I grew older, he introduce me to Lu Hsun, my favourite writer.'

Shin-tsu spoke thoughtfully throughout, sometimes pausing, looking straight into me – those piercing eyes on his handsome face – as if to check that I am taking in not just his words, but also the implications behind the words. He seemed eager to open up to me, making my heart flutter.

Thinking about his pauses now, maybe he was expecting me to correct his English! Oh dear. But Shin-tsu has a way of making me forget it's a lesson: his appealing mixture of candid innocence and deep intelligence makes me focus on what's he's saying, and I forget about how he is saying it. How I'd like to know more about Chinese literature – to know what it tells me about Shin-tsu that Lu Hsun is his favourite writer.

Wednesday, 24 June

The days are getting excruciatingly hot. We are fortunate to have high ceilings and ceiling fans, but one step outside, and the body immediately becomes sticky from the heat and humidity. Kazu is getting prickly heat all over his body, and now always smells of talcum powder. Sachi, on the other hand, isn't bothered at all. They spend more time indoors because of the heat, and Sachi has taken to her new game, playing 'house', where she is the wife and Kazu the hen-pecked husband.

Tamiko and I were in hysterics, watching the two of them, Sachi ordering Kazu to 'do this', 'do that', and Kazu faithfully running around the room obeying. Even the usually protective Amah seemed bemused. She let out a soft cackle and said, 'She little Shanghai *tai-tai*.' Tamiko laughed and explained that Shanghai matrons are known for their pushiness. Our amusement encouraged Sachi to boss Kazu around even more.

Amah is completely recovered, back to her sweet usual self, only even more devoted. She is always saying 'Missy savey me from die' at every opportunity.

Friday, 26 June

I haven't seen Anne lately, and don't know what's happening with Daddy's situation, but Tamiko heard from her Quaker friends that the *Gripsholm*, a Swedish liner, left New York last week carrying over a thousand Japanese on board.

'In a few days' time, the Americans in China will head back to the US on the *Conte Verde*,' she said.

'They must be keen to get away from this war, and how lucky to be going on the *Conte Verde*,' I said, remembering the dazzling sight of the liner on the Whangpoo.

'It won't be as comfortable as you think. The *Gripsholm* left with three times more passengers than capacity and the *Conte Verde* will be the same. Even so, there will be many disappointed Americans left behind,' Tamiko said.

'In a month's time, all the boats – the *Gripsholm*, the *Conte Verde*, and the *Asama-Maru*, leaving Yokohama any day with Americans in Japan on board – will be gathering at a port called Lorenço Marques in Portuguese East Africa, where the exchange takes place. Can you imagine, Eiko, what a strange scene it could be? Japanese and American diplomats and business people who probably know each other from social functions and could be friends, filing off one boat and getting on the other. And probably not being allowed to communicate during the process because they are now enemy nationals.'

Tamiko looked in the distance, as if she were actually witnessing the exchange. The concept of 'exchange repatriation' suddenly became a physical reality to me – the *Conte Verde* offloading Americans at this East African port, and filling up with Japanese to bring them back to Shanghai or Yokohama. No wonder Anne described the preparations as a 'nightmare'.

Monday, 29 June

Yesterday, as Tamiko, Rokki, Hiro and I were heading towards Hongkew for a Japanese lunch, we came upon long queues of dock-workers carrying heavy loads, snaking along the piers. Hundreds of people were milling about with worried, frustrated expressions. Although overcast, the humidity was excruciating, and the stench from the waters made me retch.

The people assembled were all tall and fair, the area a sea of sun-bonnets and panamas. It was an extraordinary sight: the Americans waiting to board the *Conte Verde* although the boat was nearly unrecognizable. It now had a large red Japanese 'rising sun' and two equally large white crosses painted over the single green line across her body. Most strikingly garish were the two crosses constructed on the upper part of the ship, lined with what looked like hundreds of tiny light bulbs.

'They certainly made sure the boat is easily spotted as an exchange boat, even in the dark,' Rokki said. Rather than giving me comfort, it highlighted the dangers of the sea. The sheer amount of cargo being loaded was beyond imagination – hundreds of coolies nearly bent into half with heavy loads on their backs marching onto the boat. It brought into stark reality the huge number of people that need to be fed over the long journey.

'This is a historical event,' Rokki said. 'We should witness it from my office.' We marched into the Yokohama Specie Bank Building and placed ourselves in front of the large windows, with a pair of binoculars to share among us. Hiro was the first to look through the binoculars, and after a long look, gave out a little gasp.

'I see the Bakers. We must let them know that their furniture will be kept for them even if they are back in America,' he said. I was impressed by Hiro's memory – it took me a while to remember that the Bakers were the couple from whom we took over our flat.

Tamiko, too, found people she knew among the throng – some Quakers seeing off friends. There was some kind of registration going on, men with clipboards working their way amongst the crowd. A smaller boat approached, letting off more Americans, who joined the general melee. Everything seemed chaotic, with no sign of anyone getting on the *Conte Verde* for a long time yet.

Tamiko and Hiro decided to go down into the crowd. The thought horrified me – the heat and the dirt and the smell. I was relieved when Rokki said he would prefer to stay put, too.

When Hiro and Tamiko returned about an hour later, Tamiko was looking unusually subdued.

'This American widow, Mildred, who I just met, is supposed to look out for a pair of twelve-year-old twin girls when she arrives at Lorenço Marques. The girls are travelling on their own from Japan because their parents weren't released from prison in time to make the boat.'

'Why are the parents in prison?' I asked.

Tamiko heaved a sad sigh. 'There is no reason. The parents are American Quakers who have been professors at the Japanese university for many years, very well respected. After Pearl Harbor, the Special Police arrested them on spy charges. The State Department negotiated their release, and Japan agreed. But they're still in prison.'

Looking at Rokki, Tamiko said, 'The Friends Centre here think it might be because Harold Lane was a known conscientious objector during the First World War. The Japanese military don't like that. It's so worrisome for all Quakers.' Rokki's frown deepened.

Hiro, meanwhile, was busy with the binoculars, observing the endless cargo slowly being loaded on the *Conte Verde*. I joined him by the window. 'Twelve thousand pounds of meat, 4,000 pounds of poultry, 20,000 pounds of fish, another 20,000 pounds of fruit, 800 sacks of flour, 200,000 eggs...' he muttered, showing me a list a Japanese official had given him on the amount of food needed for the Japanese exchange boats reloading at Lorenço Marques.

Tuesday, 30 June

I had a strange dream last night. I was on the boat that took me back from London to Japan, only I was much younger, and felt terribly lonely and kept looking for Mummy and Daddy. I was wandering around the boat, looking everywhere, and getting increasingly frantic. It seemed that Mummy was somewhere far away, making me feel that I wouldn't find her, but Daddy seemed closer at hand. It felt that I could reach him any moment, yet I couldn't find him and became increasingly desperate. At the height of anxiety, I woke up.

For a moment I didn't know where I was, and then felt a surge of relief knowing it was just a dream.

How odd that Tamiko's story about the twelve-year-old twins and my own boat journey when I was eighteen should get mixed together into a disturbing dream.

The feeling of unease from the dream lingered on as I mulled over the events of yesterday, wondering whether the Americans were on board the *Conte Verde* by now. And thinking of the Quakers, I couldn't shake off the image of Keith and Joyce – their baby due any day now – overlapping with the fate of the Lane girls.

The phone rang breaking my trance. It was Shin-tsu, saying that instead of our regular lesson next Tuesday, Midori wanted to invite Tamiko and me for lunch at their house. I will miss my little tête-à-tête with Shin-tsu, but how exciting to see the Maos' residence!

7

A bonnie baby girl born to Joyce and Keith! Happy news that dispelled the unease from my disturbing dream.

We celebrated over tea at Jiro and Sayako's, where Irma was bubbling with excitement, as if she was a proud new grandmother. 'The most beautiful baby mädchen! Such an easy birth, too, baby popped out in less than an hour!' Keith, unable to get a word in edge ways, smiled contentedly.

Keith left shortly for the hospital to join baby Anna May and Joyce, and Irma's tone suddenly changed. Turning to Masaya, she said, 'I didn't want to bring up gloomy news in Keith's presence, but tell me Masaya, what do you know about man called Meisinger being here in Shanghai? Refugees are worried he will push Japanisch to treat Jews in same way as Germany. And they hear that Jews there are being shipped by trainloads to concentration camps.'

Irma bore her eyes into Masaya's face, making him look down into his whisky glass.

After a long pause, he finally said that Meisinger had been in his office meeting people, but his intentions were unclear.

'We think he's here to collect information on Germans,' Masaya said, 'to root out any spying activities that's anti-Nazi. You know how complicated Shanghai is, with thousands of Jews and Russians and underground activities, never sure where people's allegiances lie.'

'We don't think he's here to be involved with the treatment of the Jews,' he added.

Irma persisted. 'But Masaya, rumours are flying, the refugee community is very much distressed!'

His expression was so pained, I could barely look at him. He closed his eyes for a while, and I wondered whether it was to suppress tears. From the corner of my eye, I noticed Tamiko's hand softly reach over and give his forearm a gentle squeeze, but Masaya appeared lost in a still numbness.

Irma quickly saw the distress she was causing, and reverted to her motherly persona. 'Masaya, Liebling, I know you are doing what you can, and all Jews are grateful to your office for showing real care. Don't take what I say to heart. I speak just to let you know refugees' concerns.' She gave him a sturdy pat on the shoulder.

Masaya responded with a grateful nod, but after she left, he looked at Tamiko as if appealing for understanding.

'We don't know what pressure the Nazis are putting on Japan because the Army is suspicious of our office and information doesn't flow our way. And to some Army young hotheads, Meisinger's hard-line approach is appealing. We want to protect the Jews, but if my office seems too sympathetic, it could backfire – a mighty difficult balancing act. I can only offer my prayers, and believe me, I am praying almost every minute of the day.'

I feel exhausted from so many topsy-turvy emotions – the joy of Anna May's birth quickly overshadowed by Irma's distress and worries about the German situation. If Meisinger is collecting information on Germans, would they become suspicious of Frederick Ringhausen because of my ignorant mention of Irma and her refugee work at Ayako's tea party? And if the Germans are tightening control over fellow Germans, the Japanese might be doing the same towards us civilians. And I still have Kimmy's book in the wardrobe...

Tuesday, 7 July

It was the Mao lunch today.

I had expected something grand, but not quite as grand as the elegant four-storey grey stone mansion with two lower wings. Tamiko really should have left Sachi behind at home, I thought, as we entered the grounds through imposing wrought iron gates, crunching our feet over the gravelled driveway. Suddenly, out of nowhere appeared two gobbling large turkeys, one charging straight towards Sachi, making her shriek and burst into tears. Tamiko swiftly lifted her up, and chuckled in amusement. Had it been Kazu, I would have been horrified, but I laughed, thinking see what happens when you bring a child to a lunch for grown-ups.

Seated in the large dining room, Mr Mao, Midori and Shin-tsu on one side and us on the other, we were treated to a sumptuous feast of dish after dish of exquisite Shanghai cuisine. Tamiko told me later that the carp dish, called *congshao jiyu*, would have taken days to prepare, needing to be soaked in vinegar, then deep-fried, then stewed with scallions for a very long time. As tender, rich fish melted in my mouth, I felt sorry that Hiro was not there to sample such delicacies.

Mr Mao was a gregarious host, telling us of his travels in China inspecting sugar cane plantations, and of his love of Japan and the Japanese ever since his student days there in the 1920s. I couldn't tell whether it was my imagination, but Shin-tsu seemed unusually withdrawn, almost as if he was embarrassed by his father. There was discomfort in his attitude that I had never noticed before.

At the end of lunch, Shin-tsu made a hasty exit, remembering some student meeting he was to attend, and Sachi was excused from the table to wander around. It must have been a good thirty minutes before we noticed that Sachi was nowhere in sight. Tamiko just smiled and continued her conversation, so I volunteered to go and find her.

Despite the heat outside, the whole mansion felt remarkably comfortable, ceiling fans twirling high above in the large common rooms and corridors, with a cross breeze coming from the open French windows. I ascended the magnificent staircase, to the first floor without seeing Sachi, and then on to the second floor where there was a half open door. As I approached, I could hear low voices, and thinking that Sachi might be there, I pushed the door slightly and peered in.

Two middle aged Chinese ladies, quite heavily made-up, in silk gowns, were reclined on a large platform bed with a table in the middle. A young servant girl was busy dipping what looked like a knitting needle into a ceramic pot, and then burning the tip on a bluish white flame from a lamp. In the meantime, the ladies smoked long delicate pipes, eyes half closed in contentment. As I took in the scene, briefly inhaling the faint sweet, slightly sickly aroma, I knew I shouldn't be there and yet felt glued to the spot in fascination. Never would I have imagined Mr Mao's first and second wives spending their day smoking opium. Which of them was Shin-tsu's mother, I wondered.

By the time I returned downstairs, Sachi was back at the table, and it was time for us to leave. Neither Mr Mao nor Midori seemed the least concerned that I had wandered off to the far regions of the house, but I felt I had pried into a dark secret.

Saturday, 11 July

I'm enjoying a wonderfully quiet moment, alone in the flat – Hiro off playing tennis, Miyo, Kazu and Sachi in the courtyard, no sign of Amah and Chokugetsu-ken. The day is hot, but not so humid, and I see Sachi chasing Kazu. When Tamiko brought her over earlier, Sachi said to Kazu, 'We play turkey!' Perhaps that's what they are doing now.

The papers report promising news of Japan's war efforts, making advances in the Aleutians and New Guinea. I wonder if the war could end soon. How nice that would be, if the fighting stopped and Japanese and Westerners and Chinese could lively peacefully together. Sitting here in this comfortable setting, looking out on a beautiful summer's day, it all seems possible – Japan ending the war while she is ahead. If Japan followed what she preached in the true spirit of a Greater East Asia Co-prosperity Sphere and governed justly, could everyone start afresh together? I pray this is not just wishful thinking.

Sunday, 12 July

Being a Sunday, the Uchiyama Bookshop was busier than my previous visit with Tamiko, and it seemed we had joined the backroom tea-gathering in the midst of an ongoing conversation.

A man dressed in a typical Chinese gown barely acknowledged our arrival and continued talking. 'As I was saying, the China Film Company and the Manchurian Motion Picture Company are making a joint film, with the Manchurian film star, Li Koran, featuring in it.'

The mention of Li Koran captured my attention, making me think of Mother Kishimoto who was a big fan. How she used to pour over the newspapers when Li Koran came to Japan for concert performances! She'd read some article that hinted that Li was actually Japanese rather than Chinese. 'That can't be true. Look at her face, no Japanese woman has such big eyes and distinct cheek bones!' Mother had exclaimed.

'Daisuke-san, perhaps you should let our guests settle down first,' said the perky lady who was busy pouring us tea. 'Excuse my husband, he gets carried away when it comes to films. I am Michiko Otsuka – everyone calls me Cheeko – and this is Daisuke. Everyone thinks he is Chinese, but he's really Japanese!' She spoke good naturedly in a rapid twitter, the name Cheeko seeming totally appropriate as she reminded me of a little chick busily chirping away.

Daisuke ignored the interruption. 'I'm telling you, the process of a joint production between the Manchurian Company and the China Film Company will be interesting to watch. I bet the Chinese actors at the China Film Company won't be so comfortable performing with Li Koran. Quite intriguing. Ha, ha, ha.' What a curious man, I thought, especially since I couldn't understand at all what he was talking about.

Rokki later explained that Daisuke went to university in Peking, and became part of the Peking opera set. 'He mixes not only with opera singers but with actors and critics. So knows a lot about films too. He's friendly with the Japanese head of the China Film Company, a liberal man committed to pure movie-making, but of course the Manchurian Motion Picture Company is known as a Japanese propaganda machine.'

Tamiko voiced my impressions. 'A rather unusual man. Especially since his real job is senior sales manager at one of the largest Japanese cotton mills. With such a delightfully friendly wife.'

Tuesday, 21 July

Shin-tsu came over today, the first time since the lunch at their mansion. There was no trace of the uneasiness I had detected then, and we began our English conversation over tea as usual. But I felt constricted in bringing up anything personal in our conversation, the strange atmosphere of their household still fresh in my mind.

During a lull in the conversation, Kazu unexpectedly toddled into the room, and to my surprise, Shin-tsu's face lit up.

'I would like baby brother or sister very much,' he said, with a sigh. '*I*-Mama, after me, have no more children. *Er*-Mama, no children. When Midori-Mama come, I hopeful for baby, but not yet, and already eight years.'

I wondered whether he felt heavy pressure being an only child of a wealthy businessman – perhaps the reason for the uneasiness in his father's presence.

'After university, will you work for your father?' I asked. For the first time, I saw a fierce, angry expression on Shin-tsu's smooth face.

'Never,' he said. 'Baba's business very complicated. Also, now is very difficult political situation. Baba work very closely with Japanese, making life easy for us now, but…'

He paused, as if searching for the right words to continue on. Did he not believe that Japan would win the war? I couldn't imagine that Shin-tsu, with a Japanese stepmother he is so close to, could be anything other than pro-Japanese.

His thoughtful silence was stretching so long that I was about to change the subject when he simply said, 'Chinese people, Western people, Japanese people, everyone suffer in war. I hope war end soon.'

The more I see of Shin-tsu, the more I sense that there is a depth to him beyond his tender age. I find myself wanting to know more about his inner world, feeling fascinated and protective at the same time. As if he were a younger brother I never had.

On parting, he casually mentioned that he would not be able to come during August because he will be going away.

'On summer holiday? Where to?' I asked, somewhat enviously as I hear it gets even hotter and more unpleasant in Shanghai in August. He smiled rather mysteriously and said nowhere special, just a break he's planning with university friends. I will miss him.

Tuesday, 28 July

Twenty-one years old today! I was certain that Hiro would not remember my birthday, so it was a surprise to find a bicycle in the hallway with a big red ribbon attached. Hiro was quick to point out that the ribbon was all Tamiko's idea. The thought of Tamiko persuading Hiro to do something so unlike him was a lovely birthday present in itself.

Having a bicycle has actually become a necessity these days, with more and more buses taken off the roads to save fuel. I gave Hiro a deep bow of appreciation, which was met by a slightly embarrassed but very sweet smile.

Mid-morning, I changed into a billowy skirt and simple blouse, grabbed a pair of comfortable shoes and took my bicycle out for a virgin journey. I swiftly overcame my initial wobbliness, and headed towards Jessfield Park, remembering that a Japanese grocery van came on Tuesdays to the Toyoda Cotton Mill housing compound nearby. By the time I got through the narrow, crowded lanes and reached the wider Yu Yuen Road, I had found my stride and was enjoying the warm breeze against my face.

I nearly missed the entrance to the Toyoda compound, but the van caught the corner of my eye, and I quickly jumped off the bicycle. The van was a rickety, old rusted vehicle with a canvas top, now pulled back to display the wares. But the groceries looked good, and I was rummaging through a pile of Japanese radishes, when I felt a little tap on my shoulder. It was Cheeko, the perky lady we had met at the Uchiyama Bookshop.

'Eiko-san, what are you doing here?' she asked. Before waiting for my answer, she chirped away in a high-pitched voice. 'We live in this compound. Daisuke works for the Toyoda Cotton Mills. I've never seen you at the van before. You must come more often!'

She led me to a nearby bench while continuing her chatter. 'There are a few Japanese families around us in the compound, but Daisuke socializes with his Chinese opera friends. He's lived in China since he was eighteen years old, and is probably happier speaking Chinese. But I am so happy to be speaking to you in Japanese!'

'How pretty you look in your fresh white blouse!' she went on. 'When I first arrived in Shanghai, I had no sense of fashion. Daisuke on the other hand is very fashion-conscious and has suits made for him all the time. He also loves Chinese gowns, especially in the summer – very cool, he says – and has them custom made too. He still buys most of my clothes for me, not trusting my taste.'

Cheeko's happy chatter was uplifting, and I felt drawn to her. Her attire – a floral patterned blouse and a striped skirt in clashing colours, with a Japanese-style apron smock thrown over – made me like her even more, especially after her description of Daisuke's fashion sense.

Speaking of, I must put my pen down and think of what to wear tonight – my slinky black dress or the pastel chiffon? I wonder which Hiro would prefer, for our birthday evening outing – my first visit to a nightclub with Tamiko and Rokki.

Thursday, 29 July

I am still dazzled by the glitter and the shimmer of the Paramount, the grandest nightclub in Shanghai just off the Bubbling Well Road. Although there were other entertainment establishments around, the Paramount stood out by its sheer size, and the enticing glow from the stained glass windows adorning the opulent *art moderne* building. I can still feel the rush of excitement as we entered the ballroom, softly lit by a series of chandeliers that cast an alluring sheen. I noticed a number of eyes following us, making me stand taller so that my chiffon dress could spread, feeling a bit like a film star.

The live band was playing the Charleston, the dance floor filled with people dressed exquisitely, especially the Chinese ladies in their silky body-hugging *cheongsams*. Skirting around the dance floor, we were led to a cosy table, covered with a pristine white tablecloth, on which sat a vase of pink flowers and gently flickering candles. Once I became used to the dim lighting, I could see the people at other tables – a smattering of Westerners, some well-dressed Chinese, and many Japanese including smug-looking military men, surrounded by pretty ladies.

I noticed that every time the band started a new tune, a few men would head to the side of the dance floor where a cluster of beauti-fully-dressed girls congregated, and take the hand of one of them in exchange for a ticket. The look of the girls suddenly made me think of Midori Mao, and I instinctively felt I knew how Midori had met Mr Mao. I could practically see her being led onto the dance floor by him.

How different it was from my debutante dances in London – fresh-faced young men down from Cambridge and Oxford eyeing us girls in our finery as the chaperons discreetly stood around the ballroom! Here, the atmosphere was full of shadows, stripped of innocence – perhaps befitting for a new twenty-one-year-old.

Rokki, usually serious and scholarly, surprised me by leaping up and pulling Tamiko with him. Before I knew it, they were on the floor dancing the tango, of all things! Hiro and I, left behind, sat awkwardly as the fast tempo music played away. Finally, when the waltz came on, we arose, and for the first time ever, Hiro and I were dancing together – a strange sensation. I hadn't even known he could dance.

But for Hiro, the excitement of the evening was not dancing with me. During our waltz, I spotted Li Koran, the Manchurian singer and actress, on the dance floor with a Japanese military officer. She was even more striking in person than on the screen, and Hiro and I rushed back to our table to watch her. After another dance, Li Koran returned to her table, which was not very far from ours. Most of her group were Chinese actors – all terribly good-looking, and among them an older Japanese gentleman.

Hiro suddenly stood up, muttering that he had spotted an acquaintance. It turned out to be the Japanese gentleman at Li Koran's table. Tamiko, Rokki and I watched with great amusement as Hiro made his way, and after what seemed like a brief introduction around the table, we could not believe our eyes, Hiro had Li Koran on his arm, heading towards the dance floor!

The dance was a fox trot – Li Koran was obviously the better dancer, but Hiro held his ground. Tamiko and I couldn't stop giggling over Hiro's expression as he danced - trying to appear carefree when he was so obviously over the moon, at the same time having to concentrate on his dance steps. When he came back to our table, he was flushed, and unable to conceal his triumphant expression.

He tried to appear nonchalant, saying 'She really does speak Japanese perfectly.' But we could all see through his almost child-like elation, causing good-natured teasing on Rokki's part and merriment and laughter by all, including Hiro himself. I felt an enormous surge of affection – my somewhat aloof husband suddenly became human, making me feel very grown-up.

It couldn't have been a better evening – a very happy twenty-first birthday indeed.

Friday, 31 July

Tamiko rushed over this morning with news that Daddy was on the repatriation boat, the *El Nil*, which had left Liverpool for Lorenço Marques. We embraced and remained in each other's arms for a long while.

'Eiko, we must keep faith and pray for his safety. Once in Japan, his life will no longer be in suspension. He'll be back at work at bank headquarters, and Rokki can be in regular contact through bank channels. It will be such a relief,' Tamiko said, squeezing my hand, as if willing his safe return.

Tuesday, 4 August

Ever since knowing of Daddy's repatriation, I've been wondering whether I would hear from Anne, who should be leaving Shanghai soon for the exchange, taking the *El Nil* back to England once the boat is emptied of the Japanese at Lorenço Marques. But no sight of her, no word from her.

I decided to cycle to the pier to see for myself the boat, the *Tatsuta-Maru*, scheduled to leave any day now with the British on board, the very boat that would be collecting Daddy to take him back to Japan.

When I finally got there, struggling through the crowded roads in the stifling heat, I saw only gunboats, tugs and sampans: no *Tatsuta-Maru*. Where were the British, or at least the coolies loading the boat with supplies?

I dismounted my bicycle and pushed towards the water. All that was there was a wide, empty berth, with bits of floating rubbish.

I had missed the boat.

I felt devastated, worried that my ill luck might be a bad omen for Daddy's journey. No, no, I said to myself, vigorously rejecting any such foolish thoughts. My true disappointment came from the realization that the British were gone. Anne had left, and I wasn't getting Jane after all. I hadn't even admitted to myself how much I looked forward to having a dog again. Anne's seeming trust in me had given me hope. But we were, after all, from enemy countries, and my expectation had been wishful thinking.

Monday, 10 August

Just as I was thinking how I missed my lessons with Shin-tsu, Midori rang wanting to know whether I had any word from him. It seemed a bit strange.

'No, not since our last lesson about three weeks ago,' I said. 'Hadn't he gone to the countryside with his university friends?'

'Oh, is that what he told you? To me, he said he was going away with people he knew from Uncle Uchiyama's Bookshop. But Uncle knows nothing about it,' Midori muttered.

Unsettled, I asked whether everything was all right. 'It's nothing to do with Shin-tsu. I just wanted to let him know of some trouble we've had at the house, and reassure him that we're fine.' Without any more explanation, she apologized for the sudden call, and hung up.

Worried, I rushed over to Tamiko's to see if she had heard from Midori. She hadn't, and suggested that we visit straight away in case she needed help. 'But she wasn't very forthcoming,' I said.

'She will be grateful to see us,' Tamiko said decisively. 'Much as Mr Mao adores her, he is a busy man always at work, and with Shin-tsu away, she would appreciate company.' Having said that, Tamiko collected her handbag and nudged me to follow her.

When the pedicab pulled up to the gates of Mao Mansion, it seemed a different place from the one we had visited just a month ago. The grillwork of the wrought iron gates was covered from the inside with sheets of dark metal, shielding the house from the outside world. It looked very unwelcoming, and I felt like pulling Tamiko away to go back home.

But she charged straight ahead, trying to push the gates open, and when they didn't budge, started banging fiercely. A heavyset Chinese man peeped through a small square opening, and upon seeing us, released the bolt. Tamiko spoke to him in Chinese, and to my relief, he nodded and led us to the front door. Another man, thin and dark, was standing ominously by a makeshift guard box, a rifle hanging over his shoulder.

Midori appeared at the door, looking beautiful in a simple but elegant floral cotton summer dress. Only the bags under her eyes indicated something amiss. Her face lit up with appreciation as soon as she saw us, just as Tamiko had expected.

Leading us through the grand hallway into the living room, she pointed to a few holes in the wall. 'This is what happened. A car came roaring into the driveway, and a couple of men, faces hidden under deep caps, charged into the house with pistols in their hands, shooting randomly. Shanghai violence is nothing new to me. But not in my own home,' she said.

She calmly continued: 'We don't know whether the shooting was meant to be just a threat, or whether Wen-tsu was actually being targeted. He was taking a bath at the time, and could have been killed if the men went into all the rooms. Fortunately, they remained in the stairwell, shooting into the air. So it probably was only a threat.'

When Tamiko asked whether she had any idea who the attackers might be, Midori said it could be anyone as her husband wasn't without enemies. 'Wen-tsu works closely with the Japanese, so he is obviously an irritant for Chiang Kai-shek's side. At the same time, with so many food short-ages now, sugar is a precious commodity. There's lots of smug-gling between Free and Occupied China and people make huge profits. I'm not saying that Wen-tsu is involved in ille-gal trade, but there are all sorts of people, including military officials, who, I am sure would like to get their hands on his sugar.'

I was struck by Midori's cool-headedness, a different side to her from the flamboyant lady at the racetracks. Recalling Mr Mao's shrewd-looking eyes and mysterious air, I felt their world was beyond my comprehension.

'And then there are the communists,' Midori continued. 'It's impossible to know who is an underground activist, and of course they are the most anti-Japanese of all. Their network is broad among the intellectuals...'

I shuddered by the mention of communists. Hiro always seemed disdainful, and even liberal Daddy, a regular participant at Fabian Society meetings in London, never had anything nice to say about communists.

When we were leaving, Midori took my hand and said, 'Do let me know if you hear from Shin-tsu. He enjoys your lessons and is very fond of you.'

Wednesday, 12 August

Kazu had another upset tummy today, with a slight fever – a reg-ular occurrence every few weeks, especially since the weather has become so hot. Why is it that my poor Kazu is so prone to illnesses? The saving grace is that Miyo knows exactly what to do and remains calm and cheerful – probably the reason for Kazu's relatively quick recovery each time. I have learned not to be overly concerned, although I feel wretched when I see his discomfort.

Friday, 14 August

I ruffle the coarse hair of the little creature on my knee to make sure she is real, still in wonderment at what happened today.

The front doorbell rang mid-morning, and standing in front of me was Anne, with a big box in her arms and Jane by her feet. I blinked in disbelief, so certain that she had already left Shanghai.

'I'm sorry I didn't ring in advance, but things have been so hectic, I just thought I would pop over when I had the chance. I'm so sorry,' Anne said, misunderstanding my startled look.

She seemed even more gaunt since the last time I saw her, and her hair and clothing were dishevelled, as if she really had been running around frantically. But her eyes had a bright gleam.

'We are finally leaving Shanghai, Eiko. What a relief! The repatriation negotiations finally came to a close, a huge weight off the shoulders. The Japanese now have a list of all the British who are to leave, and the British have seen off the Japanese from Liverpool!'

I told her that we had word that Daddy was on the *El Nil*. 'And I thought you would have left on the *Tatsuta-Maru*,' I added.

'No, no, we will be on the *Kamakura-Maru*, which picks up 900 of us from China. The *Tatsuta-Maru* stopped in Shanghai, but only picked up a few British because it was already full with Brits from Japan,' Anne said.

'We leave in three days' time, and once we arrive at Lorenço Marques, we won't be getting on the *El Nil*, as that will be filled with everyone from the *Tatsuta-Maru*. Our exchange boat is the *City of Canterbury*, which is picking up Japanese from Australia and the Dutch East Indies.'

From the way she spoke, she must have explained the complicated arrangements many times, probably to the numerous British people seeking to secure a place on either of the boats.

'Goodness, how I am going on when my reason for being here is to hand over Jane!' she said, catching herself.

'Eiko, it will be such a comfort to know that she is with you.' She picked Jane up and placed her in my arms. Jane was quivering and looking towards Anne, as if she sensed a life change. Kazu, who had been shuffling around my legs, jumped up and down trying to touch her, and I gently turned aside to protect Jane from his eager hands. How vulnerable Jane seemed at this moment.

'I've been so caught up in our own affairs, I haven't seen or spoken to you for ages. And now I am dumping Jane on you at the last minute,' Anne said, as if having Jane would be a burden on us.

I sheepishly confessed that I had been longing to have Jane, and when I thought Anne had left, I harboured the tiniest doubt that perhaps being on opposite sides of the war mattered.

Anne took my hands into hers and gave me a soft smile. 'Eiko, Jane sensed your qualities from the outset, and brought me closer to you. You are a person I respect, and nationality doesn't matter.' I squeezed her hand back and held Jane ever so tightly.

'Jane's things are in here,' she said, handing me the big box. 'I must be going now.'

She leant over and kissed Jane, who was still in my arms, and then gave me a peck on the cheek and dashed out of the door.

Although I wanted to see her out to the lift, I thought it better that I didn't and remained on the spot, putting my face close to Jane to take in her smell. How comforting doggy smells can be! Even when I heard the lift door close I couldn't make myself move, totally overwhelmed by Anne's unexpected visit.

When I finally got around to opening the box, I found not only Jane's basket, leads, a bowl, but also some English tea and biscuits – items that have become so difficult to obtain these days, especially for Westerners strapped for money. I said a silent thank you to Anne in my thoughts and prayed for her safe journey back to England.

Saturday, 15 August

I could spend all day just watching Jane and Kazu. Jane seems to think of Kazu as a rival. If I show any interest in what Kazu is doing, she comes rushing over and brushes against my legs. Kazu on the other hand is totally fascinated, constantly sticking out his hand to touch her. But Jane is disdainful. She slips away as fast as she can, with Kazu still reaching over calling 'Jay-jay, Jay-jay'.

But it is Hiro's reaction that tickles me most. I will never forget his surprised expression as he saw her rushing towards him upon entering the flat yesterday evening, and then the big smile and gleaming eyes as he bent down to give her a pat. He took a long time saying goodbye to Jane when he left for his tennis game this morning, with just a quick wave of his hand at Kazu and me.

Monday, 17 August

Even with the departure of many British and Americans, I was amazed by how cosmopolitan Shanghai still is as we gathered for the Shanghai Philharmonic Orchestra's summer concert held in the lawns of the former racecourse. Everyone was dressed in their summer finery – women in kimono, *cheongsam* and flowing dresses with matching shawls, men in linen suits or elegant Chinese gowns.

We sat on deck chairs under the stars as the music – ranging from jazz to popular opera pieces from *The Merry Widow* and *La Traviata* – played away. It was pure bliss: the breeze, the music, the applause, the gentle rustling of the trees and bushes, and hushed voices of appreciation between numbers. It brought back memories of Hyde Park on a beautiful summer's evening, and I closed my eyes to absorb the wonderful atmosphere.

During intermission, I ran into our German upstairs neighbours. 'You are enjoying the concert?' Herr Schmidt asked in his accented English. 'Very generous of ze Japanese Army to allow ze concert on zese vunderful grounds,' he said, with a slight bow. Frau Schmidt, barely acknowledged me, pulling at her husband to steer him away to a group of Germans nearby.

I don't know what came over me – I had the urge to win over this older woman with an intimidating hauteur. 'We are having a party soon, and I would be delighted if you could come,' I heard myself saying.

Frau Schmidt seemed taken aback, but quickly regained her composure, and said stiffly, '*Danke*. Ve look forward to it.'

I was still questioning my rashness for inventing a dinner party for people we barely know as we walked out of the racecourse grounds onto Nanking Road, which seemed somehow different from usual. It took me a moment to realize that the neon lights were out, creating an eerily dark atmosphere. I grabbed on to Hiro's sleeve to keep from tripping.

'It's the blackout,' he said. 'Because of increased air activity over Shanghai, they decided lights out after ten.'

8

Tuesday, 1 September 1942

Shin-tsu is back. Despite Midori's concern, he returned, just as he said he would at the beginning of September.

I greeted him with much fuss, which he accepted with an amused grin. Apart from the suntan, I detected an air of added confidence and a certain determination in his eyes. 'You have grown!' I teasingly exclaimed.

'Midori Mama very grateful you and your sister visit her after attack on house,' he said. 'I sorry I not home. Did Midori Mama talk about me?' He cast me a concerned look.

I shook my head and he seemed relieved.

'Midori Mama has sharp sense and she worry I no like Baba's business,' Shin-tsu said, with his old unaffected openness, which relieved me.

'She take me to Uchiyama Bookshop when I a boy. Uncle and Lu Hsun put on art exhibits – woodblock prints. Place always full of energy, people looking, talking. Prints very interesting for little boy – coolies pulling rickshaw, men loading boats, scene I see every day in Shanghai.' Watching him talk, I could almost see his wide-eyed younger self fascinated by the prints.

'Prints show strong, working people, different from men around Baba. Uncle later tell me Lu Hsun interest in woodblock print is very brave and new.'

'Eiko-san, I now know what Uncle mean by brave,' he continued, giving me a serious look. 'Lu Hsun sympathy for worker make him target of Nationalist suspicion. Chiang Kai-shek men round up many people those days, and Uncle Uchiyama always keep eye on street and let Lu Hsun know if see any strange person. Now, I never like Chiang Kai-shek, who always on side of big money and power.'

I suddenly thought I was starting to understand and asked, 'Is that why you are critical of your father? Because he favours Chiang Kai-shek?'

Shin-tsu waved his hands in front of me and vigorously shook his head. 'No, no, Eiko-san. Baba not on Chiang Kai-shek side, but on Wang Ching-wei side.'

Of course, I should have known, for Mr Mao worked closely with the Japanese.

With a deepened frown on his otherwise smooth face, Shin-tsu said, 'Actually, Baba is careful to be on both Wang Ching-wei and Japanese side, and maybe little bit on Chiang Kai-shek side, too, to be safe. People call Wang government Japanese puppet, but I don't know if Japanese trust him.'

I didn't fully understand what he said, but was impressed by Shin-tsu's political sophistication. 'And where do you stand, Shin-tsu?' I hesitantly asked.

Shin-tsu lowered his eyes, and his delicate hands rounded into fists as he stared down at the floor. I wished I hadn't posed my question.

After a few uncomfortable moments, he looked up straight at me and said, 'I like Japanese people very much. I love Midori, and Uncle and Auntie Uchiyama, and you, Eiko-san. But I hate what Japan is doing to China. And I hate Japanese military. I have no respect for Wang Ching-wei. I want China be able stand on its own.'

It was so straightforward, a sentiment I could fully share, even as a Japanese.

The Japanese papers say Wang Ching-wei stands for peace, although Shin-tsu didn't seem to think so. From his photos, Wang seems a cultured, good-looking and gentle mannered man – unlike Chiang Kai-shek, who has an unpleasant devious air. That's the thing about this war. Wars in times past had heroes: people one believed in, causes to stand up for. But I can't see any in this one.

Saturday, 5 September

I'm still swooning from last night's outing to *Gone with the Wind*. It was a special military-organized screening, for which Masaya managed to get tickets.

'The military confiscated all Western films after Pearl Harbor, but kept them for internal screenings. I might as well make the most of my privilege as an officer to invite you,' he said with a little snicker at the irony.

I had put on a colourful cotton frock for the occasion, and felt out of place as soon as arriving at the cinema entrance: in the queue were men in dark suits or military uniform, and the few women there were in kimono, looking down at their feet. Tamiko whispered, 'Oh dear, not like going to a normal cinema! Let's quickly slip in.' Fortunately, the lighting was dim inside. There was a hushed atmosphere, the only occasional voices coming from military officers.

When the lights went out, the military marches began, and the hitherto subdued crowd erupted in applause. Then came the news-reels – scenes of Japanese planes dropping bombs, and soldiers marching behind a Rising Sun flag bearer in some Chinese town, raising their arms repeatedly in victory *banzai*s. It was easy to be swept up in the atmosphere, to join the thunderous applause. But Shin-tsu's face fluttered in my mind's eye, preventing me from clapping. I turned to Hiro, curious of his reaction, and found him bent over, fiddling and twisting his arm, distracted by some problem with his cuff-link. This filled me with relief and affection, and I sat on my hands, letting the patriotic fervour pass over me.

Thankfully, the screening of the film began before too long. What a film it was! I still tingle recalling some scenes: the pillaged Tara; a railway yard filled with dead and injured soldiers; Bonnie's fall from her pony; and the charged love scenes between Scarlett and Rhett Butler.

We couldn't stop talking about the film on the way home: Masaya, Jiro and Rokki saw Scarlett as a disagreeable character;

Hiro thought she was very pretty. 'Eiko has rounder features, but there's a definite resemblance. She's your type,' Rokki teased, making me blush and Hiro pretend he didn't hear.

Sayako surprised me. 'I loved Scarlett's amazing spirit. So strong!' she exclaimed. Jiro glanced knowingly at his normally meek wife, making me wonder whether Sayako actually has a steely strength beneath the gentle surface.

But it was Masaya's parting sober comment that stuck in my mind. 'A remarkable film, the scale, the wealth, everything. To think that Japan is foolishly at war against a country that can make a film like that…'

Wednesday, 9 September

I've finally settled on the guest list for my dinner party with the Schmidts. I'll have the Maos and Cheeko and Daisuke Otsuka in addition to Masaya, Jiro, Sayako, Rokki and Tamiko. I've ruled out Joyce and Keith and Irma; I don't know how the Schmidts would be with a British couple and a Jewish refugee. And reluctantly, I've also ruled out Mona and S.P., as they might not be a good mix with the Maos.

Shanghai is so complicated.

Sunday, 13 September

I am exhausted but relieved and content with last night's dinner party. Hiro too seemed to think it went well.

My nerves had been on edge all afternoon. After much thought, so as not to be overdressed but properly respectful to our guests, I put on my black and white silk dress with the dynamic geometric cut, and a gold necklace. Then I fretted the guests might not show up.

The doorbell rang two minutes early, making me jump. It was the Schmidts, tall and erect, beautifully attired for the evening. They reminded me of Daddy, always arriving too early at functions, standing at the door with eyes on his pocket watch. As Hiro greeted Herr and Frau Schmidt, I realized we had never before hosted a Western-style dinner party at home.

Drinks in the living room took me back to London days: the din of simultaneous conversations peppered with soft laughter; the clinking of ice; the warm air mixed with perfume and alcohol.

Chokugetsu-ken announced dinner at the perfect moment, leading us into the dining room where he had laid on a marvellous buffet spread of Chinese and Western dishes: five appetizers, including spring rolls and delicate dumplings, much favoured by the Germans, and intricate Shanghainese main dishes, including shrimp with Dragon Well tea leaves, which impressed even the Maos.

What took me by surprise was the set of unfamiliar plates on the sideboard. Had Chokugetsu-ken spent food money buying such beautiful plates? Slightly irritated, I handed out the plates as the guests filed in. Frau Schmidt's eyebrows rose as she entered. When everyone was busy eating, she came by my side and said, 'Do you like these dinner plates? They are mine.'

I froze. Frau Schmidt, straight backed and serious, said, 'The house boys in the building help each other when employers have guests. Dinnerware and cutlery move backwards and forwards. Our plates are popular.' If it hadn't been for the bemused look in her eyes, I would have been crushed.

'It took me a long time to adjust to Chinese servants,' she continued. 'In Deutschland, servants are orderly, never out of line. Here, they are noisy and cunning. My German acquaintances say their things go missing. I counted my silver once a week when we first arrived in Shanghai. But now, I am fond of our boy.' With that, she held her head high and went to join her husband in the other room. I warmed to Frau Schmidt, and the rest of the evening passed in pleasant bonhomie.

The Japanese guests stayed on after the others left, and we sunk into the sofas with a general sense of fulfilment from an evening gone well. Cheeko congratulated me on my skills as a hostess, and I noticed Hiro looking proud and content. Excited by the buzz of the evening, I felt a second rush of energy, wishing the party not to end. The room filled with lively Japanese chatter.

Daisuke Otsuka suddenly said, 'We have a good group here. Why don't we put on an amateur dramatic production to entertain Japanese troops?' Giddy from the evening, everyone agreed. Amidst further excited chatter, it was decided that Masaya would arrange dates with the Naval Office, Sayako and Cheeko would put together dance routines for the show, and Rokki and Daisuke would produce and direct.

The party and post-party left me in a state of over-excitement. Only after listening to Hiro's even breathing for ages was I able to fall asleep.

Tuesday, 22 September

I saw Cheeko this morning at the Japanese grocery van. 'Eiko-san, your dinner party, it was lovely. Such a beautiful mix of East and West – so sophisticated! I don't know how you manage at such a young age,' she chirped, as she led me into their house.

'Daisuke is so excited about the amateur theatre production. He's going to ring Rokuro-san soon to start preparations. It should be lots of fun, and we'll get to see each other all the time.' As she rattled on, Cheeko placed a cup of fragrant jasmine tea before me, together with a bamboo tray of delicious-looking almond cookies.

The house seemed totally Chinese: the well-thumbed Chinese books on the bookshelf; the carved ebony furniture and faded red and gold colour scheme; the smell of Chinese spices. It almost seemed strange to be speaking to Cheeko in Japanese. I was fascinated by how a Japanese household could become so transformed.

'I never think of myself as having become Chinese.' Cheeko laughed. 'It's all Daisuke's influence. I'm glad you find it interesting! Some of our Japanese neighbours don't approve because they think the Chinese are beneath us. They forget that so much of Japanese culture originates from China. I just love being here, surrounded by Chinese friends.'

As I was leaving, Cheeko said, 'Eiko-san, you must think of what part you'll take in the performance for the Japanese troops. I think you'd be a beautiful dancer!' I'd nearly forgotten that the performance was to be for Japanese soldiers. Being in such comfortable Chinese surroundings, it felt incongruous that we should be talking about a performance to boost Japanese morale in a war against China.

Monday, 28 September

'Daddy arrived safely in Japan!' Tamiko exclaimed, as she came bursting into our flat. We embraced, and I could almost physically feel the relief going through our bodies. Kazu and Sachi must have sensed the joy, for they held hands and started jumping up and down.

'Rokki said the boat was met by a large welcoming delegation at the Yokohama piers,' Tamiko said.

I could picture the scene, people excitedly waving little Rising Sun flags like in the newsreels as the passengers disembarked from the boat.

'Our brothers were there to greet Daddy and Sachiko-sama,' Tamiko went on.

I felt as if a pin had pricked my happiness balloon, suddenly being reminded that Daddy wasn't alone. How could he bring home another woman to the large Kanda compound, with loyal retainers from generations ago still serving the household which Mummy had managed with graceful dignity!

'I bet our brothers won't like her,' I pouted.

Tamiko laughed good-naturedly. 'Knowing them, I'm sure they're being jokingly rude. But Eiko, they're certain to be relieved that Daddy is being looked after by the woman he loves.'

I felt my face tighten into an even bigger pout.

Friday, 2 October

News of the sinking of the *Lisbon-Maru*, dominates the papers – unusual to read about a Japanese boat being hit by an American torpedo. 'The paper says Japanese patrol boats in the nearby waters carried out an impressive rescue operation. The story is all about Japanese efficiency,' Hiro said, speaking from behind the spread paper. It brought home the dangers on the waters – and that Daddy's safe return to Japan wasn't to be taken for granted. I felt somewhat ashamed for having thought ill of his wife.

Tuesday, 6 October

Shin-tsu came today looking unusually downcast. 'Is everything all right at home?' I asked.

'Yes, ever since shootout, Midori worry about Baba, and Baba respond by spending more time at home. *I*-Mama and *Er*-Mama always in own room upstairs, so very peaceful,' he responded with a sweet smile. I wondered whether Shin-tsu knew what his mother and other stepmother were up to in their quarters – the image of their smoky contentment still so vivid in my mind.

'But something is troubling you, Shin-tsu.'

'How you can tell, Eiko-san?' I smiled knowingly, and he smiled back. But his expression immediately turned serious.

'Eiko-san, you know there is new Japanese policy,' he said. I couldn't tell if it was a question or a statement, but shook my head.

'Japan make all Chinese schools, elementary to university, teach Japanese language. Everyone now have to learn Japanese,' he said.

'Oh.' I didn't see what the problem was, especially since Shin-tsu already spoke some Japanese.

He must have sensed my lack of sympathy. 'Eiko-san, for Chinese people, we learn Japanese if we want, but not to be forced. Many Chinese lose business or in gaol or taken away under Japan rule. Making people learn Japanese language is big insult.'

I was struck by my own insensitivity.

On his part, Shin-tsu seemed to feel he might have been too forceful. He softened his tone and changed the subject.

'Eiko-san, you know Lu Hsun my favourite writer, I tell you why. He study in Japan when young man. China still Ching Dynasty then and Lu Hsun have queue pig tail. But he believe China need to modernize and he even cut off queue, very radical to do,' he said.

'Instead of joining political party, Lu Hsun become teacher and writer. He believe each Chinese person must use willpower for change, and he try make it happen through writing. His writing very powerful, and make me feel I too can bring change.' Shin-tsu's passionate sense of involvement in China's destiny shone through his soft features.

'People like Lu Hsun and Uncle Uchiyama my heroes. Lu Hsun was Chinese patriot but respect Japanese knowledge, and Uncle can speak out when he believe Japan wrong.'

By the end of the English lesson, my mind was too overworked to deal with Chinese tones and phrases. I learn so much from just listening to Shin-tsu. When I suggested skipping the Chinese language lesson, Shin-tsu too seemed relieved and took his leave while it was still light outside.

The days are getting shorter, and quite autumnal now.

Monday, 12 October

Tamiko prepared a splendid meal of *shaolongbao* dumplings yesterday. With Shanghai crabs now in season, the dumplings were stuffed with pork and crabmeat, and we made much fuss trying to eat them without spilling the oozing delicious soup.

In between mouthfuls, Rokki suddenly said, 'Daisuke Otsuka and I are ready to put together the amateur production. You're all expected to take part.' Such eagerness from my bookworm-ish brother-in-law surprised me.

'I'd like a big part!' exclaimed Tamiko, responding to Rokki's enthusiasm. Not for the first time, and with a little envy, I noticed how they shared interests and seemed to have fun together.

. Jiro spoke up. 'Sayako is accomplished in traditional Japanese dance. She'll find other Japanese ladies to form a dance group. I'll be back stage support.' Sayako shyly gave him a smiling glance.

'Just as well you're not performing, Jiro,' boomed Masaya. 'Do you remember that family play, where you not only forgot your lines, but managed to trip and fall flat on your face in the middle of the makeshift stage?'

'I was seven years old then, and my accident became the high-light of the performance. Everyone remembered it,' Jiro retorted.

Masaya let out an affectionate chortle, and Tamiko looked on with a pleased expression. I knew she was worried about Masaya ever since Erna spoke of Meisinger's visit to Shanghai – 'His work puts too much pressure on him,' she had said – and I sensed her relief at his light-heartedness.

'How about you, Eiko, what will you do for the performance?' Rokki asked from across the table. I fidgeted, glancing over at Hiro. 'You, too, Hiroshi-kun,' Rokki persisted.

Hiro laughed lightly. 'I'm too busy with my tennis and golf. I could make a special appearance as a tennis and golf enthusiast, but I don't think that would go down well in military circles. Eiko can take part for the two of us.' He gave a little shrug and reached over to eat the last of the *shaolongbao* dumplings.

All I could do was smile. 'I'll think of something and let you know later,' I said, annoyed at Hiro for extricating himself and putting me on the spot.

Saturday, 17 October

Lunched at the French Club today and watched Hiro play tennis. Being the only wife there, his tennis friends – well brought up Japanese men who'd studied or worked abroad – teased him about his 'exotic bride from London' or my being 'too pretty and too young' for him. Pretending not to hear, but obviously pleased, Hiro urged everyone back onto the courts, and I left the Club feeling uplifted.

As I walked through the gate, I noticed a new sign I hadn't seen earlier. *No Americans or Britons allowed,* it said. Shocked, I ran straight to Tamiko's.

'Oh dear, the notices are up in Frenchtown now, too, are they? They appeared a few days ago in the International Settlement, on the doors of cinemas and dance halls,' she said with a heavy sigh.

She suggested we go and visit the Leighs tomorrow. 'If their movements are restricted, we should go and see them. Besides, I owe them an apology,' she said.

I looked at her questioningly and she blurted, 'It's wretched. The Japanese have frozen enemy assets, meaning the Quakers have to register their possessions and aren't able to take out money from their bank accounts. But worst of all, Eiko, it's Rokki's bank that's doing the freezing, and Rokki's been put in charge.'

Sunday, 18 October

Despite the mounting inconveniences, there seemed nothing that could rock the peacefulness of the Leigh household. When Tamiko and I arrived, Anna May was fast asleep, looking angelic with her chubby rosy cheeks, filling the place with warm serenity.

'Not being able to go to the cinema or nightclubs is hardly an inconvenience. Nor the freezing of assets since we don't have many possessions anyway,' Joyce said.

Keith was more concerned for Tamiko and Rokki. 'Being in charge of enemy assets is a heavy burden for Rokki,' he said, folding his large hands. 'Tamiko, you shouldn't worry about us. We knew this was coming, and are prepared both materially and spiritually. I know it might feel awkward for you and Rokki, but just think, Tamiko, we should be delighted that our money is in good hands!' He chuckled reassuringly.

'The only real inconvenience is the red armbands,' Keith said. 'The Japanese guards are more vigilant in checking our identification papers. Crossing Garden Bridge has become particularly difficult with more inspections. We rely more and more on Irma to run errands for us. As a refugee, she doesn't wear an armband, so she ends up making the rounds between the refugee camps, the relief organizations and the authorities.'

Gazing at Anna May, he said with a smile, 'Sometimes what appear to be hardships turn out to be blessings. If we can't go out easily, we are able to include more people into our circle of activities at home. Have I told you of our monthly Shakespeare play-reading?' I pricked up my ears – Rokki and Daisuke's production in the back of my mind.

'We had a bigger "cast" in the early days, but we still have a growing collection of refugees, Chinese, German and some Americans and British who take part.'

'Some of the readers are so good we can imagine ourselves at Stratford-upon-Avon,' Joyce said. 'And then there'd be Shakespeare in such heavy accents we can hardly make out the words. It could get quite funny!'

Keith smiled, saying that the readings provided relaxation in tense times, and the genius of Shakespeare was a solace that transcended national boundaries.

'We are also working on a performance. A group of us are preparing a production to entertain Japanese troops,' Tamiko said. I looked at her in disbelief. How could she mention a performance for soldiers to the Quakers, and to them, enemy soldiers, no less?

To my surprise, Keith and Joyce in unison exclaimed, 'What a wonderful idea!'

'It will be a great comfort for the soldiers so far away from home and family. Whenever I look at Anna May these days, I think of all the mothers who have sent their sons off to war, and my heart aches for both mother and son,' Joyce sighed.

It was a moment of revelation. Entertaining troops wasn't about supporting the war, but about bringing joy and comfort to soldiers, many of whom were young men, hardly out of boyhood, even younger than Shin-tsu, risking their lives for their country. Was it the Quakers' faith that enabled them to focus on what really mattered, rather than on how people might see things? I couldn't help being impressed and hope that I, too, will learn to worry less about appearances, and be able to see through to the core importance of things.

Saturday, 24 October

We had our first meeting of the amateur production, starting with an announcement of responsibilities.

'Eh-hem.' Daisuke, asserting his authority, cleared his throat and read out the list:

Daisuke, director and script-writer; Rokuro, producer; Tamiko, main part; Sayako, dance coordinator; Cheeko, costumes and organizing rehearsals; Masaya, location and publicity; and Eiko, fund-raising.

I giggled, daunted by the prospect of asking around for money, secretly suspecting I might be rather good at it.

The show would take the form of a grandmother recounting Japanese folktales to her granddaughter, each story to be followed by a dance. Each tale would represent a season: *Hanasaka Jī-san*, the story of a kind old couple who magically revive a dead cherry tree; *Urashima Tarō*, a young fisherman who disappears from a summer beach into a deep-sea kingdom, only to return to earth as an old man; *Kaguya Hime*, the baby girl found in a bamboo grove who, upon adulthood, flies into the autumn full moon, leaving behind a trail of suitors; and finally, the tale of the snow ghost who breathes on travellers and freezes them on the spot, to be followed by a dance of a kind snow spirit that brings all back to life.

Tamiko will be the grandmother, the granddaughter to be played by Cheeko and Daisuke's eight-year-old daughter, Hanako.

Saturday, 31 October

The production is moving ahead apace. The actual performance is to be on 29 December at the barracks of the Special Naval Landing Forces in northern Hongkew. 'It's perfect timing as an appropriate year-end treat for the troops, and gives us a two full months to prepare,' Masaya said.

For the first time, I met Hanako, who looked a typical Japanese schoolgirl, with hair in a bob, the nape area unappealingly shorn high, and her knobbly knees peeking from her pleated skirt and her well-worn plimsolls. Unlike her parents, I don't think she could ever be mistaken for a Chinese.

'I'm in the third grade at the Japanese school,' she announced, as if speaking at school assembly. 'My brother, Taro, is in the fifth grade, and he wants to be a fighter pilot to fight for our country. As a girl, I can't be a pilot, but I am pleased that I can be in my father's show and contribute to the war effort even before Taro!'

I was taken aback by her patriotic fervour. Cheeko must have seen my expression.

'Eiko-san, it's what the Japanese schools teach - Japan gallantly fighting to free China from Western imperialism, that sort of thing,' she said.

'As Christians, we don't like the belligerence the children pick up, but can't do much about it unless we take them out of the school. At least Taro and Hanako don't look down on the Chinese. For them, the war is against the West.' She shrugged her shoulders resignedly, and flashed me an apologetic smile.

I don't think I would want Kazu to go to Japanese school here.

9

Sunday, 8 November 1942

Kazu turned two today. He looked adorable in his sailor suit, basking in the attention he was getting. I still think of this day as the anniversary of my giving birth, filling me with fragments of emotions: the bittersweet loneliness of not having my own mother to share the experience with; the kindness and concern from Hiro's parents; the relief and sense of responsibility giving birth to an heir; and overwhelming love for the little creature born. To think Kazu is now two years old!

The birthday party consisted of Sachi and Tamiko and Rokki, Betty Ringhausen and her parents, and the Leighs. Hiro surprised me by cancelling his golf game to be at home for the party, 'to make sure that Jay-jay doesn't get in the way' he'd said. Indeed, he had Jay-jay on his lap most of the time, quite oblivious to the birthday celebrations.

Chokugetsu-ken baked a beautiful chocolate cake, and Kazu looked bewildered when it was placed in front of him with three lit candles. Betty told Kazu to make a wish, and discreetly helped him blow out the candles.

Keith and Joyce cut a soothing presence with rosy-cheeked Anna May contentedly snuggled up with one or the other of them. But I noticed deeper lines on both of their faces. Before touching his cake, I noticed Keith close his eyes and bow his head over clasped hands, making me realize how much I simply take for granted.

What will the world be like for Kazu's third birthday? I wonder.

Thursday, 12 November

Rokki reminded me of my fund-raising duties, so I rang Midori Mao to ask for a donation.

'What a lovely idea! I'll get money from Wen-tsu straight away,' she said.

Laughingly, she added, 'It sounds like fun. I wouldn't have minded taking part in it, too. But of course that wouldn't do, having a professional among amateur dancers, the wrong kind of professional at that!'

Her words reminded me of the attractive girls in *cheongsam* dresses waiting for ticketed dance partners at the nightclub. How amazing that she so light-heartedly confirmed my hunch.

Sunday, 15 November

Rehearsals today at Hanako and Taro's Japanese elementary school, a stark and grey place, especially without any heat. But the atmosphere brightened when Sayako appeared with two attractive Japanese ladies – Hisako and Kyoko – for the Japanese dances. We women instantly found mutual acquaintances and other things to talk about, leaving Daisuke, Rokki and Masaya huddled in a corner overwhelmed by the female presence. I felt giddy being part of a close-knit group of similar aged Japanese women, a new experience for me.

Daisuke eventually managed to impose some discipline and tone down the chatter.

'We have enough dancers now. Let's add a song-and-dance scene of flower-selling girls as the finale,' he said.

I immediately thought of *Pygmalion* with Leslie Howard and Wendy Hiller, which I had seen in London. The same thought occurred to others too, and we broke into singing and high-pitched excitement that even Daisuke couldn't control.

At the end of the day, Cheeko and Daisuke's cook and *amah* came over with a huge pot of piping hot jasmine tea and *yue pin* – bean-filled moon cakes. As we gratefully tucked in, exhausted from our efforts, someone brought up the latest Japanese gossip – the burning of the most expensive Japanese restaurant in town, and the subsequent copycat fires at other establishments.

Cheeko said, 'The fire in the middle of the Japanese entertainment district lit up the whole sky! Uncle Uchiyama thinks it might have been some Japanese civilian disgusted by the extravagance of military officers.'

Hisako, delicately refined, spoke softly. 'Fortunately no one was hurt, but the little daughter of the proprietor has nothing to wear now except her school uniform.'

In a slightly gossipy tone, Kyoko, the beautiful wife of prominent businessman, said, 'The joke within my husband's circle is that an army man set fire because the Army didn't like the Navy having exclusive use of the best restaurant. It makes sense, don't you think? All the establishments are either exclusively Navy or Army, and the two subsequent fires were both at Army places, probably Navy retaliation.'

I turned to Masaya, expecting a light-hearted brush-off of the various rumours involving the military.

But Masaya had gone to the table where the teapot was, and I could tell from his ashen profile and slightly shaky hands that our conversation was deeply upsetting him. Tamiko was the only other person who seemed to notice. In a second, she was by his side, positioned as if to shield him. To us, she cheerfully called out, 'Would anyone like more tea?' By then, everybody was ready to go home, attention focussed on collecting belongings, the fire incident seemingly forgotten.

Friday, 20 November

Tamiko came over with Sachi today looking worn, making me wonder whether she was still concerned about Masaya. But her voice was bright. 'It's such a nice crisp autumn day, let's go for a walk,' she said, already on her knees putting a lead on Jay-jay.

We walked by the Grosvenor Garden's arcade and across the road towards the French Club, the children shuffling their feet in the fallen leaves. As Jay-jay pulled me, I tilted my head upwards to feel the soft rays of sun on my face. Tamiko gently yanked my arm and brought her face close to mine. 'Eiko, I think I am expecting,' she said.

Seeing my expression, Tamiko started laughing and said, 'I don't see why you should seem so startled. I may be older than you, but I am still only twenty-nine, not too old to have a baby, silly!' I came to my senses and gave her a congratulatory hug.

But why had her announcement given me such a jolt? Did I not want any change to our cosy *status quo* – us two sisters with Sachi and Kazu? Or envy? Perhaps.

Tuesday, 24 November

The minute I saw Shin-tsu's face, I could see he was not happy with me. I knew why, and it hit me like a physical blow. I'd hoped he would never hear of my asking Midori for a donation, but he obviously had.

We silently took our usual seats at the table by the window. As he sorted out his notebook and pencils, I caught myself repeatedly glancing at his handsome face, worrying about the gloom I had cast upon it. Being a polite young man, he tried to hide his feelings, but his discomfort was obvious – avoiding my gaze, sitting at an awkward angle.

'So Shin-tsu, you are angry with me.' The words came tumbling out before I even knew I was going to raise the subject.

After a moment of startled hesitation, he blurted, 'Yes, Eiko-san how you can ask money from my parents to support war? This is war by Japan against Chinese – my people, my country!'

And then he caught himself. 'Sorry, Eiko-san. Not mean to shout at you. So sorry!'

'I am the one to be sorry, Shin-tsu,' I said. 'I should have discussed the matter with you.'

Yes, it would have been good to sound Shin-tsu out, have him help me sort out my own feelings about putting on an elaborate performance for Japanese soldiers fighting a war I don't like.

I explained to Shin-tsu that the peace-loving Quakers had helped me see the good in entertaining young men far away from home. But then, eight-year old Hanako unsettled me again, being so proud to be helping Japan's war effort.

Shin-tsu listened thoughtfully and was slow to respond. He finally said, 'Eiko-san, you very good person. I not upset with you.' He made me tearful.

'If everyone is like you, things be all right. But in reality, life getting tougher for Chinese people. Short-wave radios, cameras, field glasses all prohibited now, more difficult to get news.' He gazed out the window into the far distance.

'And means *kempei-tai* can make search against us Chinese,' he added.

There was something in the way he said 'us Chinese' that made me stare at him. Again, the determined look I had seen before, when he returned from his summer trip. But I couldn't pry further.

Saturday, 28 November

An exhausting but satisfying day of rehearsals. I did my part in the flower-girl song routine, and then served as stagehand for the Japanese dances – complimented by all for being wonderfully efficient.

I was fascinated to watch Tamiko and Hanako go over their lines under Rokki's direction. 'You should use hand movements as if you are caressing the little bird when you talk about the old man's kindness,' he said, and by obligingly incorporating the gesture, Tamiko brought the scene even more to life. I envied their total absorption.

Hanako's brother, ten-year-old Taro, appeared at the end of the day. A solid boy, looking mature for his age with closely cropped hair and an intense gaze, I was reminded immediately that this was the boy who wanted to be a fighter pilot. Such determined children – so different from Cheeko, their sweet, bird-like mother.

Thursday, 3 December

We ladies of the performance had lunch today at the Palace Hotel. It was Kyoko's suggestion as she knows the manager, a Mr Kanaya, from a famous hotelier family in Japan. We took care to dress simply, but I felt the eyes of the other diners, mainly Japanese military officers and businessmen, follow the five of us as we were led to our table in the corner of the grand dining room.

Mr Kanaya, a genial man in his mid-thirties, came out to greet us, and Kyoko flattered him by explaining to us that his grandfather had founded the famous Kanaya Hotel in Nikko, the very first establishment to cater to Western travellers in the nineteenth century. Mr Kanaya beamed appreciatively, and with several gracious bows, withdrew.

When we were well into our main course, he again appeared, but this time, he seemed ill at ease. Looking embarrassed, he apologetically asked if some screens could be put up around our table to ensure our privacy. Ignoring some puzzled looks, Tamiko swiftly responded with a reassuring smile. 'How very thoughtful of you, Mr Kanaya. Please do go ahead.'

Relieved, Mr Kanaya told the hovering waiters where to place the screens, and before we knew it, we were shielded by four wooden framed panels – the kind one hides behind when undressing in a doctor's surgery.

We started talking at once, wondering what this was about. Tamiko spread both hands, palms down in a gentle up and down movement, telling us to quieten down. 'There must have been a complaint. It was practically written on Mr Kanaya's face!' she whispered.

Peeking out from in between panels, we speculated as to which of diners might be the culprit. We rolled our eyes and giggled as quietly as we could, unwilling to admit that perhaps a ladies' lunch party in public was inappropriate for the times.

By dessert time, the dining room was almost empty, and Mr Kanaya came back. Seeing us in good spirits, he visibly relaxed. 'I do hope you ladies have enjoyed your lunch,' he said. 'In times like this, it is so important to have uplifting pleasures now and then, and nothing pleases me more than to have the Palace used for such occasions. Just the other day, I arranged a tea party here for about a hundred invited guests.'

Motioning the waiter to replenish our coffee and chocolates, he continued. 'I arranged for an orchestral performance of Japanese folk music to introduce Japanese culture. We had many Chinese, some Germans and a group of Japanese dignitaries, and everyone had a lovely time.'

'How wonderful!' Kyoko said, encouraging Mr Kanaya to elaborate further.

'Not only enjoyable, but I felt I was somehow contributing to the Japanese war effort,' he said. 'What happened later in the evening made me realize the significance of the afternoon's event.' He looked up at the chandeliers, recalling the scene.

'An American lady with a red armband approached me in the lobby. "That was some party you had today," she said. "I was so disappointed not to be included. All that music, the cakes, the tea, the whisky... Even Victor Sassoon's parties didn't serve so many delicacies. All I could do was try to breathe in the smells that wafted from the ballroom."'

I felt crestfallen for the American lady, and ashamed of tucking into my dessert. I leaned forward to hear the rest of the story, hoping that the lady at least got some cake in the end. It turned out I was completely missing Mr Kanaya's point.

Taking in a deep breath, he said, 'I just stared into this woman's face. My party was hardly an elaborate affair, just a simple get together with a sprinkling of ordinary snacks. But to people who are losing the war, I suppose even a simple party gets turned into something much more grand in their minds. In the olden days, it was the Japanese who were excluded and had to satisfy themselves with just the smells of Western riches.'

He straightened his slight frame and stood to attention. With eyes shining brightly, he said with emotion, 'The American lady made me realize that the tables have truly turned, and I was overcome by our government's great achievement.'

I was dumbstruck. I avoided looking at the other ladies, afraid they might be concurring with Mr Kanaya's sentiment.

'Your concert party must have been wonderful.' This was Tamiko, effortlessly charming Mr Kanaya. 'In fact, we are gathered here today because we, too, have been busy preparing for a performance of Japanese folktales and dances to entertain Japanese troops. Interesting how, as we approach the end of the year, we feel it's time for appreciation and gratitude. Speaking of which, we are

grateful to you, Mr Kanaya, for making our lunch today so special.'
She tactfully gave us the cue to stand up and thank him with bows.
He contentedly escorted us out of the dining room.

Pouring out of the hotel, we reminded each other of Saturday's
rehearsal and said our goodbyes.

As soon as we were on our own, I asked, 'Is it just us, Tamiko,
who feel saddened by the plight of American and British people?'

'We don't all have the same upbringing, and people have different points of view,' she said. 'Mr Kanaya, even if we can't share his
view, is a decent man, doing his job as he sees fit. We have to be
respectful. But certainly not agree. Come on, get rid of your frown!'

We popped into the Cathay Hotel to see if Mr Hsu was there – I
hadn't seen him in ages, and felt a sudden desire to see his friendly,
wise face. But alas, he was off duty until later in the evening.

Tuesday, 8 December

The headline in Hiro's Japanese newspaper celebrated the first anniversary of Pearl Harbor, extolling Japan's sacred Greater East Asian
War, 'liberating the peoples of Asia from the clutches of Western
imperialism'.

'Mr Kanaya at the Palace Hotel must be celebrating with fellow
Japanese guests there,' I said.

Without looking up, Hiro muttered 'Why would he be
celebrating?'

'Because he believes Japan's war is reversing the injustices of the
past,' I said, repeating the story of the American lady with the red
armband. I couldn't think of her without feeling pity. How I wish
Japanese leaders would get on with it; end the war and bring about
'liberation' by being fair, and then they wouldn't have to humiliate
people who would no longer be enemies.

Hiro continued reading, and I wasn't even sure if he was listening, until he peered above the paper. 'Is that what he says? Being
anti-Western seems strange coming from a Kanaya Hotel man with
its history. Hope the American woman at least got some leftovers.'
His head then disappeared back behind the paper.

Sunday, 13 December

I was in Sayako's kitchen, relishing the peace and quiet after a busy afternoon sorting costumes and props for the performance. With Jiro and Masaya clumsily hovering about as Sayako prepared the tea, I felt an added intimacy and attachment to the dear Sekines.

'How are the Jewish refugees?' I asked Masaya, having had little opportunity to catch up during rehearsals.

'Even though life is harsher with price rises and food shortages, they manage to lift their spirits, looking forward to the festive season of Hanukkah and Christmas,' he said. 'I'm invited to a small piano concert, and it's bound to be beautiful – there're so many talented musicians among the refugees.'

This gave me an idea. I asked whether we might invite the Quakers and some refugees to our dress rehearsal, saying how wonderful it would be to share our efforts with such a deserving audience.

'What a brilliant suggestion!' Masaya said, with a clap of hands.

But Jiro cast a worried glance. Speaking softly, almost apologetically, he said, 'Where could we have the dress rehearsal? Japanese sentries are constantly checking Japanese school premises and it would be impossible to invite red armbands. I'm afraid all public places have to be ruled out.'

Masaya glared at his brother, his temples throbbing. I held my breath, taken aback by his violent mood swing. In the next instance, Masaya went pale and clenched his hands, desperate to control his emotions.

'Perhaps a scaled-down dress rehearsal would be possible in someone's home,' Sayako swiftly said, as if she hadn't noticed Masaya's reaction.

'We can have it at our place,' I offered, feeling somewhat responsible for the tension I had created.

'That would be wonderful! We know what a superb hostess you are Eiko-san, and your beautiful flat would be perfect,' Sayako said, gently nudging us out of the kitchen to let the cook prepare dinner.

The brothers went into the living room and Sayako led me upstairs to put the kimonos away.

Alone with Sayako, she quietly said, 'Eiko-san, you and Tamiko-san are like balm for Masaya Onī-sama. When you are around, he actually smiles. That is why the performance has been a godsend.'

She continued in a soft even tone. 'At the Naval office, they receive so much information on what is going on. And most of what Masaya Onī-sama hears is terribly disturbing. Jiro also gets news from his Chinese friends who listen to short-wave radios – so we learn that the war is not going well for the Japanese, completely opposite to what the Japanese papers say. Of course, we half suspect it anyway.'

I'd always sensed the strength of character behind Sayako's gentleness, but I now felt her wisdom, too.

'The kind of information that troubles Masaya Onī-sama isn't how the war is going for Japan, but has to do with human cruelty. Being a man of faith and principle, I think the knowledge sometimes becomes overwhelming, indigestible, for him.'

Sayako's kimono-folding hands stopped as she gazed helplessly into the beautiful silk fabric. I, too, stared at the exquisite chrysanthemum embroidery, which became etched in my mind with Masaya's sorrow because of what Sayako said next.

'Masaya Onī-sama has been in a particularly dark mood, not being able to sleep well, since he learned about the *Lisbon-Maru*.'

I remembered the story in the papers about the *Lisbon-Maru* – the Japanese troop transport ship that was torpedoed and sunk, but with few casualties because of Japanese rescue efficiency.

'That's not the full story,' Sayako said. 'It turns out that the boat had in its hold over 1,800 British prisoners of war, and as the Japanese soldiers were being rescued, they battened down the hatches so that the British would all drown.'

Her voice became barely audible as she cast her eyes towards the floor. 'In the end, half of them managed to get out, but then Japanese patrol boats tried to prevent them from reaching shore. The Navy didn't want any witnesses of their ill-treatment of the prisoners.'

The kimono in my hand slipped to the floor. Rather than feeling shock, Sayako's quiet delivery of the horrific event had the effect of draining away my faith, and bringing in doubts and questions. In my mind, the Imperial Navy was the civilized part of the Japanese military – in London Daddy knew Naval Officers, educated and trained in Britain, true gentlemen. How could something like this happen?

Sayako gave me a sad smile. 'Eiko-san, I'm afraid all we can do is pray – for everyone suffering through this war, all the British prisoners who drowned, and especially for Masaya Onī-sama. His desire is to help people – that is his mission. To be mentally affected by the horrors around us I am sure is a double burden on him. I know that his faith will pull him through, but this is a difficult time for him. I am hoping that our prayers during Advent in preparation for Christmas will give us much needed strength.'

I took Sayako's hands into mine, and we closed our eyes as if already in prayer.

At that moment, there were voices in the entrance hall, indicating the arrival of Tamiko, Rokki and Hide, and we switched gears in anticipation of a jollier evening.

The evening was indeed filled with banter and teasing. Tamiko and Rokki argued over the grandmother character, Rokki saying she should be wise and kind, but Tamiko wanting her to be a bit eccentric and forgetful. Of course, Tamiko will have her way, and Masaya seemed genuinely gleeful at the prospect of Tamiko as a quirky old woman.

Now, alone with my journal, I fret over my hasty decision to host the dress rehearsal. Could there be problems from Japanese authorities? The *Lisbon-Maru* has shown what the Japanese are capable of. I am haunted by the image of British sailors drowning in the sea.

Thursday, 17 December

I wouldn't have thought of approaching Kimmy for fund-raising if it hadn't been for the recent wet, cold days. Looking for a suitable pair of boots, I rummaged through my shoeboxes and came across the dreaded banned book. How I wished it remained forgotten. But it reminded me I hadn't seen Kimmy in ages, not since the day her office was raided. I decided I would return the book and ask for a donation at the same time.

We met for a quick lunch near her office. She looked slightly haggard, a little too worn for a nineteen-year-old, but once we started chatting, I found her feistiness intact. 'Oh those fellows at the office, they get worse and worse,' she chuckled. 'The mess they make with their cigarettes and papers scattered about the place. I have become the office nag, berating them for their bad habits.'

I told her about the performance, and she immediately said she would tell her mother about it. 'When it comes to this war, Mother is the one who is most emotionally involved. She wants to do what's right, and entertaining the troops is something she'd wholeheart-edly support.'

Kimmy leaned over and dropped her voice. 'You of course remember her worry over the banned books and burning them all. That's her way of behaving correctly.' This gave me the opportunity to bring out the book, wrapped in plain brown paper, and shove it across the table. I had mustered up the courage to bring it with me, my desire to be rid of it being so strong.

'Could I please give this back to you, Kimmy, I would feel so much better not having it lying about in the flat,' I said.

'Eiko, I can't take it back,' she said firmly. 'How could I have it on me and return to the office when we are under constant watch. We don't know when another raid might happen.' I felt crushed, and nervous about having the book on me.

I can hardly believe what I did. As soon as we left the little res-taurant and Kimmy rushed back to her office, I walked across the Bund into the Public Gardens. Given the miserable weather, there was no one around. I simply dropped the book by a bench and walked away.

When the phone rang early this evening, my heart skipped a beat, certain it was the authorities tracing the book back to me. But it was Kimmy.

'It was so good to see you, Eiko. Mother is delighted to contribute money towards your performance from her own pocket. She thinks what you and the other ladies are doing is wonderful.'

I still worry about the book. But surely, even if someone picked it up they could never know where it came from…

Wednesday, 23 December

Little time these days for my diary. The rehearsals are taking up lots of time, and then there are all the preparations for Christmas. I helped Kazu with his letter to Father Christmas, and of all things, he wants a toy rifle.

'Bang, bang toy,' he said, holding up his little arms in position and repeating, 'Mama, Mama, bang, bang!' I was horrified – is it a reflection of the times, or is it what every little boy wants?

We are invited to the Leighs for Christmas tea on the 25th, the dress rehearsal will be held here on the 28th, and then the REAL THING on the 29th. How am I going to get everything done?

Saturday, 26 December

Christmas at the Leighs' was magical. Upon arrival, we were greeted with lovely baking smells and Christmas carols sung by a cluster of children assembled around Anna May's pram. There were at least fifteen people gathered, but the place had a settled peacefulness – an amazing blend of serenity and a festive atmosphere.

'Christmas, or this time of year, may have different significances for different cultures and religions but it is an occasion to share love and gratitude for the blessing of being able to come together,' Keith said, as he assembled us around the tea table.

With little pomp, he offered a prayer – 'God of all gifts, we bless you and give you thanks for bringing our hearts to life this Christmas Day, Amen', swiftly followed by another – 'Blessed are You, Lord, our God, King of the universe, who performed miracles for our ancestors in those days at this time…' And then with a joyous clap of hands, invited all to tuck into tea.

Tamiko wandered over to me with an amused smile. 'Keith manages to make everyone comfortable, with his Christian grace, Jewish prayer, and easy hospitality,' she said, indicating towards Hiro. She knew my concern of being in a Christian setting for the first time with Hiro, who, coming from a Buddhist family had probably never set foot in a church. Whatever he thought of Keith's prayers, he was now completely at ease, deep in conversation with a Chinese gentleman, who was kindly piling cakes and biscuits on his plate.

Hiro was in high spirits on the way home. 'Dr Tang, he's president of a university here. Every time he visits the Quakers, he changes his route because he's marked by the *kempei*. The Christians are very brave – an impressive get-together.'

A memorable Christmas.

Tuesday, 29 December

Despite the makeshift arrangement – chairs arranged in rows in the living room, the entrance foyer made into a stage – once the rooms were darkened, a general hush descended, creating a genuine theatrical atmosphere for the dress rehearsal.

The audience consisted of the Leighs, Irma and Agnes Flynn, and various family members of the performers. For the benefit of the non-Japanese audience, the grandmother-granddaughter scenes were cut, and in place, Tamiko recounted the folktales in English. Pregnancy suits her, as she glowed in good health under the spotlights. Seemingly without effort, she brought the stories to life, and the children squealed and laughed at every turn as Tamiko transformed herself into characters in the stories. Once the dances started, our foreign guests gasped out loud at the beauty of the kimonos.

Judging from the audience's reaction, the dress rehearsal was a success. But I couldn't help noticing how Irma and Agnes looked much frailer, Irma in particular, with dark bags under her eyes. How little I knew of their plight. I suddenly became self-conscious that the show and Chokugetsu-ken's delicious spread that followed could seem like flaunting Japanese affluence. Of course, our guests saw their invitation as nothing but an act of friendship, but I still felt discomfited by the difference in our circumstances.

Wednesday, 30 December

Now it's all over – all that work of the last two months.

Early in the afternoon, we arrived at the Naval Landing Force headquarters on a military bus, and poured into a building used as a gymnasium/auditorium. It was huge – hundreds of seats lined in neat rows, filling the vast space.

We spent a good three hours working on the scenery and props, and by the time we put on our make-up and costumes, the adrenaline was flowing. When Tamiko finished dressing, there was a big 'aaaahhhhh' in unison. As if by magic, we had before us a shrunken old woman, bent in half over her walking stick, only her mischievous eyes reminding us who she is. Hanako immediately addressed her as '*obāchan*', seemingly unaware it was Tamiko!

Despite my tiny part in the finale as one of the flower girls, I found myself getting more and more nervous, especially when I heard people coming into the hall taking their seats. When the stage lights went on and Tamiko and Hanako started their dialogue at the front of the stage, I peered at the audience from the wing and froze. It was bad enough to see all those empty seats – now, every one of them was filled with a young man with short cropped hair in khaki-coloured uniform, eyes glued to the stage. I felt my knees go weak.

Tamiko and Hanako's cherry blossom story received a huge round of applause, but nothing compared to the thunderous roar and sound of stamping boots, when the ladies in bright coloured kimonos appeared for their dance. Even after the classical Japanese music started, there was still applause and hooting at every possible turn.

By contrast, during the final snow dance, I sensed a more sombre response, as if the eerie snow fairies in a distinctly Japanese winter landscape transported the soldiers momentarily back home. When the number ended, I could almost physically feel the emotion that filled the hall.

But there was no time to be sentimental. I was now on stage with the others in our frilly Western costumes, the scenery quickly transformed into modern times. Perhaps it was the contrast from the previous subdued dance, but when the curtains went up, the eruption from the audience was astounding. My jittery nerves were immediately replaced by sheer amazement and then giddiness, as I sang at the top of my lungs.

'Glowing red lanterns, evening in Shanghai; the flower-selling girls sweetly roam, white baskets in hand with trailing pink ribbons...' The familiar melody, a big hit song from a couple of years back, carried the mood, and I found my body easily swaying in tandem with the waving arms of the soldiers, some who were now standing, and others whistling away. We had to repeat the last twelve bars three times before the audience was ready to let us end the show.

We were elated by our huge success, and moved about in a continued state of excitement. Even Daisuke was talking at an unusually high pitch. He suggested, and we all agreed, that the show should be repeated for other troops, too.

We were still a little too drunk from our success to notice the perfunctory thanks given to Daisuke and Rokki by a senior naval officer as he saw us back on the bus. Despite the blacked out dark roads, spirits were high, and not wanting the evening to end, Tamiko, Rokki and the Sekines stopped by at our house for a nightcap.

'Good show! The flower dance was spectacular,' Hiro said. By then, he was the only one with any energy left, having been a spectator.

'You liked it because Eiko was in it. I bet you're thinking she was the most beautiful of them all,' Rokki teased.

With an embarrassed chuckle, Hiro said, 'All the dancers were good. Eiko did well with her fund-raising, too.'

I was too tired to say anything, and closed my eyes in a half-smile. Hiro had shown little interest in my involvement with the show, but he was actually proud of me! I felt a surge of contentment, and wanted the moment to last forever.

Masaya, nursing his favourite whisky, broke the silence and quietly said, 'I sat next to a young officer just back from the front. He'd lost three of his colleagues – enlisted boys even younger than him. He kept sighing while the rest of the hall was hooting and clapping. At the end, he turned to me and said it was the most comforting time he had had in the last two years.'

Staring at his clasped hands, Masaya went on. 'This is what he said: "I've been reminded of what a normal world is like – tales of childhood, beautiful kimonos and young women trying so hard. Especially at the very end, when the ladies didn't know when to finish and kept looking at each other, one of them threw her head back and laughed gleefully when she took a wrong step. The kind of spontaneity lost in my world. We only blindly follow orders."'

'I knew we'd done a good thing when I heard this,' Masaya said, making me tearful.

'We must repeat our show for other troops,' Tamiko said eagerly. At this, Masaya's face clouded over.

Looking at nobody in particular, he said, 'I was called into the Commander's office while you were clearing up, and was told that the flashy show had been totally inappropriate for these austere times. "Your rich ladies flaunting their finery was a total disgrace," were his final words, and I was dismissed from his office.'

We sat stunned, lost for words, except for Rokki. 'That's ridiculous! It's the stupidest thing I've ever heard,' he stated angrily.

'I wish I could have said that to the Commander,' Masaya muttered. 'Whatever the higher-ups say, there is no doubt we brought joy and comfort to the troops.'

He gulped down what remained in the glass, and seemed to retreat into his own distant world as Tamiko and Sayako exchanged worried glances.

*

Only one more day left in 1942. What a year it has been – a new city, new friends, and above all, being with Tamiko. I am filled with gratitude for my privileged existence, pray for a speedy end to the war. In the meantime, may God give me guidance and strength to be able to distinguish good from evil and not be swayed by prejudices and sentiments of war. May I have the moral courage to treat all those around me with respect and fairness.

10

Friday, 1 January 1943

I can finally breathe easily, having shed my formal kimono. What a perfect Japanese New Year's Day it was, starting with the *toso* wine toast at 9 a.m. with the entire household. Amah and Chokugetsu-ken seemed bewildered by the formality, being offered the large shallow *sake* cup in turn by Hiro, dressed up in a well-cut dark suit. When the cup came to Miyo, Kazu eagerly stood on tiptoe, antic-ipating his turn next. But Hiro's gaze passed over Kazu towards me, and for a moment I worried that he would skip Kazu, perhaps thinking him too young to be given the ritual wine.

But in the next instant, Hiro was on his knee handing Kazu the cup with a token drop of wine. Kazu held it with both hands, beaming me a proud smile, as his father encouraged him to drink up for good health and prosperity. When my turn came, I received the cup from Hiro with gratitude and respect.

It was a bright, crisp day, just like Japanese winter days, and we strolled the neighbourhood paying visits to friends. The Sekines were dressed in their finery, and I was struck by how handsome Masaya looked in his naval uniform. I sensed it wasn't just the outfit that gave Masaya an added glow. Sayako mentioned that Masaya's office was working on a new beneficial policy for Jewish refugees, which she hoped would bring peace of mind to her over-worked brother-in-law.

Our final call was Tamiko and Rokki's. We exchanged formal greetings, expressing gratitude for the past year and best wishes for the year ahead. Tamiko was dressed in kimono, her *obi* sash accen-tuating her growing belly. She gave me playful looks as we bowed to each other, making it difficult to keep a straight face. But my New

Year's greeting to her was heartfelt, filled with prayers for a healthy birth and happiness.

Tuesday, 12 January

Shin-tsu appeared today in a smart navy-blue blazer, looking dashing. I took it for granted that he was dressed up because it was the first lesson of the New Year. I, too, had taken care to look my best, putting on a nice suit. I bowed deeply before sitting down for our lesson. He looked puzzled.

'Eiko-san, what is happen today? Is some special occasion?' It was my turn to be baffled.

'I wanted to start our lesson with proper New Year wishes,' I said, sounding slightly defensive even to my own ears. Shin-tsu swiftly took my hand into his, and shook it with a respectful smile.

'Wish you healthy and prosperous New Year, Eiko-san, so sorry I don't know Japanese custom. Midori-Mama never tell me about Japanese New Year and we celebrate only Chinese New Year, very noisy occasion. You bow so serious, I thought something the matter.'

'Why are you looking so smart today then, Shin-tsu?' I asked, feeling a bit foolish.

'Oh, just some small ceremony at university,' he said dismissively. The more he denied its importance, the more I wanted to know, thinking he had received some citation or award.

Finally, with a pained expression, he said, 'University was celebrating return of concessions to China and end of extraterritoriality.' I went blank.

'You see, Eiko-san, just yesterday, America and Britain sign treaty and return all territories they have in China back to Chinese.' There had been something in the papers last week about Japan helping China achieve independence.

'Following what Japan did?' I asked.

Shin-tsu let out a big sigh. 'Japan pretend to respect Chinese by returning old rights it has from old treaties. But return to Wang Ching-wei government, which Japan control anyway. And America and Britain also give up old treaty rights – to Chiang Kai-shek,

Nationalist government – because they don't want appear imperialist. Today, at university, we celebrate China getting back all her rights.'

I detected an expression, like a sneer, which I would never have imagined on Shin-tsu's face. With a wan smile, he said, 'Is "ironic" right word, Eiko-san? China now supposed to be no longer anyone's colony. But Chinese people continue suffer under foreign control.'

Wednesday, 13 January

I was so busy in December with the performance, I seem to have lost track of my monthly visitor – but I am pretty certain it didn't come, and no sign yet this month either. Could I be expecting? Could it be possible that Tamiko and I might have babies close in age again? No, no, I mustn't get my hopes high. I shall wait a few more days to see if the visitor comes…

Friday, 15 January

We went to the Palace Hotel for our third wedding anniversary, and sat at the same table as exactly one year ago – which seems a lifetime ago, so new to Shanghai I was then.

What a change a year makes! With the Palace Hotel dining room now a Japanese hangout, Hiro was constantly getting up to say hello, and the men would scurry away as soon as they saw me, a rare female presence. Mr Kanaya, the hotel manager, diplomatically said, 'Mr Kishimoto it is a pleasure to have the two of you here. The entire dining room is in admiration of your beautiful wife.'

Despite the interruptions, I enjoyed seeing the social side of Hiro, and found it convenient not having to talk much to him. Had it been an intimate dinner, I know I would have had the urge to tell him about my possible pregnancy. But I didn't really want to until it was certain.

Towards the end of the evening, an older military officer came straight up to Hiro, exchanged a few hushed words and left with a brisk bow. Seeing my curious look, Hiro said, 'Captain Okada wants to see me in his office next week.' I sensed that he knew the reason for the meeting, but didn't inquire further.

I knew Hiro wasn't telling me because it wasn't the right moment, just as I felt reluctant to mention my pregnancy just yet. And I could sense that just as I was keeping quiet out of consideration for him, he was doing the same towards me.

Wednesday, 20 January

It's been confirmed – a baby due in August! And now I can't wait to see Hiro's expression of surprise and joy when he receives the news.

Friday, 29 January

I was at Tamiko's, flopped on the sofa, watching Kazu and Sachi play 'house'. 'Just think, Sachi will soon have three underlings to boss around,' I said.

Laughing, Tamiko responded, 'And you will be getting all worked up about germs and cleanliness for two children!' Unlike when pregnant with Kazu, this time I feel tired all the time, and whiling away the day with Tamiko helped ease the discomfort.

Irma was expected for tea, and I looked forward to being energized by her motherly bubbliness. But she came looking unusually downcast. 'Japanisch military start confiscating office property. I'm afraid Quaker office will be taken soon, and I am packing up Quaker belongings. Keith and Joyce feel bad for me but they can't do anything because of red armbands, stuck at home. So much chaos, with Japanisch guards going round the streets making people leave buildings. And people being sent to camps.'

Tamiko took Irma's hand and said, 'The Quakers couldn't manage without you, Irma. Let us know if there's anything we can do to help.'

'Your friendship, my dear Japanisch Lieblings, gives me much strength,' Irma said, her expression brightening. As if suddenly noticing, she exclaimed, 'Tamiko, you are so big now!'

Tamiko smiled and pointed to me with a knowing nod. Irma leapt up to give me a kiss on the cheek and said, 'Babies coming into the world is most beautiful thing. They make everything else seem insignificant.'

Friday, 5 February

I went to the Shanghai General today, at Hiro's urging. 'They say it has a superb maternity ward, better than St Marie's Hospital,' he said. Much as I'd tried to hide my fatigue and lethargy, he must have noticed.

I entered the examining room with trepidation, certain there was something wrong with me, but Dr Ruben, a burly middle-aged obstetrician, assured me that how I felt was normal in early pregnancy. I suddenly felt better from relief, and even enjoyed the return pedicab ride, feeling the cold air against my cheeks.

As the pedicab turned onto Kiangse Road, I noticed Japanese guards with bayonets scattered around a long queue of Westerners shuffling towards the docks. The people were of all ages, clad in layers of clothing and laden with luggage and bedding.

I instantly remembered what Irma had said. These people must have been made to leave their homes. Where were the camps they were heading for?

In contrast to the sombre-looking adults, two little boys giggled away as they chased each other. They moved awkwardly because of the amount of clothing they had on, looking like overstuffed teddy bears, which seemed to be the cause of their merriment. The children's happy innocence accentuated the overall grim atmosphere, filling me with a sense of foreboding.

Friday, 12 February

It was Miyo's day off, and I tried my best to entertain Kazu, mustering up what little energy I had. I realized how dependent on Miyo I'd become, not just for looking after Kazu, but also for her calmness and reassurance.

So I was alarmed when she came home appearing flustered, not rushing over to Kazu as she normally does, and asked if she could have a word with me.

My mind swirled: had I done something to upset her, and was she going to hand in her notice? Appearing as calm as I could, I led her to the sofa, leaving Kazu to play on his own. He was absorbed in placing a red block on a blue one, desperately trying not to topple the pile – a sight that helped me collect myself.

Once seated, Miyo looked down on her lap, rearranging the folds of her skirt, as if finding her words. Turning pink in the cheeks, she quietly said, 'Oku-sama, there is something I must inform you of.' She took a couple of swallows before continuing.

'I am most grateful to you and Danna-sama for my comfortable situation, and I would not wish to cause you any inconvenience. But there has been a minor development. Mr and Mrs Uchiyama said they would tell you, but I wanted you to hear it directly from me.' I could almost feel the heat from her flushed face.

'The Uchiyamas have kindly introduced me to one of their longtime trusted managers, and it has been agreed that we would marry. Please rest assured, Oku-sama, that I fully intend to be here for the birth of your baby, and will continue to work for you as long as you want me.'

I felt giddy from relief, almost forgetting to congratulate her.

But I'm left with conflicting emotions. I feel a sense of accomplishment: having been responsible for bringing her to Shanghai, what more could I wish than to see her happily settled in a home of her own. At the same time, would a married Miyo be the same for us? Surely, we can't expect her to live with us, and how will we cope, with a new baby on its way?

Sunday, 14 February

With rumours spreading of more and more Westerners being taken to camp, Tamiko insisted that we visit the Leighs, although I wasn't feeling well. 'A walk will be good for you,' she said, taking my arm into hers. Because of her size now, we waddled awkwardly along the rubbish-strewn roads.

Turning off Avenue Joffre, we came upon a particularly large mound in a darkened corner, and I had to let go of Tamiko to walk around it, keeping my eyes on the ground so as not to trip.

Suddenly a pair of eyes stared right up at me from the rubbish. I felt a rush of nausea and grabbed on to Tamiko's shoulder.

Tamiko swiftly pulled me away from the dead body and rubbed my back. 'The winters are too harsh for people who live on the streets,' she muttered. 'The war keeps the Municipal Council too busy to remove the bodies early in the mornings as they used to do.'

Once I recovered from the shock, I felt ashamed for being repelled by the sight of the corpse, forgetting that he was once a human being. Where was my compassion?

It was a relief to reach the Leighs' cosy home, where Irma was in the middle of an animated conversation. 'I'm telling Keith and Joyce of Japanisch Navy men coming to the Quaker office. Before they come, when clearing the place, I found a drawer full of anti-Japanisch pamphlets, and stuffed them into a suitcase. Just as I am doing this, there is a knock at the door, and I jump!' Irma knocked on the table and rolled her eyes.

'My heart is pounding, but I say "Come in" and in come five Japanisch Naval officers and interpreter. They begin to question: "Who are the Friends, and who are you, what's your nationality, your religion?" I say I am Austrian Catholic, born Jewish, and they give me a puzzled look. One fellow makes the sign of cross, so I nod. And then he asks, "Do you like Shanghai?" and I answer, "Very much, everyone is very kind", and he gives me a smile and a bow. He thinks I compliment the Japanisch!' Irma chuckled gleefully.

'Then he suddenly says s-s-s-!!! And I panic thinking he is going to inspect my suitcase. But instead, he says, "Sausage, Weiner sausage very good!" I think fast and say, "Japanisch flowers very beautiful!" He nods with a big smile.'

Irma imitated the man's smile and nod, making us laugh out loud.

'But that was not the end. They start looking through things in the office, and when they come near my suitcase, my heart beat faster, and I worry they can see my chest heaving,' she continued.

'My heart stopped when one of them stumbled over the suitcase, but they prepared to leave ignoring it! We are spared! I thought. But before I close the door on them, the senior office said, 'I give you three weeks to vacate these offices. The Imperial Navy needs these rooms.'"

Irma drooped her shoulders, deflated that her amusing story had to end in disappointment.

'They didn't close the office, Irma, it has to move but can continue to operate. That is all thanks to your witty encounter with the naval officers,' Keith said encouragingly. 'And you know how grateful the entire Quaker community is to you.'

The topic of internment camps was never mentioned during our visit, although surely, it must weigh heavily on the Leighs' minds. Instead, Joyce's parting words to us, after finding out that I, too, am expecting a baby were, 'How I look forward to all our children playing together!' It didn't seem like stoicism, just a natural outcome of faith, and once again, I couldn't help being impressed by the Quakers.

Thursday, 18 February

The Sekines threw a celebration dinner for the Proclamation issued today for Jewish refugees.

'I thought we would stick to the theme,' Sayako said playfully, as she brought out plate after plate of food from the Jewish delicatessen – blinis, soured cream and caviar, *piroshkis*, *borscht* and *stalanka*.

Masaya held up a bottle of vodka and said, 'A prominent Jewish leader gave this to me as a token of friendship. Let us drink to the Proclamation for the protection of the refugees.' He seemed exuberant, despite having more lines around his eyes.

'Could you explain what the Proclamation does?' I asked, ready to expose my ignorance.

'It's a good question,' Masaya said, his benign smile exposing even more his premature wrinkles. 'On the face of it, it's a policy that appears to create inconveniences for the refugees, who have to move to a designated area in Hongkew. It was extremely difficult to come up with an agreed policy, but in the end, I think we have attained the best way to protect the refugees from ill treatment.' I cocked my head not understanding.

'You see, Eiko, there's a strong pro-German faction within the Army,' Masaya explained. 'Some young Japanese army hotheads talk of taking drastic measures against the Jews, as the Nazis would wish. There were lots of heated discussions between the Army and Navy. I'm confident that we reached a workable solution. By gathering the refugees in a specific area where we have control, we can ensure that no harm is done against them.'

The vodka flowed, and with Masaya in excellent form, there was the usual teasing and banter. Except for Tamiko, who seemed unusually quiet. Even when Masaya twirled his tumbler with a contented expression, she hardly seemed to notice. It must be her pregnancy catching up on her – she's suddenly looking much bigger.

Monday, 22 February

Tamiko, now full of energy again, whisked me off for another visit to the Leighs. 'Internment is becoming imminent. We must see them as often as we can,' she said.

When we arrived, the house was in some disarray, with boxes scattered around. Sachi and Kazu rushed straight to Anna May's cot, and once the children settled into their own little world, Joyce gave us an apologetic smile. 'We thought we lived simply, but look, we seem to have accumulated so many things! And not knowing when we might be summoned makes us terribly inefficient at sorting things out.'

'Packing isn't much of a problem,' she went on. 'We won't be able to take many things anyway. The problem is what to do with the things we can't take. My first thought was to give as many things away as possible to the Jewish refugees, but now with this Proclamation, they are having to scramble, and in some ways are in an even more uncertain situation than us.'

I looked up in astonishment, wondering whether I had heard correctly. Was Joyce talking about the same Proclamation celebrated just the other evening? Tamiko, her eyes fixed on Joyce, asked very gently, 'What have you heard from Irma?'

It was Keith who answered, his tone unusually grave. 'Irma was here two days ago, ready to take on the world. Her natural resilience seems to increase in face of mounting hardships. But this new policy is a huge blow, for her personally, and adding difficulties to the work she does for the Friends. She can't live with Agnes any longer outside the Designated Area, and finding accommodation in the already heavily crowded district won't be easy.'

'Where is the area?' I asked, the Proclamation becoming something real in my mind rather than an abstract idea.

'Towards the east of Hongkew, close to some factories and municipal works, a very Chinese neighbourhood not far from Japanese military headquarters,' Keith replied.

'The Proclamation goes into effect in May. Once in the Designated Area, the refugees will need permits to go in and out. Unfortunately, our clothing distribution centre and library are outside the area, so we'll have to find somewhere within the area for the refugees to have access. This, I'm afraid will all fall on Irma's shoulders. A real headache and heartache.'

I never saw Keith look so troubled. I realized Tamiko had already sensed the implication of the Proclamation, which was why she seemed so quiet the other night. Would she challenge Masaya about it, I wondered. Tamiko and Masaya seem to have a remarkably close relationship, which intrigues me. A relationship that seems even deeper than a simple friendship. Would I ever be able to find such a close tie to someone of the opposite sex?

Saturday, 27 February

Walking along Avenue Joffre, attracted by the aroma of coffee, I peeked into the steamy windows of a Viennese café, and caught a glimpse of Tamiko at a table not far from the window. I was about to tap on the glass to get her attention, but stopped midway seeing that she was deep in serious conversation.

I wasn't surprised to see Masaya seated across from her. His shoulders were slightly slumped, and he was leaning into the table, his eyes fixed on hers. I was certain that Tamiko was discussing her visit to the Leighs, bringing up the painful subject of the effects of the Proclamation. How could she do that, to the very person responsible for the new policy? I could see though, from the way Tamiko looked at Masaya – concern, filled with compassion – that they shared complete openness with each other.

Sunday, 28 February

Tamiko collected me on her way to visit Irma and Agnes. I hadn't been to Agnes's since my first Quaker Meeting last Easter, and was pleased to be back at the charming little house tucked away in a quiet corner of the Frenchtown.

'Such a blessing to see friendly familiar faces appear at the door!' Agnes exclaimed in her lovely Irish lilt. Irma came bustling into the hallway to add her greetings: such a contrast between the two ladies' physiques and personalities – petite and elegant silver-haired Agnes and exuberant, dynamic wild Irma – making up the cosy household. I found it difficult to believe that Irma would really have to move out because of the Proclamation.

It soon became obvious that Agnes and Irma had been carefully avoiding the subject of the Proclamation, and only with our presence, Agnes found the courage to bring it up. Maintaining a light-hearted tone, she casually asked, 'By the way, Irma, how is your house-hunting coming along?'

Irma looked down at her plump hands resting on her knees and twiddled her fingers. Taking a little breath, she looked up at Agnes with a reassuring smile.

'I did manage to find a room, dear Agnes, a sweet little place. I was lucky to get the first one I looked at. A romantic attic room, with my own ladder to reach it!'

Even I could tell that she was putting on a brave face for Agnes's benefit. I felt a sudden anger at those bringing misery to the lives of people like Agnes and Irma.

'What on earth does Masaya make of the hardships the Proclamation is bringing about?' I blurted to Tamiko on our way home.

Tamiko softly squeezed my hand, and with the saddest eyes, said, 'Believe me Eiko, Masaya is torn, feeling the deepest sorrow he has ever known. Long time ago, when Rokki fell ill shortly after our marriage, it was Masaya who showed me how to be brave and look on the bright side of things. How I wish could do for him what he did for me then.'

She gently shook her head as if to disperse the helplessness she felt.

11

Wednesday, 3 March 1943

Masaya has taken to his bed. 'Sayako didn't say in so many words, but it's a nervous breakdown, Eiko,' Tamiko said. 'The final straw for Masaya was learning about Laura Margolis' internment.' It took me a moment to remember that Laura was the petite but dynamic American lady who coordinated refugee relief efforts.

Tamiko said that Laura was in the Chapei Camp, a derelict old school building, squeezed in one room with forty other women. 'Masaya feels betrayed by the military he serves. For all he's done believing it was for the refugees' benefit, and now this,' she said, with a big sigh, her eyes cast downwards with her arms draped around her large belly. I rushed to hug her, never having seen Tamiko so forlorn.

Monday, 8 March

And now the Leighs are interned.

At Tamiko's urging, we joined a group including Irma to see them off to their camp – which turned out to be the old British Public School on Yu Yuen Road, within walking distance, and right next to where the Japanese grocery van comes. Given the bright spring day and the Leighs' positive attitude, it seemed like a picnic outing at first.

But as soon as the buildings came into sight, reality set in. There was barbed wire around the whole block, and the main building and scattered huts looked ill-maintained and desolate. 'Poor little Mädchen Anna May growing up in such a prison-like place!' wailed Irma.

Pressing her handkerchief on her eyes, she said, 'They are gone. Only an occasional twenty-five-word Red Cross message will be allowed.'

The proximity of the camp now seemed a cruel irony – being physically so close and yet totally isolated.

Monday, 15 March

As soon as Hiro came home from the office today, he led me to the bedroom, and closed the door behind us. I instinctively knew it had to do with the military man who approached Hiro during our anniversary dinner. That was two months ago, and although nothing was mentioned, I could never believe the matter had disappeared.

'The Japanese are taking over foreign companies here in Shanghai,' Hiro began, as I sat anxiously on the edge of the bed. 'The Kishimoto Company has been told by the military to take over management of a former British shipyard. At some point, I'll be transferred to work there. Going to the shipyard means that I will be technically on secondment to the Navy.'

I remained silent, sensing he hadn't finished.

'They are sending me on a two-month inspection mission around Southeast Asia, and I am to leave in a fortnight.'

The shock felt like a physical blow, and I wrapped my arms around my growing belly by reflex. Hiro was quick to notice. 'I'll be well looked after during my travels, so you must not worry. Just take good care of yourself, especially with the baby.'

Hiro travelling through war zones – alarming images filled my mind: all those pictures in the newspapers, of bombs being dropped from aeroplanes, of soldiers with rifles positioned on their shoulders running through dusty battlefields. I wanted to cover my eyes to make the images go away, but didn't want to make things difficult for Hiro by showing distress. I silently bowed, and Hiro responded with a grateful nod.

Tuesday, 16 March

Hiro's impending trip made it difficult to concentrate on anything. Only when Shin-tsu came and started pounding Chinese pronunciation into me was I able to see that life could go on as normal.

I became stuck on the syllable 'si', pronounced 'see', failing to get it right. In frustration, Shin-tsu finally said, 'But Eiko-san, you must say "see" in high single tone to mean "think", I don't want you say "die" by adding wrong intonation!'

The ridiculous coincidence that the dreaded word 'die' should pop up triggered an uncontrollable giggling fit, and tears streamed down my face as Shin-tsu stared in bewilderment.

I felt refreshed after the release of tension, and told Shin-tsu of my pregnancy, which was met by unexpected delight. 'I am so happy! Feel like own baby brother or sister coming!' he said, taking my hand for a congratulatory handshake. It's nice to know I will have Shin-tsu to cheer me up in Hiro's absence.

Tuesday, 23 March

Less than a week until Hiro's departure. Spent the morning at Shanghai General, collecting medication for his trip, and getting a check-up from Dr Ruben. Hiro was visibly relieved from hearing the doctor's verdict that all was normal with my pregnancy. Running around preparing for Hiro's trip takes my mind off worrying, and makes me feel useful.

Monday, 29 March

Hiro looked dashing in his tweed jacket, an Aquascutum raincoat draped over his arm, as he hopped onto the awaiting military jeep. The khaki-clad soldier gave us a military salute before taking the driver's seat, and off they went as we – Miyo, Amah, Chokugetsu-ken, Kazu and I, all lined up in the driveway – bowed deeply. By the time I rose up, I saw only the rear of the jeep and a cloud of dust.

At least I know a little more about Hiro's mission from his send-off dinner last night. 'So you're off to Vietnam, Singapore and Thailand! Should be very interesting,' Rokki had said.

'I fly to Vietnam tomorrow. It'll be my first plane ride, on a Navy aircraft, the Mitsubishi K3M,' Hiro responded, barely able to conceal his enthusiasm. Perhaps for my benefit, he added, 'It's a well-flown route. Vietnam's safe. We have 30,000 troops there working with the Vichy Governor General.'

'Since you'll be in Japan-controlled stable countries, you might need a dinner jacket,' Rokki said. I couldn't tell whether he was serious, or teasing – knowing Hiro's care with his wardrobe.

'I'm told most dinners will be hosted by the military, in Japanese establishments, so I didn't see the need,' Hiro replied, in all seriousness, and Tamiko let out a gleeful chuckle.

The light-hearted mood comforted me. It seemed travel to Southeast Asia was nothing unusual – people were doing it all the time. Hiro's trip was just a normal extended business trip.

But after everyone left, other bits of conversation swirled in my mind: 'Vietnam's rice and rubber are important, so Japanese troops are vigilant about protecting transport routes'; 'Fortunately, Chennault's Air Force can't quite reach beyond Haiphong'; 'Even though Thailand's a Japanese ally, it seems British and US supplies are reaching anti-Japanese training camps in the north'; 'Singapore, now renamed *Shonan-tō*, remains rife with anti-Japanese activities...'

Normal war-time conversation among the men, I told myself. But uneasiness kept me awake long into the night. Unlike Hiro, who, after giving me a tender pat on my swelling belly, was out like a light.

With Hiro gone, how empty I feel.

Wednesday, 31 March

Sayako rang with news that Masaya was admitted to hospital.

'The doctor said Masaya Onī-sama's physical problems all come from his mental state. It is good to have a foreign doctor – you know how it is in Japan, with illnesses of the soul. Onī-sama's doctor, Dr Ziegler, is from Vienna and trained in psychiatry.' Sayako's frankness about Masaya's condition surprised me.

'Eiko-san, I mention this because Hiroshi-san is now seconded to the military. Accepting military values as a civilian could be very difficult. I am praying that Hiroshi-san won't find working for the Navy as troubling as Masaya Onī-sama does.'

I was touched and a bit amused by Sayako's concern. It seemed inconceivable that Hiro might ever need a Dr Zeigler with his easy-going ability to accept or let things go – a quality I increasingly appreciate.

Friday, 2 April

Tamiko organized a tea party to cheer me up in Hiro's absence. All the ladies from the performance gathered, and not having been together in months, everyone talked at once trying to catch up with one another, creating a lively din. But the war situation was never far from the surface.

'Taro still wants to be a fighter pilot,' Cheeko said. 'Only eleven years old, and my son can't stop going on about wanting to fly a Mitsubishi Zero. He loves the dark green colour with the big red circles on the wings and body. I have to say, the Zeros really are good-looking aeroplanes!'

'I never thought I'd be talking about aircraft, but having boys does that to you,' she said, reminding me of Kazu's toy rifle from Father Christmas.

'Speaking of boys,' she chirped on, 'you know how our house is very close to the internment camp on Yu Yuen Road. Some neighbours of ours complained that stones were being thrown at their windows from behind the camp walls. I told Taro about this, and next thing I know, he collects some friends to stake out the culprits. Of course they couldn't see anything – the walls are high and covered with barbed wire. But they heard footsteps and voices, and then down came the stones.' I held my breath, thinking about the Western families – including the Leighs – in that forbidding-looking place.

'The boys could sense that on the other side were lads about their own age, and Taro's friends were about to throw the stones back at them. But Taro said, "No!"' Cheeko paused, and proudly said, 'My boy who wants to be a fighter pilot. Instead of stones, he threw back a ball he had in his pocket!'

'He wanted to go back and throw more balls over the wall, but our neighbour's complaints seemed to have put a stop to the stone-throwing. Taro hasn't heard any boys' activities since.'

I felt crushed that Taro's connection with the boys on the other side had to end so soon, the flicker of a tie between the outside world and the internment camp extinguished without a chance.

Monday, 5 April

Kazu asks after Hiro all the time now. Having waved him goodbye, he knows Hiro has gone away, but seems to think it's time his Papa was back home. He pulls at my skirt and asks, *'Papa doko? Papa doko?'* How I wish I knew! I am in the same boat as Kazu, and also want to ask, 'where is Hiro?'

I scan through the papers every day, looking for any bits of news on Thailand or Vietnam or *Shonan-tō*, but see nothing. I asked Rokki whether he knew anything, but all he said was, 'Eiko, Japanese newspapers focus on actual battles and report victories, even if they aren't real victories. Hiroshi is travelling through Japanese-controlled areas, so there's no real fighting, no news. The papers don't report incidents like resistance against Japan or guerrilla operations, nothing that makes Japan look weak.'

I know he meant well, but I became more alarmed about dangerous possibilities one would never find out about from the papers.

It's now a full week since Hiro left, but not a word from anywhere. Being a military mission, I can't even ring his office. I just try to be calm and reassuring, tell Kazu that Papa still has important business to do before coming home, and pray that no news must certainly mean good news.

Friday, 9 April

Tamiko rang, her 'Hello, Eiko,' sounding so subdued that I thought Masaya might have taken a turn for the worse. But in fact she had surprising good news. 'Daddy's coming to China in about three weeks' time,' she said, 'He's been promoted to Director in charge of China.'

'How long has it been? Not since before all those years in London, Mummy dying, Daddy remarrying, Sachi and Kazu being born, and war and internment. It's like a lifetime,' Tamiko said with a sigh.

I realized that she was overwhelmed by the prospect of Daddy's visit – an emotion that went beyond simple joy. In her mind, because of the distance of time, and the many changes, Daddy had perhaps become a somewhat abstract, giant presence.

But to me, Daddy is Daddy, disciplined but with a mischievous sense of humour, my companion and anchor, especially in the years since Mummy's death. I can't believe that I will be seeing him so soon – a most welcome ray of happiness!

Friday, 16 April

Masaya is now allowed visitors. Despite having barely six weeks till her due date, Tamiko was practically skipping to reach the hospital. Once on the ward, though, our pace slowed, not knowing what state Masaya might be in, tension mounted as we followed the numbers on the doors in search of his room.

Tamiko knocked softly, and pushed open the door. Our worst fears were instantly dispelled by the sight of Masaya, dressed in normal street clothes, sitting comfortably in a corner armchair in the sun-filled room. Although thinner, with more strands of grey hair, he had regained his calm, reassuring air. He smiled broadly when he saw us walk in.

'Well, well, how wonderful to see the two of you, or is it the three of you!' he said, marvelling at the sight of bulging Tamiko. Noticing my loose clothing, he teasingly added, 'It's the four of you! Unless Eiko-san, Shanghai suits you so well that you are putting on weight.'

'Masaya, you've spent time in England, and should know it's rude to call a lady fat!' I retorted.

'But in Japan it's a compliment, a sign of contentment and well-being!' Tamiko and Masaya spoke almost in unison. I left them on their own to find Sayako, who was in the washing area putting flowers in a vase.

'It's a blessing to see Masaya Onī-sama smile again,' she said, giving me a heartfelt gaze. 'Dr Ziegler says his recovery is remarkable, due in large part to his faith and will to recover. Still, the doctor calls for caution – not to expose him to upsetting matters.'

We ran into Irma on her way to Masaya's room, arms full of bags, hair wild and face flustered from her walk along the corridor. 'I am on my way back from Holy Trinity Cathedral. Just handed over keys of the old clothing centre to Bishop Abe. All done within deadline!' she exclaimed triumphantly.

'It was not easy because Japanisch Navy is right across the road and I had to move things bit by bit so they didn't notice. But I succeeded!'

Sayako and I glanced at each other, worried about the effect of Irma's words on Masaya.

But Tamiko, seemingly oblivious, said, 'Marvellous, Irma. Keith and Joyce would be so pleased. You'll now be able to focus on a new clothing centre in the Designated Area where refugees will have easy access.' I couldn't believe how Tamiko could talk so openly about the Jewish refugees in front of Masaya.

The bustling Irma gave Masaya a peck on the cheek and, blowing us kisses and collecting her numerous bags, was out of the door as suddenly as she came in. Masaya was looking tired and Tamiko indicated that we, too, should take our leave.

Back in the corridor, Tamiko said, 'Irma's visit was timely. Masaya is ready to face Jewish reality – a thorn, which he sees as a challenge to strengthen his faith.'

I had the feeling that Tamiko understood Masaya even better than Dr Ziegler.

Monday, 19 April

When Chokugetsu-ken announced that there was a call for me from Hiro's office, my heart started to pound fiercely. I braced myself as I heard the voice on the other end say, 'Hello, this is Yamada from the Kishimoto Company. The Naval Attaché has informed us about a communication from Bangkok.' I clutched the receiver with both hands, and tried to steady myself for whatever news was to come.

'Kishimoto-san has just completed a very successful mission in Vietnam, and arrived safely in Bangkok last night. He is staying at the Oriental Hotel, now a Japanese officers' club. He is safe and well. Please take care. I will ring when I hear again.'

I leaned heavily against the wall feeling the relief sink through me. After all this worry, my mind full of images of Hiro amidst war rubble, it turned out he was staying at Bangkok's renowned Oriental Hotel!

I was about to find Kazu to tell him about *Papa,* when the phone rang again. The sharp ring made me jump, and for a moment I wondered whether it was a call to retract the wonderful news I was cherishing.

It was Tamiko. Before I could tell her about Hiro, she said, 'Daddy left Yokohama yesterday, and will be arriving here the day after tomorrow.'

I feel as if I am floating on air.

Tuesday, 20 April

Could it be the sudden relief of learning about Hiro's safety and the anticipation of Daddy's visit affecting my body? I ought to be refreshed. Instead, I feel as if all my energy has drained away.

Wednesday, 21 April

I woke up feeling weak and chilled to the bone, but nothing was going to keep me from greeting Daddy at the pier. Was it my condition that made the chaos seem unbearable? The jostling crowds, rubbish everywhere, hawkers shouting and beggars blocking the pavements. Tamiko nudged to humour me, but made me even more irritated.

How I wished I could simply pluck Daddy from the crowds, bring him home and relive our cosy time together in London! But a big delegation from the Bank, including Rokki, was lined up to greet him, and a shiny black Chrysler awaited to take him to the

Cathay Hotel, where he was to stay. Even his private time wasn't to be entirely mine. Tamiko had taken it for granted that his first family meal would be at her place, and she was making preparations for the last two days.

When he finally emerged, Daddy quickly spotted Tamiko and me at the front of the queue, and his face glowed with delight, instantly melting my heart. He had aged, but in a nice way that added a distinguished air. I felt proud to be his daughter.

Before I knew it though, the Bank delegation swiftly whisked him into the car, and he was gone.

'We might as well leave now,' Tamiko said. 'Didn't Daddy look wonderful? I'll hear from Rokki later about the rest of Daddy's day with the Bank people. Come Eiko, let's go!'

I felt cheated – such little contact with Daddy after all that effort. Tamiko had her dinner preparations and news through Rokki, but I had nothing. Dejected, I said, 'Go ahead without me. I'll stop by to see Kimmy as I'm right nearby.'

I hadn't even thought of seeing Kimmy. Instead, my feet automatically took me to the Cathay Hotel. Even if Daddy had work, I could say hello to Mr Hsu.

Mr Hsu was there, welcoming me with a 'Good afternoon, Madam,' and a warm nod. 'I can see that Madam now well settled in Shanghai,' he said, about to say more when his attention shifted beyond me towards the lifts. He broke into an unexpectedly open smile, and from behind me I heard a familiar voice approach.

'My good friend, Hsu-hsien-sheng! Long time no see. How are you my friend?' Mr Hsu rushed from behind the counter, and there was Daddy, the two of them exchanging affectionate handshakes. 'Huh, huh, huh!' Daddy chortled.

'Daddy!' I exclaimed.

'Eiko, I didn't know you were coming here,' he said with a surprised look, immediately giving me an English-style hug. How good it felt! Mr Hsu stood by agog.

'I never know Madam Kishimoto is daughter of Viscount Kanda. Fine young lady, just like father,' he said nodding.

'Your father, stay here many times. I am caught in crossfire in Chapei during fighting of 1937, and have big gash in forehead. Other Western hotel guests pay no attention but Viscount Kanda show great concern, at time when Japanese and Chinese killing each other.'

'Hsu-hsien-sheng, do not exaggerate,' Daddy said. 'It is you who looked after me so well every time I came here.'

There was little time to dwell on the coincidence. Mr Hsu had already resumed his position behind the counter, and Daddy saw that the Bank officials were at the entrance to collect him.

Before heading off, he flashed me a wink and mischievous grin, just like he used to in London when he left to attend what he called his 'boring functions'. I did well to drop by at the Cathay.

Friday, 23 April

I ended up crying myself to sleep after Tamiko's sumptuous family dinner surrounding Daddy. Was it my lack of energy and physical discomfort that made me so emotional?

The evening started out fine. Daddy was in good spirits, more relaxed than I have ever seen, perhaps because of the grandchildren. Sachi and Kazu jumped up and down, competing for his attention, and when Sachi slurped her soup noisily, he simply chuckled.

'Daddy, how you've softened in your old age! You used to be a demon when it came to table manners,' I teased.

'Huh, huh, huh, grandchildren are different,' he laughed.

Over dinner, Daddy held court. Recalling his internment on the Isle of Man, he said, 'Life was basic, but not harsh. We organized lectures, sports events, quizzes, you name it, to keep busy. During cleaning duty, I'd swoop around with my mop and make everyone guess which *kanji* character I wrote on the floor – a pretty good game!'

He managed to make even dark developments in Japan sound entertaining. 'Do you know what "golf" is called these days? We can't say "golufu" any more – since "enemy" nation words are forbidden. It's *dakyū* now, literally "hit the ball". We had lots of fun at a recent Bank golf outing, inventing Japanese equivalents for "tee" or "putter" or "green". Huh, huh, huh.'

During the meal, I noticed how protective Daddy seemed of Tamiko. 'Eiko, you go and help,' he'd say whenever Tamiko prepared to get up. I wanted to remind him that I, too, was expecting a baby, and having a more difficult pregnancy than Tamiko.

It was over coffee when Daddy said, 'Apart from attending Bank business, I've been given some shopping tasks. And here, I really need your help, Eiko.'

'What a shame Hiroshi isn't here,' I said. 'He's the one who knows the best places for men's clothing.' I suddenly missed Hiro very much.

'No, no, it's not for me. I have precise instructions on the make and the size of the brassieres that I am supposed to buy. I am told that they have every style here in Shanghai. This is the sort of thing you can help me with, Eiko. Besides, Tamiko is too busy.'

I could hardly believe my ears. For Daddy to even mention the word brassiere seemed out of character: to ask his daughter to buy undergarments for his wife was unthinkable. I felt completely put upon.

Of course, I couldn't show my feelings. I just nodded assent, hoping that he might notice just a bit of my unhappiness. Even more, I was hoping Tamiko, always sensitive to others' feelings, would understand my predicament. But she seemed completely under Daddy's spell.

'Eiko really knows the fashionable stores here and is always telling me I should get better clothes. I'll come with her tomorrow – I'll enjoy it. I hope we will find exactly what Sachiko-sama wants,' she said.

That she genuinely meant everything she said irritated me even more. How could Daddy be so blinded by his wife – could he not see how ridiculous her request is in the middle of a war?

Saturday, 24 April

Tamiko and I remained silent during the walk to Yates Road, I, because of my foul mood, and Tamiko probably because she was enjoying the warm spring sunshine. My spirits lifted briefly as we passed shop after shop of silk and lace displays in the windows, but plunged again as we stood before a high-cheek-boned Russian shop attendant in one of the classiest shops. Why were we doing this?

The shop lady, taking my sullenness as a sign of dissatisfaction with the displayed items, brought out beautiful bra after beautiful bra from under the counter. 'Madam, perhaps this black one here would meet your approval?' I was now annoyed being taken for a woman hard to please.

Tamiko told the woman what we were looking for.

'Ah, Mesdames, not for yourselves!' she said, staring at our chests: even in our pregnancy, our Japanese bosoms could hardly fill a C-cup. Is that why Sachiko asked Daddy to find bras for her – to make sure his daughters knew how endowed she was?

With the money Daddy had given me, we could afford only two, but Tamiko insisted we buy three as requested, swiftly taking money out from her purse. The shop lady seemed relieved to see us leave, after handing us the carefully wrapped 34-inch C-cup brassieres made by the Warner Brothers Corset Company of Connecticut, USA.

Once out of the door, Tamiko said, 'Eiko, what is the matter with you? Ever since last night, you just don't seem to be yourself. Please think of how much it means to Daddy to fulfil Sachiko-san's wishes.'

I found it difficult to hold back my tears.

'Daddy was never like this with Mummy,' I blurted. 'You weren't in London to see how Mummy was Daddy's backbone, how digni-fied a couple they were. After Mummy died, for as long as I know, Daddy continued to act according to what he thought Mummy would have advised. But now, he makes his daughters run after bras for his new wife!'

Tamiko's eyes were full of sympathy, and something else – hurt or longing, perhaps. 'It's true, Eiko, you have spent far more recent years with the two of them, and then with Daddy on his own. I envy you and can see how Daddy's new circumstances are upsetting. But, Eiko, you have to accept that Daddy has to move on. It's different, but he is obviously happy now. As loving daughters, who've received so much from him, we should accept and celebrate his happiness.'

We walked arm in arm on our way home. Again, it was a silent walk, but having let off steam, and having Tamiko by my side, affectionately squeezing my arm from time to time, I felt comforted. I couldn't be angry and grumpy in her presence for long. Yes, Daddy would be happy with our shopping success.

Sunday, 25 April

It was Easter Sunday, and Daddy's final lunch in Shanghai. We celebrated with a Bible reading and some hymns before the meal, just like the olden days in London. In prayer, so many thoughts floated through my mind: the day Mummy died – Daddy away on a business trip, Mummy and I, with Benji by our side, reading the Bible and singing hymns, the same late spring sunlight as today, shimmering through the window; the peacefulness followed by sudden tragedy. It made me pray desperately for Daddy's safety – I couldn't bear the thought of anything happening to him during his travels in China. My annoyance with him was so trivial in the grand scheme of things. I thought of Hiro, sadly missing Daddy's visit, but allowing me to revert to daughterhood in his absence.

When it came time to leave, Daddy said, 'Tamiko, you have your family to look after, and you should rest. Hiroshi-san is not around, so perhaps Eiko can see me to the station.'

In the car, Daddy seemed content. 'So good to see my two daughters, well and settled together in Shanghai. It is a great comfort that you are here, Eiko, such good company for Tamiko.' Daddy's words surprised me. I never considered myself good company for Tamiko, only the other way round: she, the older sister, whom I count on all the time.

'Seeing Tamiko thrive is a great relief. I felt I could never forgive myself for the dark early years of her marriage, when Rokuro-san was so ill.' Looking vacantly out the car window, he seemed to be talking to himself, rather than to me.

'It appeared to be such a good match, Rokuro-san from a highly respectable family. Tamiko barely knew him, but was happy to go along with whatever we felt best for her. And we really did believe it was the best for her. But soon after the wedding, Rokuro-san took ill, and Tamiko was thrust into being a nurse, rather than a wife. So much time spent in hospital, and then a very long convalescence at home, and a big financial strain. But never a complaint from her, all through her youthful years between age nineteen to twenty-five.'

After a pause, he turned to me with a smile. 'But with you, I have been spared the heartache,' he said, patting me on the hand. 'Huh, huh, huh, marrying you off to an Osaka merchant family was a shock for us Tokyo people from a different social class, but look at you, so poised and polished, so happy! Seeing you so well settled is a great joy, especially as I did not have your mother to consult on your marriage. I am very proud.'

'Of me, or of yourself?' I giggled, somewhat embarrassed by his gaze full of praise.

Chuckling he said, 'With Sachi and Kazu the same age, and younger ones coming along later this year, the age gap between you and Tamiko seems to have disappeared. You have blossomed. I didn't get to see Hiroshi-san during this visit, but I can tell he is looking after you very well.'

I now understood why Daddy had been so protective of Tamiko. And his demands on me I realized were only a reflection of how he saw me as a grown-up, independent woman.

We were approaching the station, little private time left to share. I squeezed Daddy's hand tightly, as I used to as a child whenever I wanted something badly. 'Ouch, Eiko, I thought I was just complimenting you on your poise and maturity. Maybe I spoke too soon. Huh, huh, huh, what is it that you want!'

'For you to be safe, to keep well, and to know that your visit here has been so special,' I said in as steady a tone as I could manage. He gave me a mischievous smile and a wink before getting out of the car to meet the Bank delegation lined up to see him off.

The train departed with a whistle and a jolt, and I bowed until my back ached – towards the departing train, and to the Bank people.

12

Thursday, 14 May 1943

'I won't be mobile for much longer,' Tamiko said, 'So let's pay a visit to Irma in the Designated Area.'

Despite her enthusiasm and the beautiful early summer weather, the journey was fraught from the outset. We stood in a long queue at the Garden Bridge checkpoint, and finally, just before our turn, the Japanese sentry started shouting at the Westerner in front of us. Right before our eyes, the man was forced to the ground and slapped across the face. The impact made me jump back, but Tamiko stood firm, with a stone-cold expression while the sentry held down the prostrated man with a dirty boot. After what seemed an interminable period of time, the sentry kicked the Westerner away. My knees were shaking as the guard checked our papers and dismissed us with a grunt.

Our foray into Hongkew and the Designated Area did not get any better. Eastern Hongkew was even more crowded than the Japanese area to the west, the streets and alleys filled to the brim with people, rubbish, mangy dogs, children squatting and men urinating against walls. Even the weather seemed to have turned hot and oppressive.

Irma's place was tucked in a narrow alleyway off Tongshan Road – a dingy rundown building which was a stark contrast from the pretty house she shared with Agnes in leafy Frenchtown. We were about to bang on the door, when Irma came bouncing out.

'Lieblings! I had a hunch there was nice surprise outside,' she exclaimed, waving her arms in excitement. Her hair, now half grey, seemed to have absorbed the humidity and curled wildly in different directions.

'Ah, you have brought me soap from Agnes. *Danke*! Now I can clean my place for your next visit.' My heart sank, thinking how nice it would be to have a cup of tea after our trying journey.

'Irma, if you don't mind, we would love to come in now,' Tamiko said, to my relief.

With a furtive look, Irma said, 'It is not easy to get to my room, especially for you, Tamiko.' Tamiko said she would be fine, and Irma had little choice but to invite us in.

It was pitch dark in the windowless corridor, and we gingerly followed Irma towards the back of the building. At the very end, where the passageway narrowed, a dim bare light bulb exposed a small wooden ladder. 'We climb up here. I go first. Tamiko, you follow, and Eiko, come last so you can push Tamiko from below if she needs help.'

Before her ascent, as if reminded, Irma said, 'If you need the washroom, better to go now before we climb up. It is on other side of the corridor.'

I went in first, and had a retching fit from the smell. The WC consisted of a wooden, barrel-like 'honey pot' and a cracked washbasin. No flush, no bathtub, no sign of hot water. I grimaced at Tamiko as she took her turn to go in, but she coolly ignored me.

The place was barely large enough for a bed and a table, but Irma had made it cosy with a bright bedcover and a flower-patterned curtain. The one tiny window high up near the ceiling let in enough daylight to give the room a soft glow. She boiled water over a small portable charcoal stove, making the room stiflingly hot.

'I should go down to the hot *wasserman* next door, but climbing the ladder carrying boiling *wasser* is scary,' Erna said, wiping sweat from her forehead.

'The tea is delicious, and you've done wonders to this place,' Tamiko said.

Irma smiled gratefully. 'Yes, I am lucky to have a whole room to myself. Many families live in one room, and if the room is big, they hang a sheet as a partition, and two families share the space. This is a very populated Chinese area to begin with, and now thousands of Jews are moving in before the deadline in four days' time. Yes, I've been very fortunate.'

On our way home, I said to Tamiko, 'Do you think it's just that one washroom for the whole building?'

'Yes, I am sure it is. Is that all you can think of?' she replied with a sisterly nudge.

But yes, it's the dismal washroom that sticks in my mind as summing up life in the Designated Area.

Wednesday, 19 May

Masaya appeared at Tamiko's today, looking remarkably well. He had regained some of the weight he had lost, and his greying temples gave him a distinguished air.

'I'm a liberated man now. Free from hospital and free from the Navy' Masaya said, relaxing into the sofa.

'Have you been fired?' Tamiko asked, teasingly.

'Actually, yes!' Masaya replied. 'I no longer have a job.'

Tamiko's enquiring look made Masaya turn serious. 'The Army has completely taken over the Jewish Affairs Bureau. The Navy has let the refugees down. I hope I can be more effective in helping the refugees through prayer. Christian groups have asked me to lead Bible studies and prayer meetings, and that's what I will devote myself to,' he said.

His calm expression was that of a confident man, and his recovery filled me with optimism. If only Hiro were back, it would be like the happy earlier times.

Tuesday, 25 May

As if in answer to my prayers, Hiro's office rang saying that he is due back on the 27th, in just two days' time! He flies back from Singapore, again on a military aircraft.

'There is no time given of his arrival. The Navy's instructions are for you to wait at home,' the man on the phone said apologetically.

Thursday, 27 May

Kazu was my distraction, filling the void awaiting Hiro's return. I wondered how much of Papa Kazu actually remembered – a two-month absence being a big chunk of a child's life.

'Papa sits in that chair, reading his paper, and he pats Jay-jay, always sitting by his feet. Do you think Jay-jay will be happy when Papa comes home?' Kazu nodded vigorously. 'Remember, how Papa likes the chocolate tin?' I pretended to open the tin and pop a chocolate into my mouth. Kazu giggled out loud.

'But do you remember how he gets quite cross if your toys are scattered on the living room floor? You must put your things away.'

Kazu pounded my knee in mock anger, and quickly stated, 'I'm a good boy!'

Although I couldn't make the time pass quicker, my little game with Kazu had a comforting effect, taking the fretfulness away. When the doorbell rang shortly after teatime, I could reach the door calmly, with only a slight flutter in my stomach.

Hiro walked in, with a deep tan and perhaps just a bit wider smile than usual. '*Tadaima*, I'm home,' he said, with his usual slight nod in lieu of a bow. I responded with my normal bow and '*Okaeri-asobase*' greeting – a homecoming not much different from his daily return from the office.

But Jay-jay howled, as if the joy of seeing Hiro was more than her little body could contain, her tail wagging in frenzy. Kazu, not to be outdone by Jay-jay, jumped up and down squealing, 'Papa, papa, papa, papa!'

Overcome by the commotion, Hiro picked up Jay-jay to quieten her down. While she was licking his face and wriggling in his arms, he took a good look at Kazu and said, 'How you've grown!' Kazu beamed proudly at his father, stretching his back to appear even taller.

Hiro then formally thanked Miyo, Chokugetsu-ken and Amah, who were lined up to greet him, for their work during his absence. Finally, with a glance at my belly he softly said, 'It seems you've looked after yourself and the whole household well.' It was a statement of appreciation, which made me happy.

Hiro unpacked in his orderly manner. Anticipating piles of dirty laundry, I was surprised to see most of his clothes washed and neatly folded. 'The hotel in Singapore was very efficient,' he said. 'But the Chinese working there don't like the Japanese.'

'Thailand was easier, the Thais being on our side,' he added, as he rummaged around the bottom of his suitcase. 'Ah, here it is! I bought this for you. Thailand has very good gemstones.'

In my hand was placed a ring with a beautiful star sapphire. I put it on, and he looked pleased. 'Perfect fit. Just as I thought.'

Before I had a chance to thank him, he said, 'I wonder if dinner's ready. I'm hungry!'

Chokugetsu-ken had painstakingly prepared a proper Japanese celebratory dish on occasion of Hiro's safe return: sea bream stewed in aromatic juices, head and all. The accompanying dishes were Hiro's favourites – broad beans lightly seasoned with soy sauce and *mirin*, baby aubergines new in season, and deep-fried *tofu* – and he ate with relish. By the end of the meal, he could barely keep his eyes open.

As I listen to his even breathing, deep in sleep, beside me, I am filled with gratitude. I thank God that he is safely home. Despite his unfussy homecoming, the deeper lines on his forehead and his obvious physical exhaustion speak of a mission that was more trying than he makes it seem. Given his easy ways, I may never find out everything he went through, but he seems a bigger presence now – filling me with happy reassurance.

Saturday, 29 May

Only two days since Hiro's return, but it feels as if he never left – life has settled back to the comfortable old ways – Hiro out playing golf, me popping over to Tamiko's, stopping in the courtyard to watch the children at play, and discussing the dinner menu with Chokugetsu-ken. Tomorrow is the special dinner to celebrate Masaya's recovery and Hiro's homecoming.

Sunday, 30 May

The evening started light-heartedly, like the good old days. 'Still dressed impeccably, even after gallivanting in the dust and heat in Southeast Asia!' was Rokki's comment as he arrived, eyeing Hiro's tie.

'I actually received compliments. Some officers have good taste,' Hiro retorted.

'Trust Hiroshi to return from a military mission with an increased sense of humour,' Tamiko said, gently patting Masaya on the arm. Masaya responded with an understanding smile, accepting that Hiro's nonchalance was precisely what he lacked.

The informality and warmth among friends and family made me giddy with happiness. Hiro entertained us with stories of his travels. 'Going to Angkor Wat was scarier than being in a war zone. Tigers could appear any minute. We had to be accompanied by soldiers with rifles, walking deep through the jungle. We reached an area covered with old tree roots that looked like giant snakes, and suddenly, the temples magically appeared before us.'

After the satisfying meal, as we were settling for coffee and brandy, Jiro said, 'I almost forgot! There's supposed to be some announcement from Military HQ in Japan on the wireless.'

'Do we really want to listen to those monotone voices that we know always stretch the truth, telling us of our victories?' Masaya asked, in a brotherly taunt.

'Normally not,' Jiro responded, his tone serious. 'But my Chinese friends who listen to shortwave broadcasts from Chungking seem to think something is going on.'

We listened in anticipation, but only crackly noises came through. We were about to give up when a scratchy male voice came through the airwaves.

'Since 12 May, the small Imperial Japanese Northern Army garrison in Attu Island...' Crackle, crackle... '...fierce battle against superior enemy forces under extremely difficult conditions...in the night of 29 May ... spectacular attack against the main enemy force… display the true spirit of the Imperial Forces…' Crackle, crackle… 'Communication has ceased, and we acknowledge *gyokusai* for all…'

No one spoke, only the interference filling the void until Hiro turned off the machine.

Tamiko appeared to have understood everything. 'All dead, those poor soldiers, stuck in the freezing Aleutian Islands. And they say *gyokusai* to make it sound noble.'

'What does it mean?' I asked, feeling left in the dark.

Sayako answered in her soft, thoughtful tone. 'If I remember correctly, the word comes from the Chinese classics of the Tang dynasty, on how men should live: more noble to be a glass bead – jewel – and be crushed in honour, than survive and live on as a simple roof tile. *Gyokusai* literally means "crushed jewel".'

Rokki started pounding the sofa armrest, fist clenched with protruding whitened knuckles. I looked in alarm at Tamiko, but she sat, arms huddled around her belly, looking elsewhere with a frown between her brows. 'They're doing it again,' Rokki muttered. 'Making it sound like noble deaths. But they abandoned those soldiers in that bare, remote, island with no reinforcements or supplies, encouraging death rather than capture, in the name of *gyokusai*. It's a disgrace.'

Jiro seemed crestfallen, not just by the news but by having ruined the evening.

'You were right to turn on the wireless,' Masaya said with authority, sensing his brother's dismay. 'We have to face reality, and we are here assembled together. Let us pray for the soldiers who lost their lives, may their souls rest in peace.' His deep, commanding voice provided comfort, as we bowed our heads in prayer.

Then came a sudden, sharp groan from Tamiko. For a split second, I thought it was because of the radio announcement.

'Sorry,' Tamiko said, forcing a cheerful tone. 'I think I'm in labour.'

That was two hours ago. Rokki swiftly took her to the Great Western Hospital, and I haven't heard anything since. No wonder I can't fall asleep.

Monday, 31 May

A baby girl: born at 5.43 a.m. I was awoken by Rokki at 7 a.m. with the news, and am now trying to catch up on sleep. My body is exhausted, but my nerves are still on edge.

Tuesday, 1 June

Tamiko was looking radiant, with little Asako in her arms – a big baby with a round, sweet face. She was peacefully asleep, and I stared in amazement at the tiny fingers, even tinier fingernails, and the millimetre-long eyelashes, all so perfectly formed. I felt wistful with still three months to go until my turn, but feeling unbearably heavy and dull.

Tamiko, glowing in health, said, 'We named her Asako, because she arrived at dawn – 'morning child'.

Friday, 4 June

No energy. Found out only after a long nap that Masaya had dropped by. The single pink rose he left lifted my spirits, and I was sad to have missed him.

Wednesday, 9 June

Cheeko kindly dropped by, hearing that I had been unwell. 'We went to the opening night of Li Koran's new film, "The Opium War",' she chirped, as soon as she arrived.

'Li sings the "Candy-girl Song". I'm sure it will make her a big star throughout China even if she's from Manchuria,' Cheeko went on excitedly.

'I'm not quite following you,' I said, wondering if my poor physical state affected my brain as well.

'I'm sorry Eiko-san, I get so carried away. You see, the film is a joint production between the Manchurian Motion Picture Company and the China Film Company, and the Chinese tend to be suspicious of stars from the Manchurian Company. But in Li Koran's case, it's a bit different because many people think she is actually Japanese. The curious thing is, if Li was Chinese, the China Film Company people would see her as a betrayer, but if she was Japanese, they'd accept her as a colleague!'

I found it difficult to get my head around, but whether she was Chinese or Japanese, I wondered how she felt about the two countries being at war. Like me, born in Britain, growing up there, even holding a British passport – a fact I could never mention now – but being Japanese: an existence of torn allegiances. I couldn't help feeling affinity for Li Koran, who according to Cheeko, is only a year older than me.

Tuesday, 15 June

It is a struggle to get myself out of bed in the morning. But for Hiro's sake, I make an effort to dress nicely and look as fresh as possible. That gives me a little pick up, until the slightest physical exertion, and my energy ebbs away. This has been the pattern for the last few days.

The one big boost to my spirits has been Masaya's visits. He says the walk is good for him and drops by without warning, always bearing a flower or two that he buys from a pedlar on the street. He sticks it in a vase himself, and says, with a wink, 'Eiko-san, I've given the flower a good sprinkling so it has no germs from outside!'

Today, he caught me at a good moment, and stayed for a cup of tea. 'I've been offered a teaching position at St John's University, to start in late August,' he said. 'It will be good to work with students again. Tamiko-san says it's about time I'm gainfully employed.'

Tuesday, 22 June

I mustered up my energy for a Shin-tsu lesson, and was taken by surprise when he announced, as soon as our lesson began, that he was going to work for his father's company.

'I still not interested in sugar business, but want office experience,' he said. I was puzzled, given how disapproving Shin-tsu had been towards his father's business.

Shin-tsu must have read my thoughts. 'You see Eiko-san, I discover strange coincidence which make me think working for Baba is OK. Man named Liu Bin-ro who in my study group, happen to be manager in Baba's company! Very clever man, ten years older than me. One day, we have drink at Hotel Park bar, and he say why not come work in his department.'

Why was I so surprised to hear that Shin-tsu went to bars? I had never imagined clean-cut and polite Shin-tsu in smoky, intellectual hangouts, deep in debate.

'Liu Bin-ro is man who think about China future, like Uncle Uchiyama. He help me understand what is happening in war and Nationalists and Communists. I decide I want to work for him.'

'Baba wants me in different department. He says Liu Bin-ro office work not interesting, just buy supplies from small traders, like boy in our house who buy food for family.' Shin-tsu shrugged with a resigned smile.

'But Midori-Mama manage make it all smooth. She say to Baba, "Wen-tsu, he has to start somewhere, and you mentioned what a fine man Liu-hsien-sheng is." When Midori-mama talk, Baba listen.'

Although my energy was deserting me by the end of the lesson, I felt uplifted by Shin-tsu's bright smile.

Wednesday, 23 June

I am aching all over and feeling feverish. How this scares me! I am terrified of losing the baby. God, please give me courage.

Sunday, 27 June

When I opened my eyes, I saw Hiro and Tamiko peering into my face with worried expressions, and it took me a while to work out where I was.

The unfamiliar pale green walls, the smell of disinfectant. As soon as I realized I was in hospital, I became gripped by panic. And the vague memory of a high fever, discomfort and an ambulance ride came back to me.

I felt a strange dullness throughout my body, and was afraid to move. No, I wasn't ready to hear the fate of the baby. I turned my head away from Hiro and Tamiko.

Tamiko took my hand. 'Finally awake! Amazing how you can sleep,' she said softly. To Hiro, she said, 'Hiroshi, you can go and take a rest now that she's awoken. You look like you could do with some tea.'

He gave her a grateful look, and I sensed his huge relief at being dismissed. Our eyes met, and he gave me an awkward, apologetic wince. My heart sank. So it was up to Tamiko, I thought, to give me the bad news.

'You had a very bad infection, and ended up delirious on Friday,' Tamiko said. 'Miyo rang the ambulance, and Dr Ruben was waiting for you at the hospital. He gave you intravenous medication, and you fell into a deep sleep. He was sorry he hadn't nipped the infection earlier thinking you would naturally shake it off. In any event, you are awake now and the fever is gone!'

She pulled my hand closer to her, and I stiffened, unsure whether I had any feeling below my waist. I closed my eyes tight in fear.

'Eiko, what on earth are you doing?' Tamiko said lightly. 'Can you not open your eyes? Is this some kind of a game?'

I shook my head and started to sob. 'Just tell me the truth. I have lost the baby, haven't I?' Tamiko gently swept a strand of hair off my face, and peered into my tear-filled eyes.

With great tenderness, she said, 'You are very silly, aren't you.' She gently led my hand down to my belly from above the blanket. I stroked my taut, large bulge, while tears of relief trickled onto the pillow.

Upon leaving the hospital, Dr Ruben said, 'The baby is healthy, but you are frail. We can't give you strong medication. You just have to endure any discomfort for baby's sake.'

I will endure anything to keep the precious life growing within me.

Thursday, 1 July

I'm still confined to bed, quite dependent on Miyo, who discreetly brings Kazu to my side to cheer me up and ensures I take plenty of fluids. Only ten more days to her wedding – will I be able to cope without her?

I'd like to get well enough to attend her wedding. With something to look forward to, perhaps I will start feeling stronger.

Monday, 19 July

Over a week now since Miyo went off on honeymoon. How disappointed I was to miss the wedding, but I could barely get out of bed.

Fortunately, Kazu is adjusting to life without Miyo, perhaps better than me. He has taken to Amah in a way I hadn't imagined. He takes full advantage of Amah's soft nature, giggling more, poking her when he wants attention. At the same time, he seems to sense she is more vulnerable than Miyo, and does everything he is told straight away: a curious mixture of becoming more spontaneously childish in some ways, and more independent and responsible at the same time.

I could hear their lively exchange in the corridor as they returned from a walk in the rain, Kazu shouting, 'Amah, splashy, splashy! Water in boots!' and Amah saying, 'Takey off! No wetty boots in housey! Missy no like messy.'

And then sounds of Kazu's happy squeals as his wellies were being pulled off. Had it not been for the obvious fun he was having, I might have leapt up to dry his feet – the last thing I want is for him to catch cold. But I am learning to contain myself, and besides, I had no energy.

So many things I should be doing to prepare for new baby's arrival, but just the thought exhausts me.

Tuesday, 27 July

I had to tell Shin-tsu that I was too big and too weak to continue lessons. 'Good for me, too, Eiko-san. Baba want me to see sugar plantations with him during summer,' he said.

'Travel with Baba won't be like trip with study group. This time will be nice hotels and good food.' Instead of looking pleased, he appeared troubled.

'I not happy, having comfort when many other Chinese suffering,' he said. 'Last year, we help injured woman return to village south of Yangtze River. Beautiful place, with mountains and lakes, but people there very poor. We walk everywhere, and eat simple vegetables and rice. Hard journey, but study group friends learn much, and old woman we help is wise teacher. She been with Helpful Friend Society – our study group name – for long time.'

Perhaps he sensed my lack of energy, for he kept on talking, saving me the effort of making English conversation. 'Eiko-san, I tell you why I join study group. All because of what Nationalists do against own Chinese army. You know about united front?' I responded with a completely blank expression.

'When Chiang Kai-shek became leader of Nationalist Party, Kuomintang, he try to get rid of leftists, and he against communists, so Nationalist Party and Communist Party always fighting. But when Japan wage war against China, Nationalists and Communists decide to come together and fight Japan. They call that united front, and Communist New Fourth Army and Eighth Route Army, join Nationalist forces. But Chiang Kai-shek still always try to weaken liberal forces.'

Like the rivalry between the Japanese Army and Navy, I thought.

'In January 1941, unbelievable thing happen. Nationalists attack New Fourth Army, nearly wiping them out.' Shin-tsu fixed his eyes on mine.

'This is when I hate Nationalists. For them, own power more important than China independence. Many school friends feel same way and we start going to Helpful Friend Society meetings.'

I looked into Shin-tsu's face – such soft, handsome features, behind which existed unexpected passion and determination. I always thought of him as someone younger, but now saw his maturity. Unlike me, growing up in relative peace until recent times, China had been turbulent for Shin-tsu's entire life.

'Study group teach us many things. Old woman tell us much about rural conditions in China, things students in city don't know.' Shin-tsu looked dreamily out the window. How I will miss him, I thought.

As if responding to my feelings, he said, 'Eiko-san, I able talk about these things with you. You are good friend and understand. At home, Baba thinking different from me, and much I can't say.'

Before leaving, he gently took my hand and said, 'Eiko-san, I look forward to come back after baby born. Please keep very well.'

Yes, I must keep well so that our cosy lessons can resume after the summer.

Wednesday, 28 July

Turned twenty-two today. But I feel like forty-two, worn out and listless. Masaya came mid-morning, bearing a birthday bouquet of pink roses. He stayed for just a few minutes, making it sound as if he had many errands, but I know it was out of consideration for me.

At teatime, Tamiko came over with baby Asako strapped on her back, one hand holding Sachi, the other bearing a huge birthday cake. I managed to eat a decent sized piece, which pleased Tamiko. 'With an appetite like that, there is nothing wrong with you,' she said, taking my hands into hers. But I noticed her concerned look, which told me that despite putting on a brave face for me, she was actually very worried.

They say it's the wettest and coolest summer here in recorded history. I can't shake off the thought that something will go terribly wrong with the birth.

Friday, 13 August

I can barely take up my pen, but I am determined to record my gratitude for the life I have been given, surrounded by people I love, and who love me. Their faces pass one after the other in my mind's eye, making me smile and tearful at the same time. I have been given such a happy life. Whatever might happen to me in this last stretch of pregnancy, I shall have no regrets. My physical discomfort is hard to bear, but my soul is at peace.

13

Thursday, 9 September 1943

It is now three weeks since Takao was born, ten days since being back from hospital. I can hardly remember the last days of confinement, feeling so tired and unwell that all I wished for was the misery to end.

When I finally went into labour, I remember wondering whether I would have the strength to endure the birth. But Dr Ruben managed to nudge me along, and with the help of forceps, the baby came sliding out, only after three hours.

Takao – born on 19 August.

The moment he was placed in my arms, I felt the same incredible rush of joy and relief and surge of love as when Kazu was born. But whereas Kazu was a beautiful, handsome baby from the moment he was born, this one came out with a scrunched up face, looking like a monkey, with mischievous slanted eyes.

He's never still, always wriggling. Perhaps he was using up all my energy, making me so tired while he was inside me. Now that he's out, I feel perfectly fine again, and much amused by this new creature. Before his arrival, I couldn't imagine being able to love another child as I love Kazu. But here is Taka, as precious to me as Kazu. It seems that God gives us infinite capacity for love.

Hiro suggested the name 'Takao', the *kanji* character meaning the one to rise and prosper, perfect for a boy coming into a challenging world. Now, at three weeks, Taka focuses his determined gaze, already looking as if he is up to something naughty – a true fighter.

Friday, 10 September

'Italians sink the *Conte Verde*!' was today's headline, with a blurry photo of the vessel tilted and half sunk in the water. 'Can't believe they sunk their own boat,' Hiro said, head stuck in the paper.

'The crew switched sides right after Italy's surrender. They obviously didn't want Japan to take over the boat.' Hiro shook his head in disbelief as he munched on his marmalade toast.

Straight after breakfast, I phoned Tamiko. 'We must go and take a look,' I said. It was the boat that had opened my eyes to a larger world – giving me my first real impression of Jewish refugees arriving here, showing me what repatriation meant.

'Such interest and energy all of a sudden!' Tamiko teased. The trams were too crowded so we meandered our way through the congested streets. It was good to be out in the hustle bustle, feeling light and free of health worries. I felt eager to re-engage in the world about me.

The crowds became even thicker as we approached the pier. We weren't the only ones to come and see the overturned boat. All around us were excited Chinese, everyone talking loudly.

The sight was shocking: the huge inert body of the *Conte Verde*, looking like a beached whale; the murky yellow waves of the Whangpoo hitting against her belly and portholes as if trying to coax out her last breath.

The Chinese voices nearby brought me back to reality. A group of men were shouting and laughing and pointing at various parts of the boat. Tamiko tilted her head, angling her ear in order to catch the words.

'They're taking bets on whether the Japanese will pull the boat up or not,' she said. 'They seem very excited by what the Italians did. That man over there, the one who's showing his missing tooth, he says there's no way the Japanese could lift the boat. "No *Conte Verde* for the Japanese!" That's what he's smiling about.'

The turn of events was difficult to keep up with – Italy surrendering, ceasing to be part of the Axis. Did all Italians suddenly feel they were against Japan now, like the *Conte Verde* crew?

'It depends whether they were Mussolini supporters or not,' Tamiko said. 'In any event, now that Italy is no longer an ally of Japan, most Italians in Shanghai will probably be treated as enemy nationals.'

Even a boat's fate was affected by war. I couldn't bear to think that the *Conte Verde* would simply disappear under water.

Tuesday, 14 September

Shin-tsu appeared early evening, neatly attired in a light grey suit, bearing a bunch of red roses. 'Congratulations, Eiko-san! In China giving birth to son is biggest achievement. I am most happy.' Perhaps it was the shadow from the hallway light that made him seem older and graver.

At our table by the window, I was relieved to find his smile as bright and youthful as before.

'Travel with Baba was good,' Shin-tsu reported. 'He tough businessman, but I see other side of him, too. He show concern over peasants working condition. Baba inspect plantations and I stand by and watch. I would have liked to work in field with peasants, but not possible with Baba there.'

'I much like job with Liu Bin-ro because not desk work. I go all over Shanghai to buy paper and ink and printing equipment. Meet traders, and go to factory and get to know workers.' His eyes shone with enthusiasm.

'But your outfit, Shin-tsu, you look too elegantly dressed for someone rushing around town all the time,' I teased.

I thought I sensed an uneasy flicker in his eyes, but he quickly responded, 'Eiko-san, you notice everything!' with a louder than expected laugh. 'I change clothes to come here. Work clothes much too dusty for your home. During day, leave suit in office, and at end of work, put on,' he said.

With a sly smile, he added, 'Better be in suit when Baba see me, and also for Hotel Park bar.' I couldn't tell whether he was teasing me: perhaps he did grow up in the two months I hadn't seen him.

Friday, 17 September

The doorbell rang mid-morning, and it was Herr and Frau Schmidt from upstairs, standing ramrod straight in front of the door. From their stern looks, I thought they had come to complain about noise from the children, and felt embarrassed.

'I hope we are not bothering you,' Herr Schmidt said, sensing my discomfort. Frau Schmidt pushed a nicely wrapped box into my hands and said, 'Zis is for your new baby. Ve hear from our boy about ze birth.'

I was deeply touched. I had worried that the baby's crying was keeping them awake.

'No, no! Ve hear nossing, and vundered whezer Japanese babies do not cry,' Herr Schmidt said, with a twitch of a smile.

'When ve hear ze baby cry in the distance, ve are reminded of our little *enkelkind* in Deutschland,' Frau Schmidt said, oblivious of her husband's comment. I suddenly felt sorry we hadn't made more of an effort to see these lovely neighbours regularly.

Monday, 20 September

Miyo, now a live-out nanny, keeps me abreast of what goes on in Japan Town.

'Oku-sama, the atmosphere in Hongkew has changed for the worse recently. Japanese plainclothes policemen are entering residential lanes,' she said today, as she handed me Taka for his feeding.

'I was approached by this man while hanging out the laundry the other day. He seemed friendly and eager to engage in conversation. I soon realized he was trying to get information on some of our Chinese neighbours, and kept asking about our landlady's son, who is a university student.'

For some reason, her mention of a Chinese university student made me think of Shin-tsu and I felt a wave of unease. 'What did the policeman want?' I asked.

'It wasn't clear. He asked when I'd seen the boy last, whether he goes out a lot, those sorts of questions. Of course, I had nothing to tell him.' Noticing that I had become distracted from Taka, Miyo reached out to turn baby's head towards my breast, and gave me a reassuring smile.

'Mr Uchiyama says this has been happening for years and is nothing new,' she said. She reminded me how Uncle had helped many Chinese under suspicion, and with his intervention they were always released. Of course, I thought, Shin-tsu would always have Uncle Uchiyama behind him, and as I relaxed, Taka started sucking again with gusto.

Amah, Kazu and Jay-jay, appeared, back from the courtyard, and Kazu immediately leaned over to watch Taka feed. He looked at me and said, '*Itakunai-no?* No hurt?' He's taken to repeating everything he says in Pidgin English for Amah's sake. '*Boku mo kōshitano?* I do same when baby?'

Being surrounded by Kazu, Taka, Miyo and Amah is domestic bliss.

Tuesday, 28 September

I wish my lessons with Shin-tsu could revert to those leisurely afternoon sessions of the past. Now, everything is rushed. Today, he insisted on starting with Chinese and grilled me on pronunciation. 'Eiko-san, I think maybe time off with baby makes you lose Chinese tones. Baby is *ying-er*, same *ying* as in *Ying guo* – England – but way you say, sounds like "hard child" or "hard country".'

I detected some impatience on his part, which made me even more flustered and unable to get the tones right.

There was little time left for English conversation, and given Shin-tsu's lack of enthusiasm – so unusual – I wondered whether he had actually engineered it that way.

'Sorry Eiko-san, very tired today,' he said. 'Had to cross Garden Bridge, and even with papers show I work for Japan friendly company, sentry still don't like Chinese. And I carry heavy machine today.'

It broke my heart to imagine Shin-tsu being humiliated by the arrogant sentries at Garden Bridge. Was this the kind of work he really wanted to do? His whole body seemed slightly slumped forward in exhaustion, and I noticed how hardened his hands looked – no longer those sleek delicate fingers, but skin coarsened with ingrained grime. It was strange seeing the roughened hands sticking out of his clean white shirt under the well-tailored suit.

I asked, hesitantly, whether he thought he could continue to come to lessons with such a tough job.

'I continue, Eiko-san. Come here always my big pleasure. Only today, I so tired. But job not too tough, is best work for me,' he said with determination.

Thursday, 7 October

Tamiko came over this morning with Sachi and Asako, transforming the flat instantly into a nursery. Squeals, gurgles, cries, and Jay-jay's barking created such a cacophony that Tamiko and I looked at each other and burst into laughter. Asako at five months has started interacting with the older children, reaching out and babbling. Amazingly, little Taka only seven weeks old today, follows the others with his sharp slanted eyes, seemingly missing nothing. How wonderful for the children to be growing up together; and for Tamiko and me to have each other!

After lunch, with babies asleep and Amah and Miyo on hand, Tamiko and I went to see Irma at the new Friends Centre on Museum Road. Compared to the old place confiscated by the Japanese, the new centre was cramped and stark, but made warm and welcoming by the presence of Irma and a couple of Chinese ladies busy sorting out bits of clothing. As soon as she saw us, Irma came bouncing to the door to give us hugs. 'Look at the two of you, so slender now. What a change!'

The next minute, she rushed back to the large wooden desk, pulled open an ill-fitting drawer, making lots of banging noises as she took out two packages. 'This is for your baby-Mädchen, Tamiko, and this for your baby-Bübchen, Eiko.'

My chest tightened. Despite all her hardships, Irma had gone out of her way to prepare gifts for us. They were beautifully knitted woollen baby boots, pink for Asako, blue for Taka. 'Made by one of my creative neighbours,' she said.

'It is not all doom and gloom in Designated Area. We live on top of each other, but there is so much talent, poetry and book readings, music. Ersatz concerts everywhere – Beethoven, Schubert, Mendelssohn, always lifting our spirits.'

She made life sound so attractive that when she suddenly said she needed to rush back home, I imagined it was for some interesting cultural event.

'Oh how I wish, Eiko,' she chuckled. 'I don't think Sergeant Goya would fit in the cultural category. You see, we need these passes to leave Designated Area.' She showed us a blue card, and pointed at a flimsy coin-like medal on her chest.

'This little pin we have to wear at all times. Goya is the man who gives out these passes, and is very strict about curfew. He is an erratic man, and I cannot afford to displease him!'

Her hurried departure belied her light-hearted tone.

Friday, 15 October

'I'll be working at the factory from November,' Hiro casually mentioned as he brushed his suit jacket before putting it on. Glancing in the mirror for a final check of his tie, he said, 'At the shipyard, I won't be wearing suits.' Before I could ask any questions, he was out of the door.

'It must be the Company Control Act,' Tamiko said, when I told her about Hiro's new assignment. According to her, many businesses were coming under direct military command, and the Kishimoto Company was most likely being made to run the shipbuilding factory for the military.

'Hiro just doesn't seem cut out for rough work,' I moaned, trying to picture him in a dirty factory filled with unfamiliar machinery. But Tamiko narrowed her eyes with a knowing smile as if she didn't agree.

Upon his return from the office, Hiro showed no sign of being worried about his new assignment. 'Will it be hard work for you at the factory?' I finally asked, wondering whether he really was so unconcerned.

'The commute will be longer to the eastern Hongkew industrial area,' he said. 'But it's a factory so I'll be finished earlier. It's not a huge factory – about 100 workers, with good Chinese foremen. Making wooden boats on military instructions. I'll have two Japanese supervisors under me, fellows I know from the Kishimoto Company. Could be better than now - no more kowtowing to military officers as a go-between,' he said, reaching into the chocolate tin. He popped a chocolate into his mouth, and went back to reading his paper.

Tuesday, 26 October

Shin-tsu was in good form today, telling me that he now had a young underling to accompany him on his rounds. 'Good! You won't be so tired for our lessons then,' I said.

'Will be less tired, but Eiko-san, I cannot continue lessons for next few months because have to travel.' This was so unexpected, I struggled not to sound too disappointed.

'Will you be travelling with your father again?' I asked, wondering why travel would be required for buying things like paper and ink for the office.

Shin-tsu looked slightly evasive. 'No, I am doing same job with Liu Bin-ro, but some of company warehouses further out in countryside, and prices going up every day, better to buy and store supplies when possible.'

What he said made sense – we are doing the same thing, really, especially with toiletries, buying what we can because prices change daily and shortages are starting to appear. Still, I wanted a little more explanation for having to stop our lessons so suddenly. Would there be no evenings when he'd be back in town? Even sporadic lessons would be preferable to none.

'Eiko-san, it will be just for short period. When I come back, I sure to have interesting stories to report.'

We clasped hands tightly when he was leaving. He tried hard to be reassuring, repeating that the travel was only temporary, that he'd be back before long. But his reassurances had the opposite effect, making me anxious that he might not come back. I hope I'm just being silly.

14

Saturday, 6 November 1943

We were gathered at the French Club, and Hiro, cheeks flushed from exertion on the tennis court, offered to get drinks from the bar. He was away a long time and when he returned, he said, 'There's lots of commotion at the bar. A former bartender's been murdered in broad daylight, somewhere not far from here.'

'Would we have known him?' Tamiko asked.

'You might have, Tamiko-san. They say he left the French Club in mid-1941 and went to the Hotel Park,' Hiro responded.

I felt a jolt at the mention of Hotel Park – where Shin-tsu went for drinks with his boss. Shin-tsu would have known him, I thought. How shocked he'd be with the news.

Rokki collected more details from the bar. 'Apparently it happened around 2 o'clock this afternoon – after the lunchtime rush. Hong was clearing up, went outside briefly to take out empty beer crates, and that's when someone came from behind. One single bullet, and that was it. The perpetrator apparently disappeared into the crowd.'

Settling into the wicker chair with beer in hand, Rokki went on. 'One of the French fellows said Hong was a superb bartender, remembering the tastes of all his clients, and good at picking up languages from bar conversations – French, English, Russian, even Japanese, apparently. There're rumours of involvement with gangs and spies. They say he never lacked for anything, had a string of street boys willing to run errands and procure whatever he needed.'

It all sounded like something from a film. I tried to picture Shin-tsu being served drinks by this man Hong. It felt incongruous, but I could also imagine inquisitive Shin-tsu finding the shady bartender fascinating. To think that such violent things were happening so close to us! It suddenly occurred to me that even innocent civilians, with nothing to do with gangs and spies could be caught in crossfire and I felt a shudder run through my spine.

Tuesday, 9 November

Midori rang this morning. 'Eiko-san, has Shin-tsu been in touch with you?' she asked in a concerned tone.

'Not since our last lesson, but I didn't expect to hear from him because he said he'd be travelling,' I responded.

'Oh, good, so you expect him to be away,' she said, with a little sigh of relief. 'It's just that he wasn't around at the weekend, so I started getting a little worried. I know he goes over to you on Tuesdays, and if you are not expecting him, I feel much better.'

In a lighter tone, she said, 'Wen-tsu tries hard not to show it, but he's very pleased about Shin-tsu. And Shin-tsu, too, has become more mature. He doesn't sulk or make faces when Wen-tsu says things he disapproves of. Family meals have now turned into happy occasions.'

I smiled. How I would like to hear Shin-tsu's version.

Wednesday, 10 November

Miyo is pregnant – a blessing for her and her husband. But we will be losing her. Will we be able to cope? Amah is more than capable of looking after the two boys. Actually, Taka is strapped on her back all day long, as if he were a part of her. And Kazu is an easy child, obedient and content to play on his own. And I am full of energy. Above all, Tamiko and the girls are around for support and good company. Yes, we will manage. I must reassure Miyo that we'll be fine, and what's most important is for her to look after herself and her husband.

Friday, 12 November

Another phone call came from Midori early this morning, and this time she sounded eerily subdued. 'Eiko-san. Something serious has happened. I'd rather not speak over the phone. Do you think you could come over with Tamiko-san sometime today?'

Alarm bells ringing in my head, I rushed to fetch Tamiko. We hadn't been to the Mao Mansion since the break-in, over a year ago. The house was still heavily protected, with the guards and the metal sheets covering the wrought iron gates, and the chill autumn wind added to my sense of foreboding.

Midori appeared, dressed immaculately in a bright green jumper ensemble over a tight fitting skirt. The elegance of her clothing created a stark contrast to the gloom in her expression.

'We are pretty certain Shin-tsu has been kidnapped,' she said.

'No!' I gasped, covering my mouth.

Tamiko, in a controlled voice said, 'Midori, please tell us what happened from the beginning.'

'You're right Tamiko-san. I'm sorry. After speaking to Eiko-san the other day, I rang the office and spoke to Liu Bin-ro, Shin-tsu's superior. Just as Eiko-san had said, Liu confirmed that Shin-tsu had left Shanghai for a few days to store things in some far-away warehouse. So I thought nothing of the matter.' She swallowed, and shifted her gaze into mid-air.

'Then yesterday, Wen-tsu came home quite agitated. He said that Liu received a call from Shin-tsu the day before, asking for Liu to come out and help him sort some problem with a supplier. Shin-tsu was back in the city, calling from Chapei, so Liu went rushing over. As I said, this was the day before yesterday. Neither Liu nor Shin-tsu have been heard from since.' Midori sank into the sofa, covering her face with both hands.

'Do you suppose Mr Liu has also been kidnapped?' Tamiko asked.

'Yes, yes, Wen-tsu is pretty convinced that the two of them were kidnapped together,' Midori said. 'Shin-tsu could have already been in captivity when he made the call. Such shortage of supplies now, and with an active black market, Shin-tsu would have been an easy target.'

'Not only have they stolen the supplies, but now the kidnappers have two captives for whom they can demand ransom,' she muttered, shaking her head.

We sat in silence, trying to digest the horror. I shook my head, willing this to be not true, for Shin-tsu to be safe.

'The problem is that we don't know who is behind this. It could be petty thieves, or gangs, acting for themselves or on behalf of some bigger power. Wen-tsu is convinced that if only he could find out who they are, there would be a way out, that he could get Shin-tsu back. But nobody has made any move,' Midori said. She added in a low hiss, 'It is so frustrating!'

Tamiko took Midori's hands into hers. 'Midori, you must tell us how we can help. I know we are powerless in terms of finding Shin-tsu, but there must be something we can do to ease your pain,' she said.

Midori squeezed Tamiko's hand, and looked gratefully into her eyes. 'Just having you here and talking to you is a great comfort. Thank you for coming at such short notice.'

Turning to me, she said, 'Shin-tsu is so fond of you, Eiko-san. His face always lit up when he talked of his lessons with you. Your being here makes me feel he's around too!' She gave me a soft, solicitous smile, making me feel that I ought to say something.

I had been sitting there, in denial, praying that this wasn't happening. How I wish I could have given Midori some comfort, telling her of the things Shin-tsu and I talked about during our lessons, of his sense of humour, of his intelligence and sensibility, reassure her that he would do nothing rash.

Instead, I just broke down in sobs.

Monday, 15 November

Every time the phone rings, I jump in anticipation. The days seem to drag by – still no word on Shin-tsu. I find it difficult to think of anything else.

Hiro came home with grease stains on his trousers, so unlike him. He said he had to go to the docks to oversee the unloading of timber and machinery. 'We need to buy parts for building the boats. The stains must be from that rundown factory,' he said, carefully inspecting his trousers.

I hadn't realized Hiro was doing the same kind of thing Shin-tsu had been doing, and was gripped by panic. 'What if you are kidnapped, too?' I blurted.

'Not very likely. I go around in Japanese military jeeps, accompanied by soldiers,' he responded, patting Jay-jay. I felt reassured by his nonchalance.

Thursday, 25 November

There's more work for me without Miyo, but what with the shortages and difficulty in finding basic necessities, everyone is working harder, and I don't really mind. I set off to Nanking Road this morning to buy underwear for Kazu, and found the streets even more chaotic than before.

I had to dismount my bicycle several times to avoid running over the deformed beggars sprawled with their palms stretched out. How used to these street scenes I've become! In the past, I would have gagged, but now I pass by stony faced, focussing on staying alert – street urchins and pickpockets are everywhere these days.

Before reaching the Wing-on department store, I saw two Japanese soldiers ordering Chinese policemen to disperse a crowd clustered around what looked like a bonfire, in front of a large dancehall. I rushed to steer my bicycle around the edges, trying to avoid the mayhem.

In my haste, I nearly bumped into a slender Chinese youth, and did a double take because of his resemblance to Shin-tsu. I instinctively gave him a friendly smile, and was met by a look of bewilderment and a flash of deep hatred. From the Chinese characters on the piece of paper he held, I realized it was an anti-Japanese flyer.

Shaken to my core, I wobbled along as fast as I could to Wing-on, only to find that they no longer had any decent children's underwear.

The look the student gave me still lingers in my mind's eye – piercing hostility because of my nationality. I never found out what the bonfire was about.

Wednesday, 1 December

It was wonderfully warm and steamy inside the small café, the aroma of coffee and chocolate filling the air. 'Ooh, this is lovely,' Tamiko said, as we took seats at a table by the window.

'Such a nice little break away from Sachi!' Tamiko laughed. 'She's decided to take charge over her sister. It is so exhausting! We have to keep watch every moment. You should see the way she shoves the spoon into Asako's mouth, or plonks her down on any hard surface when she decides its nappy-changing time.' I laughed out loud.

'How are you getting on without Miyo?' Tamiko asked.

'Amah is wonderful with the boys,' I said, picturing the three of them together. 'But it's interesting how she treats the two differently.'

I was voicing my inner observations for the first time. 'With Kazu, she's very careful, knowing how fussy I am – meticulous hand-washing and water-boiling, that sort of thing. But with Taka, everything is easy. He's almost a part of her, always on her back. She seems to know what he wants instinctively. She'd suddenly stand up, and there'd be a giggle and a squeal of delight. Or, she'd be eating her own lunch of rice and vegetables, and without a thought, mashing some up and popping it into Taka's mouth. Again, gurgles of contentment, little arms flailing all over the place.'

Tamiko gave me a teasing look, and I knew what she was thinking. 'I'm not spying even if Amah doesn't know I am watching! I just peek into the kitchen sometimes. Okay, I *was* concerned a bit about sharing food, but Taka seems so healthy, I let it be.' Tamiko smiled approvingly.

We turned our gazes to the window, and happened to catch, in a flash, the sight of a Chinese policeman chasing someone down a small alleyway.

The two figures disappeared around a corner, as if in a silent film. 'Could it have been an anti-Japanese agitator, like what I saw the other day near Nanking Road? Curious that it's a Chinese police-man after another Chinese,' I said.

'All the policemen are part of the Wang Ching-wei operation, on the Japanese side,' Tamiko said. 'That bonfire you mentioned, apparently a group of anti-Japanese elements raided a dancehall, and burned everything they took. I suppose dancehalls are worthy targets because they are filled with Japanese officers and protected by Nanking policemen.'

'The anti-Japanese student looked so much like Shin-tsu,' I said, almost in a whimper, thinking of Shin-tsu.

'A lot of the affluent, educated Chinese students hate the idea of the Settlements coming under Wang's Nanking government,' Tamiko said, gazing out of the window. 'Many of them don't like Chiang Kai-shek either. Brought up in international Shanghai, many of the sophisticated students probably identify most with the West, and now Japan is trying to wipe away the West.' She let out a deep sigh.

Friday, 10 December

Exactly a month since Shin-tsu's disappearance, and my day started by a phone call from Midori. I felt my heart pounding in my throat as soon as I heard her voice.

'We do have some information now. Would it be all right if I dropped by to see you today?' She spoke calmly, with little urgency in her voice. I felt marginally relieved, and said Tamiko and I would be awaiting her at teatime.

Midori arrived with a steely facial expression, as if by effort to keep her emotions in check. We sat at the table by the window, where Shin-tsu and I used to have our lessons. The familiar setting heightened my anxiety – what could Midori possibly have to tell us about Shin-tsu that required such stern formality?

She began in a low, even tone. I had to lean forward so as to catch her every word.

'For the first couple of weeks, we were on tenterhooks. Wen-tsu stayed at home every other day, wanting to be around in case of a ransom demand. Every time the phone rang, we jumped. When there was any delivery, we anticipated the worst, prepared to find a body part.' I winced, but she spoke detachedly, almost as if we were not there.

She told us how desperate they were for some indication from the kidnappers, but also dreaded what they might learn. As the days went by without any information, Midori had to urge Mr Mao to spend time at the office because she couldn't bear his anger and frustration.

As Midori's monotonous tone droned on, I was getting impatient to find out what might have happened to Shin-tsu.

She continued at her own pace. 'I think Wen-tsu felt equally restless at the office, too. He decided to go through Liu Bin-ro and Shin-tsu's desks and papers. And that's when Wen-tsu found some chits that didn't make sense – IOUs for supplies in excess quantities, far more than they should have been buying.' Midori's story was taking an unexpected line, making me more attentive for fear of losing the thread.

Apparently, Mr Mao went through all the books and found that while the correct amount of goods was being purchased, the money paid for them showed to be nearly twice what it should be, even in these inflationary times.

'Wen-tsu is now convinced that Shin-tsu and Liu were siphoning off supplies, mainly paper and ink and printing equipment, from the company,' Midori said.

It took a while to digest the meaning, and I could only stare in total disbelief.

Tamiko, who had been listening with her head bowed at a slight angle, looked up and quietly asked, 'Does this give Wen-tsu any idea what might have happened to Shin-tsu and Mr Liu?'

Midori did not answer immediately, looking through the window into the grey winter sky. 'At first, Wen-tsu was livid, saying he didn't even care what happened to them. Once he calmed down, we wracked our brains trying to work out why they were doing this. Surely, it couldn't have been for money,' she said. Mr Mao, with his vast network of business and government connections, was now searching for clues as to what might have happened.

'One thing Wen-tsu is quite certain about is that it is not a kidnapping. They must have disappeared of their own accord. This is the good news part, if you can call it that. It doesn't necessarily mean they are safe, but I suppose they knew what they were doing,' she said, letting out a long sigh, as if in resignation.

As she was leaving, Midori said to me, 'Eiko-san, Shin-tsu was so close to you. If you can remember anything he said that might shed light on his activities or state of mind, do let us know.'

After she was gone, I yanked at Tamiko's hand. 'Do you really think Shin-tsu is all right? If Midori is asking even me for some insight, maybe Mr Mao isn't finding anything out,' I said. Tamiko's gaze was elsewhere, in deep thought, as she absent-mindedly squeezed my hand.

'I would agree with Midori about Mr Mao's ability to gather information,' she finally said. 'Perhaps there is so much to sift through. If Shin-tsu really was improperly collecting supplies, for whom would it be? Not for the Japanese or the Wang Ching-wei regime – Mr Mao is already working for them. Not for money, surely, so it would be for some group, the Kuomintang or the Communists, or someone else? Either way, it's probably highly disturbing for Mr Mao.'

It seemed too far-fetched to imagine gentle Shin-tsu being engaged in direct political activity. Of course he was passionate when talking about China's destiny, but then he was equally passionate about his family. He would never knowingly hurt anyone. So what could all this be about? There had to be some good reason for whatever Shin-tsu was up to.

Sunday, 12 December

It was dinner at Tamiko's today. Being the tail end of the Yangchen River crab season, and knowing how fond of them Hiro is, Tamiko spent half the day preparing the creatures to be steamed – binding them in straw so that the legs don't fall off while cooking, and keeping them in a pail with sesame seeds at the bottom so that they would remain plump until the last minute. I helped arrange the crabs in the bamboo steamer.

When the steamer lids came off, Hiro broke into a huge smile at the sight of the juicy-looking crabs and Rokki busied himself pouring warm golden Chinese rice wine into our cups. In lieu of a toast, he teasingly said, 'Hiroshi, I hear you're wearing workman's clothes to the factory these days. Here's to the new look!'

Hiro smiled, and Tamiko and I giggled. 'He actually looks rather stylish in them,' I said. 'He even manages to keep his shoes clean after a day at the docks.'

'The trick is to step on other people's feet before they step on yours,' Hiro said good-naturedly, as he poked his chopsticks into a crab claw to pick out the flesh. He then dipped it into the delectable vinegar and ginger sauce and slid it contentedly into his mouth.

When we were into our last crab, Rokki suddenly said, 'Oh by the way, that bartender incident from Hotel Park, it turns out he was a Communist agent. Jiro heard something about it on the shortwave radio from Chungking.'

I felt as if some heavy object had come crashing down on me. Ever since Midori's visit, I had been mulling over bits and pieces of things Shin-tsu had told me, and his mention of visiting the bar at Hotel Park with Mr Liu had stuck in my mind. I kept on telling myself that the murder was just a coincidence.

But now, I felt almost certain there was a connection. 'Tamiko,' I said desperately, 'Shin-tsu used to go to the Hotel Park bar with Mr Liu.'

Tamiko's eyes widened, but she casually said, 'You hadn't mentioned this before.' Sensing my anxiety she kept a light tone. 'Why don't you tell us some of the things Shin-tsu said to you.'

I swallowed hard. 'Apart from mentioning the Hotel Park, I can't think of much else. Of course, he was always very passionate about China's fate: critical of his father, and of Japan. When Japanese language teaching became compulsory in Chinese schools, he was very cross about that.' I was frantically trying to remember specific things he had said to me, not very successfully.

'You know his heroes are Uncle Uchiyama and Lu Hsun – his eyes always brightened when he spoke of Uncle Uchiyama's bravery – helping Lu Hsun and other Chinese intellectuals evade Nationalist spies, that sort of thing,' I muttered.

Rokki was now leaning forwards, mulling over every utterance that came from my mouth. 'What else, Eiko,' he demanded.

Tamiko let out a soft admonishment. 'This isn't an interrogation, Rokki.'

Checking himself, Rokki said, 'Sorry Eiko, it's just that you probably know more than you are aware of. Take it easy, but just think whether he might have mentioned names or places.'

I closed my eyes, trying to get my brain to work harder. 'Well, he mentioned his study group – what was it called, the Helpful Friend Society, that's where he knows Mr Liu from too, I think he said. It's such a while ago when we talked about this – before Taka was born.'

Everything before the birth felt covered in fuzz, but I now saw that Tamiko was looking almost as anxious as Rokki, and I forced myself to concentrate. 'Oh, I remember. He spoke of the New Fourth Army, how the attack against it made him hate the Nationalists. About an old woman the study group assisted, to get her back to the countryside…' As I spoke, I realized how stupid I had been, so many hints as to where Shin-tsu's sympathies lay.

Rokki voiced what was just coming to me. 'Eiko, I don't think there is any doubt that Shin-tsu was working with the Communists. The Helpful Friend Society is a known Communist underground organization – I'm surprised Shin-tsu mentioned the name, but then he probably thought it was safe with you.'

My head was spinning. I thought I saw Hiro flinch when Rokki mentioned Shin-tsu working with the Communists. Would it have made any difference had I realized this earlier? Did a Communist connection involve danger?

'Rokki, please explain to me what you think has happened to Shin-tsu,' I pleaded.

Staring into his hands, Rokki said, 'First, tell me when Shin-tsu disappeared – was it before or after Hong was killed?'

I tried to think. The day we went to the French Club was the Saturday before Kazu's birthday, and Midori rang the following Tuesday. But she hadn't seen him during the weekend, so perhaps it was exactly around the same time – this had never occurred to me until now.

Rokki went silent, leaning on the table, head rested on one fist. Eventually, he said, 'Well, it's total conjecture, but this is what I think. Hotel Park is known to be a gathering place for spies of all ilk – Japanese, German, French, Chinese, Russian, you name it. Countries spying on each other, and each nationality would have spies from different factions, the Japanese Navy trying to collect information on the Army, or the *kempei* on citizens, or the Nazis on the Jews or the Chinese Nationalists on the Communists, etc. etc.' Rokki was describing a world totally alien to me. I wished he'd hurry up and focus on Shin-tsu.

Rokki straightened himself and looked right into me. 'I have a feeling that Shin-tsu, Liu and Hong all worked together, Hong the one giving instructions on where to drop off the goods they were collecting. There are all sorts of underground networks for contraband to move to different destinations. Hong's network was most likely supplying the New Fourth Army.'

The image of Shin-tsu's hardened hands came to mind and made me shudder to think of the danger he must have been exposed to as he made his drop-offs in unsavoury corners of Shanghai. 'Do you think he's safe?' I barely managed to utter.

'As a matter of fact I do,' Rokki said. 'If the Nationalists had broken the whole ring, they would have announced it, just as they did Hong's death. My guess is that Liu, by all accounts an experienced hand, had enough warning, either before or immediately after Hong's murder, to get himself and Shin-tsu out of Shanghai, to the Communist base.'

I wrapped my face in my hands. The relief of hearing that Shin-tsu was likely to be safe quickly dissipated at the thought of such a narrow escape from dangers I couldn't imagine.

'I can well understand how Shin-tsu might have felt, hearing of all the corruption within the Kuomintang and seeing how they are more interested in crushing the Communists than fighting Japan,' Rokki said. I noticed that Hiro, who until then was quietly listening with little involvement, turned his head towards Rokki, eyebrows raised.

Oblivious, Rokki continued. 'If I were a young, idealistic Chinese patriot like Shin-tsu, I would be inclined to go over to the Communists, too.'

Hiro, face unusually rigid, hissed under his breath, 'I'd be grateful if you kept your radical ideas to yourself.'

I was stunned, not knowing where to look. Tamiko sat rock still, hands folded on her knee. Nothing seemed to move for the longest time. Until some spell seemed to have broken, and Rokki and Hiro simultaneously said, 'Didn't mean to …' The coincidental timing made them look up sheepishly.

'You didn't mean to what?' Tamiko asked lightly.

'Get carried away,' Rokki said, with Hiro, nodding. Tamiko smiled and stood up to clear the dishes, and I followed.

Staring at the aftermath of the sumptuous dinner – the piled up empty crab shells, the scattered bamboo steamer lids, splashes of ginger vinegar sauce on the white table cloth – I couldn't help but think that it summarized exactly how I felt. Totally spent and left in a mess. The tension may have eased but nothing was resolved. We left shortly thereafter.

Preparing for bed, Hiro casually muttered, 'Rokki is such an idealist sometimes. I hope he's more practical as a banker.'

That was my chance. 'You were so angry with him, I didn't know what to do.' Hiro looked startled.

'Why do you think I was angry?'

'Well you certainly sounded angry, telling him to keep his radical views to himself.'

Hiro looked sheepish. 'Did I say that? Maybe I lost my temper when he went on about how he wanted to be a communist.'

He paused, as if trying to recall Rokki's exact words. 'Really! He's a banker, financing this war. I'm manager of a factory making war supplies. As if we have any choice. It's ridiculous to wish to be a communist or whatever.'

'What about Shin-tsu?' I asked.

'He may be an idealist, but Rokki's also knowledgeable and analytical. Much as I hate communism, I do hear the Chinese Communists are more disciplined and less corrupt than the Kuomintang. He's probably right that Shin-tsu is safe at some Communist base.' Hiro narrowed his eyes, emitting a little snort of affection towards Rokki, and climbed into bed.

I hope sleep will come as easily to me as it has to Hiro.

Monday, 13 December

Tamiko was busy in the kitchen putting things away from last night, and gave me a big bright smile as soon as she saw me. 'Is Rokki upset with Hiro?' I asked hesitantly.

'Of course not, silly, why would he be? Rokki was naughty to wind up Hiroshi, who's usually good at remaining aloof.' Tamiko chuckled. 'What Rokki wanted to do was to reassure you, that by saying what he did about the Communists, he thought you would worry less.'

I cared about Shin-tsu's safety, not where his allegiance lay: I trusted Shin-tsu's judgement.

Oblivious to my inner thoughts, Tamiko was still explaining Rokki's thinking. 'Of course, given how the war is going, Rokki wants a negotiated peace settlement. But his idealistic side admires what the Communists are trying to do. They are much more sincere about uniting China to fight the Japanese and to bring more equality within Chinese society. There is so much poverty.' She looked thoughtfully into her teacup.

'For a businessman like Hiroshi, communism goes against the grain. And if the Communists and Nationalists really united, it wouldn't be good for Japan. The Communists are an added complication to reach peace, and Rokki well knows that, but he's an idealist!' She took a gulp of tea. 'So there's you, married to an easygoing, practical-minded businessman, and me, to an eyebrow-knitting idealist, stuck in a banking job. But we do have fun together,' she said, patting my hand.

Wednesday, 22 December

We put up the little Christmas tree today, and what joy it was to see the boys' reaction. Kazu clapped his hands, and, to get Taka's attention, pulled his foot, which was sticking out from a side of Amah's back. Taka was about to bawl, but Amah swiftly turned so he could see the tree, and out came a squeal of delight.

Watching the boys made me think how sad and lonely the Maos must be with Shin-tsu gone. I decided to include the Maos for our Christmas celebration with Tamiko, Rokki and the Sekines.

Sunday, 26 December

Had it not been for Masaya, our Christmas dinner would have been a trying affair. Mr Mao was a changed man. He has lost his expansive charm, which used to make even his shifty eyes part of a mysterious allure. Now there was bitterness and evasiveness. The minute they walked in the door, I felt the tension between Midori and Mr Mao, which took me aback. Out of his earshot, Midori quickly whispered, 'Please don't mention Shin-tsu at all. Tell Tamiko, too.'

From then onwards, I felt like walking on thin ice, worried about inadvertently causing hurt or offense. Even the topic of children made me nervous lest it would remind Mr Mao of his son.

But Masaya somehow managed to make the evening a warm, convivial gathering, reminding me of our Christmas last year at the Leighs'. Although he didn't seem to be saying much, people congregated around him, drawn by his charisma. It made me think of the power of faith: both Masaya and Keith exuded a sense of reassurance, which seemed to come from deep within. Masaya's faith perhaps has deepened having overcome his illness.

When everyone left, Hiro said, 'That was a successful dinner party you put on.' I was touched that he thought the success was due to me.

15

Saturday, 1 January 1944

Unlike last year, there were no formal social rounds of New Year's greetings due to directives calling for 'restraint' in wartime. So we had a cosy family gathering at Tamiko's over a feast of Japanese and Chinese symbolic dishes to welcome in the New Year.

'Do you know what these little black beans mean?' Tamiko asked the children. 'The Japanese word for bean is *mame*, but if you say someone is *mame* it means they're hard working. So we eat black beans to be diligent throughout the New Year.' Whereas Sachi appeared to be not listening, Kazu nodded, as if taking in Tamiko's every word.

The Japanese cold dishes were followed by Chinese delicacies, starting with spring rolls – according to Tamiko, a must for New Year as a symbol of wealth, with chicken, shrimp, mushrooms and bamboo shoots, chopped all wrapped in a delicately fried parcel. Next came noodles for long life, made Shanghai style, with thick noodles, slivers of beef and shredded greens. The final dish was sea bream, steamed with a touch of ginger and scallions.

Masaya explained the meaning of the fish. 'The beautiful fish before us, from head to tail, is whole, as this coming year should be, good from the beginning to the end. Tamiko-san, you have provided us with a meal with so many blessings. May they last throughout this year!' He raised his little *sake* cup, turning to us all to do the same, and then heartily downed every drop.

The rest of the evening was spent playing *fukuwarai*, from Sayako's box of New Year's games. Kazu and Sachi were quick to grasp the idea of being blindfolded and placing paper pieces of eyebrows, eyes, nose, mouth and ears onto a large empty face drawn on a board.

The merriment lasted long into the evening, as each of us took turns creating some ridiculous-looking faces, especially Hiro, whose pieces all ended up bunched in a corner. Rokki couldn't help teasing him saying, 'How could an ace tennis player have such poor spatial sense!'

A happy beginning to a new year, which we all hope will bring an end to the war.

Thursday, 6 January

Passing the Whangpoo pier, I noticed a huge transport cargo ship moored where the *Conte Verde* used to be. As I got closer, I saw a row of young Japanese Naval cadets neatly lined up on the front deck, looking fresh and full of life. With the clear blue sky in the background, the sight was uplifting.

As I was ready to pedal away, a voice called out, 'Eiko-san, what are you doing here?' It was Cheeko, coming from the direction of the boat with Daisuke and their son Taro.

'We've just been to see my youngest brother, Osamu, aboard that ship,' she said before I could even say hello. 'He's finished his training as a Navy air force pilot and is on his way to be stationed in Chingtao. He'd been spared the draft as a university student, but now they're all being recruited. Amazing how they've been turned into fully-fledged soldiers, looking rather dashing! Taro couldn't take his eyes off his uncle.'

Taro indeed looked flushed, and I could almost feel the heat coming out of his bright red cheeks. For a young boy, who wants to be a fighter pilot, seeing his uncle and colleagues in full military uniform must have been a dazzling experience.

Sunday, 9 January

Miyo came for a visit, braving the cold, damp weather. She arrived rosy cheeked from the bicycle ride, not yet showing her pregnancy. Greeted by a flurry of excitement from the boys and Jay-jay, she glowed. Marriage suits her well.

'I have missed the boys, and look forward to spending time with them today,' she said, picking up Taka and placing him on her knee.

'There's also something I have to report to you. Oku-sama, Tanaka has been called up. He will be leaving Shanghai in a week's time.'

I was at a loss for words. 'Miyo, I am so sorry – at such an important time for the two of you,' I managed to say. "You must tell us how we can be of help. You can of course come back here to stay.'

She tilted Taka to one side and graciously bowed her head, maintaining her smile and composure. 'That is kind of you, Oku-sama. But I will hold the fort in our little abode in Hongkew and await his return. Tanaka is not the first to be called up among the Uchiyama employees. In fact it has been a steady trickle and there are a number of us in the same boat. Mr and Mrs Uchiyama are always there, the biggest moral support.'

I remembered how lonely it felt when Hiro was away on his Southeast Asia tour while being pregnant with Taka, and felt awed by Miyo's stoic demeanour.

'There's not much to prepare, but I do want to get the *senninbari* finished in time,' she said.

'The *senninbari*?'

'Oh Oku-sama! Do you not know what it is? You have been so lucky it seems,' she smiled. She took out a piece of white cloth, the size of a tea towel, covered with small red stitches and tiny embroidered knots. 'I have actually brought this with me to ask you for a stitch, too.' She explained that soldiers are sent off with the cloth with a thousand stitches collected from a thousand women as a good luck talisman.

'The only women who can contribute more than one stitch are those born in the year of the tiger – and they can sew in as many stitches as their age for good luck,' she said. 'The legend is that a tiger wanders a thousand miles but always returns, and so the soldier, too, will return. I happen to be a tiger, and put in my twenty-nine stitches,' she laughed.

She handed me the cloth and a needle with bright red cotton already threaded. I closed my eyes briefly, saying a short prayer for Tanaka-san's safety, before sewing and knotting the stitch. Miyo bowed deeply in gratitude.

Resting her chin softly on Taka's head, she said, 'us women stand on a street corner and collect the stitches. It is a common sight now all over Japanese Hongkew. For those whose husbands are departing, it is an activity that bonds us together. And the ladies we approach, they could soon be in the same boat, or perhaps may already have husbands at the front. The time it takes to make the stitch turns into a moment of silent prayer.'

Would I, too, be soon making a *senninbari* for Hiro? The thought sent a shudder through my whole body.

Friday, 14 January

Hiro looked up from his newspaper at breakfast and said, 'Listen to this. They're encouraging all Japanese women to wear *monpe* from now onwards. It says so many women have switched from kimono to *monpe*, they're "shaming men who walk around in Western suits or smart Japanese outfits". Humph.'

The papers recently have been filled with advice for women in wartime: how we should look after the family; how we should avoid extravagance; what kind of foods we should be storing, etc. etc. And now, we are being told we should wear baggy cotton peasant trousers meant for work in the fields – all for the sake of 'enhancing our determination for victory!'

The constant bombardment of morale-boosting advice has been getting on my nerves. I *know* we have to make adjustments to cope with the realities – one only has to go out on the streets to see that life is getting harder for everyone. But the papers seem so manipulative, making me resentful. And feeling resentful brings guilt – am I being intolerant, lacking in cooperative spirit? The thought of *monpe* heightened my irritation.

Oblivious, Hiro, sipping his tea, said, 'I wonder how you'd look in *monpe*.'

'I don't own a pair. Do you think I should go out and get one?' I asked.

'Don't be silly,' he said affectionately. 'You'd probably look fashionable even in *monpe*, but I wouldn't want to follow directives

194

aimed at fanning war fever. You'd think the authorities have more important things to worry about than what people wear,' he said, head buried back in the paper.

Thursday, 20 January

Miyo came to report on her husband's departure. She was wearing a bluish-grey everyday woollen kimono, which she said kept her warmer in her poorly-heated house.

'The atmosphere is getting very warlike, Oku-sama. The Japanese community leaders are busy rallying public sentiment to support the war effort, calling for sacrifices to contribute towards Japan's advancement. We are to be proud of living in cold houses, paying more taxes.'

'It's not a very nice atmosphere, even worse for the Chinese. Japanese soldiers are increasing their searches, and some of the searches seem to be for the sake of intimidation. In a mixed neighbourhood like ours in Hongkew, where we have good Chinese neighbours, it is heart-breaking to see them treated so badly.'

'And now, my husband has been sent off to fight the Chinese,' she said, with a heavy sigh. 'It is an impossible situation, Oku-sama, to know how one should feel. Many of the Japanese in Hongkew welcome the brutal treatment of enemy nationals, and I can only close my eyes and wish the nastiness away.'

'I was privileged to be in your household – you and your sister Tamiko Oku-sama, with your international background and open-mindedness have taught me to see the ugliness of prejudice and hatred.' I was touched by her words but hardly felt worthy.

'And the Uchiyamas are truly exceptional. Usually, when men leave for war from the neighbourhood, their parting words, with a salute to the Rising Sun flag, are: "I am off, willing to fight to death for my beloved country!" Tanaka thought that's what would be expected of him. But Mr Uchiyama's send-off was completely different,' Miyo said.

'"We live in an unhappy age. You will most likely be sent into the interior of China to fight. But the person on the other side of your rifle is our brother, our friend. Keep that in mind, and I beg you to refrain from shooting." With those words, Mr Uchiyama shook Tanaka's hands to send him off.'

'Can you imagine, Oku-sama, I quickly looked around to make sure no stranger was overhearing – they might think Mr Uchiyama was being disloyal! But for us, it was a message that resonated in our hearts. Tanaka will remember what Mr Uchiyama said, and will come back with a clear conscience – if he does come back.'

Miyo cast her eyes downwards, and then sniffed the top of Taka's head before planting a soft kiss. Taka had been sitting remarkably quietly on her knee, as if transfixed by her words.

Saturday, 5 February

Upon hearing that Japanese sweet shops are now being closed and converted into businesses that would contribute to the war effort, I took the boys to Tamiko's to shake off the gloom.

'Perfect timing! I was about to make shortbread biscuits. Kazu and Sachi can do the mixing, and licking the spoons,' Tamiko said, busily taking out the ingredients.

'Are you sure we should be using up precious provisions at a time like this?' I asked. Even with Rokki and Hiro being paid in hard currency, it is getting increasingly difficult to buy basics such as flour and sugar.

'At times like this, it's all the more important to create fun for the children – and for us, too. I still have the sugar Mr Mao gave us for Christmas. If we run out of things, well, we can worry about that when it happens,' Tamiko said, cheerfully

She found some colourful boiled sweets, which she crushed with a hammer, making broken bits for decorating the biscuits.

'Mama, smile!' Sachi demanded, as she tried to make a smiling face on the shortbread. 'Auntie, be sad!' It became a game of creating different expressions on the biscuits. The older children's excitement passed on to the little ones, who joined the merriment with lots of banging and babble.

Saturday, 12 February

Sayako rang this afternoon. 'Eiko-san, Masaya Onī-sama has received his call-up letter. He is to join a regiment on 20 February.' Her words were like a punch in the stomach.

Sayako went on to say, 'I worry that it might be too soon for Masaya Onī-sama to be part of the military again. He has been so happy teaching at St John's, always talking about his bright Chinese students with whom he can discuss anything. I know the students look up to him, and I feel he is doing enough for China and Japan through his teaching without having to go to war.' And then I heard an almost imperceptible sigh.

'How did Masaya react to the letter?' I managed to ask.

'Very calmly, as if he knew it was inevitable. He acknowledged the letter with a nod, gave us a reassuring smile, and uttered in prayer, "Lord, I am ready for your next challenge for me".'

After Sayako's phone call, I sat for a while in a stupor. Unlike Sayako, concerned only for Masaya's wellbeing, I self-ishly thought more about my own loss, remembering those days before Taka's birth, when Masaya often dropped by, never staying long, but bringing much needed comfort. Tamiko must be devastated.

Sunday, 13 February

I rushed over to Tamiko's only to find her out. As soon as I walked into the door, Sachi came running over, reporting, 'Daddy is in Nanking and Mama out with Uncle Masaya.' She then held out her arms and jumped up and down squealing, 'Auntie Eiko, take us home with you! We want to play with Kazu and Taka.' So I ended up bringing the girls and their Amah home with me, leaving a note on the door for Tamiko.

With the two Amahs looking after the children and Hiro at the factory even though it's Sunday, there is little for me to do, so here I am, scribbling in my journal, while I wonder where Tamiko and Masaya have gone, a little peeved that they didn't include me.

Friday, 18 February 1944

Tonight was Masaya's farewell dinner given by St John's University – a grand affair at the Sun-ya restaurant, with faculty members and students, most of them Chinese. I saw what Sayako had meant when she said his students looked up to him. The students clustered around him, competing for his attention, making it impossible for us to get nearby.

Hiro and I were assigned a corner table, slightly removed from the main action, and as I was about to sit down, a familiar-looking couple approached. It was S.P. and Mona, whom I hadn't seen for over a year. Mona seemed even prettier than before, in a well-tailored light grey woollen dress with soft ruffles at the collar. Her hair was shorter, making her look younger than I remembered.

'Eiko, our husbands have been playing tennis and golf together from time to time, but failing to include us!'

S.P. cast a protective glance towards her, and said, 'Mona was away quite a lot this past year.' Ignoring his comment, Mona pulled me to her side and indicated that we should sit next to each other.

'Isn't it nice to be back at the same restaurant where the four of us first dined together? We must catch up. Tell me about your adorable little son, Kazu. He must be quite a grown boy now.' I was impressed by her memory, and happily rattled on about Kazu and the arrival of Taka, in between nibbles of jellyfish, thousand-year eggs, and moist cold steamed chicken. Mona was paying much more attention to my stories of the boys than to the food.

As the appetizer platters were taken away, and the Peking duck was served, the speeches began, and our attention was turned to the event at hand.

'It's impressive, Eiko, how all these Chinese are here to give Professor Masaya Sekine a send-off,' Mona whispered in my ear. 'It goes to show how much respect he's gained. After all, he is going off to fight in the war against the Chinese.'

Mona's words hit me like a stone. I felt ashamed for overlooking the significance of the event. Mona's openness gave me the courage to ask how she felt about the occasion.

'To be frank, a bit mixed,' she said, looking straight at me with her thoughtful eyes. 'I couldn't tell my non-Christian Chinese friends, for example, that I was attending a dinner for a Japanese man, to wish him well in war.' She nibbled on her Peking duck to keep the tone light.

'But Eiko, Professor Sekine is no ordinary Japanese man. I think every Chinese here wants him to be safe, because we believe he has a role to play when war ends. He has done so much to promote understanding between our two peoples. Yes, Eiko, we Chinese are here to wish him well, and pray for his safe return.'

I felt proud of Masaya, whose public persona I was seeing for the first time, realizing his special presence beyond close family and friends. He was part of the lives of so many people, and I understood why the aftermath of the Proclamation had been such a devastating blow to him: his sense of betraying the Jewish refugees who had trusted and respected him.

While the speeches went on, I bowed my head in private prayer – may Masaya's time in war be spared from the impossible dilemmas he had to endure while in the Navy Jewish Affairs Bureau.

Saturday, 19 February

Unlike yesterday's big event, tonight was an intimate dinner at the Sekines on the eve of Masaya's departure.

'Although the Japanese papers make it sound as if Japan is making good advances in China, the truth is, we are in a stalemate,' Masaya said. 'Apart from the north and coastal regions, we occupy only dots around China, not even lines, let alone major areas. I fear there will be massive offensives to secure land routes to French Indochina and destroy American airbases in China.'

Sayako deftly shifted the tone as she encouraged everyone to concentrate on the food, a variety of home-style Japanese food – deep fried prawns and vegetables, slow-cooked pork, tofu hotpot –

things she knew Masaya would enjoy with his whisky and probably miss the most away from home.

'It was a wonderful send-off St John's had for you, Onī-sama. With all the goodwill from the Chinese people there, I am hopeful that the war will not go on for much longer and you will be home again soon,' she said.

'You are right, Sayako,' Masaya nodded. 'There are many fine Chinese professors and students at St John's, and I owe it to them to return and work for peace. The university has managed to stave off military interference, and that's why good Chinese faculty members like S.P. Chen can remain and Japan Christian educators like myself were welcome.'

'It was wonderful to see him and Mona yesterday,' I said.

Masaya smiled. 'A wonderful couple – come to think of it, a Chinese version of you and Hiroshi-san. Such a shame that Mona lost her baby during a very difficult pregnancy. It was their first, and they had been so excited.'

I was stunned, shuddering to think how I went on and on about Kazu and Taka.

Oblivious, Masaya continued. 'Teaching at a Japanese-run university isn't easy for the Chinese, often judged by other Chinese as giving in to the Japanese. S.P. teaches international law, equipping his students to make their own judgements. He does what he believes in, without succumbing to outside pressure – which requires far more courage than it seems.'

'Like the Quakers,' Tamiko said. 'Wasn't it amazing, Masaya, what they had to say when we visited the group at Agnes' last Sunday?'

'Oh, so that's where you'd gone when I couldn't find you last week,' I said, perhaps with an unintentional hint of accusation, for Tamiko flashed an apologetic smile.

'It was a spur of the moment decision to go and visit. Masaya and I were discussing what it meant for a man of faith to have to go to war, and all of a sudden I thought of the Quakers. They believe that war and conflict are against God's wishes, and are dedicated to pacifism and non-violence. So what to do when one is called up? As it was Sunday, I thought there might be a Meeting at Agnes' and off we went!'

Masaya looked affectionately at Tamiko. 'I hadn't had much exposure to the Quakers till then, and am very grateful to Tamiko-san for introducing me to the group. A dedicated Quaker may become a conscientious objector, but that is not a path for me. But the Quakers helped me realize that even as a soldier, I can do what's required of me, which is talk to people. It will be a personal challenge to preserve peace through spreading reason, a challenge I can live with.'

On this note, our evening quietly ended, and early tomorrow morning, Masaya will be off to join his regiment.

Wednesday, 1 March

The wireless reported that Japanese businesses are to give up every other Sunday, and work thirteen consecutive days to increase production for the war effort.

'Does that apply to you?' I asked Hiro.

'Yes, but it doesn't make much difference. With increased demands from the military, we'd be giving up Sundays anyway, with or without any directive.'

I sensed a degree of resignation in Hiro's tone. 'I hope the work isn't dangerous,' I said.

'No, I wouldn't think so. Only a matter of developing different kinds of boats and increasing production,' Hiro said matter-of-factly.

Wednesday, 8 March

Shortly after lunchtime, Tamiko rang to say she would come over with the children to spend the afternoon with us. 'Now that it's getting warmer, the *amahs* can take the children to the courtyard and you and I can enjoy a peaceful tea-time together,' she said.

I loved the idea, but after putting down the receiver, I felt unease – something in Tamiko's voice seemed different.

When they appeared, it was the usual happy commotion – Sachi overexcited and Asako poking her fingers into Tamiko's face. 'What a relief to get these girls off my hands now!' Tamiko chuckled.

When all was quiet, and I was preparing tea, Tamiko pulled out a small packet of Walker's shortbread from her handbag. 'Goodness, where did you get those!' I exclaimed, such goodies being a rare treat these days.

'I thought you'd be impressed. You see, even if we don't save provisions, things magically appear!' Smiling, she said, 'Actually, Mrs Yamamoto, the wife of the Deputy General Manager at Rokki's bank came over this morning bearing this gift. The Bank made its annual personnel movement announcements, and Mr Yamamoto has been promoted to become General Manager at the Tientsin branch. Mrs Yamamoto is making the customary rounds to those who worked closely with her husband.'

'So eat up Eiko, there's plenty!' It was typical of Tamiko to ignore the fact that there were only eight pieces in the packet. She smiled as I took a bite. It was delicious – rich and buttery, a taste that took me back to the happy times in London. I closed my eyes as I savoured the crumbs melting in my mouth. I was about to take my second bite, when Tamiko said, 'Jiro and Rokki also received their transfer orders this morning.'

I didn't trust my ears. 'Excuse me?' I muttered.

'It's a good transfer for Rokki, to Nanking,' she said. Her casual tone made me believe Rokki would be going on his own and Tamiko and the children would remain in Shanghai.

'Well, congratulations. I suppose Nanking isn't so far away and he'll be coming to see you and the girls regularly.'

'Whatever are you talking about, Eiko? Of course we are all moving,' Tamiko said, wide-eyed.

I felt the ground fall from under me. How could Tamiko not realize how devastating the news would be to me? Did she not feel any sadness not being together anymore? Living in Shanghai without Tamiko seemed unimaginable. Did I mean so little to her? Hurt, and numb from just thinking of her departure, I let the remaining half biscuit drop from my fingers onto the table.

Tamiko peered into my face with smiling eyes. 'You're not sulking, are you? A move to Nanking is hardly worth getting worked up about. Not much different from being transferred to Tokyo from Osaka. You yourself said how close it is!'

I remained silent.

'Rokki will be back here on business trips, and we'll be in touch. Not at all as if we're being sent to the front and cut off from each other – as so many people actually are.'

Tamiko remained smiling, but her last comment was spoken with deep compassion, and I realized she had actually given much thought to this transfer. After all, it was she who had to uproot her young family to another city in the middle of a war. Typically, she focussed on the bright side, and perhaps expected me to do so too.

'I will miss you so,' I managed to say.

'Me too, of course!' she said, taking my hand. 'I've had the best time of my life since you came to Shanghai, and the thought of Kazu and Sachi not being able to play together breaks my heart. But it may not be a very long separation, and Nanking and Shanghai being firmly under Japanese control, we'll be able to communicate. I'll meet new people, and you'll broaden your circle, and we'll have lots to talk about and laugh over!'

I had no choice but to nod and give her an acquiescent smile, although I could hardly contain my sadness.

'Jiro's transfer orders are to Canton,' Tamiko said, her voice now subdued. 'Canton isn't as stable as Nanking, and with Sayako expecting a baby in October – which I just found out about when Rokki rang – it's likely to be a more difficult move.'

It suddenly hit me that I was losing not only Tamiko and family, but Jiro and Sayako as well – so shortly after Masaya's departure. Starting with Shin-tsu's disappearance last December, I'm being stripped of every person dear to me. I was overcome by sadness, and a sense of desperation to cling tightly on to those I loved most, a prayer that at least Hiro, the boys and I should never be parted.

Tuesday, 15 March

With Tamiko's move imminent, I went over to help, wanting to spend every possible minute with her, to keep physically busy so as not to brood.

When I arrived, she was sorting out her clothes. 'Oh good! You came at just the right time to help me decide what to take to Nanking. We'll be living in a Japanese diplomatic compound so I don't want to look too shabby – but one has to be practical too. What do you think of this one?' she said, holding up a worn-out grey woollen suit that had seen better days.

I glanced at the giveaway pile. 'You should swap that one with this,' I said, pointing to a smart tweed suit.

'That's practically new, so I thought it should go to Irma's clothing centre.' Before I could say anything, she quickly added, 'Besides, it's a bit tight around the waist.'

I felt a bit envious of her new situation, to be living in a diplomatic compound, no doubt with many social functions.

'Oh, and I must make sure I pack all the stuff needed for the air-raid training sessions,' she said. 'I'll get more cotton wool and bandages, they'll be useful for the refugees, too.'

Tamiko seemed to view her packing as an opportunity to gather up as many things as possible for Irma.

Friday, 17 March

We had to get a pedicab to take all the bags of clothing to the Friends' clothing centre in the Designated Area.

'Are you sure we'd be allowed in?' I asked, the memory of Irma's dismal living conditions making my feet feel heavy.

'Of course we will,' Tamiko said. 'It's the stateless refugees that need permits to leave the Area, but the Chinese are free to go in and out, and we will be too. There aren't gates, just Japanese patrols keeping an eye on refugee movements.'

Nevertheless, once in the Area, on Seward Road, we were stopped by a Japanese guard. '*Oi!*,' the man growled, asking us what business we had. He told us to open the bags, and we had no choice but to obey. Fortunately, seeing we only had women's clothes, he made a disgusting hiss, and shooed us away.

We continued along the crowded streets, flooded with local Chinese activity – a shrivelled old woman selling individual strands of embroidery yarn, men hawking hair brushes, and children running around as their mothers sat on low stools in front of houses. The normality and Chinese-ness of the neighbourhood felt strangely reassuring.

When we approached the corner of Seward and Alcock Roads, we saw the tail end of a long queue of refugees, everyone with anxious looks.

'The Japanese administration building must be around the corner. What Irma mentioned – people applying for passes to go out of the Designated Area,' Tamiko said.

The clothing distribution centre was just a room on the ground floor of the Seward refugee shelter – a run-down two-storey brick building, with laundry hung from bamboo poles strung along the verandas. The atmosphere was livelier, but there was an edge to the boisterousness. People pushing and shoving, giving us disapproving looks as we proceeded to the entrance. The room had a distinct whiff of a mixture of sweat, dust and old perfume - the smell of a long unopened drawer full of forgotten clothes.

'*Willkommen, willkommen!*' Irma, looking thinner, trundled over in her motherly gait, and gave us each a hug and a peck on the cheek.

'Tamiko, the thought of you not being in Shanghai makes me sad. I will miss you.' Even as she spoke, she deftly kept an eye on the refugees picking through the clothes, and her warm tone instantly switched into a loud shout. 'Hans, that will be far too large for you! You cannot hide that garment under the other one.'

'As conditions get worse, the ugly side of human nature comes out,' Irma sighed. 'Lack of food, awful weather, bad sanitation, it makes people sick and irritable. And Mr Goya only exacerbates the situation. He's the Japanese guard who calls himself "King of the Jews" and hands out passes as if by royal command. At the moment, he's the bane of my existence.'

As there were several refugees needing Irma's attention, we left the bag of clothes and took our leave. When we turned the corner, I caught sight of a small figure, puffing away like a chimney. In contrast to his diminutive bearing, the man had a big, ruddy face, sunned and lined, probably from years of work in the fields. Even off duty, there was a restlessness to him, hands moving jerkily, mouth opening as if talking to himself. He must have sensed he was being observed. He turned towards us and emitted a guttural growl.

'That must be Goya,' Tamiko said, as we quickly walked away.

Wednesday, 22 March

Taking Sachi and Asako off Tamiko's hands to let her pack, I spent the exceptionally warm afternoon with all four children in the courtyard. Kazu and Sachi quickly went off to play with other children, and as I sat on the bench with Asako on my knee, watching Taka bounce up and down on Amah's back as she walked along the pavement, I wished that time could stop, that Tamiko and family didn't have to go to Nanking, and we could continue having these peaceful afternoons in the garden.

I was awoken from my reverie by Jay-jay, who sprang up and pulled the lead as she saw a large, handsome German shepherd. It reminded me of yesterday's headline: 'Dogs too mustering up the spirit!' It was about a judging session to buy up dogs to train for military use. Would this shepherd be one of them? Jay-jay was excitedly wagging her tail at the bigger dog. What a blessing she's a useless Scotch terrier, of no interest to the military.

Sunday, 26 March

Today was the farewell dinner for Tamiko and family. I couldn't concentrate on anything beforehand, the thought of their imminent departure, in two days' time, weighing over me like a big black cloud. What would we talk about? If it were about Nanking, I'd feel left out and envious; reminiscing on our life together in Shanghai would add to my sadness.

In the end, I needn't have worried about conversation topics. There were enough other things that needed attention.

'We can't decide what to do,' Jiro said, about his transfer orders to Canton. 'The Bank assures me that Canton is safe. But my Chinese friends say air raids from the US bases are fiercest around Canton. Apparently, the US have new aircraft – the Grumman F6F Hellcat, supposedly faster and more heavily armed than the F4F Wildcat.'

'It's also possible that the Canton area will be in line for a major Japanese offensive to capture the land route to Indonesia. Japanese air power is said to be weakening and there may be some desperation to carry it out soon.' Jiro, always the quiet, serious voice amongst us, was in an unusually agitated state.

'How I wish Masaya Onī-sama were here to advise us,' Sayako said softly.

Rokki suddenly stood up and glowered at Jiro. 'If you left the Bank, what would you do? You'd be drafted in no time, and be in the same boat as Masaya.'

Jiro looked as pale as a white sheet. 'You're probably right, Rokuro-san. I've been asking around, but no job to keep me in Shanghai has materialized. I'm at a loss.'

Hiro, who was mixing a whisky and soda, looked up and said, 'Someone said there're civilian jobs in Japanese public enterprises – transport and utilities. Have you tried them?'

'No, I haven't. It hadn't occurred to me,' Jiro said. 'Thank you, Hiroshi-san,' he added, with a hopeful look. 'I really don't think going to Canton is an option, for the sake of Sayako and the child to come, of course, but also for my parents. It would be too much for them to have both sons in war zones.'

'Jiro-san, you mentioned America's new aircraft,' Hiro said, changing the subject. 'I've recently been asked to start looking for car engines. I'd heard that the military were planning new types of boats, but they haven't been specific. Do you know anything about it?'

Jiro seemed hesitant to reply. 'Not really. Masaya, before he left, said something about the military wanting to compensate for inferior air power by other means of attacking enemy boats. I don't know if your shipyard has anything to do with that.' Nobody was inclined to pursue the matter further.

Friday, 31 March

Tamiko is gone. I don't even want to think about the parting at North Station. So many well-wishers to see them off, the Yamanakas all smiles, thanking everyone, Sachi and Kazu excited in the atmosphere – everything running counter to my inner feelings, but I myself putting on a happy face to send them off to their new, promising future.

And yesterday, Sayako rang to say that Jiro had tended his resignation from the Bank, and would be starting a new job in Peking with the North China Railroad Administration.

'Hiroshi-san's mention of civilian jobs started the whole process. We have much to thank him for. Jiro's contacts in the Manchurian Railroad Administration found a position for him in their sister company. He starts almost immediately, so we have to pack up in a great rush.'

They are to leave next week, and all the people close to me will no longer be in Shanghai.

Part II

16

Monday, 3 April 1944

'Missy, Kazu sad no Sachi. I takey him ousai,' Amah announced, helping him put on his shoes. Despite her attachment to Taka, she's also devoted to Kazu, and I was impressed how she read his feelings. Had he mentioned Sachi to her? Was my missing Tamiko so obvious, too?

Just as Taka was waking from his nap, the two of them returned, Kazu holding something preciously in his hand. Panting as he flew into my lap, he looked up gleefully and proceeded to put on a pair of sunglasses made of hideous bright green plastic. I was about to scold him for picking up such a cheap-looking toy, when Amah, who had finally caught up with him, said, 'Missy, Kazu choose, my gift make big boy happy!'

Kazu hovered over Taka's pram, sticking out his face to his brother. Now completely awake, Taka reached out to grab the sunglasses off Kazu's face. Kazu jumped back, face still stuck out, just out of Taka's reach. Taka squeaked and reached over, only to make Kazu take a tiny step backwards. It became a wonderful game for Kazu to taunt his little brother.

I envied Kazu for so easily being distracted from missing Sachi. I felt I should wash his hands and the sunglasses – thinking of all the germs from the pedlar's cart. But I let it pass. Watching the two little ones squabble was a welcome distraction for me, too.

Tuesday, 11 April 1944

At a loss for company without Tamiko, I phoned Cheeko, who suggested I come over straight away. 'The grocery van is here today,' she said. I cycled over as fast I could.

She was waiting for me by the van, dressed in a non-descript grey frock and wearing rubber-soled Chinese cloth shoes, making her indistinguishable from the Chinese women rushing about. As soon as she spotted me, she said, 'Eiko-san, hurry, hurry, not many things left!' Taking my hand and pulling me closer, she whispered, 'There's a tin of Rowntree's chocolates if you are willing to pay.' I couldn't resist the opportunity to obtain Hiro's favourites, although the black market prices made my eyes water.

Over tea and almond biscuits, Cheeko heaved a sigh. 'I tell you Eiko-san, having a son is not easy. After seeing his naval cadet uncle, Taro insisted he was going to drop out of school and join Flight Crew Training.'

'If it was just a matter of hero-worshipping Osamu, we might have talked him out of it, but you see, Taro is very stubborn. He did his research and found out that, in fact, even at the age of twelve, he could join a training programme run by the Ministry of Telecommunications. He knows he's too young for official Navy Training, you know, the *yokaren* cadets who wear the uniform with two rows of seven buttons, made famous by last year's romanticized film. Anyway, when Taro digs his heels in, he can be quite impossible. We thought for a while he'd end up in Japan to join one of those programmes.'

Cheeko stopped to catch her breath. 'But then, one day, suddenly, he changed his mind,' she said. 'We learned from Hanako that Taro's favourite science teacher convinced him that a high school education would make him more useful for serving the country.'

'So now Taro commutes to the Japanese Middle School which is at the north end of Hongkew. It takes him two hours one way on his bicycle, and he does it every day, four hours on the road, without complaining. Even in the rain. Last week, he came home soaking wet, dripping all over the hallway.'

In an unexpectedly sombre tone, she said, 'I think what motivates him is the idea of "serving his country". I hope Japan lives up to being worth all these young men serving her. You know, the pilots' age is getting younger and younger as the war gets tough for Japan. If Taro had gone to Flight Training, who could say the five-year training wouldn't be shortened to four or even three years, and he could be going to war at barely age sixteen or fifteen. Eiko-san, you are lucky that your sons are still so little.'

Sunday, 16 April

Hiro came home past 7 o'clock, working on a Sunday, covered in dust and short-tempered. I thought it best to get the children out of the way as quickly as possible, but Kazu's brief reluctance to change into pyjamas caused a fierce 'Do as Mama says, don't cause her trouble!' Poor Kazu scrambled into his pyjamas and ran for Amah.

Restored after a refreshing bath, his bad-temper forgotten, Hiro eagerly tucked into Chokugetsu-ken's fried tofu. 'It's been difficult finding motor engines,' he said, in between mouthfuls. 'There're hardly any more cars around, and I spent all day looking for hidden garages.'

'What happens if you don't get enough engines?' I asked.

'What can't be found can't be found. Nothing I can do about it,' he said, sounding not particularly bothered. I can't help but admire Hiro's ability not to dwell on matters that can't be helped.

Monday, 17 April

Is it my imagination that I see fewer large dogs around? I certainly haven't seen the beautiful German shepherd in the courtyard lately. Now the papers talk of horses: how they, too, are contributing to the war effort. I think of the horses I have known – Cindy, the mare I rode regularly in Hyde Park, from the Smith Riding School in Cavendish Square, and Mummy's chestnut-coloured horse, whose name I can't remember. And the sad-looking horse Tamiko and I bet on at the racetracks that ended up winning – the memorable outing with the Maos, which was my first encounter with Shin-tsu. I must contact Midori and find out how she is coping.

Tuesday, 18 April

I rang Midori. 'Oh, what a surprise,' she said, sounding rather distant and not particularly pleased to hear from me.

'I'm sorry, am I ringing at an inconvenient time?' I hesitantly asked. After a short pause, she said she had people at her house and couldn't speak, but would ring me back to arrange a get-together.

From her tone, I wondered whether that would ever happen. I felt rejected and wished I hadn't bothered ringing. Had Shin-tsu's disappearance changed things completely within the Mao household? Oh Shin-tsu, please stay well and out of danger, wherever you are.

Friday, 21 April

Still feeling dejected by Midori's cold response but desperately wanting company, I gathered my courage and rang Mona – something I had meant to do ever since Masaya mentioned her miscarriage. To my relief, I sensed genuine delight as soon as she heard my voice, and instantly suggested I come over for lunch. 'Now?' I asked. 'Yes, now!'

I felt a spring in my step, walking along unfamiliar little roads in Frenchtown, looking for Mona's house. I was surprised at how little of my own neighbourhood I knew. But come to think of it, most of my strolls through Frenchtown were usually with Tamiko, always huddled tightly by her side, lost in conversation and paying scant attention to the scenery around me.

When I approached a tasteful stone villa shimmering in the filtered light from the plane trees, I instinctively sensed it was Mona's. She greeted me with a hug, and led me through a formal dining room to a bright smaller room. By the bay window was a beautifully laid round table, and as soon as we sat down, Mona asked, 'How are your little boys?'

It was a question I was dreading – how could I talk about them, knowing Mona had lost her baby? It was Mona who spoke first. 'You know I had a terrible pregnancy and then a miscarriage. It was a rough time, but I am healthy now, and you mustn't worry about hurting my feelings. I really want to hear all about your boys!'

Her magic way of putting me at ease made me tell her of how Kazu taunted Taka with his new gaudy sunglasses. The room filled with laughter.

Over lunch of shepherd's pie – 'to remind you of London' – Mona said that her grandfather had been educated at a Christian missionary school in Hong Kong and from him, their family came to love English boarding school food. 'My grandfather worked for Jardines and invested in steamships. He was one of the early modernizers of China.'

'I don't know much about your family, Eiko, but I sense we're similar. Orientals with a Western and Christian upbringing,' she said. I, too, had been struck by the parallels between her background and mine, probably why I felt such affinity for her.

'My grandfather's position put us in touch with other Christian families, like the Soongs. You know of Mei-ling Soong, I'm sure, who is Madam Chiang Kai-shek,' Mona said.

Surprised to hear the names of public figures suddenly come up in casual conversation, I wanted to know how Chiang Kai-shek and Madam Chiang came across as ordinary people.

'Mei-ling is such a strong-willed woman, not much to my taste, and Chiang is clever, shrewd, and not very nice,' Mona said. I was somewhat thrown by her candour.

'Eiko, the business community has learned to view politicians with a cool eye. Politicians want money to promote their policies and pay for their armies, and so they woo businessmen. As a little girl visiting my grandfather's house, I'd run into many nationalist leaders. My grandfather used to complain that Chiang Kai-shek and others, including Wang Ching-wei, were always fighting for power, and his company had to keep neutral, otherwise whoever was in the ascendancy might stop them from doing business.'

I chewed over her words, as she explained that the power struggle was always over how to deal with the enemies – the enemies being the communists and the Japanese. 'They'd quarrel over which was the bigger enemy of the two. Chiang was accused of appeasing the Japanese at one time, and now Wang is labelled a collaborator. But the business community, regardless of what they really think, have to go along with the flow. Now, they cooperate with the Japanese if they're to survive.' She stopped suddenly.

Throwing me a concerned glance, she said, 'You don't mind me talking like this, do you, Eiko? I want you to understand me.'

'Of course not. There's so much I learn from you,' I quickly responded. I loved the way she explained things in a way that made sense to me.

'I sound rather spineless, don't I – no firm belief, just going with the flow,' she laughed. 'I'm neither a staunch Nationalist nor a Communist, nor a believer in Japan's Greater East Asian Co-prosperity Sphere. It may sound silly, but I feel each has a certain appeal, and I can't denounce any of them outright.' Again, she stopped abruptly.

Placing a hand over her mouth in mock alarm, she said, 'What I'm saying is for your ears only, Eiko. Most Chinese people would denounce me out right!' She lifted her shoulders in an impish shrug, then reached out and patted my hand.

'The thing is, I don't want to be caught up in complicated politics and be dictated by ideologies I don't fully understand or like – I just want to live in an upright way, follow my heart and do the right thing on a day-to-day basis.'

She articulated my own feelings so perfectly. How comforting to know that, although she's Chinese and I'm Japanese, we both feel exactly the same way. But in the end, I suppose, with our two countries at war, only one of us will be on the winner's side. What would it mean to be on the winner's or loser's side, I wonder? As far as Mona and I are concerned, if the war could end soon without too much devastation, I feel it might not even matter which side wins. We would be friends in a freer world, and the two countries could focus on repairing relationships and building a future.

Tuesday, 2 May

It was mid-morning when Amah, with Taka on her back, came rushing into the living room, where I was reading Kazu a book. 'Missy, light no turnee. Water stop, too.' I switched on the lamp, and sure enough, nothing happened.

'Amah, please no flush toilet,' I said, hoping to preserve at least what was still in the tank. My next impulse was to pick up the phone to Tamiko, but of course Tamiko was no longer on hand for advice.

I heard commotion in the corridor, and realized the lifts were no longer working. When I poked out my head, one of the Chinese janitors said there was a well in the corner of the courtyard. 'Amah, collect all the buckets we have, and please put Taka in his cot. We shall go downstairs to get water,' I said hurriedly. Amah duly brought several buckets, including, much to my amusement, a little plastic pail for Kazu, which pleased him greatly.

But his excitement didn't last long. After descending three flights of stairs, he asked, '*ido mada*?' No, there was still a long way to go to the well. I had to think of ways to encourage him.

'Can you count up to twenty-two? We're on the eleventh floor. That means twenty-two flights of steps!' I smiled cheerfully, but saying the number out loud made my own spirits sag.

We ran into neighbours in the stairwell, making the journey tolerable. The Schmidts, despite panting as they climbed the stairs, gave us formal greetings, Herr Schmidt putting down his bucket to offer a handshake. Frau Schmidt sat on a step, bringing her face down to Kazu's. 'You are a good boy, helping your Mutter,' she said, making Kazu proudly puff out his chest.

The power was out for the rest of the day. I went down to the well once again on my own to ensure that Hiro would have enough water to wash after his day at the factory.

Wednesday, 3 May

Thank goodness the electricity came back early this morning. But the papers warned of the need to save energy – no private household should think of having ice even in the summer. 'A single piece of coal strengthens Japan's military power!' was the headline.

Sunday, 14 May

Rokki, in town on business, came over for dinner. I was dying to hear news of Tamiko and the children, but in typical fashion, Rokki's head seemed filled only with political developments. 'Just last week, we had big celebrations for Wang Ching-wei's birthday, and lots of official talk on Wang's improving health,' Rokki said, addressing Hiro rather than me.

'It makes me suspicious. I think the Japanese are feeling over-extended, and want the Wang government to take over more day-to-day operations. So the Japanese are finally giving the Wang Ching-wei government more authority, but typically, too late. By depriving Wang the power to govern all this time, his stature among the Chinese is so low, most see him only as a puppet of the Japanese. Argh! Japanese policy is so frustrating!'

Rokki's deep frown and typical outburst made me realize how I'd missed him. Even if I understood little of what he said, his passion gave me hope that with people like him, Japan could be put on the right track. I wished he was around more to help me work out what was going on in this complicated war.

Chokugetsu-ken had prepared an array of Shanghai dishes. Popping a whole *shaolongbao* dumpling into his mouth, Rokki closed his eyes briefly in total contentment and said, 'Shanghai cuisine is so much better than Nanking food. How I miss it. Our *amah* over there refuses to cook anything other than local dishes, and doesn't much like Tamiko in the kitchen. This is a real treat for me.'

'So what is Tamiko doing every day?' I swiftly asked, eager not to miss my chance to find out about life in Nanking.

'We live in a Japanese diplomatic compound. There are some families we know from Japan. Tamiko and the girls seem to be at someone's house every day, though I'm at the Bank all the time so I don't know what exactly they get up to.' It sounded so jolly and fun, I felt almost crestfallen with envy.

'So you've settled in pretty quickly, it seems,' I said, forcing a smile.

'Yes, you know how Tamiko is, always giggling and cheerful, appearing not to be doing much. But somehow, the house – which is quite spacious – got sorted out very quickly, and it now feels as if we've been there forever,' Rokki said.

The more I heard, the more I felt left behind, missing Tamiko terribly, and quite certain that in her new environment, she hadn't had the time to miss me. Once the conversation reverted to politics and business, I excused myself to put the boys to bed.

I lingered in the boys' room, picking up *The Adventures of Tin tin: The Black Island* – a book I'd found with Tamiko in a little book-shop on Avenue Joffre. She laughed at my excitement upon seeing that the story took place in Britain, featuring little Snowy, the fox terrier. I leafed through the pages, admiring the clear, expressive drawings until Kazu's eyes started to droop.

By the time I returned to the living room, Rokki was ready to leave. As Hiro was seeing him off to the door, Rokki suddenly swerved around and said, 'Oh dear! I almost forgot. Eiko, I have a letter from Tamiko for you.'

I was so happy, I let pass the irritation with Rokki for being so absent-minded.

The letter was not long, and much of it contained what Rokki had already reported, about the to-ing and fro-ing among the Japanese diplomatic community:

But Eiko, so much of it is superficial socializing. How I miss not being able to run over to you and have a giggle over some of the silly rituals involved! And it's very Japanese here, I can't really speak my mind. Sachi, too, misses Kazuo. She hasn't managed to find a soul-mate – the children around us are very meek and cry when she speaks in her bossy tone!!

Thinking of you all the time. With Love, Tamiko

I am happy.

Monday, 22 May

To my surprise, Midori Mao phoned, speaking in warm, solicitous tones – a marked contrast from when I spoke to her last month. 'Eiko-san, I'd like to see you. I've had so little contact with Japanese people these days. I miss Tamiko-san, and would be grateful if we could get together.'

She came at tea-time dressed in a *cheongsam*, over which draped a light black cape, looking more like a Chinese *tai tai* than the elegant, exotic Japanese woman of times past. Her mysterious classiness – hint of a shady past, mixed with confidence as the favoured wife of a powerful businessman – was replaced by a certain hard edge, although she was still beautiful.

'I have another engagement after this visit, with some Chinese ladies, so I'm not exactly appropriately dressed for tea,' she said, as if she needed to explain her heavy make-up and bright red lips.

Kazu came running out to say hello, hoping, I suspect, for some adult attention, but there was something about Midori that made him lose his tongue. He swiftly retreated to find Amah and Taka.

Over tea, Midori dropped her guard and quietly said, 'Eiko-san, things started falling apart in our household after Shin-tsu's disappearance. Wen-tsu became a changed person. I don't know what it is. For me, Shin-tsu going over to the Communists is upsetting, but at least I know he has a purpose.' Her mention of Shin-tsu made me warm to her.

'But for Wen-tsu, Shin-tsu was everything despite all the differences of opinion and tension that existed. I hadn't realized it, Wen-tsu the overbearing businessman, strong, successful – that losing Shin-tsu would change him so. Outwardly, he's not much different, even more commanding. But it's as if he doesn't have a centre anymore.'

She looked straight into my eyes, and then shifted her gaze downwards. 'He hardly comes home anymore. I am certain he has a new mistress.' I stared in disbelief. Midori had been Mr Mao's pride and joy.

'He doesn't cast me aside as he's done with his other wives. Instead, he showers me with gold and jewels and insists that I socialize with wives of Nanking government officials. I don't really mind – I quite like playing mahjong. And because Wen-tsu is a major funder of the government, I am accepted as one of them. He's succeeded in transforming me into a status conscious, gossipy Chinese *tai tai.*' Midori looked at the rings on her fingers and smiled ironically.

'But the truth is, Wen-tsu is using me. He wants me to pick up information – always asks me which *tai tai*s are most friendly with whom, what they say about their husbands, that sort of thing.' I stared into her face. What she was saying seemed so far-fetched.

'You know that Wang Ching-wei is ill, and there's lots of scrambling going on in his camp,' Midori said. 'If he were the old Wen-tsu, the wily, brilliant strategist, I wouldn't be so worried. But Shin-tsu's disappearance made him lose focus. Especially this involvement with a young woman makes me anxious – that his judgment might be clouded and he will lose his position.'

She suddenly looked at her watch – a big chunk of gold with diamonds studded on the rim – and said, 'Goodness, time flies. I must leave. But tell me, how are Tamiko-san and Rokuro-san?'

I rattled on about Tamiko mixing with the Japanese diplomatic community, and could tell from her expression that she wasn't interested. 'What is Rokuro-san's specific job in Nanking now?' she asked, rather abruptly, and a trace of impatience showed when I said I didn't know.

Her abrupt departure left me with a strange aftertaste. Why had she come to see me? Despite her confiding tone about Mr Mao, I couldn't help feeling she had an ulterior purpose. Was she trying to find out about Rokki's job? I wished I'd paid more attention to what Rokki was saying the other evening. If only Tamiko were around, she'd know what to think.

Friday, 26 May

The newspapers report the new light regulations. Shops have to be closed at 2 p.m., and the night-time curfew is 10 p.m. – even nightclubs have to close by then. Not that that will affect us – we hardly go out in the evenings.

What affects us most is the blackout – all windows to be covered with thick curtains to prevent any light being spotted by enemy planes. I will have to find dark cloth to line our existing curtains.

The papers also outlined the air-raid signals: a precautionary long blast; seven short blasts the actual air raid; and two medium blasts the all clear. Will we really hear sirens in residential Frenchtown, I wonder.

Monday, 29 May

Having thrown tablecloths over the curtains as a temporary black-out measure for the last few days, I finally set off to Wing-on to get some fabric. I'd never seen Nanking Road so crowded as this morning – perhaps everyone was trying to get their shopping done before shop closure at two. It was impossible to manoeuvre my bicycle, and I ended up pushing more than riding.

Frustrated, I took a detour and went along Hankow Road. Riding along a relatively uncrowded stretch, a warm breeze brushing against my face and arms, I felt a tingling sense of freedom as my skirt billowed around my legs. Had I closed my eyes? Suddenly, I was about to ram into a man who'd appeared from nowhere. I quickly gripped the brake hard, and my body heaved forwards. My arms were sore from the impact, but I was not hurt.

The man I nearly ran over was steadying my handlebar, looking at me with great concern. After a moment's hesitation, he quietly asked, '*Daijobu desuka?*'

Unexpectedly being spoken to in Japanese, I started babbling, apologizing for not having paid attention, explaining that I was headed to the Wing-on Department store. I recall words pouring out of my mouth, not knowing what I was saying. The man, unusually well built for a Japanese, dressed in a simple cotton grey suit with no tie, had a reassuring presence and soft smile.

'I think you might have had a bit of a shock. Would you like to come in for a cup of tea?' he said, in a deep, mellow voice.

'I run the Japanese YMCA activities here at the Holy Trinity Cathedral, and we have a little café inside. My name is Akira Ikemoto.'

I followed him as he pushed my bicycle up the few steps towards the Cathedral entrance. I had never set foot in the imposing red stone church, although its tall spire was a familiar sight, being so close to the Cathay Hotel. Mr Ikemoto secured my bicycle against a wall and held open the heavy wooden door.

'Let's sit over there,' he said, leading the way through a large hall towards a cluster of tables at the far end. A Japanese lady who runs the café brought us two cups of piping hot green tea.

The tea brought me back to my senses. 'Forgive me, thank you so much for your kindness. I am Eiko Kishimoto. I shan't take up much more of your time. I should be getting on my way,' I said.

Mr Ikemoto scrunched his tanned, fleshy face into a warm smile. 'I had a feeling you might be Mrs Kishimoto. Your husband is famous among the Japanese community for his tennis, and you have a reputation as his beautiful wife. I am honoured to have this occasion to meet you.'

Had it not been for his natural, easy manner of speaking, I would have felt embarrassed. Instead, I was able to accept what he said and look straight at him. Although not handsome in a conventional way, his large face and deep black eyes that shone through the slits of his eyelids seemed to reflect his inviting personality. I knew time was running short for the shops, but I indulged a little longer in his company.

'The Holy Trinity Cathedral is now in Japanese hands, being looked after by Bishop Abe as the Right Reverend Dean Trivetti is interned in camp,' Mr Ikemoto explained. 'Bishop Abe opened the premises for the YMCA to carry out activities in this ideal location close to many Japanese businesses. Our own place is in Hongkew, which isn't very convenient for people to drop in at lunchtime. And the curfew no longer allows evening activities.'

'If you are in this neighbourhood again, please come to some of our lunchtime lectures. There is a young woman who works at the Yokohama Specie Bank who is a regular, and others too whom you might enjoy meeting,' he said, as he saw me off to my bicycle.

He reminded me of Masaya – a slightly younger version. If Tamiko were around, I'd have gone to tell her straight away.

17

Friday, 2 June 1944

Irma rang this morning. 'Eiko, Liebling, Agnes has been taken to hospital, the one close to you – what is it called, St Marie's. She's well looked after by the Chinese Quakers, but it would be good if you could drop in to see her,' she said.

Alarmed, I rushed to the hospital, tracing the mottled shadows on the pavement cast by the plane trees along Route Père Robert. The heat and humidity had already risen although it was only mid-morning. The ceiling fans weren't working in the hospital lobby, teaming with humanity, from little babies to the very old. Everything looked shabbier from the last time I was there – when I found out that I was pregnant with Taka.

Agnes was in a private room, a little island of peacefulness, propped up against her pillows. A Chinese gentleman, Dr Tang, who I'd met at the Leighs, was by her side. 'Agnes's bronchitis has gone to her lungs, and it is not very easy for her to talk,' he said, as Agnes cast me an apologetic smile. Although frail, she still looked elegant, her fine features framed by her soft silver hair.

'Before leaving her house, Agnes collected some things for Irma. Mrs Kishimoto, would you be so kind as to deliver them to her at the Friends Centre on Museum Road?' Dr Tang asked. 'As my university is in the other direction, I have little occasion to go into town.'

'I would be more than happy to,' I said, pleased to be given an actual task.

'Thank you. And please tell Irma that Agnes is doing very well. The doctors have managed to secure antibiotics, still very rare, and say that, with rest, she will be better soon.'

I felt uplifted on the way home: from relief that Agnes was on the mend; or that I'd be seeing Irma soon? Yes, but there was something else that I couldn't immediately pinpoint. Then it dawned on me that going to the Friends' Centre would put me in the vicinity of the Holy Trinity Cathedral, its tall spire etched in my mind ever since meeting Mr Ikemoto.

Saturday, 10 June

There is no distinction now between weekdays and weekends. Hiro is at work all the time, and our daily routine is dictated by the curfews and blackouts, having to do whatever shopping is needed early in the day, and keeping the flat as dark as possible after nightfall. Still, with Amah and Chokugetsu-ken looking after us, I have plenty of time. Today was a beautiful Saturday, just the kind of day Tamiko would have suggested an outing, so off I went to Irma's bearing Agnes's bundle.

'*Willkommen, willkommen!*' Irma boomed, as soon as I arrived. She had lost weight again, but was exuberant as ever. When she opened Agnes's box, she became childlike in her excitement. 'Ooh, look at this! Agnes's linen tea towels from Ireland! Mine are still useable, but Mrs Braun next door was mending hers. How happy she will be to have one of these!' The way she thought of others rather than herself reminded me of Tamiko.

'More to lift our spirits, just like recent news from Europe,' Irma said, then cast me a hesitant glance. 'Eiko, you don't mind me talking about war, do you? Even though Japanisch on the Deutschland side.'

'Of course, not.'

'The Designated Area is abuzz with news of Allied landings in Normandy. America and Britain are retaking Frankreich from Hitler. Das is good news, and everyone is excited, although some worry that if fighting eases in Europe, the Americans will focus on China. Maybe more bombings in Shanghai.'

Irma's mention of America attacking Shanghai loomed on my mind as I mounted my bicycle. Life was inconvenient enough with all the restrictions, but would it become too dangerous to even go out, I wondered. I shook my head vigorously to wipe away such thoughts. No, there would be warnings, we would surely be able to move around, I told myself, as I headed towards the Holy Trinity Cathedral, hoping there might be a YMCA lecture.

It seemed the right time, a little before noon. I felt shy pushing open the heavy doors, and peered through a small opening before entering. As far as I could see, nothing was happening. The place was completely empty – not even any sign of the catering couple, although the tables were properly laid for lunch. Feeling disappointed and relieved at the same time, I swiftly turned around to make my exit.

As I pulled open the door, I nearly collided with Mr Ikemoto, piles of papers in his arms, about to push open the door with his mighty frame. I jumped back, and I felt my heart leap up to my throat. After a surprised look of recognition, he chuckled, 'another near collision! Have you been here long?'

'No, no, I was in the neighbourhood, so I just dropped in to see if there was a lecture,' I said, trying to appear as nonchalant as possible.

'I'm pleased you are interested. I must give you a schedule of the lectures,' he said, creasing his face into a smile that made his dark eyes nearly disappear in the fold of his eyelids. 'People drop by as they like, for lunch, or to use the piano, or our badminton equipment. But the lectures are on set dates.'

Putting his papers on the ground, he rummaged through a slim folder. 'Ah, here it is, a lecture schedule for the next few months. I would have liked to offer you lunch, but the hall is closed today because we are about to hold our board meeting. If you have time, perhaps you'd like to stay and meet some of the board members.'

Feeling foolish to have managed to pick a day the YMCA happened to be closed, I swiftly declined.

'Perhaps another time then. We have board members who are very knowledgeable about China, like Mr Uchiyama and Mr Otsuka. Do come again.'

Hearing that Uncle Uchiyama and Daisuke would be there, I regretted my hasty decision, but it was too embarrassing to change my mind. Bowing repeatedly, I hurriedly made my exit.

Once on my bicycle, I turned back and caught sight of Mr Ikemoto picking up his papers. He must have been watching me cycle for a while. It was my turn to watch him, as he shoved open the heavy door with a strong shoulder and disappeared within.

Monday, 12 June

I ran into Midori and Mr Mao, walking arm in arm outside the Astor Hotel. Midori rushed over and gave me an exaggerated hug, as if trying to mask her surprise and embarrassment. She had on a stylish black crepe cape over a tightly fitting sky blue *cheongsam*, and was decked with even more jewellery than when I saw her last. Mr Mao had perhaps aged a bit, but hardly seemed the changed man of Midori's description. He appeared proud of and devoted to Midori as before, and if anything, even more a man of stature.

He tipped his Panama hat, giving me a bow and said, 'we have just come from an important ceremony at the hotel. The Japanese have given more power to the Chinese in governing Shanghai, which will probably keep me even busier than I am now.' He gently patted Midori on the arm, while she looked the other way with a barely perceptible wince.

Towards me, she widened her bright red lips into a smile. 'We must get together again soon, Eiko-san.' I can't help wondering what is going on.

Thursday, 15 June

Mona came over for lunch – a breath of fresh air after my strange encounter with the Maos. When the doorbell rang, there was a flurry of excitement as the boys sensed I was expecting a special visitor. She came in, dressed in a simple cotton frock, looking fresh and cool despite the outside heat and humidity. Her face broke out into a huge smile as she saw the welcoming party. 'How wonderful to step into such a lively scene! I am already envious of your perfect domestic environment.' Her spontaneity put me instantly at ease.

I had Chokugetsu-ken prepare a Japanese lunch of *chirashi sushi* – seasoned rice mixed with cooked carrots and *shiitake* mushrooms, and topped with strands of thinly sliced omelette eggs – which I thought was appropriately light and cool for a hot summer's day. Mona's easy manner allowed the conversation to flow.

'Do you know anything about some ceremony that took place at the Astor Hotel?' I asked.

'Not much. I think the Japanese authorities handed over the utilities operations to the Wang Ching-wei government.'

'Does that mean Japan and China are getting closer to ending the war?' I asked hopefully. 'It seems the war isn't going that well for Japan, and perhaps the military are more willing to negotiate.'

Mona lightly shook her head and said, 'Eiko, if peace were to be worked out, I doubt it would be with the Wang government. Wang Ching-wei hasn't been given the chance to establish himself as representative of the Chinese people. Dislike as I do Chiang Kai-shek, I think he's managed to persuade America and Britain that he represents China.'

'Do you know of Mme Chiang Kai-shek's trip to America last year? She's really quite something!' she said with a laugh.

'I get these reports from my old Smith College friends, who tell me about how China is viewed in the US,' Mona continued. She explained how Mme Chiang Kai-shek, a graduate of Wellesley College, had been a most effective promoter of China's cause in America and had much to do with getting American support behind Chiang Kai-shek. 'She stayed at the White House as a guest of the Roosevelt's, gave lectures, went to parties and mingled with many politicians. And the American papers reported as much about her beauty and her exquisite style as they did her cause.'

It made me sigh, as I thought how wonderful if some elegant Japanese lady was able to travel around the world and speak for Japan. Daddy in London had tried his best, appealing to the British that Japan was a resource-poor country with an expanding population, and needed markets and access to the world's riches, just like the Western countries. Would someone like Madam Chiang Kai-shek have been able to make a better case and gain more sympathy?

'But according to the latest reports, Mei-ling's excesses are starting to attract attention,' Mona said. 'She stayed for months in the Waldorf Astoria Hotel in New York, taking a whole floor for herself and her staff. Even the most adoring fans of Mme Chiang in America came to notice that her jewellery and furs were somewhat incongruous with her appeal for more American money to help the poor, starving, war-torn Chinese nation.'

Chokugetsu-ken brought in the dessert, a cool tangerine jelly, which we savoured in silence for a while.

'You said the war wasn't going well for the Japanese, but I wonder. It doesn't seem to be going well for the Chinese, either,' Mona said. 'Some Chungking sources say that Chinese morale is almost rock bottom, and that Chiang Kai-shek doesn't seem keen to send troops to fight the Japanese. They say he's hoping the Americans will win this war for him, and that he himself is saving up for fighting the communists when it's over. Can you imagine? It really makes me wonder who is fighting whom for what gains.'

In Shanghai where Japan rules, we're led to believe that the Japanese and Chinese work together, against the Western imperialists, although one could hardly believe it the way the Japanese soldiers treat most Chinese on the streets. Oh how complicated things are! I let out a loud sigh.

'I know, Eiko, I feel the same,' Mona said, imitating my loud sigh, but in a long, exaggerated manner, making us burst into laughter. She took my hands into hers. 'The war is too difficult to understand, and we know so little, are told so little of what is really happening. But at least you and I can gossip and speculate, say things we never would in public, and share a laugh. It means a lot to me, thank you Eiko.'

Mona manages to articulate my own exact feelings in a most natural way.

Wednesday, 21 June

It was a YMCA lecture day, and I pondered whether to go or not. Even after heading to the Cathedral, I wondered whether I should just turn around and go home. I felt torn – on the one hand feeling a big attraction towards the Cathedral, and on the other, an inexplicable shyness. Was it the prospect of seeing Mr Ikemoto again?

The big heavy doors were wide open, and a sprinkling of people were milling around the chairs in front of the lectern, set up at the far end of the large hall. A pretty young woman was arranging flowers, making the stark surroundings more welcoming. As I took a seat in an inconspicuous corner, Mr Ikemoto walked towards the lectern with the speaker, a middle-aged Japanese gentleman, dressed in a Chinese gown. I was relieved that there was no time to say hello.

Once at the lectern, Mr Ikemoto adjusted his broad shoulders and cast a relaxed, welcoming smile towards the audience. 'I am glad to see you all here, and especially to see new faces,' he said, looking directly at me. I felt a thud in my heart – I didn't think he had noticed me.

I remember little of Professor Tagawa's talk itself – something about 'The State and Religion,' a title that made me decide from the outset that it would be too difficult. I was perhaps too busy soaking in the new surroundings, feeling proud to have ventured out on my own. My mind wandered, wondering who the other people were, and I couldn't help notice that the pretty flower-woman was sitting next to Mr Ikemoto and exchanging words with him from time to time even during the lecture.

Once the talk was over, people got up and left the hall immediately, and I took my time to avoid the crowded doorway.

'I'm sorry you didn't get here earlier,' a voice said from behind me. I nearly jumped when I saw that it was Mr Ikemoto, who I thought was back in the hall putting away the chairs. 'Most people work in the neighbourhood and have to rush back to their offices.

They usually come for a quick lunch before the lectures. Did you enjoy it?'

I was tongue-tied and felt blood rushing to my cheeks. 'Yes, but it went a bit over my head,' I managed.

Mr Ikemoto smiled affably. 'Tagawa-sensei was an influential politician before the war. But he fell out of favour with the Japanese military and couldn't stay in Japan any longer. He's in exile here in Shanghai, and apart from giving talks at the YMCA and teaching part-time at St John's University, he lives quietly with a Japanese Christian family and spends his days practising calligraphy.'

I wished I had paid more attention to the talk. As if reading my thoughts, Mr Ikemoto said, 'It's not easy to follow Tagawa-sensei's talks without some knowledge of him and his thinking. Come on a non-lecture day and I'd be happy to give you some background.'

I thanked him and quickly took my leave. Would I have the courage to take Mr Ikemoto up on his offer?

Thursday, 29 June

Hiro came home earlier than usual, took a long bath, and during the quiet lull before dinner, closed the bedroom door.

'The news from Japan is not good,' he said. 'Everything is being hushed, but it appears the Americans landed in Saipan earlier this month, and ten days ago, there was a decisive defeat in the Marianas.'

I was alarmed by the news itself, but knew it had to be a prelude to something else for Hiro to bring the matter up. I waited for his next words, perched on the edge of the bed with palms growing sweatier.

'You know I've been trying to collect motor engines. I was called in to Naval Headquarters in Hongkew today. They told me the kind of boats we are to build. Our aircraft carriers are too damaged to be replaced. So instead, they've decided to concentrate on building special attack boats: *tokkō heiki*,' Hiro said.

'They're still working on the design, but the small boats will carry explosives, and charge into enemy ships.'

I pondered the meaning of his words. The literal meaning of *tokkō heiki*, was 'special attack weapon'. I realized Hiro was telling me that boat and operator together made up the weapon. Who would be put on those boats – be part of the weapon itself? Cheeko's words – 'Eiko-san, the pilots' age is getting younger and younger as the war gets tough for Japan' – flashed through my mind, and I shook my head in horror.

Hiro, having imparted his news, was more sanguine. 'I won't feel so bad now if I can't find motor engines,' he said, holding the bedroom door open for me. 'Let's eat, I'm hungry.' Yes, how desirable it would be if Hiro never found motor engines for the boats that would send young men to their death.

18

Monday, 3 July 1944

At first I didn't know what awoke me – a faint siren far away in the distance, lasting a very long time. But the papers have been so full of air-raid information recently, it didn't take me long to work out it was a precautionary alarm. Because of the blackout curtains, I had no idea of the time, and quietly got up to peer through the window. It was just starting to get light – perhaps six o'clock or so.

Hiro was sound asleep. I'd wake him if the precautionary alarms progressed to a real air raid alarm, I thought, remembering to listen for a succession of seven short blasts. In heightened anticipation, aware of my beating heart, I lay completely still, concentrating on the distant sounds. After perhaps as long as half an hour, instead of short blasts, I recognized the sound of the all-clear. Hiro had managed to sleep through the whole thing.

'Of course I heard it, but saw no point of getting up, it was so far away,' he said when he got up. 'Even Jay-jay didn't stir, though I'm sure she heard too,' he smiled, patting her as she jumped on the bed.

Noticing how shaken I was, Hiro suddenly seemed to realize I had little exposure to air raid alarms.

'I guess you don't hear them much here,' he said. 'In Hongkew and the eastern industrial areas, we've become used to the sirens.' He gave me a soft nudge on the shoulder to comfort me.

But rather than being comforted, I now knew that he was exposed to so much more danger at the factory.

Friday, 7 July

I went to the Holy Trinity Cathedral yesterday, via a roundabout route. First I visited Agnes at the hospital and then went on to visit

Irma, and then to the Cathedral with the excuse that I happened to be in the neighbourhood. My motives? Of course I wanted to pay Agnes a visit and report on her progress to Irma at the Friend's office. But deep down, was it the Cathedral that attracted me, the desire to see Mr Ikemoto again?

When I reached the Cathedral, the hall was empty, not even the café people were there. Feeling an urge to see the Cathedral itself, I walked to a side door, which linked the hall and the church part. The door wasn't locked, and I entered, awed at the sight of the interior, which reminded me of the Anglican Holy Trinity Church in London, where we had Mummy's funeral.

But here in this Cathedral, there was a distinct unused atmosphere, a musty smell of dust and damp, and the huge pipe organ looked dulled from neglect. Self-conscious of my footsteps echoing against the high ceiling, I walked closer to the altar, entered a pew and sunk to my knees. Resting my forehead against my clasped hands, I prayed – for peace, for the war to end.

I don't know how long I remained in that position. I heard the side door open, and a puzzled deep male voice, '*Oya?*' and then footsteps coming my way. It was Mr Ikemoto.

'I was just about to leave,' I said, feeling blood rush up my cheeks as I stood up.

'I'm sorry if I interrupted you in prayer. Can I offer you a cup of tea?' Acceptance of his offer came most naturally, as if I had subconsciously been expecting it.

'I'm afraid you'll have to make do with tea made by me since the café people haven't arrived yet,' he said, putting on the kettle. 'Did you like the Cathedral? The church part isn't available for YMCA activities, so I was rather surprised to see you there.'

His genial manner made me relax, and I asked whether it was the Japanese authorities that kept the church part closed. 'You are very perceptive Mrs Kishimoto. Bishop Abe, head of the Japanese Anglican Church here, is entrusted with the Cathedral. But he can't run it as a church, which from Japan's official point of view is an enemy religion. The Bishop is in reality only the custodian on behalf of the military.'

Mr Ikemoto leaned on his elbows and slowly shook his head. 'Bishop Abe is a good man, and he tries to lessen the negative impact of the military in everything he does. That's why he so readily agreed to let the YMCA use these premises. But, to the Japanese authorities, he stresses the usefulness of YMCA activities in making Chinese participants more sympathetic to Japan. Whether he believes it or not, I'm not sure, but he knows that the authorities would approve, because for them, the church is a propaganda vehicle to make Japanese occupation more palatable to the Chinese.'

He looked into my face with a soft, concerned smile, almost as if he were apologizing for the position the Japanese churches were taking.

'And does using the Cathedral hall for our authorized activities put us, the Japanese YMCA, also in a compromised position?' he asked, to himself it seemed rather than to me. 'I believe not. I hope not. But as a layman dedicated to Christian values, I find myself always questioning.' Despite the serious nature of the talk, he had a way of making it seem like a friendly conversation between close friends.

'I went to divinity school in Tokyo, and graduated in the spring of 1938,' he continued. My mind moved quickly, calculating that he was thirty-two, one year younger than Hiro.

'During my last year, a letter written in English came to the university from a divinity school in Nanking. It claimed that poppies were being grown in Japanese occupied Manchuria, and that the Japanese military was distributing opium among the Chinese. It asked whether we knew anything about it, and if so, what was being done,' he said. He wanted to respond to the letter, and desperately tried to find information, but to no avail. He realized that the Japanese military and government kept a tight lid on what was actually taking place.

'They only reported the good things that promoted their grand plan of the Co-prosperity Sphere for the region. But I needed to know the truth. Studying the Old Testament was no longer a priority for me. I felt my calling was to see for myself, and to make it up to the Chinese if they were suffering at Japanese hands. As soon as I graduated, I set off to Peking,' he said.

Even though he was telling me of a turning point in his life, the conversation never seemed to lose its light touch, perhaps because of his relaxed manner and his big build that accentuated his warm personality. But he had dropped everything to follow his principles. Although different in personality, he reminded me so much of Masaya. Was that why I feel drawn to him?

Tuesday, 11 July

Hiro announced over dinner that he was put on the reservist list, and had to go on training in four days' time. The shock made me immediately lose my appetite.

'It's not as if I've been called up,' he said light heartedly, tucking into Chokugetsu-ken's *mao-bo dofu*, his favourite tofu dish. 'Most men are reservists now, and we just have to go through the exercise.'

It crossed my mind that Mr Ikemoto might have been more understanding of my anxiety.

Hiro continued in his nonchalant manner. 'The thing is, besides a khaki shirt and trousers, I'll need *gētoru* to cover the calves. The Navy will provide the cap. Could you try and find some *gētoru* fabric for me?'

I was pleased to be asked, but hadn't the faintest idea what a *gētoru* was.

Hiro chuckled at my ignorance. 'You've seen soldiers walking around with the bottom part of their legs wrapped up with strips of cloth – the effect, like wearing breeches, think of me in my plus-fours for golf. The things that wrap around the calves are *gētoru*.'

Still with an amused look, he said, 'I think it's the French word, "*guêtres*". I guess the military don't consider French as an enemy language.'

Thursday, 12 July

I managed to find some *gētoru* material at one of the backstreet merchants off Nanking Road, and before dinner, Hiro tried on his full outfit. The thick white cotton *gētoru* strips, carefully rolled up to just below his knees, stood out jarringly from the darker khaki trousers and shirt, but he still managed to look rather dapper, even with the common foot soldier's cap. Kazu was fascinated to see his father in such unusual attire, and begged to try on the cap.

After the boys were in bed, Hiro rummaged through his satchel. 'There's something else I'd like your help with. I need to memorize "The Emperor's Instructions to Soldiers". It's probably easier if you read it out to me.'

I broke into laughter, saying my Japanese was probably too unreliable for such a lofty text.

Hiro let out a soft chuckle in agreement. 'But you might as well try. If you stumble, it could help me remember better,' he said.

The text, in old formal Japanese, was difficult to read. 'Two thousand five hundred years ago the Emperor Jimmu personally led the forces of …'

'Skip that part and go to the actual instructions,' Hiro said.

'One, soldiers must pledge allegiance. Those given birth by their country are obliged to repay their country…' The paragraph went on and on. I'd read a few lines, Hiro would repeat, and we'd do it all over again. Even after four tries, it was still impossible to get all the words right.

There were many more Instructions – soldiers having to be courteous, courageous, faithful and humble, with detailed reasons and examples – but Hiro decided he'd had enough after the first. 'We can continue the rest tomorrow,' he said, and headed for bed. I was tickled by his method of learning.

Sunday, 16 July

I write as I overlook the courtyard, where the boys are out with Amah on this hot, stifling day. Hiro is fast asleep, having returned early this morning from his first reservist training.

He came home covered in mud and grime, hardly a white patch on the *gētoru*, shirt smeared with grease stains. Preparing for the training had become a pleasant diversion for me, but I felt crushed by the reality of training, seeing Hiro totally exhausted, with barely enough strength to carry his rucksack.

'We moved bombs from one warehouse to another throughout the night. I don't know whether it served a real purpose or was just an exercise to make us use our bodies. Some men were quite old, and I felt sorry for them. Really couldn't see the point,' he said wearily, as he polished off the last of his ham and eggs before heading to bed.

Beyond the courtyard, I see the grounds of the French Club and the tennis courts – covered with weeds and cracks from disuse. Hiro, the elegant tennis player now made to do harsh manual labour. On a day-to-day basis, I accept the deteriorating conditions, the realities of war without much thought. But at moments like this, when I see the stark contrasts, it is difficult not to feel shock at how the world is changing.

Monday, 17 July

Back from his morning's shopping, Chokugetsu-ken excitedly said, 'Missy, Japanese almost bling up *Conte Verde*. Stake vely high now.' It must be nearly a year since Tamiko and I went to see the boat, sunk by her Italian crew after Italy's surrender to prevent the Japanese from taking over the boat.

'My bet Japanese can do,' Chokugetsu-ken said. 'Many tink boat stay in water. They say Japanese try put rope on Customs Building and pull boat up and maybe building break. If Amelica prevent Japan put up boat, I lose bet. No wantee.' He smiled good-naturedly.

Sweet Chokugetsu-ken, in on the betting game. Is he on Japan's side because of us? Yet, I'm not sure where I stand. For the beautiful boat to remain sunk in the murky Whangpoo is heart-breaking. But do I want it to be transformed into a war machine to do hurtful things to the 'enemies'?

Wednesday, 19 July

Still apprehensive of my strong attraction to the YMCA, I mustered up courage to attend a lecture. Upon my arrival at the Cathedral entrance, I ran into Cheeko, much to our mutual surprise.

'Eiko-san! I didn't know you come here. Daisuke is a regular, but I only come for special occasions. It's Uncle Uchiyama's lecture today, not to be missed. I'm so pleased you're here. We shall sit together,' she chirped.

Nice as it was to see Cheeko, I felt the wind taken out of my sails – all that gathering of courage, a tickling sense of adventure, only to find myself greeted by comfortable familiarity.

At that moment, Mr Ikemoto appeared at the door.

'Ah, Ikemoto-san. Do you know Kishimoto Eiko-san? She and her sister Tamiko-san are dear friends of ours. Tamiko-san has moved to Nanking and we all miss her…' Cheeko twittered, as Mr Ikemoto smiled patiently, gently trying to get us to move into the hall. He acknowledged my presence with just a soft nod, and I felt faintly dismayed by Cheeko's presence.

As soon as we took our seats, Cheeko said, 'Do you know that schoolchildren in Japan are now being mobilized to work in factories? Even here, Taro's school makes the students do "field duties". They cut grass to make hay to feed the warhorses. The boys are out in the gruelling heat with no shade, bent over all day long. At least Taro has physical strength, built up from his daily bicycle commute to school.'

'I'm hoping Uncle will talk about something uplifting today, and make us smile. He's so good at telling stories,' she said, finally ready to stop her chatter as Uncle Uchiyama approached the lectern.

His lecture was indeed entertaining. The entire hall rippled with laughter when he talked about the Manchu queues, the braided long pigtails that had been compulsory for all males under the Ching Dynasty. With the fall of the Dynasty in 1911, he said the queues had to be chopped off, and even to this day, the remnants of the pigtails were circulating in women's hairpieces and hairnets the world over. Cheeko gasped and clutched the hairnet that covered the neat little bun at her nape. I burst into giggles, and was happy after all to have her at my side.

Will attending YMCA functions feel more of a routine activity from now on? I wonder: I still feel a tingly mixture of pull and shy hesitation at the thought of another visit; and can't help noticing how Mr Ikemoto and the young woman who arranges flowers seem always together.

Friday, 28 July

I'd learned to ignore distant air-raid alarms until a phone call came shortly before lunchtime from Hiro's shipyard. 'Please don't be alarmed, Mrs Kishimoto. I'm just ringing to ask if Mr Kishimoto might have returned home,' the voice said.

'There has been heavy bombing around the factory and nobody seems to know where your husband is. There are no casualties that we know of, and people are looking for him, but the streets are clogged with people and debris. Please let us know if he returns.'

I leaned against the wall taking deep breaths. I didn't want to think the unthinkable, but should I be prepared?

Kazu was absorbed with his toy trains, and Taka was playing piggyback with Amah. Leaving them engaged in their activities, I checked that all our documents – passports, birth certificates, insurance forms, etc. – were in one place in case of an emergency. What else could I do?

I wished Tamiko were around. I would run over, pour out my anxieties. She would make me a cup of strong English tea. Yes, that's what I needed. I went to the kitchen and felt somewhat better as I sipped the hot steaming tea.

'No use getting your nerves in a tangle with so little information to go on. How about a walk around the courtyard, or a visit to Agnes at St Marie Hospital,' I could imagine Tamiko saying.

Yes, I'll go and visit Agnes, I thought. Without telling him why, I asked Chokugetsu-ken to be near the phone and fetch me if Hiro happened to ring. On the way to the hospital, I concentrated on the pavement, watching the shifting shadows of the plane trees as I prayed for Hiro's safety, and the safety of all others affected by the bombs.

Try as I did, I couldn't overcome my restlessness, and stayed with Agnes for only a short while. Even so, she seemed to greatly appreciate my visit, and I was encouraged to see her looking much stronger, with good colour in her cheeks.

I hadn't been out long, and my mind knew it was unlikely there'd be any news, but my feet sped on automatically. When I returned, Chokugetsu-ken poked his head from the kitchen, and with his wide bright smile said, 'No phone call Missy, all vely well.' How I wished that were true.

As the afternoon passed, my anxiety rose. The boys' suppertime was a welcome distraction, but once they were taken for their bath and bed, my spirits fell. The time that Hiro normally comes home came, and went. Sitting by the window, wrapped in the gradually fading summer evening light, I clasped my hands in prayer, desperately willing Hiro to be safe.

I don't know how long I was sitting there, when Jay-jay's head perked up and I heard keys rattle by the front door. Then Hiro's voice: 'Is anyone home? It's so dark and quiet in here!' I flung myself towards the door, about to switch on the lights, then suddenly remembered the blackout curtains needed to be closed first.

'Sorry I'm a bit late. Took longer than I expected to get home,' Hiro casually said.

I tried to act normal, with the usual welcome home bow, but felt compelled to say, 'I was worried because the factory rang this morning saying they couldn't find you after the bombing.'

'Couldn't find me? I'm sure I told the foreman I'd be out for most of the day. What bombing?'

'They said there was a massive air raid near the shipyard,' I said, feeling my pent up emotions rising to the surface.

'Oh. I was on Nanking Road. Had lunch with Daisuke, who took me around the Chinese jewellers he knows. I got this for you. Happy Birthday.'

I had completely forgotten the date. As Hiro watched, I opened the box: a beautiful gold brooch in the shape of a five-petal flower with a pearl centre. I quickly pinned it on my plain white blouse, and looked up to thank him, but ended up with tears streaming down my cheeks.

I could see Hiro's puzzled expression through my blurry eyes. 'I'm told gold is the best thing to buy in these uncertain times. But it wasn't so expensive that you should be concerned.'

Seeing me still tearful, he looked slightly embarrassed and said, 'Think I'll go and take a quick bath before dinner.'

I shan't easily forget my 23rd birthday.

Saturday, 12 August

Hiro left for his second reservist manoeuvres. The boys gave him an excited send-off, Kazu trying on his father's foot soldier cap, Taka wildly waving one arm as he clung on to me with the other. He's standing steadily now, almost ready for his first step.

Making a final check of his appearance in front of the mirror, Hiro wryly said, 'This might be the last shirt Amah has to iron. They're restricting use of electrical appliances. Wrinkled shirts are supposed to contribute to the war effort.' With a sigh of resignation, he set out for the night.

Sunday, 13 August

Upon his return from training, less tired than last time, Hiro said, 'It was so hot they didn't make us move from warehouse to warehouse. We hung around much of the time in the square behind the YMCA.' I felt a jolt at the mention of the YMCA.

'Oh, by the way, I met another reservist, who says he knows you. A Mr Ikemoto.' This time my heart nearly stopped.

'He seemed pleased that you've been attending lectures at the Holy Trinity Cathedral.'

I hadn't told Hiro about the lectures, but that didn't seem to bother him. Eyes scanning the newspaper, he said, 'Ikemoto-san's a big strong fellow, and he helped the older men carry their load. I was impressed. He was very interested in my tennis career. Maybe we should invite him over some time.'

Desperately trying to appear as nonchalant as I could, I fussed about the breakfast table, pouring more tea into Hiro's cup. My mind raced. But I managed to casually say, 'You know I've invited

Miyo over for Taka's first birthday next Saturday. Perhaps Ikemoto-san would like to come too.'

'Good idea,' Hiro said, and headed for his nap.

Wednesday, 16 August

Three days to Taka's birthday, and all I can think of is why on earth I suggested inviting Mr Ikemoto. I feel excited and frightened in equal measure. I've only thought of his existence in isolation, not connected to the rest of my world, but now he's about to come to our home for a baby's afternoon birthday party. How strange it will be to see him in so domestic a setting.

Saturday, 19 August

When the doorbell rang, I took in a gulp of air, brushed my skirt to smooth out imaginary creases, and hoped my nervousness wouldn't show upon seeing Mr Ikemoto. I needn't have worried. Having arrived at the same time, Mr Ikemoto was trying to help Miyo with her bags as she struggled to release her little baby from her back. There was much shuffling and neither of them even noticed that I had opened the door.

Once they entered, I cooed over two-month-old Mariko, Hiro joined in the greetings, Kazu squealed 'Mi-chan, Mi-chan,' clinging on to Miyo's legs, and Amah came bouncing out with Taka on her back. Such a mêlée it was that I nearly forgot to be self-conscious.

Then Miyo knelt down to let Kazu take a look at Mariko, and Jay-jay strutted over looking as if she was about to lick Mariko's face. I instinctively bent over to hold the dog back, not noticing that Mr Ikemoto had the same reaction. For an instant, my hand accidentally brushed against his, and it was as if an electrical charge ran through my body. Mr Ikemoto was completely oblivious, happily patting Jay-jay. I felt foolishly awkward.

Fortunately, once we sat down to eat, Hiro and Mr Ikemoto sat at one end of the table, deep in conversation, while Miyo, Amah and I had to focus on helping Kazu and Taka eat Chokugetsu-ken's *shaolongbao* dumplings without making too much of a mess.

Taka suddenly banged on his highchair table, spoon in hand, gurgling 'Ku, ko, ku, ko!' Amah looked on proudly. 'Baby vely clever. He say *kekou*, he likee food!' Trust Amah to interpret Taka's gurgling as the Chinese word for 'delicious'. Kazu looked curiously into his brother's face, imitating the 'ku, ko' sounds, which encouraged Taka to shout even louder.

Watching with an amused smile, Mr Ikemoto said, 'Takao-kun seems to know it's his birthday. He's a very intelligent little boy.'

In the next breath, he added, 'How nice it is to be in this happy family setting. My own son is almost exactly the same age as Takao-kun, and although he's in Japan, it's as if I am given the privilege of celebrating his birthday here as well.'

It felt as if a stone became stuck in my throat, and I was grateful that Hiro was sitting next to Mr Ikemoto, and responded in his typically unaffected way. 'Oh, where is your home in Japan?'

While the men talked about various Tokyo locations, I tried to digest the revelation that Mr Ikemoto had a wife and son back in Japan. Why did I find it so shocking? It was my reaction that bothered me, more than the fact that he was married. What had happened to me?

The rest of the afternoon passed in a haze. Miyo retreating into Kazu and Taka's bedroom, where baby Mariko was just awakening. Hiro and Mr Ikemoto sitting in the living room having coffee, me joining in from time to time, but managing to run in and out of the kitchen on some pretext or other. The guests leaving, looking content, saying what a splendid time they had, Mr Ikemoto protectively escorting Miyo and baby into the lift, and then disappearing as the lift doors closed.

Monday, 28 August

'They've named the boat *Shinyo* – the *kanji* characters for "quaking sea",' Hiro said, talking about the type of boats his factory would be building.

'Ours will be a later model they're still designing, but the early version of these special attack weapons will be going into mass production.' He let out a wary sigh before turning to his paper.

Hiro's sigh suddenly brought home the meaning of 'special attack weapon' – a weapon made up by both the boat and the person in it. Was the war prospect for Japan getting this desperate? A shudder went through my spine.

The papers never mention defeats or lack of materials, every article geared towards rallying the Japanese fighting spirit – the calls for avoiding extravagance, saving for emergencies, the highlighting of weakness and moral degeneration of the enemy. But, come to think of it, could it all be intended to prepare us for further sacrifices, including deliberate loss of human life? How I wish for peace to come, for the war to end before any special attack weapons are put into use.

19

Sunday, 3 September 1944

Shortly after Hiro left for the factory, the phone rang. It was Mr Ikemoto inviting us to the Tricolore Coffee House on Nanking Road as a 'thank you' for Taka's birthday party. 'It's not a fancy place, but the coffee is good. Would you and Mr Kishimoto be available around 3 o'clock this afternoon?'

Ignoring my beating heart, I spoke slowly and deliberately. 'Hiroshi is at work today and will not be able to make it, but I can come, if that is all right with you.'

I surprised myself with my boldness, but it was a result of some soul searching. The shock I'd felt upon learning that Mr Ikemoto was a married man had completely thrown me, and made me realize I had developed an infatuation. So exciting it had been, my naïve attraction to him! But that wasn't what I was seeking. I now felt tender sympathy and respect for a man parted from his wife and son, devoting himself to Christian activities in time of war. I wanted to get to know him better, to become a friend.

I cycled along Bubbling Well Road to the centre of town, not entirely comfortable with the prospect of spending an afternoon alone with Mr Ikemoto. The Tricolore was easy to find, with its red, white and blue, French-style awning partially covering the pavement. The colours had faded, giving the place a well-established feel. Before walking in, I smoothed out my skirt and hair, and took in a deep breath.

The place was crowded, filled with the aroma of coffee and cigarette smoke. I looked around, and found him standing by a corner table, waving at me with his reassuring smile. We exchanged Japanese bows and greetings and settled down to order. I followed his recommendation for a Viennese coffee, not realizing until later that the creamy mixture of coffee and chocolate had a shot of some liqueur, perhaps helping me feel even more relaxed and expansive throughout the afternoon. He himself ordered a plain black coffee. The conversation flowed easily. I wanted to know about his wife – how they had met, how long they'd been married, etc. – but I asked about his son. 'His birthday is only a week after Takao-kun's, and his name is Kazuya – so similar to Kazuo-kun's. I cannot tell you how thrilled I was to be at your home the other day,' he said.

In the next instant, he was looking out of the window longingly. He softly said, 'I haven't yet met my son, but I know he was born healthy, and am confident that both he and my wife are doing well.'

'My wife, Haru, is made of sturdy stuff. I met her a month after I arrived in Peking in 1938, when she came to work at a social settlement in the slums, run by the Japanese Christian Women's Association,' he went on. They both taught at the Sunday school for a few years before marrying in 1942 when he was twenty-nine and she twenty-five.

I felt a pang of jealousy, not towards his wife, but because it sounded so romantic, getting to know each other while both being involved in good works, far away from home.

'The wedding itself was simple. A Japanese minister from our local church married us, and then we had a reception at the Peking YMCA. The weather was nice, and our friends, of various nationalities, decorated the garden with streamers and provided wonderful food and drink.' I listened intently, again, almost with envy towards the casual, warm-sounding wedding so different from my own elaborate, stiff three-day affair.

'The end was the unusual bit,' Mr Ikemoto said, eyes dancing. 'I had a teacher at the College of Chinese Studies called Dr Hayes, who was a second generation American missionary. He had a Model T Ford, to which he tied many red ribbons with empty cans attached, and drove us back to our living quarters, making quite a racket. All the guests cheered and applauded as Dr Hayes slowly drove us the short distance. It was like being in an American film.'

'But our wedding was after Pearl Harbor, and Japan was requisitioning enemy property,' Mr Ikemoto continued, casting a quick glance to see who might be around us. The closest table to us was occupied by a group of well-dressed Chinese ladies chatting away, and beyond was a table with two elderly Eastern European-looking gentlemen. Mr Ikemoto and I exchanged silent smiles as the Chinese ladies burst into a high-pitched laughter, bringing frowns onto the gentlemen's foreheads.

Lowering his voice nonetheless, he said, 'To retain the College, Dr Hayes took precautions and entrusted it to the Japanese YMCA in Peking, appointing me as custodian. It was a matter of formality and everything was run the same. But then, in early 1943, Dr Hayes was sent to an internment camp outside of Peking.' I immediately thought of Keith and Joyce and little Anna May, and momentarily closed my eyes.

'I hope I'm not boring you, talking about myself all the time,' Mr Ikemoto said.

'No, no, I was just reminded of close friends who are in a camp not very far from here, and yet, for all practical purposes, they are a world away.' We focussed on our coffees, each absorbed in our own thoughts.

'Yes, I think of Dr Hayes all the time,' Mr Ikemoto said shortly. 'He was very tall, close to 190 centimetres. We used to play tennis together, and I could never return his serves. I would love to see your husband play with Dr Hayes.'

After Dr Hayes went to camp, the Japanese military accused Mr Ikemoto of illegally appropriating enemy property, and he and his wife were ordered to move out of College housing.

'The real motive was to get rid of us because the Army wanted the College premises for their officers,' he continued. 'And that wasn't the end of it. A few days later, the *kempei* came to arrest me, and confiscated most of our personal belongings, including all the wedding presents. They said nothing about the charge of illegally taking enemy property, but accused me of being loyal to the YMCA, and having done nothing for the Japanese Emperor.'

Although never tortured physically, he was in solitary confinement during two weeks of interrogation, and on the fifteenth day, was handed his sentence. He was found guilty of appropriating enemy property, and ordered to return to Japan in four days' time.

'I was forced out of China with Haru, who was four months pregnant by then,' he said. Once back in Japan, he thought he would be returning to Peking before long, but the YMCA transferred him to Shanghai. His wife being close to giving birth, he came on his own, for the family to join him later.

'But it's too dangerous to travel between Japan and Shanghai now,' he said. I let out a long sigh of sympathy.

He looked straight into my eyes. 'I am lucky to have met you, Kishimoto-san. You are a person of great understanding and compassion. It must be your upbringing and your sound family life that gives you the wisdom and poise for someone so young. I have great respect for your husband, Kishimoto-san, too.'

I was deeply moved but not sure how to react. 'Ikemoto-san, I wish you would call me Eiko instead of Kishimoto-san. Otherwise, I wouldn't know if you're referring to me or my husband,' I managed to say.

He let out a hearty laugh. 'In which case you must call me Akira.'

It was time to go. As we parted, we addressed each other as 'Akira-san' and 'Eiko-san' in a most natural way, as if it had always been so.

Tuesday, 19 September

Feeling the need to do something worthwhile, I decided to cycle to Hongkew to deliver baby clothes to Miyo and baby Mariko. The beautiful early autumn weather was uplifting until I noticed the deterioration in the streets – more hawkers and beggars at every corner of the dirt-strewn pavements and general tension in the faces I passed.

As I went deeper into Japanese Hongkew, I happened upon an opening in the midst of a commercial area, where people were digging what looked like a big pond. The diggers were mostly Japanese women, dressed in *monpe* with tea towels wrapped around their heads. Spotting an elderly Japanese gentleman standing by, I dismounted my bicycle to ask what was going on.

I thought I was being polite and respectful, but the man looked at me with disdain, eyeing me from top to bottom before responding.

'Oku-san, where on earth have you been? This project to dig a reservoir for fire prevention has been going on for a while now. You should be in your *monpe* digging too, instead of cycling around in your pretty skirt and blouse!'

Shamed, I lowered my throbbing head in a deep apologetic bow. My cheeks burned with humiliation as I cycled through the rows of low-rise terraced houses off Woosung Road in search of Miyo's building, feeling marginally soothed by the sight of clothes drying on poles sticking out from upstairs windows, creating a canopy across the narrow lanes.

'Yes, the whole of Japanese Hongkew is becoming increasingly self-righteous,' Miyo said, when I told her of the incident. 'We're organized into neighbourhood groups to keep an eye on each other. I suppose it makes sense during emergencies, but so many people use it as an excuse to criticize each other for not being patriotic enough.'

She pointed to her outfit of *monpe* and a coarse cotton top. 'Oku-sama, if I didn't wear these, there would be no end of talk by neighbours.'

With motherhood, Miyo seemed to have gained an added layer of calm and composure. She had prepared for me a simple but delicious lunch of soba noodles garnished with deep fried *tempura* vegetables, which we ate as Mariko slept in a basket by Miyo's side.

'I had word from Tanaka that he is due for leave in two weeks' time,' she softly said, after a sip of broth. It was typical of Miyo to mention such an important event simply in passing.

'How exciting for you, and for Tanaka-san to come home and see his daughter for the first time!' I said, thinking of Akira, who had yet to see his son.

Miyo smiled brightly, showing for the first time how much she was missing her husband. I made a mental note to I get something special for Miyo before Tanaka-san's leave.

Tuesday, 26 September

I rang Cheeko to ask if the grocery van driver still kept things in his front seat, thinking of getting a box of chocolates for Miyo and her husband. '*Maa* Eiko-san, you surprise me with unexpected questions,' Cheeko chirped. 'Yes, he seems to have even more secret things these days as the shortages spread. But not many people know, Eiko-san, so be careful.'

Cheeko met me at the van with a smile, but more subdued than usual. 'Taro was kicked off his bicycle, and hit with stones yesterday,' she said. 'He still went to school today – the teachers wouldn't take kindly to him being absent, they'd just see him as lacking the fighting spirit.'

She let out a big sigh. 'It's the war situation. The Chinese know that things aren't going well for Japan, and they're getting bolder in their hostility towards the Japanese. I suppose Taro, so obviously Japanese in his school hat, is an easy target.'

'It's so strange, Eiko-san. Daisuke is always hanging out with his Chinese opera friends, and more often than not, is mistaken for being Chinese. And then we have Taro, being beaten up by the Chinese.' She cocked her head and gave me a sad smile.

Wednesday, 4 October

I went to the Cathedral for a YMCA lecture, and was introduced to the pretty, young woman who arranges the flowers. 'Eiko-san, I want you to meet Shinoda Keiko-san, who works at the Yokohama Specie Bank,' Akira said, inviting me to join them at their lunch table. Upon my approach, she jumped up from her chair, and gave me a deep bow, eyes cast down in shyness.

Her timidity was surprising, so different from my earlier impression of her. 'You must know Rokuro Yamanaka, my brother-in-law, who was at the bank until he moved to Nanking in April,' I said, in an attempt to put her at ease.

'Yes, he was very kind to me in the office,' she said in a tiny voice, still shy and stiff, but catching glances at me when she thought I wasn't noticing.

Akira looked at her tenderly and said, 'Keiko-san, what's happened to you, the chatterbox who can talk even while sleeping.'

To this she giggled, and said, 'Oh Ikemoto-san, don't tease me.' He managed to break her shyness, revealing an inner liveliness and sense of humour under her delicate appearance. 'It's just that I had heard so much about Mrs Kishimoto, both from you and from Mr Yamanaka. I thought she'd be an imposing grand lady, but she's much younger than I thought and very beautiful.'

I couldn't help wondering what Rokki had said about me.

'Keiko-san's parents are long time YMCA members from my Peking days, and I've known Keiko-san since her middle school years,' Akira explained. 'I used to be so jealous of her fluency in Chinese. We did so many things in those days, even turning the tennis court into a skating rink during the winter.' His eyes sparkled from fond recollections.

'I remember you falling flat on your bottom,' Keiko said.

Ignoring her comment and looking at his watch, Akira said, 'It's lecture time soon. We'd better eat up our "sauce with hot spices over rice".' With a mischievous smile, he pointed at our plates of Japanese-style curry. 'We aren't supposed to call the dish by the name we know it – an enemy word.'

Keiko and I sat together during the lecture, which was on the Chinese economy during the Ming period, given by an exceedingly dull old professor. All I remember is exchanging looks with her and suppressing giggles whenever we became totally lost. To think that less than two months ago, I felt jealous seeing Akira and Keiko together!

Friday, 13 October

The weather has cooled suddenly, and Kazu is down with a cold and runny tummy. I'm writing my journal in his room as he sleeps, while tough little Taka is out in the courtyard with Amah.

According to today's paper, the Chinese are keen to learn Japanese and are applying in droves to take the language certificate exam. How it made me think of Shin-tsu – so upset when the teaching of Japanese became obligatory in Chinese schools. 'Eiko-san, don't believe paper!' I could hear him say, with an earnest expression on his handsome face.

This moment of quietude brings all sorts of unsettling thoughts to mind. Although Akira was half joking about not saying the word 'curry', I wonder how strictly the non-use of enemy words is being enforced. Here I am, scribbling away in English, but should I be concerned? I couldn't imagine writing my diary in any other language given my shaky Japanese, but am I safe doing so? Images of the *kempei* raiding Chinese homes in search of forbidden goods flicker across my mind. And Akira, interrogated for two weeks in solitary confinement, for simply carrying out his duties at the YMCA. Writing in a banned language would probably be considered a far greater crime.

But I could never stop writing – my diary being my precious companion. It angers me that I have to be concerned just to pursue a private, harmless activity.

Wednesday, 18 October

Café Deedee on Avenue Joffre was bustling with activity, a mixture of peoples and languages creating a reverberating din and waiters squeezing between tables with plates of Russian *piroshkis* and blinis – as if curfews, blackouts and air raids belonged to another world. I had looked forward to my lunch with Mona, and thought the convivial atmosphere perfect. But over lunch, Mona had little to say. As she wrapped her scarf over her head, preparing to walk out into the cool autumn air, I felt a wave of disappointment that our meeting was ending so soon.

Once out of the door, though, she slid her arm through mine, just like Tamiko used to do, and said, 'Shall we stroll around the area for a while?'

'There were so many people in there, I didn't want to go into any opinionated conversation,' she said, with an impish shrug of her shoulders. 'Isn't it curious that some places remain in a bygone age despite all the changes that are happening around us?'

I realized that Mona was better tuned into the times than me.

'I had an unpleasant brush with a neighbour, perhaps that's what's making me so cautious,' she said. 'As the war encroaches on our daily lives, people can get quite nasty. This neighbour, sensing that we are better off than her, made a stinging remark about us pandering to the enemy.'

I leaned closer to her, expecting more on what her neighbour had said. Instead, she seemed lost in her thoughts, and then suddenly said, 'I'm thinking of Wang Ching-wei, who is now very ill in Japan.' Her mention of Japan's favoured Chinese leader took me by surprise.

'Did I ever mention to you that he was a friend of my father's?' she went on. 'Unlike my businessman grandfather, my father became a scholar and poet, totally non-political. He got to know Wang Ching-wei in Paris, when they were both in their twenties, and remained in touch over the years. Wang is still a good-looking man, but he was stunningly beautiful when in good health.'

'There was vicious infighting among the Nationalists at the time, so my father probably provided a welcome distraction for Wang,' Mona said, shuffling fallen leaves with her feet. 'He used to talk to my father about his passions – very openly, probably because Wang believed a fellow poet would understand. Wang was an accomplished poet, and my father liked him very much.'

'It's very sad, how Wang is now vilified,' she said with a sigh. She explained that after the outbreak of the Sino-Japanese war, Chiang Kai-shek started consolidating his power within the Kuomintang and Wang was side-lined. 'But Eiko, in terms of carrying on the nationalist and democratic ideals of Sun Yat-sen, my father always believed Wang was the purer of the two.'

She cast me an apologetic smile, and I knew she was going to refer to Japan – which I didn't mind. 'It was a time when, tragically for the Chinese, Japan was gaining ground. There was the bloody battle of Shanghai in the summer of 1937, and that December, Japan took Nanking. Peking had already fallen.'

'What Chiang Kai-shek did then, is what made Wang think differently,' she said. 'In order to slow the Japanese advance, Chiang destroyed the dykes of the Yellow River, even though he knew that meant wiping out Chinese towns and villages and killing masses of people.'

According to Mona, that was what made Wang believe that the only way to end the suffering of the Chinese people was to make peace with Japan. So he broke from Chiang at the end of 1938 to negotiate with Japan.

'Chiang now has the upper hand, and Wang is seen as a traitor by many Chinese, but I don't think Wang ever believed he was selling out,' Mona said softly.

Listening to Mona helped me understand Hiro and Rokki's favourable view of Wang, and even Shin-tsu's disdain for the man.

'Wang Ching-wei was too much of a poet and an optimist, I suppose,' Mona sighed. 'Chiang wasn't going to let him easily take over the Nationalist leadership through peace with Japan. Chiang even sent agents to assassinate Wang, although fortunately Wang survived. What he hadn't anticipated was being strung along by the Japanese, who never gave him enough authority to become a true leader.'

Mona went back to shuffling leaves with her feet. 'Anyway, Wang is very ill now, and I get the feeling that, with the war not going well for Japan, everyone is busy looking out for themselves. Have you heard about the latest fashion among the rich Chinese *tai tai*?' she said, suddenly changing her tone.

'They wear black capes and lots and lots of jewellery,' she chuckled. 'The ultimate is to have the cape held fast at the neck with thick, double-gold chains. They even play mahjong dressed like that. Can you imagine, four glittering black crows, their arms reaching from under their cape wings to clack and reshuffle the tiles!' I quickly covered my open mouth, which she took as a gesture of amused astonishment.

'Oh Eiko, you don't know the half of it! The gold and the jewels, they're not just for show. They are the most transportable assets in a war situation. I'm sure high-powered Chinese are acquiring as much as they can for future eventualities.'

Of course! It now made sense – Midori was just like one of the crows. I quickly told Mona about Midori's strange visit, and the way the Maos had changed. I'd expected her to be critical, given her seeming disdain for the 'wheelers and dealers'. Instead, she spoke with concern.

'Eiko, your friends must be going through very insecure times. The outcome of the war is becoming more and more uncertain. If – I'm just saying this hypothetically – Japan should lose the war, people who have been supporting the losing side will have to face the consequences. The closer they are to the Nanking government, the harsher the outcome will be. I'm talking about Chinese treatment against the Chinese.'

She softly added, 'Even for us, the fact that S.P. works at St John's could be held against us. My horrible neighbour is just a foretaste of what could happen.'

Wednesday, 25 October

At breakfast, Hiro's newspaper displayed a huge bold headline: 'Battle clouds gathering – heading for decisive victory in the Pacific!'

'Do you think that's true?' I asked. Hiro looked up, appearing surprised by my question. I suppose it's not often that we discuss what's happening in the war.

'I don't know about "decisive victory", but there seem to be developments in the Pacific. We're getting pressure to speed up our boat production. The Americans are pushing towards the Philippines,' he said, munching on his toast, with only a trace of a frown.

Thursday, 26 October

When I arrived at St Marie Hospital this morning, Agnes was in the visitors' lounge seated between Mr Ly and Dr Tang, all three of them hovered over a paper. I sensed a flicker of concern in Agnes's expression when she spotted me, but she warmly waved me over. Apart from deep concern in her eyes, she looked stronger with good colour in her cheeks.

'Eiko dear, we were just reading this piece in the English-language newspaper,' she said, taking my hand.

Professor Tang offered me a chair, and adjusting his spectacles, softly said, 'I don't know if you have heard this news yet. Let me read it to you.' The solemn expression on the three of them sent a shiver down my spine even before he started:

The Shikishima unit at the Kamikaze Special Attack Corps, at 10:45 hours on October 25, 1944, succeeded in a surprise attack against the enemy task force including four aircraft carriers.

I blinked blankly before it hit me: the *tokkō* suicide missions had begun. I felt my blood drain away, making me numb and cold. Agnes gently put her arm around me.

Mr Ly turned the pages of the newspaper. 'Here is a bit more – an explanation of the term *kamikaze*. It says that when Kublai Khan attempted to conquer Japan in 1281, the gods created powerful typhoons that prevented the Mongol would-be invader from reaching Japanese soil, hence the divine winds – *kamikaze*. Did you know of this word, Eiko?'

'Yes, everyone in Japan from childhood is told about how the *kamikaze* saved Japan from Mongol invasion,' I muttered. But human pilots weren't divine wind, even if they were to save Japan from defeat. I couldn't help thinking of the mothers of the young boys sent on the missions – like Cheeko, if Taro were a bit older. And I thought also of Hiro's boats, whether they, too, will have to come into use for the same kind of missions.

Agnes took my hand again. 'As we are a nice little group here, let us sit in silence and have a small Meeting of Worship.' We sat together for a good half an hour, during which none of us spoke, but were united in common prayer. As I walked home, I realized how fortunate I was to have learned about the *kamikaze* missions in the presence of the Quakers.

Thursday, 2 November

I rang Cheeko, and we arranged to meet for lunch at the Holy Trinity Cathedral.

As we entered the café, I noticed how unusually subdued Cheeko was. 'The recent *kamikaze* missions, Eiko-san, those pilots who give up their lives are Taro's biggest heroes now. They are glorified at morning assemblies, and the students and teachers talk all day of their bravery, how they are taking Japan towards victory.'

'Taro's "patriotism" mounts by the day. The school has Army and Navy officers as instructors now and they pound in a military education. Taro's mind is full of ideals – liberation from Western imperialism, Greater East Asian Co-prosperity, fatherland, and the Emperor.' Cheeko's normally high-pitched voice seemed a range lower.

'What I am most worried about, Eiko-san, isn't Taro. He's too young. It's Osamu, my brother. I really fear for his future assignments.' I recalled the fresh image of the young, dashing cadets lined up on the cargo ship, giving me hope for Japan's future. Were they all to be involved in these missions?

We momentarily focussed on our piping hot *udon* noodles. After a sip of the broth, Cheeko said, 'It's perfectly seasoned, what in Japan they'd call "taste of mother's cooking" – something those young pilots will never experience again.'

She cocked her head with a wan smile. 'I suppose glorifying the *kamikaze* isn't such a bad thing. At least the mothers can be consoled that their sons died as heroes for a just cause. Believing so might be the only way to accept the situation.'

As we were emptying our noodle bowls, Keiko Shinoda came rushing over. 'Mrs Kishimoto, the bank is holding a meeting of regional senior officers in two weeks' time, and we are expecting Mr Yamanaka to be there. I thought you'd like to know he'll be in Shanghai soon.' I was grateful that our lunch ended with something to look forward to.

Wednesday, 8 November

Kazu's fourth birthday. I invited children from the courtyard, ten in all including our boys: an impromptu gathering well attended by mothers and children. Perhaps it was the rare treat of having cakes and snacks, or everyone feeling the need of a distraction from the recent gloomy news – whatever it was, the party was a noisy, jolly event, children running all over the flat, creating mayhem, mothers chatting and laughing. I am exhausted from the noise and commotion, but in a contented way.

Monday, 13 November

The papers report that Wang Ching-wei died three days ago in Nagoya, Japan. Had Mona not talked about Wang when I last saw her, this news might have passed me without much thought. But Mona's description of the young handsome Wang, a passionate idealist, developed in me a deep sympathy, perhaps also because the young Wang reminded me of Shin-tsu. A bit ironic because Shin-tsu would hate being likened to Wang Ching-wei, in his mind a puppet of the Japanese, and a major cause of friction with his father. But Wang had a dream, which was scuttled by circumstances and perhaps misguided instincts. His death saddens me.

What, I wonder does Wang's death mean for Japan? The papers are not helpful in answering such questions.

Thursday, 16 November

Midori rang and asked if she could come over. I immediately wondered whether it had anything to do with Wang Ching-wei's death. Or had she somehow found out that Rokki was going to be in town?

She was no longer wearing a black cape, but her jewellery was noticeable, especially after she took off her gloves to expose no fewer than three glittering rings. She must have followed my glance, for she folded her hands and wanly commented, 'Safer on my fingers than anywhere else.'

'You both looked well when I ran into you in the summer. How is Mr Mao?' I asked, not quite sure what to say.

'Yes, we saw you right after the Wang government was given more powers by the Japanese. You caught Wen-tsu at a good moment, when he thought things would brighten. I'm afraid it's gone from bad to worse since then,' Midori said, eyes averting mine.

'There's now a kind of desperation in the Wang camp, aware that if Chiang Kai-shek wins the war, they will all be labelled traitors. Ironically, there's wild partying, drinking and gambling going on, as if there's no tomorrow. At the same time, people are double-crossing and denouncing each other.' She sighed.

'Wen-tsu's a fighter, and he's certainly in on the game of partying and scheming. But Eiko-san, as I said to you before, ever since Shin-tsu's disappearance, he's lost purpose. He's playing the game for the sake of playing, and I even wonder if he cares about the outcome.'

'What makes you say that?' I asked, the image of the self-assured Mr Mao still fresh in my mind.

'Three things happened to Wen-tsu, any one of them a significant blow to a normal person. But Wen-tsu appears not to feel anything. I sometimes wonder whether he goes upstairs and joins his other wives in their smoking sessions.' I'd almost forgotten how Midori could be wryly blunt. It was different from her recent edgy hardness, which seemed to have disappeared.

'The least of the three bad things to happen was that I've been dropped by my Chinese *tai tai* circle and can therefore no longer be of any use to Wen-tsu in collecting Nanking gossip. I'm frankly surprised they included me, a Japanese, among their group to begin with, but of course Wen-tsu appeared more powerful then. This has now given Wen-tsu the excuse to ignore me completely.'

'The second set-back was that Wen-tsu's main ally in the Wang government abandoned ship. One day, he simply tells Wen-tsu, "I'm becoming governor of my home province. I need a territorial base so that I'll have something to bargain with Chiang Kai-shek at war's end." Can you imagine, Eiko-san, this man is basically saying that war will end in Chiang's victory and he needs to prepare to save his skin.'

Midori recounted these grim realities in a matter-of-fact way, reminding me of her straightforward, analytical powers. I knew she was being truthful, with no hidden agenda, and felt more comfortable with her.

She suddenly covered her face, and took in a deep breath. 'The third happening, Eiko-san, is the worst, the one that makes me worry most about Wen-tsu's state of mind. You remember I had told you he had a new mistress. I didn't like it one bit, seethed with anger at times. But I knew he was happy, he carried a certain glow.'

'It turns out that the young woman was an agent, probably from a splinter Nationalist group. Wen-tsu was so enamoured though, he failed to suspect anything until it was almost too late. She set a trap.' My eyes widened. Midori noticed, but continued on.

'Fortunately for him, she was clumsy, becoming too agitated when her accomplices, who were probably going to take Wen-tsu away, didn't show up at the restaurant at the arranged time. Wen-tsu's sixth sense suddenly kicked in, he excused himself to go to the men's room, and escaped from the back door.' I sat back, eyes closed, feeling spent.

'That's not the end, Eiko-san. Wen-tsu immediately used his powers to have the girl eliminated. Yes, killed.' My mouth dropped open.

'And he's not shown a trace of sadness or remorse or anything. As if losing Shin-tsu made him lose all emotion.'

I could think of nothing to say. We sat in silence.

'Oh Eiko-san, how I long for the good old days, when we went to the racetracks together. And I think of the days I spent at the Uchiyama Bookshop with Shin-tsu. I was happiest among my Japanese friends,' she finally said, with the saddest of looks.

Saturday, 18 November

Rokki was supposed to come over as soon as he got in from Nanking. We waited to start dinner, but after two hours, Hiro said we might as well eat; he wouldn't make it in time to get to his hotel before the curfew anyway. It is bedtime now, and we still haven't heard from him.

Sunday, 19 November

Rokki showed up at lunchtime, bags under his eyes. 'Sorry about yesterday. The Blue Train express took twelve hours instead of the normal seven and a half. Held up first in Chenjiang. That's where all the illegal trade between occupied and unoccupied China takes place – Nanking officials ignoring the embargo.' It was typical of Rokki to launch into political commentary before even exchanging greetings!

'Then there was a second hold-up, much longer, closer to Shanghai,' he said, remembering to take off his coat. He told us that station staff scattered along the platform the full length of the train, inspecting the sides of the coaches and under the doors, some even crawling along the tracks. Apparently, they were looking for graffiti.

'Graffiti?' Hiro asked.

'According to a Chinese officer, the guerrillas write secret messages in white chalk on trains to communicate with comrades in distant areas,' Rokki said. 'That's how they coordinate movements for planned attacks. There'd been an ambush recently, and that's probably why they were going over the train so meticulously.'

'What do you mean ambush?' I asked.

'A fortnight ago, the same Blue Train was stopped in the middle of nowhere, between Chenjiang and Nanking,' said Rokki slowly, weighing his words. 'The Japanese soldiers guarding the train were shot, and the first-class passengers were ordered off the train.'

'You could have been on that train!' I blurted. Rokki's delay yesterday was unsettling, but I had no idea that the routine train journey between Nanking and Shanghai could be so dangerous. 'What happened to the passengers?' I asked, fearful of the answer.

'Difficult to know. Of course, nothing was reported in the papers. Just rumours through the grapevine,' Rokki said. 'The attackers were most likely Communist guerrillas, and the motive money and goods. Japanese civilians are most likely exchanged for ransom. If they happen to capture someone important, they're lucky and can get big money quickly. The unimportant Japanese probably languish in captivity if no one pays for them. I don't think the Communists would kill them. They have principles and are well disciplined.'

'But the same principles and discipline are harshly applied towards people they see as traitors,' he went on, with a grimace. 'The only Chinese travelling in first class would be part of the Wang regime. They're probably taken somewhere and executed.'

I shuddered. I shook my head to erase a horrifying scenario: Mr Mao, travelling in first class, Shin-tsu among the Communist guerrillas. No, no, of course gentle Shin-tsu would never be a guerrilla fighter. But I realized that running off to a Communist base didn't mean safety, but rather, deep involvement in a dangerous struggle.

Thankfully, Hiro changed the subject. 'What was Wang's funeral like? It sounded pretty grand in the papers.'

'Yes, it was quite a show. Wang's body was airlifted from Japan to Nanking, and a huge chrysanthemum wreath arrived from the Japanese Emperor. The funeral procession was led by eight white horses, with Japanese soldiers and officials lined up in formal regalia, slowly and grandly making its way up the foothill of Purple Mountain. Aggrandisement of Wang only in death.'

Unexpectedly, Rokki scrunched his face into a smile. 'Tamiko and the girls watched, too. Sachi was excited by the Chinese national flags unfurling all over the place. The Japanese never liked public displays of the Chinese flag with its white sun against blue sky – seeing it as belittling their control over China. But on funeral day, they let everything pass. All the roads were a sea of fluttering nationalist flags.'

How I would have liked to be there with Tamiko and the girls! Such a contrast between Rokki's description of the funeral and the grim realities of the train hold-ups. It's difficult to know where the war is leading to.

Wednesday, 29 November

Went to the Cathedral for a lecture, but it had to be cancelled. 'We hadn't anticipated the trams going out of service,' Akira said, standing by the big wooden doors and apologizing to everyone who came. To me, he said, 'Eiko-san, you've come all this way. Please wait. Once I know there're no more people coming, we'll go for coffee.' I was happy to spend time with Akira instead of sitting through a lecture.

We went again to the Tricolore, sitting at the same table as before, but the scenery had changed in just two months – much greyer and gloomier. 'Winter is coming,' I said, wrapping my jumper tightly around me, feeling the early chill even inside the café.

'I don't think it's just the weather, Eiko-san,' Akira said. 'Look at those pipes sticking out of that bus. Goodness knows what it's running on, all that black smoke spewing out. Public transportation is getting so unreliable, I'll have to find lecturers who have bicycles or are close enough to walk.' He picked up the little folded card of a menu in his big hands, and eagerly checked to see what was on offer.

Although my heart no longer fluttered, I felt distinct joy being with Akira. He put me at ease while at the same time making me feel special. Comfortable in his company, I decided to have an apple strudel with my coffee. 'Just plain coffee for me,' he said, 'I've been eating too much lately.' He patted his wide middle and smiled.

'Eiko-san, I'm almost embarrassed to tell you what I do in the evenings,' he said, conspiratorially, and I could tell he enjoyed seeing my eyebrows rise. 'There are no YMCA activities in the evenings, and living alone in Hongkew can be very boring. So I go and visit my friend, who is with the *kempei-tai*.' I was taken aback to learn of Akira's association with the dreaded Japanese military police.

'Kubo is an old school friend of mine. We are very close, and our friendship goes beyond occupations,' Akira said. 'He's not a *kempei*, but a paymaster, and has to arrange *kempei-tai* parties that take place every night in the various officers' clubs. Because I'm in and out of his lodgings all the time, the guards know me, and let me in even if he's not there. I sit there, and someone comes and asks me if I'll be wanting dinner, and I say yes, and then someone comes and says the bath is ready if you wish, so I take a bath, and then the dinner arrives. Eating a full-course meal on one's own isn't much fun, but there it is, right in front of me, so I eat it all up, and then around 10 o'clock Kubo returns, in good spirits after his party and we chat. I go there almost every night.'

'It's a comfortable way to spend an evening, and I have to admit I don't feel nearly as guilty as I should. I just wonder who is paying for my meals – I've never asked Kubo.' He shrugged his shoulders and gave me an impish smile. For a man of Christian principles, there was nothing holy about him, only an appealing natural ease.

'What a convenient friend to have!' I said.

'Yes, I get to go to the cinema for free with him, too. He just shows his *kempei-tai* identity card.' After a couple of big gulps of coffee, Akira turned serious.

'It's difficult to associate Kubo with the infamous *kempei-tai*. He's an accountant doing his job. But I learn about what goes on from him, and we both feel pretty disgusted.' Apparently, there was more drinking, womanizing and extortion going on, as if there was a certain abandon in the officers' recent behaviour. Even the dinners Akira was served were surprisingly extravagant, indicating excesses within the military when Japanese civilians were facing shortages.

Staring out the window, Akira said, 'I think it was Tolstoy, writing in *War and Peace*, something to the effect that Muscovites became less serious and more frivolous with the enemy's approach; something that always happens when people see a great danger approaching.'

I hadn't read *War and Peace* so wouldn't have known, but it sounded familiar. Hadn't Midori spoken of wild partying among Wang officials, as if there were no tomorrow? Even Kazu's birthday party, I realize was gayer and noisier. I suppose we are all feeling the approach of danger and the uncertainties of the future.

20

Friday, 1 December 1944

There was ice everywhere today, and the temperature dropped to below zero. Even more to chill the spirit was the photo in today's paper of ten *tokkō kamikaze* pilots who lost their lives, seven of whom were newly recruited students. My heart nearly stopped when I saw one of the faces – such a striking resemblance to Kazu that it could have been him as a teenager. The paper extolled *kamikaze* heroism, and reported that the Americans were losing more than half of their strength: US 'quantity' overpowered by Japanese 'quality'. Were these reports meant to lift morale? Everything is terribly depressing.

Tuesday, 12 December

I dropped by at Cheeko's after buying rice cakes – an unexpected find – from the Japanese grocery van. After trying to manoeuvre my bicycle over icy roads with little mobility because of layers and layers of clothing, it was a joy to be in her home. Her hot jasmine tea and home-baked almond biscuits tasted particularly delicious.

'I don't know how you go around town on that bicycle of yours in this freezing weather,' Cheeko said, laughing at my red cheeks. 'I don't remember Shanghai being so cold in all my fifteen years here. It can't be the war changing the weather, but it almost seems as if with each crisis – first in 1932, then 1937, and now – it gets colder!'

'How are Taro and Hanako?' I asked. I heard so much about Taro, that it was easy to overlook his perky younger sister.

'They're fine, but very dark atmosphere in their schools, maybe because of all the talk about the *tokkō*. Even if they're hailed as heroes, and we hear about victories in the Philippines day in and day out, the young ones sense the desperation. I try not to think about it. It only makes me worry about Osamu. Instead, I pray for war's end to come soon,' Cheeko said with a sigh.

'Hanako said to me the other day, "Mama, I think you should be teaching me how to cook and sew. Yoshiko-chan was showing me what she learned from her mother and I want to be able to fend for myself too in case our family is caught in the fighting and separated." Can you imagine, that's the kind of things the children are talking about!'

'Hanako says almost a third of her classmates have left for Japan. Apparently that's another thing they talk about – whether to stay or leave. And this at a time when there aren't enough boats and it's become too dangerous anyway for boats to go from Shanghai to Japan because of the torpedoes! So they take the long route – train to Nanking and Peking, on to the Korean Peninsula and then finally a boat.'

'The train isn't that safe either,' I said, recalling Rokki's story of ambushes. I hadn't realized that so many people were returning to Japan.

'For many Japanese in Shanghai who run independent businesses, the grim situation calls for difficult decisions, I suppose,' Cheeko mused. 'If they can't get goods to sell, and people can't buy from them, there's no living to be made. But the situation in Japan is even worse than here. Of course people like the Uchiyamas and us, we would never leave because Shanghai is our home. Whatever the outcome of war, I'm sure there would be opportunities for us to rebuild Sino-Japanese relations.'

If the situation is really getting desperate for Japan, perhaps the military will drop its ambitions and negotiate for peace, for surely an all-out victory now seems impossible. Yes, a swift end to the war is what I hope and pray for.

Saturday, 16 December

As Kazu, Taka and I were sitting on the living room floor playing with toy trains, Chokugetsu-ken came in to announce tea with a beaming smile. 'Missy, *Conte Verde* boat up, I win bet! People see boat on water this morning, vely big, no can see dirty bottom. Tea today my treat!'

Was this a major achievement for Japan? I wondered with mixed feelings. Would it become a Japanese warship?

The boys were making a mess, happily tucking into Chokugetsu-ken's sticky Chinese sweets as he stood by watching delightedly. I didn't have the heart to prevent them eating what I feared came from some dirty street cart.

Wednesday, 20 December

The heavy bombings in the south and east areas of Shanghai yesterday made me wonder whether it had anything to do with the lifting of the *Conte Verde*. Could the Americans have aimed at the boat again? If so, not only had they missed, but ended up destroying fifty houses and wounding 100 people in a crowded Chinese neighbourhood.

The gloomy news and bitter cold weather made me determined to make Christmas a bright event for the boys' sake. A Christmas tree was out of the question, but we still had the ornaments, so Amah and I stuck bamboo sticks in a collection of glass vases to create a makeshift structure. Once we strung the lights and hung the little decorations on the bamboo sticks, it looked passable. Making sure the blackout curtains were closed although it was daytime, I tried to see if the lights worked.

And work they did! It was almost better than a tree, for the glass vases reflected the lights, catching the colours of the decorations to create a magnificent sparkling effect. Kazu and Taka sat opened-mouthed in wonderment, eyes aglow, and Amah emitted a long, 'Ahhhhh' as she knelt to the floor.

Even with the blackout, we will be able to have a moment of sparkle every day over the Christmas season.

Saturday, 24 December

There was a notice in the papers that all offices and factories are to be kept open over Christmas and New Year – 'Just as our soldiers are giving everything for victory, the civilian and production side must also work non-stop.'

At least I was able to buy two little toy cars – one each for Kazu and Taka, as their Father Christmas presents. I am willing the day to be special for them, come what may.

Sunday, 25 December

Christmas. The boys were up early, before Hiro left for the factory, and Kazu was quick to notice the parcels by the glass vases. He jumped up and down as I lit the Christmas lights, and Taka too bounced around, wriggling his bulky nappy bottom.

Urged by Hiro, Kazu first unwrapped Taka's parcel, and handed his brother a little green car. He then opened his own, carefully inspecting the little blue car. For a while, he kept glancing between his blue and Taka's green car, as if trying to decide which was preferable. Taka in the meantime began chewing his, causing Kazu to smile contentedly, no longer interested in Taka's saliva-covered mess.

How wonderful that the size of the presents made no difference to the children! Their excitement over the 'special day' was palpable. We held our hands in a little circle, and I told them that today was the birthday of Jesus, who brought joy to us, and that we should pray for everyone we loved. Kazu shouted, 'Sachi!' I said, 'Aunty Tamiko', and Kazu squealed 'Miyo!' To my amazement, sixteen-month-old Taka caught on and gurgled, 'Amah!'

By the time Hiro returned from the factory, Chokugetsu-ken had prepared a Christmas dinner, Chinese-style – roast chicken, Chinese greens in lieu of Brussel sprouts, fried rice instead of potatoes, and a soy-sauce-based gravy. Hiro claimed it was the best Christmas meal he ever had!

It might have been a perfect cosy Christmas, allowing us to forget the war - the boys in bed, us with our coffee in front of the lit Christmas lights, Jay-jay snuggled by Hiro's side. But suddenly, her ears pricked up, and we heard heavy footsteps in the corridor. They seemed to be coming our way, and the next thing we knew, there was loud knock on our front door.

Wondering whether it might be our upstairs German neigh-bours, I headed towards the door. As I approached, I felt a sudden unease – surely the Schmidts wouldn't be coming so late in the evening.

I opened the door and immediately took a step back. There were two Japanese *kempei* standing there, stretching their necks to peer inside the flat. I stood in their way to block the view, but respect-fully asked whether there was anything the matter. The older of the two, brushing his hands against the sword and pistol strapped to his uniform, glared at me condescendingly.

'We saw lights coming through your curtains. Don't you know about the blackout regulations? The smallest ray of light can be spotted by enemy planes. You should be ashamed of yourself. Next time this happens, we'll shut off your electricity.'

Both of them eyed me distastefully for a long second and then turned on their heels, clanking their weapons as they headed to the lift. I leaned against the closed door with my eyes shut, aware of the beating of my heart, and remained there until I heard the lift descend.

I went straight to the curtains to close them tight, and turned to Hiro. 'This was the problem.' He seemed relieved and smiled rather sheepishly at having made me do the dirty work. Patting Jay-jay, he muttered, 'She handled them well, didn't she.'

Saturday 30 December

I spent the last two days sorting out old clothes, as a distraction. I missed Tamiko terribly over the holiday season. Given the bit-ter cold this winter, I could almost hear her say, 'Eiko, let's collect things to take to Irma.' So that's what I did.

My bicycle wobbled with the heavy load, but the extra effort kept me relatively warm. I focussed my eyes on the crowded street immediately ahead, not wanting to see any uncollected frozen body, apparently so many more around this winter, according to Chokugetsu-ken.

Finally reaching Museum Road, I rushed up the steps, looking forward to being greeted by Irma's lively 'Willkommen, Eiko!' But she wasn't there. The Chinese lady in the office said, 'Irma has not been here for over a month. Japanese guard, Mr Goya refuses to give her pass.'

I half thought of leaving the clothes there, but decided, no, Tamiko would never allow that, I must take them all the way to the clothing distribution centre. The extra journey was well worth it as soon as I saw Irma's beaming face. 'Eiko!' *Wunderbar*! You are an *engel*, bringing us what we need most.'

It was as cold inside the clothing centre as it was outside, and everyone was wearing layer over layer of whatever they seemed to own. Irma asked the woman working with her to take over, and led me out the door, saying 'We'll go to the café round the corner.'

It was warmer in the café and I was pleasantly surprised by the lively buzz. 'See Eiko, us Europeans, we love a good gossip over kaffee, even if we spend our last penny! Everyone now talks about New Year's parties.'

Patting my hand lightly, Irma leaned over and said, 'My run-ins with Goya have become so absurd, it would be funny if only he would give me my pass. He now claims the whole world knows that the Friends Centre is only a *nom de guerre* for a "widow's club", and that I am the manageress for Shanghai!' Irma chuckled at my puzzled look.

'Eiko, he is implying that I run a brothel! Me, of all people! I am sorry to say, he is so outrageous, I answered back. And now, he does not renew my pass. He says my English is too good, it showed I am a spy for the Allies.'

I was flabbergasted. Sweet, motherly Irma, her hair even greyer and her curls running amok – this man Goya had to be worse than a mad man. I took Irma's hand into mine – how bony and dry it felt.

'*Danke*, Eiko,' she said, squeezing my hand tightly. 'Without the pass, I feel I let down so many people who count on Quakers' work. Otherwise, being stuck in the Designated Area over Hanukkah and Christmas wasn't a bad thing. There were dinners and concerts, and even if the meals were meagre and everywhere cold and cramped, the spirit of getting together was *wunderbar*. Now everyone is concocting homemade liqueurs for a merry *Silvester*. Can you imagine the hangovers on New Year's Day?' She smiled gleefully.

How I wish I could have a fraction of Irma's strength of spirit.

Monday, 1 January 1945

Were today's headlines meant to be a New Year's special to boost Japanese morale? 'Brilliant military results in Mindoro. Five *tokkō* sink ten enemy ships. Enemy plans destroyed by noble lives offered to fatherland!'

The paper went on to say that Japan's advantage was due to the strength of Japanese mothers who bring up the *kamikaze*, willing to give up all for the war, that China was weak because it lacked the spirit of self-sacrifice.

Instead of being uplifted, I feel weighed down by heavy clouds. How many mothers of *tokkō* pilots really feel willing to give up their sons? Just the thought of Kazu or Taka being in one of those pilot's shoes sends shudders throughout my body. But there *are* mothers having to go through that ordeal. Is it for their sake that the papers have to extoll their sacrifice as the source of Japan's strength? And make me feel guilty for not being able to believe in the virtue of such sacrifice? I wonder how the Quakers would resolve this wretchedness. Please God, may this year bring peace, may the sufferings of everyone affected by this war come to an end.

Wednesday, 10 January

I know the newspapers distort the facts, but I find myself pouring over them to find out what's going on. I wish Tamiko and Rokki were around – they would teach me how to better read between the lines. I don't want to pester Hiro, who is spending longer hours at the factory, and totally exhausted by evening.

I skimmed over the main feature, which was about celebrating Air Defence Day, a series of exercises carried out in various parts of the city to boost 'true fighting spirit' for Japan's victory. As my eyes idly ran down the columns, a smaller headline caught my attention. The short article reported that sixty B-29s flying from the Marianas bombed Tokyo and other major cities, causing just minor damage.

This was the first time I read of bombings of mainland Japan, and my eyes froze on the item, as if I might learn more by looking. Minor damage, minor damage, I repeated. I knew that life was harsher in Japan than here in Shanghai, where goods, however short they might seem here, were more abundant than back home. I'd also heard that the whole country was geared now for military production, even pots and pans collected for making weapons. But the war was always being fought outside of Japan. Now that's changed. I thought of Daddy and my brothers in Tokyo, and all the Kishimotos in Kobe.

Tuesday, 16 January

Hiro came home ashen faced, heaving deep breaths as he opened the door. He let out a soft 'ouch!' when I touched his left arm as I helped him take off his coat.

'A Japanese jeep knocked me over with its wing mirror. Fortunately, my satchel caught the brunt of the impact, but I might have a bruise,' he muttered.

By dinner-time, it was as if nothing had happened. After a few mouthfuls of Chokugetsu-ken's hearty fish soup, he said, 'It's so dark these days with no streetlights and cars not allowed to put headlights on. I stepped down onto the road to avoid the crowds on the pavement. That will teach me to be more careful.'

Since I am never out after sundown these days, I'd forgotten how dark the town was with the blackout. It's dim inside as well, but one gets used to it. At least Hiro wasn't hurt, but his commute is dangerous. My list of prayers grows by the day.

Sunday, 21 January

I rang Cheeko, but she was out, and I spoke to Taro instead.

'How are things with you, Taro-kun?' I asked, feeling as if I knew him, Cheeko having spoken so much about him. He sounded slightly suspicious.

'Umm. Do I know you?' he asked in a gravelly voice that sounded as if it was just breaking, making him seem even more awkward. As soon as I gave him my name, however, his tone brightened.

'Oh yes, my mother told me about you. You're the friend who comes to shop at the grocery van. How do you do.'

I was impressed by his good manners. 'Your mother has been telling me that you are busy working in the fields in addition to school lessons. It must be very hard,' I said.

'Making hay was last year. We are now working in the munitions factory four days a week. It is hard work, but I am happy to be working for Japan's victory. I hope to pass the army junior school exam in the summer and become a real soldier soon.'

I wished him good luck – what else could I do?

Wednesday, 31 January

A bitter rainy day, and the papers finally admit the dim prospects for Japan in the Philippines. If the Philippines fall, will the fighting get closer and closer to mainland Japan? I comb through the papers for news of any further bombings in Japan, but have found nothing. I pray it will remain that way.

Thursday, 1 February

Only a few minutes after he left for work this morning, Hiro came rushing back into the flat and said, 'There's a notice downstairs. The building's being requisitioned by the Army and all residents have to vacate within a week.' I blinked, taking a moment for the news to sink in.

I followed Hiro back into the lift. 'Eiko, I have to leave this to you to deal with. I'm late for the factory,' he said.

There was a cluster of residents, the Schmidts among them, huddled around the notice pinned on the wall. They were shaking their heads in disbelief, as they stared into the sign. 'Frau Kishimoto, this is most distressing. The economy in Shanghai is in a shambles. How will ve ever find anozer place to live!' Frau Schmidt wailed. She seemed to have become a shadow of the steely, composed lady she used to be.

Herr Schmidt, with his arm around her, was saying, 'Liebling, we have many friends with large houses. This is only a minor inconvenience.'

I rushed back upstairs, determined to deal with the situation systematically. I first gathered Chokugetsu-ken and Amah to explain what was happening.

'Missy no wolly. We packee everyting. Organize coolies for move. Makee new place leady fast. No ploblem,' Chokugetsu-ken said, beaming a wide smile, while Amah quietly nodded by his side. Even if it wasn't going to be so easy, his sunny attitude made me feel more positive, and I concentrated on how best to find a place to move to.

I first rang the Kishimoto office, and then Keiko at the Yokohama Specie Bank, on the off chance they might have some leads. If only Jiro were still in Shanghai, I thought – he was always so resourceful with his wide Chinese contacts. Alas, Jiro and Sayako have been in Peking for nearly two years now.

I looked around the beautiful, comfortable flat that had been our home for three remarkable years, and couldn't help feeling huge regret at having to leave so suddenly. I walked over to the table where Shin-tsu and I used to have our lessons, and gazed onto the courtyard, now so empty and grey in the bitter cold morning.

Facing the room, I let my eyes slowly wander over every detail, so as to engrave them in my memory. The elegant but comfortable sofa, the art deco mantel piece, the chandeliers. Then all of a sudden, I remembered, the furniture!

It wasn't ours, but on loan from the Bakers, the American couple who had returned to the US back in 1942. I dashed to the bedroom and rummaged through our papers kept in the bottom drawer to find the rental agreement. As soon as I had it in my hand, I sat flat on the floor in a momentary daze, overwhelmed by the amount of things that had to be done in a week – not only finding a place to live, but the packing and the sorting and the arranging of storage.

We couldn't possibly take the Baker's furniture and risk any damage during the move. Besides, with people having to leave premises in a hurry, it was most likely that wherever we ended up, there would be furniture left behind. That thought gave me a secret joy - Army officers moving into our flat and finding it empty, to their huge disappointment.

As my mind wandered in face of the daunting task before me, I felt a strange surge of energy. Before I knew it, I was up on my feet, putting on my coat to head into town. The first stop was the Kishimoto office for names of storage companies, and then, together with a young Chinese man they kindly provided to assist me, on to actual negotiations. I managed to get good terms at the third place we visited.

By the time Hiro came home from the factory, half our possessions were already packed, and arrangements made for furniture pick-up and storage. All that remains is to find a place to live. I know we will find some place that is appropriate. I feel I can will it to happen.

21

Thursday, 1 March 1945, The Picardie

Now comfortably settled in the Picardie apartments further south-west in Frenchtown, the chaos of the last month seems like a dream. The move itself was the worst: five coolie carts going backwards and forwards between the two flats, Amah and the boys at the old place, me at the new, Chokugetsu-ken on the road, all eagle-eyed to make sure the belongings were intact. Then adjusting to a much smaller space, finding amusement for the boys, getting to know the local shops – the chores were endless.

But how lucky we were to come upon this flat on the corner of Route Winling and Avenue Petain not so far from the Grosvenor House, all thanks to Keiko Shinoda. Four days before we faced eviction, she rang to say there was an available flat and she happened to have the keys. The flat had just become vacant – the widow of a Bank employee, who had been earlier conscripted, making a hasty departure back to Japan upon the death of her husband in a field hospital. Keiko looked pale and worn, having been looking after the widow, and I felt all the more grateful that she remembered our needs while dealing with the tragedy.

Surprisingly, she seemed equally grateful. 'Being able to pass the flat on to you has been a huge relief,' she had sweetly said. 'So many Japanese are superstitious and shun places associated with death.' I couldn't believe people still thought that way in a war situation.

The boys have settled easily. Culty's Milk, a nearby dairy farm, has now become the boys' entertainment, not as convenient as the old courtyard, but Amah faithfully takes them to see the cows almost every day. Kazu still remembers the old place. He surprised me by saying, 'Mama, no building!' as he looked out from our new kitchen. Children remember the oddest things. Whereas we used to look out onto the Cathay Mansions, now we see only the treetops of the park across the street.

The move has been a welcome distraction from the continuous gloomy war situation. During the time I was preoccupied with unpacking, air raids intensified over industrial areas and electricity was cut by fifty per cent. The outside world had moved on: Japan losing the Philippines, fighting shifting to Iwo Jima, and local conscription intensifying in Shanghai. I now have time to look through the newspaper and wish I were still absorbed in filling drawers.

Thursday, 15 March

Akira rang asking me to accompany him to visit Keiko Shinoda in hospital.

'It's just a precautionary measure. She's always had a weak heart, and she's been overworked lately. She always wants to do everything to perfection. People at the Bank thought sending her to hospital was the only way to make her rest,' Akira chuckled. Relieved, I jumped at the opportunity for an outing with Akira – I'd had so little time to see him lately.

The trams weren't working and the streets were even more crowded than usual. But it felt good, walking along the wide boulevards of Frenchtown instead of being squeezed into a tramcar. The leaves of the plane trees were starting to unfurl, and the sun warmed the spring morning air – so welcome after a particularly bitter winter.

When we came to a particular crossroads, Akira said, 'Look', discreetly pointing to a pretty Chinese bride dressed in a white Western-style wedding dress. She looked delightfully fresh and young, as she waited for a cluster of carts and rickshaws to pass before crossing the road towards the little church on the corner. Most of her party was already on the other side, eagerly waving for her to hurry up. We slowed our pace to admire the happy scene amidst the hustle and bustle of the streets.

Just as the bride took one step off the pavement, Akira grabbed my arm and pulled me towards him. A Japanese soldier with an 'on duty' armband came charging over, nearly colliding into me as he rushed towards the bride. My initial thought was that he was coming to help her cross the road, or prevent some accident.

But no, the soldier was actually sniggering at her as he blocked her way, poking her cheeks with a forefinger. He seemed to enjoy seeing her panic-stricken face, and continued to sneer as she froze on the spot. Then, right before our eyes, the soldier's arm started moving downwards, his hand fondling the bride's breasts and abdomen, as it slowly inched towards the bottom of her skirt.

I felt my body stiffen, and covered my mouth in horror. By then, Akira was no longer by my side, but had leapt in front of the solider, telling him to keep his hands to himself. The soldier looked astounded for an instant, but then glared at Akira and lifted his arm to strike a blow. Akira's reflex was swift and decisive. He landed a punch in the soldier's stomach, making him double over. The soldier groaned, stumbling a few steps, about to fall to the ground.

Assuming his job done, Akira turned to the bride, when the soldier half rose and plunged towards him, knife in hand. Akira bent over in pain, and the soldier scurried to his feet. Growling a stream of insults, he fled into the startled crowd.

Blood started to ooze from Akira's calf, and the bride's party was rushing from across the street. Until then, I had been watching in a stupor. But the minute I saw the blood, my body, as if suddenly awakened, went into action. Before I knew it, I was crouched on the ground, pulling up the cuffs of Akira's trousers, placing a clean handkerchief on the wound, and bandaging his leg with my scarf. 'Tightly,' I said to myself, desperate to stem the blood.

The bride, too, was on her knees, looking worriedly into Akira's face. He now seemed more embarrassed than hurt. 'It's just a small cut, nothing serious,' he said, rising to his feet. 'We should be on our way.' But an older member of the wedding party insisted that we come up to his flat in a building nearby.

Thankfully, the knife cut was small and shallow, and after a soothing cup of jasmine tea, we took our leave. Our gracious hosts expressed their gratitude to Akira, and were concerned over his injury, but tactfully, never mentioned the incident itself – fully aware that Akira and I were Japanese. In a flurry of thanks and best wishes, the bridal party rushed off again to the church, and we to the Great Western.

We spoke little during the short distance to the hospital, and as soon as we were with Keiko, the matter was put behind us. But Keiko, who looked well rested and alert as ever, astutely noticed a patch of blood on Akira's trousers.

'Oh that. I was very clumsy!' Akira said, almost too quickly, throwing her his affable smile. 'I sometimes forget my size and tried to get on Eiko-san's bicycle when I went to pick her up.'

Keiko giggled and said, 'Oh please don't make me laugh, Ikemoto-san, that's when I feel the pain around my heart!' She pressed her hands against her chest and smiled delightedly.

After leaving the hospital, Akira and I said very little. It was as if there was no need to talk – we shared the unspeakable: the anger, and the deep shame over the Japanese soldier, our countryman.

Sunday, 18 March

Hiro had a rare day off, and was taking a nap in the early afternoon when a phone call came from the Kishimoto office. My heart pounded – why would the office be ringing on a Sunday afternoon? Not meaning to eavesdrop, I couldn't help but sit absolutely still so as to catch a word, or Hiro's tone of voice from the hallway.

All I heard were occasional acknowledgements of '*Aah, so desuka,*' in between silences, and then at the end, a formal thank you for the phone call.

Hiro came into the living room looking quite shaken. 'There was massive bombing in Kobe, but the family is safe,' he said.

'Over two thousand deaths, but every Kishimoto is accounted for. No casualties among office employees either. But big damage to the warehouses.'

Having dreaded the worst, I found myself actually breathing a sigh of relief.

Monday, 19 March

The bombing of Kobe turned out to be minor compared to what had happened in Tokyo earlier. The papers had reported that many American B-29s were shot down, and I failed to read between the lines – that it meant Japan was being bombed.

From today's headlines though, even I could tell how serious it was: 'The entire population is honoured by His Majesty's tour,' the paper extolled – in fact admitting that the situation was so horrendous the Emperor had to appear in person.

The one consolation was the lack of a phone call: we'd surely be informed if something had happened to the family.

The paper has become so short – only one sheet folded over, compared to the pages and pages we used to have only a few months ago. A smaller headline read: 'Enemy Manoeuvres Nearing the Mainland' – a piece of news that sounded straightforward, as if it wasn't possible any longer to keep up all the pretences.

Thursday, 22 March

Iwo Jima has fallen. Over the last three weeks, we have been constantly told of the bravery of the Japanese soldiers, inflicting huge casualties on the Americans. But finally the paper admits that all communication was lost, filling the page with tributes to 'the heroes who gave up their lives for their country' – over 20,000 of them.

Friday, 30 March

Kimmy rang this morning out of the blue. 'Eiko, it's been ages, and I wanted to see you before we move to Nanking in two weeks' time,' she said. As soon as I heard her bright voice, speaking to me in English, I was sorry we'd had little opportunity to stay in touch. We met briefly at the Sullivan Chocolate Shop near her office, and then took a stroll into the Public Gardens – easier to talk outside of other people's earshot.

Kimmy had changed little, still lively and youthful, but I sensed sadness in her eyes. 'Our move to Nanking came about quite suddenly,' she said. 'My father doesn't talk much about it. Oh Eiko, it is so distressing, to see my active father sometimes gazing into space, looking lost. Running the cotton mills was his life, but, given the way the war is going, he knows he might lose everything.'

We chose to sit on a bench in a sunny corner, where we overlooked the Whangpoo. We silently looked far across the river, towards Pootong and the eastern shores of Hongkew, where all the major factories lay, among them Mr Noguchi's cotton mill.

'The protection Japanese businesses received from the Imperial Army is waning. I guess they have more important things to worry about – like how not to lose the war.'

Kimmy's old perkiness showed its head. 'And I have to quit my job too, but they've arranged it so that I can work in the Japanese Consulate in Nanking a few days a week. I look forward to that.'

'You might be living in the same compound as my sister then,' I said, not without a tinge of envy.

'I don't know where we'll be living, but I certainly hope I'll get to meet your sister. We've heard much about her, and my mother is particularly looking forward to having an acquaintance in the new city. You know how my mother is, she can be quite snobbish and off-putting, and doesn't adjust very quickly in new environments.' Kimmy gave me an impish smile.

'Actually though, she's been doing quite a lot for the war effort recently,' she said, looking unexpectedly solemn.

'You know the *yokaren*, the air force cadets, who are only about sixteen or seventeen years old. They used to be trained in Kasumigaura, near Tokyo. But because the bombing in Japan is getting heavier and heavier, they've been moved to Shanghai, somewhere in the suburbs.'

'Because they're so young, Eiko, some Japanese families have been recruited as volunteers to look after them at weekends. So this has been my mother's contribution to the war effort. About six or seven of them come to our house every weekend.'

'Isn't it nice having the boys over and be able to do something so worthwhile?' I asked.

'Oh yes, it is certainly fulfilling in many ways. But Eiko, this last weekend was heart-breaking, and made my mother take to her bed afterwards,' she said.

She took my arm as we stood up to walk around, taking her time to continue.

'The leader of the cadets, who's about twenty years old, asked if he could bring four young men, who had to fly off the following day. He told my mother that he wanted them to be able to spend their last evening in a pure way. I didn't know what he was talking about, but it turned out that they were members of the *tokkō-tai*.' Kimmy paused, and I swallowed hard.

'They were so young, Eiko. They didn't sleep all night. Each of them took turns to go to my mother and talk to her. They had to leave the house at 4 a.m. The cook made a lovely meal for them, including an upside down cake. Then they left on their suicide missions.'

I thought of Mrs Noguchi, how I couldn't take to her initially, with her overbearing manner. But she had contributed generously towards our troop performance, wanting to help cheer up the soldiers 'because that would make their mothers happy' – words that had stuck in my mind.

I'm sure the young pilots' mothers would be comforted were they to know that their sons spent their last night with a caring woman such as Mrs Noguchi. Would I have the mental strength to host the boys, knowing I was sharing the last precious hours of their young lives? A situation too sad to contemplate.

Sunday, 8 April

Minutes after Amah and the boys set off to Culty's Milk, I heard a panicky shout from below the open window. 'Missy, missy, pleasy come ou sai Taka cly hurtee leg!'

I rushed downstairs to find Amah hovering over a whimpering Taka, as Kazu sulkily stood by holding Jay-jay's lead. He refused to answer me when I asked what had happened. Pushing Amah gently aside, I knelt down to take a look at Taka, my heart pounding in anxiety. He was all curled up, sniffling, with one hand tightly covering his knee. I wrapped my arm around him and softly called out his name.

When he saw me, rather than Amah by his side, his body stiffened and his whimpering stopped. I removed his hand from his knee: just a small scratch with a bit of seeping blood, hardly an injury to merit Amah's panic. I saw immediately that Taka had been putting on a show for Amah. I pulled Taka's arm quite hard, and picked him up with a glare. Kazu was now inching forward, with a triumphant look.

Amah cowered, knowing the boys were about to get a scolding. As I stood firmly with hands on my hips, Taka gave me a sheepish upward glance, and Kazu stood by, biting his lips with a concerned frown. Their expressions suddenly melted my heart.

How fortunate I was to have the children around, making everyday life as normal as could be. The haunting image of the young pilots leaving Kimmy's house flittered in the back of my mind, and I couldn't help being thankful that our boys were still so young.

We walked back to the flat hand in hand, swinging our arms, a relieved Amah happily tagging along.

Tuesday, 10 April

Met up with Akira at the Tricolore this morning. 'Do you know, the Embassy is gathering people with English language ability,' he said, as soon as we sat down. 'It's peculiar, don't you think, as English has been banned these last few years.' He looked at me questioningly.

'Acknowledging the need for English sounds promising,' I ventured. When I'm with Akira, I feel comfortable expressing my opinion – he has a way of making me feel special, which gives me the confidence to say what comes to my mind.

'Perhaps Japan is starting to see sense and willing to engage in negotiations for peace. Don't wars end when one side decides to give up and seeks peace terms? Maybe it's reached that point for Japan,' I said hopefully.

Akira nodded with an impressed smile. 'Now that you mention it, it could indeed mean preparing for war's end.' We silently sipped our coffees, as we contemplated the possibility.

'I don't want to be too optimistic, but there's certainly lots to look forward to if fighting ends,' Akira said. 'At this stage, Japan probably won't get the best of terms, and there should be need to work together with former enemies towards reconstruction. Just think, Eiko-san, the YMCA might be able to resume English-language classes again soon, and then you must come and be a teacher! Keiko can be an administrator – she's well rested and out of hospital now.'

It was wonderful to think of positive possibilities, and we happily spent the rest of the time planning English-language courses for different age groups.

Saturday, 14 April

Two big headlines in today's newspaper: the death of President Roosevelt, and a huge Japanese Naval success near Okinawa, both reported as welcome news for Japan. But I sense gloom, not really believing what's reported about Okinawa, and thinking of the loss of the American President right in the middle of a war.

I couldn't say so openly, but how I loved seeing President Roosevelt's pictures in the British papers when living in London – so distinguished-looking despite his disability. After Pearl Harbor, one hears and reads only bad things about America, making it difficult to know what to think. Still, the President's death saddens me.

Wednesday, 18 April

I paid a visit to Agnes at the hospital, and to my great, pleasant surprise, found Irma there.

'Eiko Liebling, Goya is gone!' she exclaimed as soon as she saw me. 'The Japanisch higher-ups finally realized he is a madman, and his replacement has given me this!' She proudly pointed to a pink pass pinned to her chest, different from the blue one she used to have to go to the Friends' Centre.

'This is a special one-day pass to be with Agnes on her *geburtstag*.'

Agnes squeezed Irma's hand. 'The best birthday present,' she said. 'It's almost two years since Irma moved out, and I hadn't seen her since, although Mr Ly and Dr Tang and you, Eiko, have kindly kept me abreast of her news.'

Alice looked at Irma with affectionate concern. In just four months, Irma was looking thinner and greyer; the change over two years must have been a shock for Agnes.

But Irma was full of her unwavering good spirits. 'We get inklings of good news from Europe. A welcome boost, especially since the Designated Area had fallen into despair when we learned of the death of Präsident Roosevelt, a hero figure to the Jews.'

Lowering her voice, she said, 'The refugees even held secret memorial services, risking trouble from the Japanisch authorities, who have set up the neighbourhood watch *pao chia* system to keep an eye on refugee activities.'

'Sad as the Präsident's death is, most refugees are cautiously optimistic now. They get news from Soviet radio broadcasts, and – touch wood – it sounds like Deutschland is losing.'

She cast me an apologetic glance. 'Eiko, I am sorry, Deutschland is a Japanese ally, but Hitler is an evil man.'

Agnes took my hand and pulled me closer. 'As Quakers, we renounce war and violence and try to understand. Let's not worry about sides and join hands to pray for peace.' I did so with all my heart.

Monday, 23 April

Met up with Cheeko at the Holy Trinity Cathedral. She's taken to helping Keiko with the flowers, 'to keep my mind off worrying about Taro and Osamu,' she says. Today, she was abuzz with excitement over a Li Koran concert that was to take place in May.

'It really is just what we need, something to cheer us up. Something to look forward to,' she chirped.

Akira looked puzzled. 'It seems strange that the China Film Company would want Li Koran to give a concert,' he said. 'They've been careful not to appear pandering to Japanese interests, and Li is the darling of Japanese audiences.'

'That's the thing, Ikemoto-san,' Cheeko said. 'The China Film Company stopped making films altogether. The wonderful Chinese director they had, Chang Shan-kun, the one who managed to get Chinese big movie stars to work with him - he disappeared. Into thin air! So the company's disbanded, and the skeleton Japanese staff decided on the Li concert.'

'Oh! Won't there be any more China Film Company movies?' Keiko asked, as she stuck a lily into a vase. She was still somewhat pale, but her eyes shone with alertness. 'A concert won't be the same as those wonderful films. I loved the Peking accents, which enhanced the romantic atmosphere.'

'I know what you mean,' Cheeko said. 'Such a shame that Chang is gone. They say he'd been a target of *kempei-tai* suspicions for having ties with the Chiang Kai-shek government. Daisuke thinks he's escaped into unoccupied parts of China before anything horrible could be done to him. You know how it is these days, defections and suspected defections, people being eliminated.'

I was surprised to hear Cheeko speak of the same kind of things Midori had mentioned, and was reminded of her political astuteness.

'With Chang gone and some of the Japanese producers called up, Mr Kawakita, the Japanese head of the Company, told all non-essential Japanese staff to go back to Japan,' Cheeko continued. 'After the Li concert, Daisuke says Mr Kawakita will move the company to Peking, since the Americans are more likely to invade Shanghai than Peking.'

'Cheeko-san, you are remarkably abreast of what's going on,' Akira said.

'Am I?' she asked with a pleased look. 'I'm just repeating what Daisuke says, and he is always spending time with his Chinese theatre friends so I suppose he gets all sorts of information that most Japanese don't have.'

'Anyway, there's to be this Li Koran concert in mid-May at the Grand Theatre on Bubbling Well Road. We should all plan to go together. Wouldn't that be fun?' Cheeko said, humming the tune of 'China Nights', Li's signature song.

Akira laughed. 'Cheeko-san, count me in!'

And I'll go too, I thought, if Akira was going. It really would be something to look forward to.

'Is Li Koran Japanese?' Keiko suddenly asked.

Akira turned thoughtful. 'You're right to ask, Keiko-san. It's an uneasy time for Chinese who are close to Japan. Extremely brave and bold for a Chinese performer to hold a Japan-backed concert.'

'There have always been rumours that Li is actually Japanese,' Cheeko said. 'Or it could be that she's Chinese but too easily manipulated, and agreed to the concert. Or maybe she just wants to please her fans. Perhaps she's simply an innocent in a complicated world.'

For some reason, Li Koran reminded me of Midori. Midori certainly wasn't an innocent, but their vague identities – either Chinese or Japanese – and being caught in intricate politics, brought the two together in my mind. Perhaps because of Akira's mention of uneasy times, I can't shake away a sense of danger associated with them.

Thursday, 26 April

A call from Akira right after breakfast saying he received his call-up letter. I stood in the hallway, completely numb. It couldn't be true, I'd just been with him yesterday. I felt the blood drain from me, feeling sorrier for myself than for him – again, someone dear to me being taken away.

How had Tamiko reacted when she found out about Masaya's conscription? I imagined her being a source of strength to him – yes, she had taken him to a Quaker Meeting. Certainly not whining about her misfortune.

'If there's anything I can do to help you prepare, I would like to,' I managed to say.

'That would be wonderful. I don't have much time to prepare, so your offer is most appreciated. I'll let you know what I might need, and it will give me an opportunity to see you before I leave. That will give me great pleasure.'

He spoke in his usual genial way, no different from normal, and I could practically see the warm smile on his face, eyes nearly disappearing under his heavy eyelids.

Sunday, 29 April

Of all things Akira wanted me to get for him, it turned out to be *gētoru* fabric! At least I knew what it was this time.

'I remember Hiroshi-san's *gētoru* from reservist training,' Akira chuckled. 'His stood out because they were so new and clean.'

'They're washed now, unused. Would they do for you?' I asked, without much thought except of the shortage of practical goods these days in the shops.

There was a short pause, and then Akira's rather hesitant words, 'If you don't mind, Eiko-san, black fabric might be better to hide the dirt. I'm not the tidy type. Hiroshi-san should keep his.'

'Of course,' I said, embarrassed for having offered Hiro's hand-me-downs. But thinking back on what he said, I realized that despite his light tone, he was gently suggesting that Hiro's turn might come in needing his own *gētoru*.

Could that happen? Would they really call up someone spending ever longer hours engaged in weapons production under pressure from the Navy? No, I couldn't imagine it.

Monday, 30 April

With mixed emotions, I set out to the Holy Trinity Cathedral to give Akira his *gētoru* fabric – wanting to see him, and at the same time dreading the farewell it was going to be.

I pedalled my bicycle with a heavy heart, and wasn't paying much attention to the street scenes around me until I reached Nanking Road. Suddenly, there was tranquillity all around – no sign of the usual throng of people, carts and pedicabs. The street had been cleared, and a huge crowd of silent Chinese stood, many people deep, along the pavement. I dismounted my bicycle and squeezed into a little gap in the human wall to follow the common gaze.

A long string of trams was trundling slowly eastwards towards the Bund, with bayoneted Japanese guards scattered along the tracks to keep the crowds from getting too close. There was no one to ask what was happening – the Chinese around me seemed like local shopkeepers with little English. I stood on tiptoe, straining to get a look inside the trams, and was struck by the lack of black heads. Everyone had grey or brown or blonde hair, some heads wrapped in scarves or tied with bonnet ribbons.

Suddenly, a Chinese man nearby leapt out and dashed along the trams, shouting, 'See Missy Duncan? Missy Duncan? See Missy Duncan and baby? Where they?' I noticed some heads in the tram turn towards the man, but he was quickly shoved back into the crowds by a Japanese guard.

The people on the tram were Westerners, and I realized that the Yu Yuen Road camp, the one near Cheeko's where the Leighs were taken, was a short distance to the west. It must be the internees being moved, I thought, and strained even harder to get a better look. It seemed there were only women and children. I desperately scanned as many windows as I could in the hope that I might see Joyce and Anna May. But it was a futile exercise – the trams were so packed, with heads and faces closely pressed that all was a blur. But where were the men?

The trams were moving so slowly I knew I could get to the Holy Trinity Cathedral before they reached the end of the line at the Bund. Perhaps Akira would have an explanation for what was going on. I went on the back roads and pedalled as fast as I could.

As soon as I found Akira, we rushed towards the Bund. There too, around the terminus, the streets were cleared and crowds were piled onto the pavements. Motorcycle-mounted Japanese soldiers with machine guns – about twenty of them – were on guard.

We stayed long enough to witness the earlier trams arrive, and watched the internees pile out. They were shoved into line as the motorcycle engines started up with a loud roar. The human column of dishevelled-looking Western women and children shuffled across Garden Bridge, machines guns aimed in their direction from the motorcycles that crawled alongside them. It broke my heart to see how weakened every person looked. Before long, Akira gently pulled my arm to lead me away. We remained silent until seated in the café back at the Cathedral.

'What can be happening?' I asked. He took a big gulp of hot green tea, and stared into his teacup before answering.

'I don't really know, Eiko-san, but I can think of possibilities. Probably not unrelated to my being called up. Japan is running short of manpower and can't afford to lose men. Judging from the direction the internees were heading, they're likely to be housed in buildings in the factory area occupied by Japanese soldiers. They probably want to move the soldiers into the Yu Yuen Road camp, which would be safer from American air raids.' I buried my face into my hands. Joyce and Anna May among those heading for even worse hardships.

At the same time, I didn't want Japanese soldiers to be bombed either; Akira would be a soldier in a few days' time. 'Can this possibly go on much longer?' I asked, not really expecting an answer.

But Akira, looking again thoughtfully into his teacup, slowly said, 'I don't know about the war in China and the Pacific, but there seem to be dramatic developments on the European front. Though not in the Japanese papers, it sounds like Germany is completely surrounded. A YMCA member heard the Soviet radio broadcast saying the Russians and the Americans and the British were comrades-in-arms celebrating the "eradication of evil".'

I stared into Akira's face. 'What does that mean for Japan?' Akira gave me a wan smile.

'I think it means that America will soon be able to concentrate on fighting Japan to bring an end to the war in China.' He flashed me his usual broad smile. 'Which may mean my time at war could be quite short.'

While being resigned to going to war, he seemed refreshingly unconcerned over the risks involved. So much like Masaya in his commitment to serve God, but without the internal torment. I was not about to let my anxieties and sadness over his departure spoil our time together.

'Thank you for the *gētoru* fabric, I will think of you every time I wrap my calves – which I suppose will be every day!' he laughed. And on this note, we stood up to say good-bye. It was a most natural, light-hearted parting, not much different from taking leave after a YMCA lecture.

Only now, has it hit me, like a rock in the stomach, that I may never see Akira again.

22

Tuesday, 8 May 1945

To fill the void left with Akira's departure, I went to the Friends' Centre to visit Irma with a few more items of clothing. I knew that being in the vicinity of the Holy Trinity Cathedral would be heart-wrenching, but at the same time, I felt the urge to see the tall, solid, red brick spire. The warm sunshine felt comforting on my cheeks as I bicycled east along Hankow Road.

Irma greeted me with a jubilant look. 'Have you heard the news? The fighting in Europe has ended! Deutschland has unconditionally surrendered. For us Jews, the defeat of Hitler is like a dream come true. There is much rejoicing in the Designated Area.'

She suddenly covered her mouth. 'Eiko Liebling I realize this may not be good news for your country.'

I shook my head, and smiled. 'It is wonderful news for you, Irma, and it may mean that war in this part of the world will also end soon. That is good news.'

Irma patted my hands. 'Yes. But in the meantime, here in Shanghai, my beauty sleep still gets disrupted with air-raid alarms, and it might get worse before it gets better.'

Friday, 11 May

There was a tiny notice in this morning's paper that Japanese men not yet called up would be summoned for ten days of military training. I didn't think it would affect Hiro because of his work at the factory. But when he came home, I learned I was wrong.

'I'm to report for duty on Monday morning,' he said. Sensing my concern, he added, 'It's for all men not called up. Better than going to war.'

But this was different from reservist training, and I couldn't help wondering whether it might be a prelude to being drafted. I must be prepared for all eventualities.

Sunday 13 May

Today, Hiro's last day before military training, was the much-anticipated Li Koran concert – Akira now missing from the party that consisted of Cheeko and Daisuke and us.

Japanese songs and some Western pieces opened the concert, followed by a collection of contemporary Chinese popular songs, which stirred the Chinese audience into audible excitement. Then came the highlight, a medley of different musical arrangements of 'China Nights'. It began in darkness, just a distant low voice singing *'ye lai hsiang'* as if to conjure up the scent of night jasmine. As the curtain went up to reveal an eerily lit stage, Li Koran mysteriously appeared, dressed in a tight-fitting pure white satin *cheongsam*. She sang the first verse in a coloratura cadenza, with no accompaniment, so soft and beautiful, shivers ran down my spine.

The next movement, with orchestra and Li Koran taking turns as if chasing each other as the music went into crescendo, the audience went wild – Cheeko practically falling out of her seat.

Remembering Hiro's excitement when he danced with Li at the nightclub, I discreetly turned to observe his expression. To my amusement, he was nodding off, oblivious to the enthusiasm around him. It must have been the dark surroundings, or perhaps the workload from the factory taking its toll. He looked relaxed and content. I found it difficult to imagine he would be gone tomorrow.

As we walked home, I teased him about his falling asleep.

'Were my eyes closed?' he asked sheepishly. 'Maybe I just tuned out for a while. The concert was a bit overdone. It grates when they try so hard to stir people, the Japanese organizers playing up to the Chinese audience. And Li Koran is prettier when less made-up.'

I, too, hadn't enjoyed the concert as much as I thought I would, and Hiro's straightforward reaction made me understand why.

Friday 18 May

Four days since he's gone, but no word from Hiro. Was it possible that he could be sent straight to war without informing the family?

I needed distraction from my worries, and took the boys to Culty's Milk. It was comforting being in a working dairy, exposed to the smells of cattle and watching the workers milk the cows – doing what they always do, war or no war. Taka was touching everything in sight, poking his fingers into any little crevice he could find, making me wince at all the germs he was picking up.

Because the boys often come with Amah, the Chinese workers shouted greetings. One, dressed in dirt-covered work clothes approached us, shaking hands first with Kazu, and then Taka, and bowing to me. 'You boys' Mama, wanchee show insai,' he said.

He beckoned with his hands towards a large barn-like structure and led us inside. Before us was a big machine that had steam coming out of one end. Kazu pointed excitedly shouting '*kemuri*!' I told him it was steam and not smoke, and we all watched in fascination as liquid milk passed over steam-heated rollers, evaporating the liquid. Two metal plates then scraped the powder off the top to make powder milk.

'You go shop can buy,' our Chinese guide said, as he shook hands again with the boys to indicate that the tour was over. Impressed with the workings of the dairy I bought a tin of powdered milk, and gave in to the boys' desire for some ice cream. A mistake, for sure enough, in the evening, Kazu ended up with a tummy ache and diarrhoea.

Thursday, 24 May

A big photo of five *kamikaze* pilots setting off to Okinawa in the paper today – heart-breaking and filling me with unease. Hiro's military training should have ended, but still no sign of him.

Friday, 25 May

The day dragged on as I waited for Hiro's return, my anxiety mounting. Could he have been injured and unable to get home? I must have been so absorbed in my thoughts, I didn't notice Jay-jay let out a little bark and rush to the front door.

All of a sudden, Kazu and Taka shouted '*Papa!*' in unison, and Hiro walked in with a smile, although his gait sagged with weariness. His foot soldier uniform looked remarkably unsoiled, even the *gētoru* nearly as clean as when he left. But there was a whiff of un-fresh rawness about his whole being, and it was Taka who identified the odd smell.

'*Papa, osakana kusai!*' he shouted as he pinched his nose. Hiro really did smell fishy.

Instead of scolding Taka, which I thought he might do, Hiro breathed out a sheepish chuckle. 'Turns out I failed the physical on the first day of training – some unintelligible diagnosis of colour blindness – and ended up peeling squid skins in the mess the entire time. Think I'll go for a good soak in the bath before dinner.'

Once he disappeared, I fell into a helpless giggling fit, from relief and the thought of him in the army mess. Hiro, who hardly ever set foot in a kitchen, and probably doesn't know how to boil water. To think he was handling slimy squid every day! I wished Tamiko was here to share the irony and laugh with me. Instead, the boys, sensing my sudden light heartedness, jumped and skipped around me.

Thursday, 31 May

Chokugetsu-ken came to me looking unusually sombre. 'Missy, no vely good news from ol flat. Uppey stair German Master and Missy comi suici.'

I hoped I'd misunderstood him.

'Their boy say shorly after Hi'ler die and Germany lose war, they takee some pill.'

I buried my face in my hands, and Chokugetsu-ken rushed into the kitchen to make me a cup of tea.

I recalled the time the Schmidts came down to our flat shortly after Taka's birth, bearing their gift of the soft blue baby blanket, which is still Taka's favourite. I saw in my mind's eye their softened expressions when they spoke of hearing Taka's cry in the distance reminding them of their granddaughter in Germany.

How were their children and grandchildren taking this tragic news from Shanghai? Was Germany's defeat so devastating to them personally? Or was it the loss of hope and pride? Such a tragedy of war. My prayers are with them.

Wednesday, 6 June

Hiro came home early and pulled me to the corner of the hallway, out of the children's earshot. 'Kobe was heavily bombed yesterday. Mother and Father are all right, but their house was burned down. They're staying with distant relatives.' Hiro shook his head as if in disbelief.

I thought of the beautiful house, where I first stayed before moving into our own rented house after the wedding. Mother Kishimoto had lovingly prepared my room in the western wing of the house, and I recalled my first walk along the long corridor that connected the western part with the Japanese wing, thinking I had never seen such a sprawling house, arranged in a way that the manicured garden with many flowering Japanese shrubs could be seen from all angles. All of it gone. I felt a big sob arising, which I quickly stemmed for Hiro's sake.

'What will Father and Mother do now?' I asked.

'I'm not sure. They'll probably move to the compound in Shukugawa, halfway between Kobe and Osaka,' Hiro said.

'It's a property of three Western-style houses that used to belong to the First National City Bank. Father was a friend of the American General Manager, who asked him to buy the compound before war broke out,' he explained, realizing I had no knowledge of the property. 'The Americans were worried that once war began, they'd lose all their assets in Japan. Although Father bought the property, far as I know, the houses were left unoccupied after the Americans left, so I suppose they could move there, if they're still standing.'

My heart ached for Mother and Father Kishimoto. It dawned on me that Hiro and I, too, no longer had a home, as we knew it, to return to in Japan. It felt like the ground I stood on was being pulled from under.

Thursday, 7 June

Just when I thought things couldn't get much worse, we were again slapped with a notice to vacate the building to make room for the Japanese military. This time, we are given only three days.

Wednesday, 20 June, Mr Tomita's House

I can't say we are happily settled, but at least we have a roof over our heads. In fact, how can I complain, when I think of the bombings in Kobe, leaving so many dead, and even more homeless?

Here we are, at Mr Tomita's, an older employee at the Kishimoto office, who has given us accommodation in his house in Frenchtown. A widower living on his own, with an old Chinese *amah*. It was obvious from day one though, that he doesn't like the arrangement. I suppose I can't blame him, his peace all of a sudden disrupted by a young family with two little boys, and an *amah* and boy and dog in tow.

We have been given the top part of the house, normally unoccupied. Chokugetsu-ken created a makeshift pantry, with a portable charcoal stove upstairs, so that we don't have to rely on the downstairs kitchen. Mr Tomita keeps long hours at work, and I make sure the boys are in bed before his return. I, too, try to keep as invisible as possible, and go out of my way to show respect when I see him. But in these encounters, his dislike of me is obvious, and seems to grow stronger by the day.

Yesterday he deliberately ignored my bows and shouted at his housekeeper to bring him a cup of tea, as if I didn't exist. Hiro thinks I'm being over sensitive.

'Tomita-san is of the old school and isn't used to women who take the initiative. Maybe he's a bit uncomfortable because you are attractive and competent.' Sweet as Hiro's interpretation was, I am quite certain that Mr Tomita's disapproval goes much deeper.

Tuesday, 26 June

We learned of the fall of Okinawa first thing in the morning. Mr Tomita solemnly gave us the news he had just heard on his scratchy radio that picks up Japanese long-wave broadcasts. We bowed our heads, as I thought of the newspaper photo of the *kamikaze* pilots sent to Okinawa. My chest ached at the thought of all the losses.

Hiro swiftly left for the factory, and I bowed to Mr Tomita once again, saying how sorry I was for all the victims in Okinawa, and expressing my hope that such a massive defeat might trigger a settlement for peace.

'What on earth are you talking about, Oku-san, you don't know anything!' came Mr Tomita's thundering voice. He was in fact shaking with anger, and shouted, 'The American battle in Okinawa was a dirty one, an attempt at the mass murder of innocent Japanese women and children who had no connection with the fighting. Japan is a country that has never lost any war and never will because of our mental and spiritual superiority. You are smearing the Emperor's name by even mentioning the word defeat. Show more respect for your country!'

He stood glaring at me, arms crossed in front of his chest in an overpowering stance.

I was crushed for I never imagined that my attitude could be construed as being disrespectful to Japan. I always followed my instincts based on my Christian beliefs and deep affinity for the West, especially Britain, the country of my birth. Perhaps because of that, and because Rokki and Tamiko and even Hiro never accept the news we get at face value, I could only try to understand what was happening. But Mr Tomita was right that I knew little. Could there really have been deliberate killings of women and children? Do most Japanese people see the world as Mr Tomita does?

I humbly bowed again, and Mr Tomita simply nodded his head and walked away.

Sunday, 1 July

All of a sudden, Shanghai is steaming in a sweltering heat unusual this early in the summer, with more mosquitos buzzing around than ever. Worried about the boys getting malaria, Amah and I spent the afternoon going over the mosquito nets and mending even the tiniest of tears.

Seeing us sitting on the floor of their bedroom, surrounded by flowing gauze fabric, Kazu and Taka took great pleasure in prancing about, sometimes rolling under the nets and other times pulling them over their heads. They were having so much fun that I didn't have the heart to scold them. Amah and I put our needles away and savoured the mayhem they were creating, laughing out loud together.

I had assumed that Mr Tomita was away at the office. But amidst the boys' happy squeals, much to my horror, I heard footsteps coming up the stairs, and before I knew it, I saw Mr Tomita's disapproving face poke through the doorway.

'Oku-san, *chotto*,' he said, beckoning me into the hallway and indicating that I should follow him downstairs. I felt like a schoolgirl, about to be scolded by a teacher. Although sorry about the noise that must have bothered him, I couldn't help feeling resentful that I had to constantly live under the scrutiny of this objectionable landlord.

I was about to apologize, when he said, 'Oku-san, it may not be my business, but you should never let your guard down with Chinese servants. They are not to be trusted, and you must always show you are in charge.' I was stunned. It was my laughing with Amah that had offended him!

I felt instant anger at his implicit negative view of our servants, and could feel the heat rising to my cheeks. But of course I couldn't talk back at him. I breathed deeply and tried to contain my feelings, closing my eyes for a few seconds. Even through closed eyes, I knew he was waiting for my reaction, probably pleased at my discomfort. I decided that I would take my time – that would be my resistance, let him feel awkward at my silence.

I was feeling calmer, ready to acknowledge his words with a brief '*wakari mashita*,' – my intention to simply imply 'I hear what you say', but a phrase that can also be interpreted as a humble 'I understand.' How convenient the Japanese language can be! I was starting to enjoy my little game when I suddenly recalled Chokugetsu-ken mentioning that some of our food and had disappeared. I had found Mr Tomita's commandeering manner with his housekeeper distasteful, but perhaps he had reason for being untrusting. Could it be that he was trying to give me advice rather than being antagonistic?

I bowed and said '*wakari mashita*,' more heartfelt than intended at first, and slowly retreated upstairs.

Thursday, 12 July

The unbearably hot days continue, not just the weather, but the whole atmosphere in Shanghai feels terribly oppressive. It's difficult to know what's going on in the bigger world as the Japanese papers are no longer in regular circulation. There's just a general sense of deep anxiety that something is going to happen soon. But we don't know what or when, and life goes on in the stifling heat.

Just a short stroll around the crowded streets makes one's clothes stick to the body, and Amah and I are constantly running after Kazu and Taka to give them cold-water rubs. We then smother them in talcum powder to prevent prickly heat, making them squeal with laughter, calling each other 'Snowman! Snowman!' Jay-jay barks and joins in the fun. Comforting distractions at a time of unspeakable uncertainty.

Wednesday, 18 July

After his usual early morning walk with Jay-jay, Chokugetsu-ken came rushing up the stairs. 'Missy, Missy, big bomb drop Hongkew, refugee people area.' Hiro, who was about to have breakfast, looked up with a frown.

'Wonder if it's the factory area. Better rush and find out,' he said, grabbing a few slices of toast as he headed downstairs. Seeing my worried expression, he said he'd try to ring when he had any news.

For some reason, Mr Tomita was not leaving the house as usual, and I fretted as the phone was down in his hallway. When the call finally came, he was the one who picked up. I hovered at the top of the stairs as I heard him answer, '*Aah so desuka.*' His monosyllabic acknowledgements continued, and I began to think it wasn't Hiro after all, when he shouted, 'Oku-san, for you!' I rushed down the stairs.

Hiro was succinct – his factory was safe, the bombs dropped mainly in the Designated Area, with substantial casualties, a few Japanese who lived close by were also affected. As soon as I hung up, I asked Mr Tomita for permission to make a call and rang the Friends' Centre to enquire about Irma. Nobody was picking up, and with each unanswered dial tone, my anxiety mounted.

Mr Tomita was staring at me clinging onto the receiver. Once I hung up, I knew he expected me to say something. If I wanted to find out about Irma, I decided the only option was to actually go to the Designated Area. I bowed to Mr Tomita and told him that I would go to Hongkew to see about a friend who might have been caught in the bombings.

'Oku-san, you are crazy. The roads over there are probably impassable, and more bombs may drop.' Although his tone was gruff, I sensed a softening of his rigid censorial stance. I quickly made another bow as I headed up the stairs to collect some provisions for the journey. Despite the heat, expecting lots of dust, I put on a pair of trousers and a long-sleeved shirt, with a scarf around my head, and said a hasty goodbye to Amah and the boys.

Just as I was about to pedal off, to my amazement, Mr Tomita came rushing out of the house with a small bundle. 'Oku-san, since you're determined to go, you might as well take these things. I've collected an assortment of bandages, disinfectant ointments and some Japanese sweets for your friend. Have a safe journey and stop by the office if you need help.' Before I could thank him, he had turned back to the house.

What made Mr Tomita suddenly be nice to me? I wondered, as I cycled through the stifling heat, beads of sweat trickling down my face. Catching sight of the bundle in the handlebar basket, I suddenly knew: he thought I was helping a Japanese friend and therefore no longer unpatriotic!

My brief light-heartedness was shattered upon approaching the Designated Area. Initially, all I saw was rubble and dust among damaged buildings, and many Chinese people, some in torn clothing, scurrying around.

When I came to the corner of Wuhang and Muirhead Roads, I ran into a scene I couldn't have imagined even in my worst nightmares. Foreigners in uniform were laying out rows of dead Chinese, while another group of people with official armbands were moving some of the bodies onto wooden carts. I had to dismount my bicycle and cover my entire face with my scarf. I could hardly breathe as I gagged from the smell. I tried to avoid looking directly at the bodies, but there were so many, and my eye would catch a hanging limb, or a shoe scattered on the road, making shivers run throughout me. All I wanted to do was get out of the place. I desperately pushed my bicycle towards Tonghsan Road, where Irma lives.

The building stood, but the road was in shambles. A small bomb crater had appeared in the middle of the street, and most shop fronts were ruined from the explosions. As I weaved my bicycle through the debris, Mr Tomita's words, 'Oku-san, you're crazy' rang in my ears.

My tears blurred the contours of the people around me, who were poking through the rubble, perhaps looking for family members or lost possessions. Suddenly there was a huge blast of sirens – a preparatory alarm for another air raid – which shook me to the core.

But the people on the street seemed hardly concerned, making me realize that this was nothing unusual for them. These alarms were part of their daily life. When the siren changed into a continuous shrill, however, everyone started rushing about, disappearing into buildings. Instinctively, I abandoned my bicycle against a wall, and pushed myself behind some refugees as they entered a concrete building. I was overwhelmed with fright and regret at exposing myself to such danger.

I felt a yank on my arm, and a voice said in English, 'Come over here.' Bewildered, I turned around to see a small, elderly Jewish man, urging me to join two others huddled under a table. We seemed to be in some kind of kitchen, with tiled walls and a rudimentary sink in the corner. There was a collection of heavy iron pots piled on the table above us.

'With no air-raid shelters, we have to make do with this. I survived yesterday this way, so today should be OK too.' He flashed me a toothless smile. He and the other two settled themselves down and started conversing in what I think was Yiddish, chuckling at a joke here and there. The normality of their interaction helped to soothe my frayed nerves and I concentrated on their voices, which helped to block out some of the alarming outside sounds of planes, anti-aircraft flak, and distant bombings.

But time passed extremely slowly, making me increasingly anxious that only a massive bomb right above us would end this feeling of suspension. What could I have been thinking when I set out from home, dismissing Mr Tomita's warning of possible further bombings. The faces of Kazu and Taka kept appearing in my mind's eye, and I tightened my fists against my chest, praying and willing that I could come out of this in one piece.

Just when I thought I could take it no longer, the skies seemed to quieten down, and shortly thereafter we heard the all clear. The men exchanged handshakes, and one of them said something to make them all laugh heartily as we emerged from under the table. After the other men parted, my original friend said casually, 'Well, young lady, what brought you to this part of town. Hope you didn't mind us ignoring you throughout the acute alarm. One of the fellows here is rather suspicious of Japanese people, so I thought it better to distract him.'

I bowed deeply in gratitude. I felt like bursting into tears for his kindness, after all the fear and tension, and strained to hold myself together. 'I came to find out whether my friend Irma Czeska, who works at the Friends' Clothing centre here, was safe from yesterday's bombings,' I barely managed to say.

He narrowed his eyes and broke into a wide smile. 'Ah, you are a friend of Irma's. A true friend to come all this way! She is indeed safe and sound, busy running around helping those who are injured or have lost their homes.'

'Oh, you know her!' I exclaimed, as my knees almost gave way from the relief of learning of Irma's safety. I leaned against the table to support myself, and the elderly refugee gently took my arm and helped me regain my balance.

'Look,' he said. 'You've had enough excitement for a day, and should get back to wherever your home is as soon as possible. It would be difficult to find Irma anyway, as she could be anywhere in the Area. I shall be seeing her soon, probably this evening if she drops by at my Heim, as she usually does. I will tell her that I had the privilege of running into you. She will be enormously touched to know that you came in search of her.'

I knew he was right, that there was now no point in trying to find Irma. I had the news I wanted, and missed home terribly. I took his hand in mine, trying to convey all my gratitude and relief in a single handshake, for I no longer had any energy for words.

He accompanied me outside, and I let out a squeal when I found my bicycle, exactly where I had left it against the wall. Nothing had changed outside during the frightening air-raid. The packets of supplies were still in the bicycle basket, and I thrust them into my new friend's hands. As I started pushing away, he said, 'I don't know your name, dear. I'm sure Irma will know immediately when I describe you, but it would be nice to have a name. Mine is Jakob.'

I remember little of my return journey. Once home, I told Amah that I needed a bath before seeing the boys, and took a long soak, trying to wash away the dust, the smells and the fear that clung stubbornly all over me. I won't be able to speak of the horrors that I saw for a while yet, especially to Hiro. How could I let him know of my thoughtlessness, taking risks that could have left Kazu and Taka motherless? I shudder to think what might have happened, and realize that Hiro is exposed to such dangers all the time at the factory. As are the people in the Designated Area, who, despite incurring huge damage from yesterday's bombings, might still face worse to come.

Friday, 20 July

Irma rang this morning, fortunately after Mr Tomita left for the office. 'Eiko Liebling, you are a very, very silly girl,' she blurted, as soon as I picked up the phone and said 'Hello.'

'Do you not realize how foolish to come to Designated Area in these heightened times! People here have no choice, but what do you do, come all the way from safer Frenchtown, you are *albern* beyond words!' She was breathing heavily, and I could almost see her waving her arms, her greying, curly hair flying wild around her teary face. I felt ashamed for adding to her distress.

'I know, Irma, I was very foolish. I had no idea what to expect,' I said, my voice coming out even meeker than intended.

There was silence on the other end, and then some sniffling. 'The truth is, Eiko Liebling, when Jakob told me you came all the way here, I had no words. I was moved to tears. I was all day seeing hellish scenes, helping very badly hurt people, and exhausted. Before going home, I dropped by at the Heim for one last check on the sick. Jakob catches me in the corridor and tells me you were with him under a table in the soup kitchen! Eiko, my heart nearly burst from love and thanks.'

I leaned against the wall, eyes closed. My journey hadn't been a futile exercise after all! Irma's heart-felt appreciation gave me a sense of fulfilment.

'But Liebling, you act much too rashly. You must be more careful,' Irma said, reverting to her motherly tone. 'There could be more bombings. Many here worry we'll be killed by Americans before Americans win for us. You must stay away, you saw what it was like.'

'You be a good girl now, and look after your family. The next few weeks will be crucial, we must be vigilant. Take care of your husband. Say your prayers.'

Could Irma be right that the heavy American bombings meant the war was close to ending in American victory? Mr Tomita saw it differently, that the bombings were only an indication of American desperation and incompetence, hitting the Designated Area by mistake. I don't know what to think.

Monday, 23 July

When Chokugetsu-ken said Hiro was on the phone, my legs started to feel shaky from anxiety – it surely had to be some terrible news, probably another bombing. Chokugetsu-ken, too, seemed worried, and had an unusual frown on his normally smooth face.

'Just had a messenger from the Kishimoto office. There's an available flat in the Embankment House, and we can move in by the end of the week.' Having said that much, Hiro quickly rang off.

'Chokugetsu-ken, we are moving again!' I squealed, and his face broke into his jolly big wide smile.

'Missy, vely happy for evlyone. I tell Amah and we star pack,' he said, as he dashed upstairs to spread the good news.

We are going to have our own place, and in none other than the Embankment House, known to be the largest of the apartment buildings built by Victor Sassoon. The thought of being in another Sassoon building is so uplifting, I hope we can be as happy as when we were in the Grosvenor House. I can't believe our splendid good luck in these gloomy times.

Friday, 27 July

Mr Tomita didn't go to the office today and we had to move our things under his watchful gaze. I had Amah take the boys and Jay-jay outside so as not to bother him, and worked silently with Chokugetsu-ken, sweat trickling down both our faces as we made repeated trips up and down the stairs. It couldn't have been such an interesting sight, but Mr Tomita stayed put in his chair with the view of the staircase throughout. I was comforted by the thought that soon I would be free from him.

After the last box was neatly stacked in the foyer, I went over to apologize for the commotion and tell him we were now ready for tomorrow's move, thinking how he must also be delighted to see us leave.

He acknowledged me with a silent nod, and I bowed deeply. Just as I was turning towards the stairs, he said, '*Oku-san*, you're a hard worker and manage your household well. The house will seem empty when you're gone.'

I gave him another deep, solemn bow, but inside, I felt triumphant!

When I raised my head, he added, 'When Japan wins the war, you must come back to celebrate together.' Lost for words, I gave him yet another bow and rushed upstairs.

Sunday, 29 July, The Embankment House

Unlike our previous two moves, which were within the French Concession, yesterday's involved going across the International Settlement, over Garden Bridge, then west along the Soochow Creek and finally reaching the Embankment House.

Hiro had managed to secure an army jeep, which he then took over to transport the heavy luggage, the boys, Jay-jay and himself, leaving me behind with Chokugetsu-ken, Amah to deal with the remaining luggage, and organizing the team of coolies. It took ages in the excruciating heat and crowded streets. Arriving at the flat, covered in grime and sweat, I felt a tinge of irritation at Hiro looking cool and relaxed. But the comfortably furnished flat lifted my spirits.

It almost felt like being back home again, the Embankment House being similar, although not as elegant as the Grosvenor House. The large foyers and the lifts, the high ceilings, the modernity of the place brought back memories of my early days in Shanghai, filling me with optimism. How wonderful it would be, if the war ended, and we could have a normal life, with no Mr Tomita, in this comfortable place – with a veranda overlooking the Soochow Creek, and accommodation for Chokugetsu-ken and Amah on a separate floor.

Sitting with my feet up at the end of the day, I felt very happy. Suddenly, I remembered that it was my 24th birthday – a milestone completely overshadowed by the move! What a birthday present, to be in the new flat!

Friday, 3 August

We're getting used to our new neighbourhood, so different from leafy Frenchtown. Around us here is the hustle-bustle of a commercial city – shops on top of each other, some big Japanese establishments sandwiching numerous little Chinese shops, pedlars and carts and beggars and hawkers crowding the streets.

Much to Chokugetsu-ken's delight, Hongkew Market is nearby – a huge triangular, double-storey concrete structure with a dark entrance covered in shade. I ventured there yesterday, even going upstairs, where the goods are cheaper for Chinese shoppers. The air was filled with smells of frying oil and garlic and a loud din, much livelier than downstairs, where most of the shoppers were Japanese – housewives in *monpe* and a sprinkling of soldiers on leave, their dark, focussed expressions giving me a sense of foreboding.

For the boys, the veranda provides a new source of entertainment. They stick their faces against the horizontal railing and look out over the Soochow Creek, watching the big barges go up and down, as if they are aboard a ship. The sampans, with whole families living on them, are of particular interest. 'Mama, mama, baby *mite!*' Taka shouted this morning, pointing at a tiny naked Chinese boy running the length of the sampan, making me nervous that he might topple into the water.

But of course we have to close the windows early and cover the place in blackout curtains, the night scenery over the water left to the imagination. Like the swimming pool – an imaginary delight in this stifling heat – now filled with dirty water as an emergency reservoir in case of fire.

Monday, 6 August

Could it be because we are comfortably settled in our new flat that I sense a change of wind? High above the blue skies float strips of clouds that look like fish scales, and I can already feel an early autumn breeze. It seems, too, that the tide of war is changing, that things are more relaxed. The Chinese people at the Hongkew

Market this morning certainly appeared more boisterous. And I overheard Japanese neighbours in the building saying that radio broadcasts from military headquarters report important Japanese victories against the encroaching Americans. I wonder if this means that we are close to war's end, that a settlement for peace can finally be worked out.

Thursday, 9 August

The boys were out on the veranda with Amah shortly before lunch-time, when I heard Kazu summoning me excitedly, 'Mama, Mama! *Hayaku kite!*' Despite Kazu's plea for me to rush, I took my time – nothing moves very fast on the creek.

When I approached the glass door, Kazu, Taka and Amah were standing still, heads turned to the sky rather than the waters. As soon as I set foot outside I, too, could only stare, speechless. The sky had turned into a strange orange colour, not without beauty, but casting an eerie, unsettling atmosphere.

Uncomfortable, I beckoned everyone inside, and tightly shut the door.

When Hiro returned from work this evening, he said there had been hailstorms in parts of Shanghai. Is it the sudden cool weather that's bringing about such odd phenomena? I felt a shudder go through my body, and my hopes for a smooth end to the war ebb away.

Saturday, 11 August

Despite the uneasiness in the air, I went out on my bicycle to Nanking Road to find a birthday present for Taka. It was my first trip back to the big shopping area in the International Settlement, and I looked forward to dropping into Sincere's or Wing On.

The crossing at Garden Bridge was surprisingly easy, the Japanese sentries being less vigilant, letting Chinese passers-by through without inspection. I wondered whether some important person was expected, as the sentries seemed to be in nervous anticipation.

Nanking Road, although crowded with people, seemed different from usual. At first I couldn't tell what it was. Dismounting my bicycle, I saw that all the shops were closed, some with blue and white Chinese Nationalist flags fluttering in the shut doorway. There was a sense of elation all around me – that's what the strange atmosphere was, a light heartedness that permeated throughout the crowds.

Suddenly, I felt Chinese eyes staring at me, and instinctively became self-conscious of being out of place. Nobody did or said anything, but their gazes felt like needles pricking into my skin. The contrast between the overall sense of joy in the air, and the coldness of the little pocket around me was piercing. I desperately pulled tight the scarf covering my head, wanting as little of my face to show as possible, and pedalled as fast as I could out of the crowds.

When I reached Hankow Road, I allowed myself to slow down, and took in deep breaths. What had happened? The relationship between the Japanese and Chinese seemed to have changed dramatically. But there was no news, no announcement. I looked up, and before me was the Holy Trinity Cathedral, the tall red spire casting a shadow in my direction. How I wished Akira were here! I wanted to rush in, see his reassuring smile, sit in the café and have him help me understand what was happening.

Alas, I made my way straight back to Hongkew, where only a few Chinese shops were closed and all seemed normal. I went into a Japanese shop and picked up the first toy I found – a wooden boat painted in bright red, blue and green – perfect, for Taka, I thought. But my eyes nearly popped out when I saw the price.

'Oku-san, you should have come yesterday,' the shopkeeper said. 'The price has doubled since then. You should see the food prices in Hongkew Market!'

Something was definitely happening, but it was like trying to catch a cloud – why was there no information? I've been waiting for Hiro to return, for surely people at the factory would have heard something and he would be able to enlighten me.

Sunday, 12 August

Hiro didn't come home last night – no word since he left for work yesterday morning. Chokugetsu-ken came back from the market with a 4,000 yuan pork bun that cost 500 yuan just two days ago. 'Missy, must buy now, pricee go up evly minit,' he said, carrying huge bundles of provisions into the kitchen.

I couldn't bear sitting at home not knowing what was happening. Even if Akira wasn't there, I decided to go to the Cathedral in the hope that I'd run into someone with news.

Entering the café, I recognized Cheeko's back, sitting at a table on her own, crouched over a cup of tea. What luck, I thought, as I rushed over, calling out 'Cheeko-san, Cheeko-san!'

When she turned around, I realized she was actually hunched over in tears. Even before she said anything, I knew that it was her brother, Osamu. I sat down and took her hands into mine.

'So close to war's end – if only he could have held out a little longer!' Cheeko said, pressing her handkerchief to her eyes. I squeezed her hands, and we sat there in silence for quite a long while.

Eventually, she looked up, determined to revert to her usual chirpy self. 'There are signs everywhere on Yu Yuen Road put up by Japanese authorities banning public meetings and demonstrations, and Japanese armed soldiers are all over the place, some even with machine guns.' Cheeko spoke fast, as if to push away her sadness.

I was puzzled. 'Cheeko-san, what is happening? Yesterday there was jubilation among the Chinese on Nanking Road, but now you're telling me that the Japanese are tightening control?'

'Eiko-san, you're not the only one. Nobody has any definite information. But Daisuke's Chinese friends heard that Japan agreed to some declaration ending the war.

'Last night, Daisuke was at a nightclub, which as usual was dimmed dark. But around 10 o'clock, somebody opened all the windows and turned on the lights, making the place unbelievably bright, and the Chinese started raising toasts. Daisuke was in his Chinese gown so everybody thought he was Chinese, too, shouting '*gambei*!' at him. But even so, he felt uneasy, what with recent open hostility against the Japanese. I've heard of Japanese housewives having watermelon skins thrown at them, and Chinese servants turning against their Japanese employers.' Cheeko was regaining her normal tone.

She said that the celebratory mood at the nightclub was quickly put down by Japanese soldiers, who turned out the lights and barked orders at the Chinese manager of the club to restore order. Daisuke and his friends quickly left the place soon after.

Cheeko looked straight into my eyes. 'Eiko-san, even when Japan's defeat is obvious, they pretend all is normal, even talking of a final push towards victory. Apparently, some new special bombs were dropped, first on Hiroshima on the 6th and then on Nagasaki, causing unheard of devastation. And Russia joined the war against Japan on the day of the second bomb, on the 9th.'

'Special bombs?' I asked, suddenly reminded of the eerie orange sky seen from the veranda. It had to be related to the second bomb, Nagasaki being so close to Shanghai.

Cheeko was again lost in her thoughts. 'If only Osamu's mission was scheduled for a few days later! All the lives being wasted even now, the futility…' She buried her face into her hands.

23

Wednesday, 15 August 1945

Everything is clear now – Japan has lost the war, an unconditional surrender.

There was a directive yesterday for all Japanese to listen to an important radio announcement to be made at noon Japan time – 11 a.m. Shanghai time. Hiro didn't go to the factory, and we joined a group of neighbours clustered by the open door of a flat with a large wireless. There must have been about twenty of us – men, women and some older children – everyone looking extremely solemn, standing with our heads hung, hands neatly folded.

I wanted the broadcast to happen quickly, to end the ongoing feeling of suspension, to know what was happening. The few minutes' wait, while the wireless was being adjusted and volume turned up, seemed interminable.

When we heard the Japanese national anthem, it was clear that it wasn't a normal news announcement. All bodies tensed, and heads hung even lower. At the end of the anthem, amidst the crackling of airwaves, came an unexpectedly high-pitched voice, haltingly speaking strange Japanese with an unusual lilt. I was lost in incomprehension, until suddenly drawn back to reality by sudden loud sobs coming from a few men around me. I quickly looked towards Hiro, who looked surprised, whether at the content of what was being said or the men's reaction, I couldn't tell.

I focussed hard, and by the time the short announcement came to the end, I was able to catch the words: 'bearing the unbearable' in the desire for world peace. I knew then it was the Emperor himself speaking, and my heart tightened with sorrow, for all the sufferings that the people of Japan had endured over the years, and for the frail-sounding man who shouldered the entire nation's grief.

The national anthem was played again, and then an announcer read out, in simple Japanese, what the Emperor had said: that Japan accepted the Potsdam Declaration; that Japan had declared war on Britain and the United States only to preserve Japan's independence and for the stability of the East Asian region; that he, the Emperor had never wished to invade foreign territory. The statement went on to say that with the particularly brutal bomb that had caused the death of many innocent lives, and with no indication of how long this cruelty could go on, in order to avoid the total destruction of Japan, he, the Emperor, ordered the acceptance of the Potsdam Declaration.

Further sobs and groans spread among the gathering, as the reality of unconditional surrender sunk in. I couldn't help feeling a sense of detachment, recognizing I didn't share the same emotions. As if deep inside me, although I had never been able to articulate the feeling, I had sensed that Japan's defeat was a foregone conclusion. I wanted an end to the war, and this is what we were getting. How could I not be relieved, happy even! If only it had come sooner. I felt a flicker of anger at the Japanese leaders, for taking us so far.

I didn't know how Hiro felt, having had to work so hard at the shipyard for the war effort. Before returning to our flat, I bowed to him and expressed my condolences for Japan's defeat, and appreciation for his work on behalf of his country. It seemed the right thing to do.

He raised his eyebrows, making his round eyes even rounder. 'I really didn't think we were going to lose the war. Just two days ago, the Army and Navy Command issued a statement saying we were to fight for "war's achievement", and the factory was put on 24-hour operation.'

Nudging me through our door, he said lightly, 'I was as surprised by the Emperor's voice as by what he said, much of which I couldn't catch.' I should have known that Hiro would take even defeat with equanimity. I felt a surge of affection, and slight satisfaction, too, that I had had a better sense of where the war was going.

Hiro continued talking, more to himself. 'There's lots to sort out now. Chokugetsu-ken and Amah have to go. They can't be working for Japanese or they'll be shunned by other Chinese and will never find jobs.' I realized he had a far better sense of what defeat entailed.

Chokugetsu-ken was busy preparing the lunch table and Kazu and Taka were out on the veranda with Amah. Kazu came rushing over, flushed with excitement. '*Papa, Mama, omatsuri da yo!*' he said, pulling me outside. It really was like a summer festival on the Creek – the barges and sampans noisily blowing horns, children waving Chinese nationalist flags, Stars and Stripes and Union Jacks. Bamboo victory banners praising Chiang Kai-shek floated in the air, and firecrackers exploded everywhere. In contrast to the boys' excitement, Amah looked troubled, as if she didn't know what to do.

Hiro called Chokugetsu-ken and Amah over, and bowed deeply, thanking the couple for their years of service. 'We cannot have you work for us any longer because being with a Japanese family will be bad for you,' he said.

Amah broke down in tears, and Chokugetsu-ken momentarily looked down at his feet. But once his face came up, it was with its usual wide smile. 'Master, Missy, you si down, lunchee time. Amah and I talkee you eat.' He served us a large plate of fried noodles and spring rolls, and then disappeared into the kitchen with Amah.

The boys seemed to sense something was happening. Kazu solemnly ate his lunch while Taka kept looking towards the kitchen asking, 'Amah *doko?*' in between mouthfuls, searching for his Amah.

Before we finished our meal, they re-emerged from the kitchen. 'Missy, Master, we makee decision, I go, work pedicab but Amah stay,' Chokugetsu-ken said cheerfully.

Hiro shook his head. 'Amah must go too, she needs a more secure position.' But Chokugetsu-ken was determined.

'Amah small, no one see. She say won't leave. She be alrigh.' He flashed his broad smile at us, and Amah stood quietly next to him.

I was deeply touched by their loyalty. Taka wriggled out of his high-chair and flew into Amah's skirt, making her face and body crumple with delight. She would stay with us until she had to be prised away.

The rest of the day passed in a haze. Having been told by Chokugetsu-ken, 'Missy, you no go outsi', Chinese people too excite no goo Japanese out on street,' I could only imagine what the street scenes might be like from the sounds of the firecrackers.

Only at night, did the reality of war's end sink in. We had the living room curtains open until the sun was deeply set over the Soochow Creek, and the boys ran around the flat way into the night, excited over the brightness – what difference the lights made! Despite defeat, it was an uplifting experience, and I prayed there could be moments of brightness in the days to come. How I wished I could contact Tamiko in Nanking and Daddy in Japan. What was to happen to everyone in Japan with defeat? And Akira, where could he be?

Thursday, 16 August

I couldn't believe that Hiro was going to the factory as usual. What would there be to do, now that the war was over? And what might happen out on the streets amongst hostile Chinese crowds? Ignoring my frowns, he said, 'I need to see about closing the factory and look in at the Kishimoto office.'

Before heading out, he rummaged through his drawer, and pulled out a small felt pouch. 'Eiko, you take care of this. With war's end, I won't have any income, and these will have to keep us going.' I looked into the pouch and saw five small gold pieces that looked like peanuts.

To my relief, Hiro returned home before long.

'Didn't encounter any acts of hostility from Chinese on the streets,' he said. 'Japanese soldiers are still around. Apparently, Chiang Kai-shek asked the Japanese military command to administer the city until the Americans and his own forces could take over.'

'The Kishimoto office is closed and the Navy is busy burning evidence of the suicide boats before handing over the factory to the

Chinese. I'm glad war ended before our boats went into production.' He picked up Jay-jay who was snuggled by his feet, and gave her an affectionate pat.

Saturday, 18 August

Strangely, even though war is over, our daily life goes on, with a feeling of being in limbo. I wake up, get the boys up, prepare breakfast with Amah's help, Jay-jay on my heels waiting for her meal, and the boys spend hours on the veranda watching the boats on the Creek.

Amah manages to do the shopping – actually, I am pretty sure that Chokugetsu-ken, although working as a pedicab driver, collects food for us and passes it on to Amah – and we have our daily provisions. Of course there are changes – Hiro is now at home, sleeping in in the mornings, and I am busy with kitchen work. But how odd it seems, that life goes on as normal when the world has been turned upside down for Japan.

Wednesday, 22 August, Japanese district, Hongkew

The strange sense of suspension following defeat ended abruptly two days ago. Is it really just two days ago? With all the changes, it feels like months ago. We have moved yet again, and now live in the heart of Hongkew, on the upstairs floor of the home of Mr Yamagiwa, from the Kishimoto office.

I am sitting at a small table in a room that serves as living room, dining room and kitchen all in one. Hiro and the boys are asleep in the small room next door, which we all share as a bedroom. Although I am physically exhausted, I am savouring these quiet moments to myself, reflecting on the events of the last two days.

On the morning of the 20th, there was a notice in the Embankment House lobby that all residents had to move out – the building was needed for the arriving Americans. We were given only four hours, and American MPs were already stationed telling everyone to hurry. How tall and big they were! I had almost forgotten the look of well-fed Westerners. Their gruff and unsympathetic manner rubbed in the fact we're a defeated people, a humiliation I was ill prepared for.

The whole place was mayhem, with hundreds of Japanese families having to vacate their premises in such a short time. Hiro seemed lost in the chaos, and I had to ask him to look after the children on the veranda. I needed to think fast. Amah and I started throwing things into large bedding bags and pillowcases.

With belongings packed, the next challenge was to take them downstairs and load them on to coolie carts that hung around the building waiting for jobs. There were *pisse* everywhere, the petty thieves that walk off with anything they can get their hands on. A bundle would have been snatched from my hands had it not been for Amah, who, watching from above, shouted, 'Missy, Missy, watchee. No takee out!'

The American MPs checked every item that was to leave the building, and my old samurai sword, which I had tossed into a large bedding bag, caused a scene at the checkpoint. Despite my pleas that it was a family heirloom, in the end I hand to give it in, having wasted precious time for more useful packing. The place was emptying, most Japanese families having cleared out by now, and the MPs flashed us impatient looks as my frustration mounted.

Just then, a distinguished-looking Western gentleman stepped out of one of the lifts, receiving the MPs' salutes. As he walked towards the entrance door, he looked at me intently and suddenly said, 'Why Mrs Kishimoto! Is that you? How extraordinary to run into you here!'

I was completely taken aback. But how wonderful it was to hear a British voice! The clipped accent, the deep tone! The green-grey eyes looked vaguely familiar, but who was he?

He stuck out his hand, and said, 'Stacey, from the Hongkong Shanghai Bank, just back with war's end. I'm a friend of Rokuro and Tamiko. I met you briefly at their place, and I never forget a beautiful face.' I quickly shook his hand and apologized for the state I was in – covered in dust and sweat, and no doubt looking totally dishevelled.

Mr Stacey gave me a kindly look. 'These are hard times for you. You must let me know if there is anything I can do to help. Have you managed to get all your things out?' His warmth and genuine concern made me almost crumble on the spot, especially after the intense last few hours of desperation and unpleasant dealings with the American MPs.

But I realized this was a God-send, a chance to resolve the two matters that had been weighing heavily on my mind. I quickly asked Mr Stacey if he could help with taking care of the Bakers' furniture from the Grosvenor House still in storage, and Jay-jay.

'Of course,' he said, taking the furniture storage papers from me. 'Mrs Kishimoto, if the Bakers return to Shanghai, they will be more than impressed to have furniture returned to them by a Japanese couple after four years of war.'

'As for Jay-jay, I will personally look after her.' His eyes lit up as he stooped down to pick her up. Jay-jay knew immediately that she was in the hands of someone who would love her, and happily licked his face. Perhaps she was reminded of her previous owners, the English couple, Anne and her husband. But it was a sad parting for us, especially for Hiro, who looked totally forlorn seeing Jay-jay in Mr Stacey's arms. With a quick wave of his hand, Hiro pushed the boys towards the door, and Mr Stacey thoughtfully retreated towards the lifts.

But we couldn't depart just yet, for it was the moment when we had to say goodbye to Amah. She was already in tears, hovering over the boys. 'Missy, countrysi' more food. Wishee can takee boys. Amah thinkee boys evlyday,' she said, in between sobs. She had been so pleased, just the day before, to celebrate Taka's second birthday and pampered him with dumplings and sweets.

Little had we known then that our circumstances would change so drastically overnight. Amah worried the boys might not have enough to eat when we moved to the Japanese section, and I think she seriously thought they would be better off going to the countryside with her. I wanted to give her some money, but she refused, 'Missy, you nee money. You keep.'

She collected her meagre belongings and walked out of the building ahead of us. Taka whimpered, and as I saw her tiny figure disappear beyond the Creek's bend, it felt as if my heart was being wrung like a wet tea towel.

And here we are, in the upstairs of this small terraced two-up two-down, with another lodger, an unmarried middle-aged women living in the attic above us. Everything is cramped, especially as the Yamagiwas have three children, aged five, seven and ten – a lovely family, though, so different from living with Mr Tomita. I wonder what has become of him. I hope Japan's defeat hasn't plunged him into despair like Germany's defeat did to the Schmidts.

Along the staircase, large bed sheets are hung to serve as partitions. It reminds me of how people in the Designated Area live, and I suppose it's the same kind of thing, we Japanese – nearly 100,000 – all gathered to live in a small section of town, just like the Jewish refugees. Having seen what life was like for Irma, it's almost a déjà vu, as if I've been mentally prepared for the life that now faces us.

I must go to bed; my mind is no longer functioning.

Saturday, 25 August

Living in deep Hongkew, adjacent to slum-type dwellings, is a bewildering experience. How cocooned in Western comfort we've been up to now, remote from real Chinese life.

I am woken at dawn by the rumble of the two-wheeled night-soil cart rolling along the back alleys, and the night-soil man's call to the neighbourhood, followed by voices of women bringing out the red *madong* chamber pots. At first, I was appalled by the idea and the stench, but now, I have come to appreciate the almost ritualistic beginning to the day, the women's voices and the soft rattling of the seashells against the wooden drums as the women deftly polish the *madong* with bamboo brooms.

My life in the last few days has been consumed with feeding the family, trying to be as frugal as possible. Living amongst the Chinese makes it easier to put things into perspective. Most don't even have cooking stoves and after the *madong*, the women start their daily chore of lighting small coal stoves – quite an elaborate operation, getting the fire going with wastepaper and woodchips before throwing in the egg-shaped briquettes of compressed coal. How can I complain, when all I have to do is switch on the gas stove?

And there are joyful moments. Yesterday, I made fried eggs for breakfast and Hiro said, 'Maybe it's your English upbringing, your eggs are perfect. Reminds me of breakfasts in the dining hall at Cambridge.' It made me laugh, but I was also touched for I never thought my cooking would please Hiro in the way Chokugetsuken's did. Knowing I have an appreciative audience now, I find shopping a stimulating challenge rather than a chore, wondering how I could cook the available ingredients to suit Hiro's taste.

But I am physically exhausted. Not just because of the housework, but having to be constantly on the alert. This morning, right in front of my eyes, a *pisse* knocked over a destitute-looking Japanese man and ran off with the man's sack. I'm learning to strap my bag across my chest and guarding it tightly against my body.

Saturday, 1 September

As Kazu and I turned on to North Szechuan Road this morning, crowds of Chinese were lined along the road waving little Nationalist flags. We squeezed into a small gap to see what was happening, and suddenly the whole place erupted in shouts and applause as impressive American trucks and jeeps came crawling along. Behind them were rows and rows of marching soldiers clad in pristine olive-coloured uniforms bearing impressive machine guns. I realized we were witnessing the entry of the Chungking army into Shanghai.

Kazu was beside himself surrounded by such excitement, and jumped up and down to get a better look. Worried that he might start asking me questions in Japanese, I swiftly picked him up and whispered 'keep quiet' in his ear.

But Kazu thought I was carrying him for a better look – an unusual treat. He meekly wrapped his arm around my neck and quietly stared at the spectacle.

I could sense Kazu's excitement – what boy wouldn't be, seeing such magnificent machinery and powerful display of soldiers. For me, there was no sadness or sentimentality – just a feeling of defeat as a physical reality, the contrast between the spectacle before us and the emaciated Japanese soldiers wandering the streets, in their rag-like uniforms, carrying a single water flask made out of bamboo.

Wednesday, 5 September

Mrs Yamagiwa, a usually calm and composed woman, came loudly rushing up the stairs as I was clearing up after breakfast. 'Oku-sama, Oku-sama!' she called from behind the sheet curtains. 'Your sister, Tamiko-sama, is back from Nanking!'

I stared for a moment, speechless. 'My husband just ran into a colleague of Mr Rokuro Yamanaka on the street and found out that they had arrived in Shanghai the night before last,' she said. 'They are temporarily staying with a Yokohama Specie Bank family on Arbury Lane, fifteen minutes from here.'

I sank into a chair and covered my face with my hands, controlling my breathing. Kazu came over asking, '*Mama, dōshita no?*' with a worried expression. I drew him tight into my arms and, by the time I looked into his face, I couldn't contain my happiness. Kazu giggled, as if to say, oh, you're laughing rather than crying.

Leaving the boys with Hiro, who's become expert at taking things easy with no factory to go to, I dashed out of the house.

My heart beat loudly as I walked towards Arbury Lane through small alleys filled with Chinese street life. I couldn't believe Tamiko was so close by. How I had missed her! So much had happened in the last eighteen months making the separation feel much longer, and I found myself deliberately slowing my walking pace in order to calm down. I imagined myself falling into her arms and letting out all the tensions of war's end, crying and laughing over our changed circumstances, cradled in her wisdom and humour.

But it was a distant formality that greeted me. When I arrived, Tamiko was busy moving possessions out of the way from their host family's hallway, looking worn and haggard, as the owner of the house stood by. There was a momentary flash of warmth and longing when she discovered me at the doorway, but before I could dash over and embrace her, the owner stepped forward.

Tamiko took a step back. 'Mrs Shimizu, may I introduce you to my sister, Eiko Kishimoto, I had not known that she was going to drop by. Eiko, this is Mrs Shimizu, who is kindly putting us up for a few days until our flat is ready,' she said, half bent in a permanent bow. Mrs Shimizu nodded and gave me a cool look.

I heard girls' voices from the back of the house, and wanted to run in to see them. But there was no sign of being invited in, and I felt superfluous, standing in the entrance hall, barely over the threshold.

'Tamiko-san, perhaps you should sort your luggage and then get some rest. You still have so much to do,' Mrs Shimizu said coolly. She gave me a slight bow and retreated swiftly into the house.

Tamiko came over and gave me the hug that I was waiting for. But it was an embrace that lacked any force, and had it not been for the soft whisper in my ear – 'Eiko, I'm exhausted, there's so much to tell you.' – I might have felt dejected. As it was, it seemed Tamiko needed as much comforting as I thought I needed from her.

I made a hasty exit, consoling myself that she was now close by, and that our happy days together were surely going to return.

Friday, 7 September

This morning, Mr Yamagiwa arrived with his ten-year old daughter, Yumiko, who came to collect the boys to play with the other children. There was something about Yumiko, perhaps her inviting dark eyes, which made Kazu and Taka happily rush over and take each of her hands into theirs. Once the children went downstairs, Mr Yamagiwa asked if we had a moment. Being American educated, he has a natural ease, always polite, but never stiff, and we were pleased to invite him in for a cup of tea. I knew his visit had some specific purpose – living in such close proximity, we normally respect a neighbourly distance.

'You probably know, but the Nationalist Chinese Army led by Tang Enbai is taking over Shanghai, and we are from now to be identified as *nikkyō*,' Mr Yamagiwa said.

'What does *nikkyō* mean?' I asked.

Hiro traced the *kanji* characters with his finger on the table. 'The literal meaning is something like "non-immigrant Japanese".'

How strange, I thought. 'It sounds more like being labelled "Japanese who don't belong here in China",' I said, despite myself.

Mr Yamagiwa clapped his hands and said, 'Mrs Kishimoto, I think you've got it! They're organizing the *nikkyō* into groups under a *pao chia* system – ten houses forming one group with an overseer, and ten groups forming into a larger group with a higher overseer.'

It sounded completely familiar, Irma telling me about an exactly same system the Japanese imposed in the Designated Area to keep tabs on the people. It was our turn now, and it occurred to me that the Jews, too, must have felt that 'stateless refugee' had an unwelcome ring, as *nikkyō* has to me.

It is all the same – we are now to wear yellow armbands at all times when in public, and be confined to a restricted area of Shanghai. We are not to hire any person from the victor country, nor to ride any vehicles operated by a national of the victor country, meaning I can't even ride on Chokugetsu-ken's pedicab.

As Mr Yamagiwa was leaving, Hiro matter-of-factly said, 'Thank you for the information. Considering our total defeat, the measures seem civilized.'

Mr Yamagiwa nodded. 'Indeed, considering how some Japanese treated the Chinese during the war,' he said.

The big difference between us and the Jewish refugees was that they had done no harm to anyone yet had to undergo the same kind of treatment as the Japanese were now getting.

Sunday, 9 September

I heard Tamiko's voice downstairs, asking for me, and I nearly stumbled down the stairs. I had been thinking of her every minute since the frustrating first meeting, but didn't have the courage to face another constrained visit in the presence of the haughty Mrs Shimizu.

Tamiko still looked drawn and tired. She hugged me tightly and said, 'We have our own place now, and Rokki is looking after the girls so I could come and see you properly.'

Our place was nice and empty, the boys being taken out by Yumiko to play with neighbourhood Japanese children, and Hiro at some communal baseball game. Tamiko and I stood facing, holding hands, and just staring at each other for a while.

Finally, we simultaneously broke into smiles, Tamiko saying, 'I know I've aged, Eiko, I'm thirty-two! But look at you, as pretty and fresh as ever.' She squeezed my hand tightly, and I wished the moment could last forever.

Once settled, Tamiko started talking. 'When the war ended, nothing changed for a while. Then, one day, with no warning, all Japanese were rounded up for internment,' she said, staring into her teacup. 'A convoy of Chinese army trucks came into the compound, and they started shouting for everyone to get on. Sachi was so frightened, she started wailing, setting off Asako, too. Rokki was away on business. There was no time to take anything, just what we had on – all of us women in *monpe*.'

Tamiko continued in a monotonous tone, as if in a trance. 'When a truck filled up, it would immediately depart for the internment camp. We climbed into the third one, and seeing the fear in the peoples' eyes, Sachi started wailing again until suddenly she stopped, pointing her finger at the road. "Daddy! Daddy!" she shouted. Rokki was running towards us, waving a piece of paper in his hand.'

It was a certificate that spared the family from internment. Rokki was being retained by the Bank of China, which had requisitioned the Yokohama Specie Bank, made in charge of unfreezing the enemy assets he had earlier frozen. Instead of going to the camps, the family had to return immediately to Shanghai.

Tamiko's tone and expression suddenly took on a darkness I had never seen before.

'Eiko, I've never been as frightened as during the journey from Nanking to Shanghai,' she said, her hands now shaking.

'The hostility of the Chinese towards the end of the war was so piercing, I was braced during the whole journey for fear of being identified as Japanese. I almost wondered whether it would have been easier to be interned.'

She had to borrow clothes from a Japanese diplomat's wife, to get out of her *monpe*, which made her instantly recognizable as Japanese. In the middle of the night, a horse buggy took them to the railway station, where they waited on a bench for the first train to Shanghai. On the crowded train, they feigned sleep the whole time, speaking in Shanghainese only when absolutely necessary.

'Then in one of my semi-wakeful moments, I felt my pockets and realized I no longer had our papers,' Tamiko said, her voice sounding almost hollow. 'I must have dropped them somewhere in the chaos. I couldn't stop shaking. Without identification to prove Rokki was needed to help with the transition, anything could happen to us, without a trace. I clung on to the girls, almost certain they would be snatched from me and sold.'

I felt cold and numb, physically sharing Tamiko's fright. It was a while before I came to my senses and took her hands to offer comfort. She seemed to have come back to the present at the exact moment.

With a smile and a twinkle in her eye, she said, 'Arriving in Shanghai seemed a miracle, even the formidable Mrs Shimizu seemed a real blessing!' Having told me her story, I sensed Tamiko managed to purge the horror from her system.

How happy I am to have Tamiko back! I can feel it in my bones that things will be fine, despite our reduced circumstances. We are safe and together, have a roof over our heads and enough to eat. What more can I ask for!

Saturday, 15 September

Rumours of the war's aftermath are starting to spread. Apparently over 200,000 people were killed in Hiroshima and Nagasaki alone, and most of Tokyo is reduced to ashes. I can't imagine the landscape. What will life be like, when we get back to Japan? How are our families coping?

I almost feel guilty of the life we have here, hardly a hardship, especially with Tamiko around. Today, when they arrived, Sachi went straight to Kazu to resume their game of 'house', as if from the day before. Not a trace of a year-and-a-half separation.

Rosy-cheeked Asako and Taka initially stared at each other suspiciously, but Sachi was quickly in charge. 'Daughter, you make a cup of tea for your father. And son, come help me move the table,' she commanded, as she pulled Taka over to her side. Taka, not used to being bossed around, dug his heels in, refusing to move. Sachi started shrieking, 'you are a naughty son! Go stand in the corner!'

Tamiko winked at me, and I closed the bedroom door, leaving the children on their own, while we ate sticky rice cakes and became lost in idle chatter.

Suddenly, a loud bawl, and Asako came rushing out into Tamiko's lap while Taka stood by the doorway looking triumphant. Sachi stuck out her head. 'Auntie, Taka hit Asako over the head, shouting "Atomic bomb! Atomic bomb!"'

I looked at Tamiko, bewildered.

'How the children pick up everything!' Tamiko said resignedly, patting Asako's head.

Thursday, 20 September

Taking advantage of the pleasant early autumn weather, I ventured beyond Hongkew Market along Hanbury Road, and waded through the lanes full of everyday Chinese life: a tailor sewing away perched on a crate, a fortune-teller reading palms, children playing and grannies gossiping amidst the moving wheelbarrows and carts.

Suddenly, in front of me, a group of American GIs appeared – three in khakis and two in pristine white navy uniforms. The size of their bodies and the healthy sheens on their faces seemed completely out of place among the sea of shabby Orientals, including myself.

Their swagger, their confidence, felt as if 'victory' was written all over them. It was yet again, almost a physical manifestation of Japan's defeat.

How torn I felt! Having always had an affinity with Americans, my natural instinct was to be excited and optimistic by the sight of them. But I was on the wrong side. For the Chinese or the Jewish refugees or the internees in the camps, the Americans must seem true saviours, but how are we Japanese to feel about them? I recalled the contempt and suspicion of the MPs going through my luggage at Embankment House, a shudder running through my spine. Their presence in Japan is probably so much greater than it is here in Shanghai. How will they treat us? I wonder. Looking forward to repatriation is one thing, but what could await us in Japan?

Tuesday, 25 September

Having gone downstairs, Hiro came straight back up again saying, 'Amah and Chokugetsu-ken are standing outside the house!' Almost before the words were out, Taka was skidding down the stairs to get to Amah. By the time I got there, Amah was fussing over him in tears.

'Missy, wollee Kazu, Taka no enuff foo. Bringee biscui and fru,' she said, pressing a heavy bag into my hands. Chokugetsu-ken had his pedicab positioned so that Amah could not be seen from the street, and stood as if on look-out. As soon as Amah gave me the gift, he told her to get into his pedicab.

He flashed me his wide smile before pedalling off, and said, 'Missy friend, Tong *Tai tai*, she ass abou you. I tell her I visit.' And then they disappeared into the busy street.

Hiro, who was poking into the bag, sounded excited. 'They brought some almond biscuits and oranges!'

But his expression swiftly took on a worried look. 'Chinese Nationalist guards are roaming the streets. Chokugetsu-ken took a big risk coming here.'

I ran to the street corner, hoping to catch at least another glimpse of Amah and Chokugetsu-ken. I wouldn't want to put them in any danger, but how I wished there had been more time. I wanted to thank them for their precious gifts and ask about Mona Tong, find out how Chokugetsu-ken came to know her.

Friday, 28 September

When Tamiko arrived this morning, I knew immediately that something was wrong. Ashen-faced, she squeezed out her words. 'Masaya was killed in action, in mid-July. We've only just heard.'

We clung to each other in an embrace, as if trying not to crumble to the ground. I could see Masaya's various expressions in my mind's eye – deep in contemplation as he stared into his twirling whisky glass; his reassuring smile; and the way he looked at Tamiko, full of affection and respect.

As I thought of Masaya, my mind drifted to Akira. How I had come to see my relationship to Akira in parallel with Tamiko's to Masaya – a friendship that I had admired and envied. It suddenly occurred to me that Akira, too, might never return from war. The sense of foreboding made me hold on to Tamiko even tighter.

24

Wednesday, 3 October 1945

Tamiko and I decided to find Irma, to give her the news of Masaya. 'If she's still in her old place, it's within the bounds of where Japanese are allowed to go,' Tamiko said, as we headed towards the former Designated Area.

Little had changed since the massive air-raid. The crater in the middle of the road was still there, and the damaged buildings were left mainly unrepaired – just a few boards put up here and there to make them marginally habitable. War's end didn't seem to have made much difference to people's daily lives. The entrance to Irma's building was as shabby as ever, and Tamiko stood across the lane shouting Irma's name as I banged on the door.

We made louder and louder sounds, until we thought we would have to give up, when suddenly we heard a voice from above: 'Lieblings! *Wunderbar!* How did you know that Keith was here?' Tamiko and I looked at each other in disbelief – that we found not only Irma but Keith as well.

In many ways, it was a sad reunion, to have to share the news of Masaya's death, and to see the physical change in Irma and Keith. Even though I'd seen Irma not too long ago, she was now walking with a limp and had turned completely grey. But Keith's emaciation was a true shock, his face so gaunt that I might not have recognized him if I saw him on the street. What hadn't changed were his soft brown eyes with a compassionate glow.

'I still spend the days in the camp, and go back to our old house in Frenchtown for the night. For the time being, Joyce and Anna May are staying with some German friends,' Keith said.

Irma quickly took over. 'When the war ended, things were chaotic – lots of euphoria, but uncertainty too. Many internees at the camp were losing their heads. So Keith took on the role of welfare officer, to bring some order, and he still goes there to help people with nowhere to go. Isn't that right, Keith?'

Keith laughed. I had forgotten how comforting his good-natured laugh could be. 'Irma is a perfect spokesman. It's no wonder she managed to keep the Friends' work going throughout the war.'

'I cannot tell you how relieved I am that you are now back,' Irma said, in a heartfelt way that spoke of the heavy burden of responsibility she had been shouldering. Keith cast her an appreciative smile.

Irma spoke of how things were easier with Keith back and about the American relief dollars, food and medicine now trickling into the refugee community. 'All I have to do these days is remind impatient refugees, waiting for permits to get to America, how much better our lives have become!'

'And what will the focus of Quaker work be now?' Tamiko asked.

Again, Irma spoke before Keith could get in a word. 'Keith, do you know what I have here? A copy of your letter to the American Friends' headquarters. I am going to show it to Tamiko and Eiko.'

She pulled out a crumpled piece of paper from her pocket and spread it on the table. Tamiko and I leaned over to read:

Before we went into camp I wrote you a letter – whether you received it I do not know – in which I said I felt a concern to visit Japanese Friends as soon after the war as possible, to give them encouragement, and to see also the conditions in Japan after the war. Herbert was feeling exactly the same concern when we discussed it the other evening. I am sure that the Japanese will feel this defeat most deeply, even those who were not in sympathy with the military adventure, and the prompt offer of our friendship and concern to share in their mental suffering will do much to bring them through this period with a stronger sense of reality of Christian fellowship.

So the Quakers now plan to help the Japanese, after all they've been put through by the Japanese. Tamiko seemed moved to tears.

Monday, 8 October

'Shall we go for a walk?' Hiro suggested. The boys were out to play with Yumiko, and I had just finished clearing up after breakfast. Hiro's adjustment to life without work has been amazing – happy to sleep in, play baseball with neighbours and wander around Hongkew. I relished the thought of a little outing with him.

We walked around Scott and Dixwell roads, an area I hadn't been to before, and I was taken aback by the scene. The place was turned into a makeshift open-air market of Japanese stalls selling everything from food to knick-knacks to furniture.

'Reminds me of the back streets of old Osaka, when I was a child,' Hiro said, walking towards a particular stall that sold *imagawa* bean cakes. He couldn't resist buying one, and looked pleased when the shabby-looking man handed him the sweet wrapped in old newspaper.

The stalls were mostly run by men, young and old, all with sagging, tired looks – men no longer with jobs, desperately trying to make ends meet. I was grateful that Hiro shared none of the listlessness of the unemployed, and realized how lucky we were to have the little golden peanuts to live on, four out of the original five, still carefully hidden away.

As we were leaving the market area, a woman who looked vaguely familiar came rushing towards us waving, 'Eiko-san! Hiroshi-san!'

It was Midori Mao, with no make-up, wearing *monpe* with a tea towel wrapped around her head – so different from when I last saw her, in a tight-fitting *cheongsam*, covered in jewels.

'This is how to find people now, wandering the streets!' Midori said, looking genuinely happy to see us. Her deep, husky voice and handsome features behind the tired lines brought back the Midori I knew, making it all the more difficult to know what to say.

'How is your husband?' Hiro asked, without hesitation.

'Thank you for asking, Hiroshi-san,' she said, equally straightfor-wardly. 'As you know, the *han-jian* collaborator trials have started. Wen-tsu is in prison, awaiting trial. The prospects are not good, but being a broken man since Shin-tsu left, being in prison seems almost a relief for him.'

How little I knew of what others were going through, having been so caught up with the changes in my own life.

Midori continued in her matter-of-fact tone. 'In the meantime, we – me and his other wives – have been forced out of our house. With Mr Uchiyama's help, I managed to find the ladies a small, secure place to live. I wasn't close to them, but one of them is Shin-tsu's mother and I wanted to do what I could – for his sake, really.'

She said she lived in a row house dormitory for *nikkyō*, next to Li Koran. 'As if the authorities thought they'd better keep us 'suspect' ones in one place.' She shrugged her shoulders with a wan smile.

Before she rushed off to the market stalls, I suggested she came around to our place sometime so that I could take her to see Tamiko and Rokki. Her mention of Shin-tsu stirred a longing, and she was a connection to him. What could Shin-tsu's life be like now, with the war over? Where could he be?

Thursday, 11 October

There was someone at the front door, and I wondered whether it might be Midori. I looked around, but saw nobody, until Chokugetsu-ken's face suddenly appeared from around the corner. He rushed over with his big wide smile, handing me an envelope and a bag filled with treats for the children.

'Missy, letter from Tong *Tai tai*,' he said, before turning back to the corner. 'I wai' ova dere with pedicab.'

I quickly opened the letter:

Dearest Eiko,

The world has changed, and you have been in my thoughts. We are well. Despite S.P.'s association with St John's University, my family's ties with the Nationalists have protected us from being caught in the collaborator net, and we continue to live comfortably in our house in Frenchtown. I hear confiscation of Japanese property will intensify. This is a thought: if there is anything you would want us to hold for safekeeping, we are happy to do so. Chokugetsu-ken, who I've come to know by chance by riding his pedicab, can be the courier. He is very devoted to you.

With much love, Mona

I ran upstairs and reread the letter, uncertain as to what to do. I handed it to Hiro, who was lazily reading a novel in the bedroom. To my surprise, he swiftly got up and said, 'we should take up their offer. Nationalists coming back to Shanghai from Chungking see Japanese property as easy game to line their pockets. Mona's taking a risk in the current climate of Chiang's collaborator witch-hunts. It's a generous gesture.'

We quickly gathered some belongings of value – a spare watch and a few pieces of jewellery – and stuffed them into an old leather handbag, which I then put in a cloth sack, and rushed down to Chokugetsu-ken.

Chokugetsu-ken casually threw the sack into the pedicab basket, saying, 'Missy you no wolly, I takee to Tong *Tai tai*. Amah say halo. She much missee boys.' And off he went.

As I watched Chokugetsu-ken pedal away, I couldn't help feeling anxious, my precious rings and brooches taken away into the unknown. I had all the faith in Mona and Chokugetsu-ken, but anything could happen – *pisse* robbing Chokugetsu-ken or Mona and S.P.'s circumstances changing…

Tuesday, 16 October

Hiro, returning from his baseball game, said, 'I have news for you, Eiko. Ikemoto-san is back from the front.'

I stared into his face, wondering if I had heard correctly. Ever since hearing of Masaya's death, I had been preparing myself for the worst – if not death, there was always the possibility of having been sent north and taken prisoner by the Soviets, a fate feared for many soldiers whose whereabouts were unknown.

'One of the baseball players is an old YMCA regular. He said Ikemoto-san made it back to Shanghai nearly a month ago, but has been in hospital with malaria ever since.' Hiro had no further information. But at least I knew he was alive, and my heart swelled with gratitude.

Sunday, 28 October

Midori showed up this morning. We immediately set off to Tamiko and Rokki's – a fifteen-minute walk towards Woosung Lu, where they have a comfortable two-room flat to themselves, thanks to Rokki being employed by the Chinese authorities.

We joined them for lunch and a family meal seemed a particular treat for Midori, who delighted in Tamiko's simple stir-fried tofu and vegetables. I couldn't help thinking back to the time that Tamiko and I had been invited to the Mao Mansion, being served sophisticated Shanghai dishes I had never before tasted. Midori seemed oblivious to her changed circumstances, her sharpness intact.

'The way things are, I can't imagine Wen-tsu getting off lightly. Especially the way the Nationalists are trying to stop the Communists from gaining ground in Shanghai,' she said, catching Rokki's attention immediately.

'The Nationalists are very clever,' she continued. 'By making a big show of the *han-jian* trials, they are proving to the world that they, and not the Communists, are the ones who resisted Japan.'

Rokki nodded. 'I can see how rounding up collaborators would give the Nationalists more legitimacy. But with corrupt officials stripping the economy for personal gain, and so many Chinese out of work, I wouldn't be surprised if people start turning to the Communists as their hope for a better life. Which I suppose makes the Nationalists even more desperate.'

'I fear Wen-tsu will get the harshest sentence, having been so close to the Wang Ching-wei government, and being the father of a Communist,' Midori said. 'And Shin-tsu, how I worry for his safety.' The sudden softness in her tone pierced my heart.

Gazing into the distance, she spoke of how strange it was that she, a Japanese national, seemed to be in the most fortunate situation within the family. 'I'm not on trial, I have my rations, meagre as they may be, and I can return to Japan. Which isn't the case for Li Koran unless she can produce her birth certificate.' We all looked at Midori questioningly.

'Of course, by now, everyone knows that she's Japanese,' she said. 'But unless she can prove it, she will be tried as one of the biggest collaborators, having been part of the Japanese propaganda machine. Right now she's under house arrest, desperately trying to reach her parents in Manchuria.'

'But this is China,' Midori went on, her tone taking on an edge. 'Li has many Chinese fans, and a very high-up Nationalist official is promising her protection if she becomes his concubine.'

I could almost feel the air of indignation blowing from Rokki's flared nostrils. 'That's what I mean by corruption! It's incredible what's going on. Taking advantage of the post-war chaos, everyone is out for their own personal gain. Businesses, even individual homes are being raided.'

Turning to Hiro, he said, 'Some Chinese officials came to a factory not far from yours, took all the cash and machinery, and sealed the place with a note saying it was now state-owned property. Two weeks later, another set of officials came to requisition the place. It turns out that the first set were fake 'officials', some rogue, low-level officers!'

With a deep frown, Rokki said that Chinese industry would be destroyed if factories and businesses were stripped of assets without being run properly, and relief goods flooded the economy. 'There will be huge problems. It's going to take a long while for China to get back on its feet, and rebuild good relationships with Japan – which is what I want to see and be a part of.'

I felt happy to have Rokki around again, hearing his opinions, feeling his idealism, even if I didn't understand everything.

Wednesday, 31 October

I saw Akira. It was he, who recognized me as I was walking by the baseball field.

It was almost like an apparition, this man, getting up from a bench, with barely enough strength to wave my way. He was just a tall frame, of skin and bones, all his reassuring bulk having withered away. I rushed towards him, and standing at arm's length, our eyes locked, simply confirming each other's presence.

After a brief pause, Akira said, 'Eiko-san, you haven't changed at all. If anything, looking younger and more beautiful. Which certainly can't be said about me.' He let out a familiar soft chuckle, and it felt like coming home from a long journey.

We sat on the bench – standing was an effort for him – feeling the low autumn sun. There were so many things I wanted to ask but I didn't know where to start. 'I heard you were in hospital,' I managed to say.

'I was released last week – a much faster recovery than expected. I was fortunate to be in a hospital that had a supply of modern medicines. I'd been suffering from malaria and dysentery for the last two months of the war. If the war had gone on any longer, I probably would have died in the field.'

He took in several deep breaths, not because of what he was saying, I realized, but because talking was using all the energy he had. I suggested we meet again in a few days' time, after he had more rest.

'No, Eiko-san, I'm fine. I looked forward to this moment for such a long time. I would like to tell you of my time at war, for I know you would understand.' I was grateful that the sun was still warm as I awaited him to continue.

'I was lucky, in more ways than one, Eiko-san. I am truly grateful to God that I was assigned to a non-combatant unit – not because I was afraid of fighting, but because I went into war with so little thought. I spent five months moving horses around inland China, not even sure what my platoon was meant to be doing. We walked over 1,000 kilometres with our horses, under the scorching sun, day in day out. It gave me time to do lots of thinking.'

Words came pouring out, as if he needed to voice his inner turmoil. 'I realized that during my life in Shanghai, I had become an automaton, numbed by the atmosphere of war, doing what was expected with no real decision-making of my own choosing. It was life in the land of the occupier, where one lost a sense of the real meaning of war, and the passion to reject war.'

'The question that kept on coming back to me was: what would I have done if I were in a fighting unit and had to kill a Chinese?' Akira gazed into the sky, a haunted glint in his eyes. 'I was deeply ashamed that I thoughtlessly allowed myself to be drafted without resolving such a fundamental issue beforehand. It was sheer luck that I ended up a foot-soldier tending horses.'

Akira's words, at that moment, sent a shock through me, as if I was struck by a bolt of lightning. It was an instinctive realization: Masaya had died because he had refused to kill a Chinese.

Unlike Akira, Masaya had resolved before he set out for war the fundamental issue, and knew what he would do if he came face to face in combat. Hence his equanimity when he left Shanghai. I was certain of it.

I felt my energy drain, from my understanding of Masaya's fate, and from relief and gratitude that Akira had ended up looking after horses – that he was alive, by my side.

He was now leaning forward, elbows on his knees, talking with his eyes fixed on the ground before him.

'It's really only to you, Eiko-san, that I can admit my shame in not having rejected war more forcefully. Becoming a conscientious objector didn't even occur to me. And to think that the very reason I had decided to come out to China in my youth was to make up to the Chinese for the injustices Japan was carrying out against them.'

'You are now back safely, in a position to continue your life's work, which I am sure is God's wish.' I said. The words came easily, an effect Akira always had on me, confident of his acceptance.

Although in a less philosophical, much simpler way, I felt I knew exactly what Akira was saying.

Had I not felt the contradiction of hating the suffering Japan was causing to her enemies while enjoying the comfortable life of being Japanese in Japan-occupied Shanghai? And how uncertain I had been about the war itself, never being able to view Britain or America or China as true enemies, yet feeling loyal to Japan as a Japanese, believing in her right to have a bigger place in the world. All I could do was to live according to my conscience in small daily decisions because the big issues were too vast for me to tackle.

'You are right, Eiko-san,' he said, his expression brightening as if a cloud had lifted.

'I shouldn't be regretting the past, but should look forwards, see what use I can be in the future. Your *gētoru* fabric, by the way, served me well during my long walks in the rough terrain. But they're now in complete tatters!'

He smiled, making me immensely happy, even though his face no longer had the fleshiness to make his eyes disappear.

Tuesday, 6 November

A general restlessness seems to be spreading through the Japanese community, and I can see myself getting caught up in it if I'm not careful. Could it be the shorter days and the sudden cold front that make everything seem greyer and duller? Or the rumours that repatriation could begin any day now, making life seem even more in suspension?

Just getting through the day is becoming a challenge, with prices rising by the minute. Our tiny rations of rice aren't enough, but trying to find affordable supplements could be an all-day effort, even with money.

Hiro says the stalls in the open-air market along Scott Road are disappearing. Something about an American soldier and two Japanese dying from a home-brewed concoction from one of the stalls, resulting in market restrictions. With the market closed, I suppose people have little means to earn anything. No wonder everyone is so focussed on the repatriation boats.

Although I feel swamped by daily chores, with little time to spend with Tamiko or Akira, I won't let myself be swept by the general malaise. Hiro remains his carefree self, and I should follow his example.

Tuesday, 13 November

Shanghai crabs appeared in the market, and I couldn't resist buying a few small ones as a surprise for Hiro. I made sure to get detailed instructions from Tamiko so that I could prepare the crabs to perfection.

The struggle in the tiny kitchen was well worth it when I saw Hiro's delighted look as I brought out the steaming bamboo basket. The boys and I had dumplings and enjoyed watching Hiro delicately dip the crab flesh into the ginger and vinegar sauce, before sliding it into his mouth. 'Just as good as Chokugetsu-ken's,' he said.

But by the end of dinner, Hiro had broken into hives all over. Even his lips became swollen out of shape. How wretched I felt! I should have known to be more careful. Why did I ever think of buying crabs from the germ-filled market? If he isn't better tomorrow, we will have to find a doctor.

Wednesday, 14 November

I went to Tamiko's to seek her advice on Hiro's hives, and found Irma there. By sheer chance, she had with her some relief goods, including medication.

'What has Hiroshi been eating, not Shanghai crabs, I hope!' Irma said, making me scoop up my shoulders and hide my head in embarrassment. 'Eiko! The *wasser* quality is bad this year. Orthodox Jews are wise to not eat shellfish.' Tamiko chuckled at Irma's motherly admonishment.

'Give Hiroshi these,' Irma said, taking a few pills from a bottle and wrapping them in brown paper. 'They suppress histamine, which causes allergies.' I didn't understand, but it sounded impressive.

Irma buried her face back into her bag and pulled out tins of fruit, powdered milk, and some chocolates – things that were unimaginable luxuries.

'These are for you – American relief goods that are flowing into the refugee community.'

Tamiko gave Irma's hands a squeeze. 'Irma, this is too generous of you,' she said.

'It's the least I can do for my Japanische Lieblings, who helped me in difficult times!' Irma responded. 'This is nothing compared to what the Quakers are doing. Keith is now busy organizing prison visits, taking supplies to Japanese prisoners taken in for war crimes. Keith says he knows what the prisoners need because he has first-hand experience!'

'I wonder what life in camp was like for him,' I said.

'Yah, yah, I heard,' Irma said. 'His first job was lavatory cleaning. Then he got a bad attack of dysentery. Food was just one bowl of congee a day towards the end. At one point they had to move camps, the men made to walk, to a dilapidated place in the middle of a factory district near the Water Works and Power Station.'

As soon as Irma said this, I recalled the trams filled with Western women and children trundling along Nanking Road.

'I saw them! The trams passing right by the Friends' office,' I exclaimed.

'Ach so, so you know it was only months before war's end. The internees had to clear open trench latrines to make the place habitable, but most were too weak for the work. If the war didn't end when it did, many would have died in camp.'

'And Keith is helping Japanese war criminals now?' I asked, trying to comprehend the Quaker mind. How could they contemplate reaching out immediately to the very people that caused such personal suffering?

'Yah, Eiko, the Friends believe in treating all peoples equally. In a way, it's very simple, they just do what they believe is right. Keith said in the early days of camp life, they put on a production of *Twelfth Night*, and some of their Japanese captors were so moved, they asked him to lead them in Bible study. He's seeing them now in prison!'

Tamiko said little, but I noticed in her eyes an intensity I had never seen before as she leaned forward and absorbed Irma's every word.

Monday, 19 November

Yumiko from downstairs came up mid-morning. 'Auntie, there is a new 'school' for children. Not a real school, but a place where Japanese children can hear stories and play games. May I take Kazuo-kun and Takao-kun with my brother and sister?'

I'd become so accustomed to Yumiko looking after Kazu and Taka, I hadn't given much thought to how remarkable a little girl she is, so mature for her age. I could tell that she was offering to take the boys on her own initiative, despite the added bother of having two extra little ones to manoeuvre through the neighbourhood streets. Kazu and Taka were already jumping up and down, wanting to be with her.

'Auntie, maybe you'd like to come too, to see this place,' Yumiko suddenly said, perhaps because she noticed me staring rather intently at her.

'I'd love to,' I said, making her break into a smile, which reflected the pure innocence of a ten-year-old. I bundled the boys into warm clothing and set off with the five children, although it was Yumiko who was taking the lead.

We weaved through back alleys, and after about ten minutes, reached a non-descript low concrete building, which felt like a run-down community hall. There were already about twenty Japanese children seated in a circle in the middle of the room, and mothers standing around the edges. To my surprise, Tamiko was among them. As the children joined the circle, I quickly squeezed into a space by Tamiko.

'Fancy seeing you here! I just learned about this gathering organized by Uncle Uchiyama yesterday when I ran into Cheeko – who's
now living with the Uchiyamas,' Tamiko said.

'Uncle decided he'd hold a story-telling session at all the wards in
Hongkew on different days because the *nikkyō* self-governing body
is taking too long to set up a temporary school for children awaiting
repatriation. He's concerned that the children have few worthwhile
activities to keep them occupied.'

As Tamiko was filling me in, Uncle Uchiyama arrived in the
room and slowly shuffled along to the centre of the room, waving
his hand to the children who were buzzing with excitement. The
minute he sat down though, they became instantly quiet. There
was something about Uncle that commanded their attention, even
though his kindly, warm smile never left his face.

'I am Kanzo Uchiyama,' he began. 'I'm here today to share
some stories with you.' He spoke as if to fellow adults without
a trace of condescension, and the children looked towards him,
transfixed.

'You know that we have gone through a very difficult war, which
caused sufferings to many people. We must all work together so
that Japan will never go to war again. Do you know the country
called Switzerland?'

Some children shouted yes, and others shook their heads while
Uncle acknowledged the responses with a smile.

'Well, Switzerland is a country that does not take sides in dis-
putes, and because of that, they were able to help everyone during
the war by sending parcels and letters and messages. Let's hope you
can grow up in a Japan that becomes like Switzerland. I'm going
to tell you the story of Heidi, a little girl in Switzerland and her
adventures.'

The children had inched forwards, completely absorbed, and
Uncle glanced up briefly to indicate that it was the moment for
grown-ups to leave. Tamiko leaned over and whispered, 'Let's get
a cup of tea somewhere.' I was rather sad to miss the story of
Heidi.

Saturday, 24 November

I heard noise downstairs, and wondered why Hiro and the boys were home so soon after they left for the baseball field. But the footsteps coming up the stairs were too heavy to be theirs, and I felt a sudden unease.

With one loud knock, in came three Chinese army officers dressed in soiled uniforms. They barely acknowledged my presence and swiftly scattered around the small quarters, fingering every object they could find. I suddenly recalled Rokki mentioning homes being raided.

I managed to remain calm, worrying only about the three remaining golden peanuts, surely to be confiscated if found. I had hidden them carefully – even Hiro didn't know where they were – and held my breath as I stood in a corner of the kitchen during what seemed like an interminably long search. I couldn't see through to the bedroom, but sensed from the noise that they were opening every drawer and cupboard, and turning over the bed. I thought, nothing under the mattress, I'm not that silly!

They came out looking irritated, not having found anything of value, and stormed through the kitchen cabinets. With only my best kitchen knife as their prize, the leader of the pack grunted as he jutted out his chin towards the door, and they retreated down the stairs.

I didn't dare move from my corner until I heard the front door bang shut, certain that they were gone. From their expression, I was almost certain they hadn't found the golden peanuts. But I needed to be sure. Ignoring the bedroom mess, I went straight to the window. As soon as I opened it, a gush of cold wind blew in, giving me the shivers.

I gingerly slid my fingers along the outside windowsill, and the moment I touched the piece of string, I felt triumphant. Our golden peanuts were safe, still hanging from the nail I had hammered into the ledge. I quickly closed the window again, leaned against the wall and let out a long breath of relief.

How lucky we were that all they managed to take was a kitchen knife! It suddenly hit me that it was all thanks to Mona's foresight and generosity that there were no items of value in the house.

Friday, 30 November

Mr Yamagiwa came up this morning to tell me that Yumiko had come down with a slight fever and wouldn't be able to take the boys out to play. 'She should be better for the next Uchiyama story-telling session,' he smiled.

'By the way, the first repatriation boat is scheduled for early December,' he said. 'This time, it looks pretty certain to happen, and people from Wards One to Four have been told to be ready. It couldn't have come sooner. People are getting pretty desperate these days, running out of money and goods to sell.'

So the much awaited repatriation is finally happening.

Tuesday, 4 December

I saw Cheeko at the market. 'Eiko-san! I can't believe it took so long to run into each other. Not quite like shopping at the Japanese grocery van, is it.' How nice it was to hear Cheeko's cheerful chirping again!

'You know that we are now living in Mr Uchiyama's house, together with Tanaka Miyo-san and her baby Mariko,' Cheeko said.

How caught up in my own life I'd been, having had little time to think of others like Cheeko and Miyo, who had been such a part of my life before war's end.

'Miyo-san and baby are fine, but Tanaka-san hasn't returned, nor has he been heard from,' Cheeko said, with a frown. 'We fear he has been captured by the Soviets. But Miyo-san is remarkable. She is always calm and reliable, a great help in the house. You can imagine how busy Mr Uchiyama is, administering the *nikkyō* self-governing body and running children's story-telling sessions. Daisuke is helping him, and even Taro and Hanako, now that they have no school, are helping with food distribution. So Miyo-san and I are kept busy cooking and keeping house – no easy task with so many people crowded together!' Cheeko twittered on, and I was grateful to be filled in on all the news.

Cheeko said that the first repatriation boat, the *Meiyū-Maru* left this morning, taking over 4,000 back to Japan. But more and more Japanese were pouring into Shanghai from inland China, the dormitories were getting really crammed, and illness was spreading.

Just as I was about to ask her when the next boat would be, she looked at her watch and said, 'Ooh, I must rush!' Off she went, leaving me to wonder when our turn will be to catch a repatriation boat.

Sunday, 16 December

Rain today. I felt the chill air even in the house, as we have no fuel for heating. Was it the damp cold that was preventing Yumiko from getting better? I was hoping that she might be able to take the boys to the new Sunday school that was recently started by two young Japanese teachers. Instead, seeing how tired Mrs Yamagiwa looked, I ended up offering to take her younger children along with Kazu and Taka.

It wasn't easy walking in the puddle-filled lanes with four children, but the little ones helped each other, and we eventually made it without getting too wet. I was bent over, peeling off the children's coats, when I heard a familiar, clear, pretty voice behind me. 'Mrs Kishimoto, is that you?' I turned around to find Keiko Shinoda approaching with a surprised smile.

'I'm the junior teacher running this Sunday school,' she said. 'We decided to follow in Mr Uchiyama's footsteps, and provide additional tuition for neighbourhood children. It gets more difficult to keep children occupied as the weather gets colder.' Keiko seemed more grown-up, with an added air of confidence.

'How is your health?' I asked.

'I am much better, thank you. I'm learning to take care of myself, be more independent, with no longer the Bank to look after me,' she said. 'I live in a crowded house full of single people. We share our rations, and try to find whatever work we can while we await repatriation. I'm very excited about being part of this Sunday school operation.'

Just then, Akira walked through the door. Although he was still looking frail, his sallow look had disappeared. 'What a happy coincidence to see you, Eiko-san,' he said. 'I came here to check up on Keiko. Make sure she's as good with children as she was with flowers.'

'Ikemoto-san, don't tease me. I am grown up, you know,' Keiko giggled.

After observing the class for about ten minutes, Akira suggested that we leave. 'I'd like to catch up with you while the children are being looked after,' he said.

We found a dreary café nearby, which was cold and had little to offer, but it was at least a place to sit. Over tasteless tea, I learned that Akira was running an English-language school.

'I've been walking around to build up my strength, and one day, in one of the discarded English-language newspapers, I saw this tiny piece saying that since the Allied Occupation of Japan, there's a huge demand for English speakers. It said an English speaker could earn a dizzying amount of money, like looking down from the Empire State Building!' Akira's laugh made the chair rattle.

'So I thought, "This is it!" I needed to find a way to make money. If people heard how useful English would be when they got back to Japan, they'd flock to learn the language.' I laughed out loud. For a man with religious faith and high morals, I always found Akira's worldliness endearing.

'We use the YMCA building for classrooms, and have 100 students now. Eiko-san, do you remember we had fun planning English classes before I went to war? You were supposed to be a teacher, too. If only war had ended then...'

He clenched his fist, the cheerful demeanour gone. 'I get angry when I think of how the military leaders, and the Emperor, too, allowed the war to drag on until the very end. A negotiated peace earlier on would have saved so many lives.'

As if to prevent himself from sinking into deep anger, he took a sip of tea and said, 'Not quite the same as the coffee at the Tricolore! Those were precious times for me.'

We remained silent for a while, each of us lost in our own thoughts, until Akira suddenly looked at his watch and said, 'Eiko-san, it's time to collect the children!'

Thursday, 20 December

We had to stand out in the bitter cold this morning, to be counted for a census. Kazu was half hidden under my coat, and Taka under Hiro's as we waited for the Chinese police, still a long distance away, to inch forward with their clipboards. How authoritative the Chinese policemen looked, in contrast to the thousands of Japanese, standing meekly, heads bowed while being counted.

The Yamagiwas emerged from the house, Mrs Yamagiwa with the two younger children in each hand, and much to my shock, Mr Yamagiwa carrying Yumiko in his arms. She was all bundled up, with her head leaning against her father's shoulder, the little of what I could see of her face parched and red. I hadn't realized that her condition had deteriorated so much. On the few occasions we ran into each other, they had been saying she was making slow progress, and I didn't want to pry, for fear that they might feel I was missing a babysitter.

We exchanged nods for a greeting, and Mr Yamagiwa, with a wan smile, said to me in English, 'Not very convenient, this census. I hadn't realized how heavy Yumiko is, despite all the weight she's lost.' I didn't know what to say, and simply nodded, trying to convey all my sympathy and concern in the small gesture.

Mr Yamagiwa nuzzled his face against Yumiko's head, and muttered, 'You're being extremely courageous fighting this infection, aren't you. I'm so proud of you.' Turning to me, he said, 'It's auto-toxemia. Without medication, the infection spreads and further weakens her immune system.'

Thankfully, Mr Yamagiwa didn't have to stand outside with Yumiko for very long as the policemen finished with us relatively quickly.

Monday, 24 December

Tamiko and I took advantage of Uncle Uchiyama's storytelling session to deposit the children and visit Irma. We couldn't help notice the difference in atmosphere between Japanese Hongkew and the Jewish area – adjacent and in similar Chinese neighbourhoods – but the latter now filled with an air of hope. There were more American GIs wandering around, and a group of them were talking animatedly with some Jewish girls as they sauntered down the street. Following their movements, Tamiko remarked, 'So nice to see young people having fun!'

Irma invited us up to her little attic room, still accessible only by the precarious ladder, but now with a charcoal heater upon which was a boiling kettle. 'Lieblings! It is so good you came to see me at this very difficult, trying time.' Tamiko and I looked at each other in puzzlement.

'So many good things are happening. With the Americans and relief goods coming, job opportunities arrived, too, and many Jewish refugees are working as secretaries as they await United States entry applications to be processed,' Irma said. Although she was talking about such bright prospects, her tone was unusually subdued.

Irma swallowed hard before continuing. 'The news from Deutschland… Every day, official documentation arrives via the Swiss Red Cross, and more refugees learn of the deaths of family members. Deaths met in gas chambers. The information comes in a just a few words written on a piece of paper; the approximate dates, and the names of the concentration camps where it happened.' Tamiko took Irma into her arms, I bowed my head in prayer.

After our moment of silence, Irma gently pulled away from Tamiko. She put on her bright, motherly smile. 'Lieblings, your love is what helps overcome sorrows. Hanukkah and Christmas this year is very special, and it is my turn to give you some gifts.'

She bustled around the small living quarters, putting various items into a bag.

'Here are some chocolates and biscuits and tea. And you must give the children kisses from me to wish them a happy Christmas!'

I suddenly remembered Yumiko, and asked Irma whether she had any medicine. 'No antibiotics, I'm afraid, but give her this powder that restores strength.' She sent us off with blessings and a kiss.

Monday, 31 December

Could there be a sadder way to end the year, with a funeral for a beautiful ten-year old girl. She fought her illness so courageously, giving me the sweetest smile when I brought her Irma's medicine on Christmas Day. In the evening, Mr Yamagiwa came upstairs to say that the medicine seemed to be working, that Yumiko felt strong enough to sit up, and for the first time in weeks, there were smiles and laughter as the family ate Christmas cake. Hearing that was the biggest present I could wish for.

But two days later, Yumiko had a relapse, and since then until her death yesterday, I had the two younger Yamagiwa children with me while the parents took turns nursing her. Her fever was so high that the cold compress on her forehead had to be changed constantly, and at one point, Hiro had to look after all four children while I ran to the doctor's to request a call-out visit.

What a scene the doctor's office was, so crowded that some had to wait outside in the cold, despite their illnesses. The nurse at the reception desk said that the earliest the doctor could make a house call would be late in the night. Seeing my desperation, she kindly went in to see the doctor and came out with a packet of pills – a futile effort that provided a modicum of comfort.

It was a quick, simple funeral. Yumiko looked beautiful at her final rest – a child who managed to brighten everyone around her during her short life.

What a year this has been. God, please give me the courage to face whatever challenges lie ahead, and not let my spirits falter.

25

Saturday, 5 January 1946

Even in difficult times, spirits seemed to pick up at New Year, being the most important holiday in the Japanese calendar. The weather also helped – sunny bright days making strolls along the streets a pleasant pastime. But was it my sorrow, following Yumiko's death, that made me sense forced gaiety on the faces of passers-by?

Such were my thoughts as I approached Hongkew Market, when I heard someone call out to me in English: 'Is that you Eiko? Eiko!' Before my eyes appeared Kimmy. I instantly dropped my shopping basket, and we fell into a tight embrace.

'Since when are you back from Nanking?' I asked.

'A few months now. When the war ended, we were taken to an internment camp for a few days. Horrible food eaten from cleaning buckets! Then we made the journey to Shanghai, where we were cramped into a small house, not far from our old house, with two other families. Torture, living in such a tight space! The good news is that we will be on the next repatriation boat, the *Enoshima-Maru*, which leaves later this month.' It was good to hear Kimmy's perky voice.

'Oh Eiko, I can't wait to be on the boat. Living with people who've lost everything isn't good for my morale. I wish I'd met you earlier, and we could have spent some time together.'

I, too, would have liked to have run into her sooner. We promised each other that we would meet again in Japan. I wonder how long it will be before it is our turn to be repatriated.

Sunday, 13 January

Not a raid, but a burglary this time, while I was at the market and Hiro had taken the boys to Sunday school. At first I noticed nothing. But when I opened the kitchen cupboards, I realized all our rice was gone.

In the bedroom, most drawers were opened, but there was no mess. All that was missing was one of Hiro's thick jumpers. Our last golden peanut was still hanging outside the window, much to my relief.

I felt strangely resigned, no sense of the violation I'd experienced during the raid, only a pitiful sigh at the desperation of the burglar, stealing just rice and a jumper.

Wednesday, 16 January

I went to Tamiko's and knocked repeatedly, but there was no answer. Finally, the door of the adjacent flat opened, and a distinguished-looking Chinese lady poked her head out, asking me in perfect English, 'May I help you?'

'Tamiko has gone out with Rokuro, and the girls are with a neighbour,' she said. 'Would you like to leave a message for Tamiko with me?'

I thanked her and said there was no need for a message. Where could Tamiko have gone? I just wanted to see her, hoping she would cheer me up. I'd become impatient to go back to Japan ever since seeing Kimmy, and wanted Tamiko, always unconcerned about the boats, to pull me out of repatriation fever.

Sunday, 20 January

On my way home, after dropping off the boys at Sunday school, a boy and a girl on bicycles pedalled past me, each pulling carts laden with luggage. The girl was struggling, and when I caught up, I saw that it was Hanako, Cheeko's daughter. How she had grown since the troop performance, when she played granddaughter to Tamiko's grandmother!

'Hello, Hanako-chan,' I said.

It took her a while to register who I was. 'Oh, you're Mrs Tamiko Yamanaka's sister. Taro! Stop! Don't go ahead without me. Come say hello.' Hanako shouted towards Taro, who approached in a half bow.

'We're helping with the luggage for people going on the next boat, which leaves tomorrow,' he said. 'Come on, Hanako, we better get on with our rounds.'

They gave me a quick bow and were off. Taro seemed just as enthusiastic about helping with repatriation as he was to be a fighter pilot. What a change in a matter of a few months. Cheeko must be proud of her hard-working children.

Wednesday, 23 January

The news that the *Enoshima-Maru* sunk just beyond the Yangtze spread like wildfire all over Hongkew. But I couldn't find out anything more apart from the fact that the boat had hit a mine in the East China Sea. Nothing on the whereabouts of the over 4,000 passengers, including Kimmy and her family. I walked over forty minutes to see Cheeko, in the hope that she'd have news. But she was equally in the dark. Apparently, Uncle Uchiyama hasn't been home since the accident happened.

Saturday, 26 January

The Noguchis are safe, housed with a family not far from us. I ran over to see Kimmy, and after a tearful embrace, she asked to come home with me to escape the chaotic aftermath of being rescued.

'It's been a nightmare, not just the accident, but after getting back to Shanghai, too. I'm so glad to be sitting in this calm room,' she said. Once she had some tea, she regained her old perkiness.

'Look at me, Eiko! This is the new fashion called *Enoshima* survivor style,' she said, pointing to the pair of grey trousers too big for her, and the padded jacket, the kind old Japanese men wear in the house. 'Provided by the elderly couple putting us up. Everything we owned was lost at sea.'

'But I'm alive! Considering what we went through, it's amazing that only twenty lives were lost. The boat was like cattle transport – the lower decks divided into layers, like bunk beds, and whole families in one bunk. I managed to find an old school friend in a nearby bunk, so we were keeping each other company, chatting away,' she recounted.

'Then suddenly, there was a huge bang, people were thrown all around, and the lights went out. Everyone tried to get up to the deck, almost pulling each other off the tiny ladder. I didn't know where my friend had gone, or where my parents were. By the time I finally reached the deck, the place was overflowing with people, and some men were starting to pull wood off the panels – to use as rafts. The boat started tilting and the emergency horn was blasting away, making so much noise that nothing else could be heard. But the strange thing, Eiko, was that I didn't feel scared, it was like watching a scene from a film.' Kimmy looked into space, as if reliving what she had gone through.

'The panic around me mounted as the time went on, the sun began to sink, and darkness descended. It was getting colder too. It seemed only a matter of time before we would all be thrown into the freezing waters.'

It hadn't occurred to me that the much-awaited return to Japan could be so dangerous. But here it was, laid bare before me. What would happen to Kazu and Taka in such a situation? My hands involuntarily grabbed the edge of my chair, as if I was hanging on to the boys determined not to let go.

'I thought I would never see my parents again, that this was going to be the end of me. I wasn't frightened, but overcome by huge sadness. People started shouting, I thought because the boat was sinking. But they'd seen another boat, approaching us at full speed. And we were rescued by an American cargo ship called the *Brevard*.'

Once back in Shanghai, she thought she would be going back to her old house. 'Well Eiko, no way!' she said, getting animated. 'The Chinese Nationalists are moving into Shanghai in droves from Chungking, so as soon as a repatriation boat leaves, the vacated buildings are quickly taken over. I couldn't find my parents for two whole days!'

It was Uncle Uchiyama's organization that found accommodation for the *Enoshima-Maru* victims, putting lost people in touch and feeding and clothing them.

'Well, maybe we should get you some decent clothes,' I said, pulling her into the bedroom. We spent the next half hour picking out things that would suit her, both of us trying on this and that – an activity that allowed us to momentarily forget the horrors of the sinking boat. In the end, we selected a number of items for her to take, including those she put on immediately – a pair of brown trousers, a simple white blouse and a woolly beige jumper with small flower patterns at the collar and cuffs, a favourite of mine.

'Are you sure I can have all these things?' Kimmy asked, her eyes dancing with glee as she admired herself in the mirror and daintily fingered the flower patterns. I would have been happy to give her more.

Thursday, 31 January

The *Enoshima-Maru* passengers, including Kimmy and family will be on the next boat, due to leave in a few days' time. Still shaken by Kimmy's experience, I went to Tamiko's for comfort. This time she was in.

The children launched straight into their game of 'house', and I tried to find out what Tamiko had been up to, without sounding too nosy.

'Oh yes, Dr Wu told me you had been around,' Tamiko said. 'She's an amazing lady, a Chinese medical doctor who studied in Japan. She's been silently treating Japanese patients throughout the war, and even now, with Nationalist agents always on the lookout for collaborators, she continues to help the Japanese.'

Tamiko seemed full of admiration. 'The Friends' Ambulance Unit is also active in helping sick Japanese, mainly transporting them to doctors and hospitals. They're also looking to expand their activities to support the particularly vulnerable, just like the Friends are doing for Japanese prisoners. I'd like to get involved, help where I can,' she said, staring at me intensely.

So that's what Tamiko had been doing – finding out about Friends' activities. She seemed so absorbed, hardly thinking about her own family's repatriation.

'Do you think you'll be able to help the Quakers and get ready to go back to Japan at the same time?' I asked.

'I don't know yet, just thinking,' she said.

'Well, if you're going to be busy with your good works, I can help look after the girls and do the packing for you – I'm very good at it,' I said. At that moment, I had a strong hunch that we would be assigned to the same repatriation boat.

'We'll be going back to Japan together I'm sure. Oh, Tamiko, it will be wonderful!'

'You make it sound like we're going on a cruise, Eiko!' Tamiko laughed.

'I know about the boat conditions from Kimmy. But if we're together, it will be fine.'

The uncertainty and wait for the boat now seemed quite bearable.

Monday, 4 February

I heard a sharp tinkle of a bicycle bell as I approached our lane, back from the Hongkew Market. Alarmed, I turned around, and there was Chokugetsu-ken's wide face beaming a friendly smile. 'Missy, happy I find you!' he said, dismounting his pedicab.

Hunching over so that people wouldn't see, he quickly handed me a small package wrapped in old newspaper. 'Missy, Tong *Tai-tai* say givee this. She givee letter too.' He then pointed to the end of the lane saying, 'I wai' ova der, smokee cigare. Takee time.'

I ran upstairs and immediately opened the package, which turned out to be a wad of cash. I then tore open her letter:

Dearest Eiko,
I have taken the liberty of selling the watch and the leather handbag, thinking you might need money with sky-rocketing

prices. What news of repatriation? Let me know what I should do with your other valuables and how I can help.

Love, Mona

I sat tightly holding the money. How did Mona know we were starting to run low on funds? I could picture her pretty, intelligent face and imagine her mind working, her determined look as she took swift action. I was overcome by gratitude, but there was little time to dwell. Chokugetsu-ken was waiting. What ought I do, not knowing when repatriation would be? Should I ask her to start selling my jewellery, or ask to have them back? In the end, I could only think of leaving it up to her:

Dearest Mona,

I am sending a few more leather handbags and shoes with Chokugetsu-ken, and would be grateful if you could sell them in the next couple of weeks. As for the jewellery, please keep them for the time being until I have a clearer idea of repatriation timing. Should there be no opportunity to communicate before we leave, I entrust you with the remaining valuables to make the best use of them.

With more gratitude than I can possibly express,

Love, Eiko

Yes, Mona would know what to do. Even if I didn't know what the next few weeks might hold for us, Mona allowed me to feel confident that all would be well.

Saturday, 9 February

Kazu has come down with a fever, and complains of a toothache. At least it's just a toothache. But how cramped our place becomes with an unwell child. Taka won't go to sleep, curious about Kazu's whimpering and the attention he's getting. In the end, Hiro had to bundle Taka up and put him to bed in the sitting room, where Hiro, too, is having an enforced early night. And I am here, sitting by Kazu, writing my diary in between changing the icepack on his cheek.

Tuesday, 12 February

Kazu's toothache turned out to be a bone-marrow infection in his mouth.

Just mentioning his condition gives me the jitters. I haven't allowed myself to sleep – how could I stop keeping vigil while Kazu is in a delirious state, with little sign of improvement.

By Sunday night, we knew that something was very wrong, as Kazu's fever kept shooting up. I can't remember how many times Hiro had to run over to the fishmonger in the market to get ice. Mr Yamagiwa, noticing the heavy foot traffic, came up discreetly to ask if there was anything we needed, and taking one look at Kazu's feverish face, quickly said, 'We must find a doctor immediately.'

He rushed downstairs, and I knew it was out of kindness, but his instinctive reaction alarmed me. After all, he had experience with Yumiko's illness – he must have sensed the severity of Kazu's condition. It then hit me: I could lose Kazu, given the shortage of doctors and medicine, and the spread of all kinds of diseases in Shanghai.

Shortly, Mr Yamagiwa came rushing upstairs, saying there was one dentist still open, about twenty minutes away. We bundled Kazu into warm clothes and blankets, Hiro carrying him on his back, with me at his heels.

The twenty-minute walk took much longer. How heavy an inert child could be! I was determined to do my share of carrying, hoping that my efforts would somehow transfer to Kazu and give him strength.

When we finally arrived, an unassuming, slight dentist in his late thirties, appeared, and swiftly placed Kazu into the dental chair. After prying open Kazu's mouth and poking around for a while, he gently put down his tools, pulled Kazu's blanket up to his chin, and turned to face us with a sad, resigned look in his eyes. My heart sank. I lowered my head, and awaited the verdict.

'Your little boy has an abscess in his mouth caused by an infection of the bone marrow. It is serious, and can be cured only with antibiotics.' The dentist paused.

'*Ah so desuka*,' Hiro said, in simple acknowledgement. For me, the dentist's pause meant only one thing – that antibiotics weren't available. We would have to rally round Kazu to fight his illness, just as Yumiko had done, and hope against all odds that he would come through.

Although I had to fight back my tears, I bowed deeply and said, 'Sensei, you have been kind to see us at this late hour. We would be grateful if you could give us whatever medicines you have that will help Kazuo gain strength to fight his infection.'

The dentist stared at me for quite a long time and finally said, 'Oku-san, even with antibiotics, many children are so weakened these days from lack of proper nutrition, and can succumb to illness. I myself lost a son two months ago.' I now understood his sad expression, and was deeply moved. I bowed again with heartfelt condolences.

The dentist spoke softly. 'I have one packet of antibiotics left, having refused to hand them over to an arrogant *pao chia* leader for a large sum of money, knowing that he would just turn them around for even more money on the black market. I am happy to give them to you, in the hope that your boy will pull through. Bone marrow infections require a longer administration of antibiotics, and the packet may not be quite enough, only ten days' worth, but let's give it a try. My boy was just a little older than yours, and it would make me very happy to save a child's life.'

Without waiting for our reaction, he went over to a cupboard at the other end of the room, and fiddled with what looked like a small safe.

Hiro and I watched with our heads bowed, and I knew that Hiro was as touched and grateful as I was. After taking out a little bottle from the safe, the dentist walked over to Kazu, and gently patted him over the blanket to get his attention. Until then, Kazu had been half asleep the whole time. But he now opened his eyes. Pouring water from a jug into a small cup, the dentist pulled Kazu forward in the chair and told him to be brave and swallow the pill. Kazu blinked several times, as if he were trying to shake off his grogginess, and then did what he was told. Before letting him sink back into the chair, the dentist deftly stuck a spoonful of syrup into Kazu's mouth.

'Three pills a day, after a meal, and the syrup every four hours if the fever doesn't come down,' he said, handing me two bottles. 'The syrup is a mild form of aspirin suitable for children. I wish you the best.' He gave us a bow, and then turned to fetch Kazu, intending no doubt, to help put him on Hiro's back. But Hiro stopped him.

'Sensei, please take this as a token of our gratitude to you,' he said, reaching into his coat pocket and producing an envelope. In my panic over Kazu's condition, I hadn't even thought of what might happen at the dentist's office, but Hiro must have prepared the money while I was dressing Kazu. I was grateful for Hiro's foresight, and comforted by his dependability. How timely Mona's cash was! Kazu was just as heavy going home, but somehow, my footsteps felt lighter from having encountered such a fine, decent dentist.

Since then, though, my heart remains heavy. It is two full days since Kazu started taking the antibiotics, with little visible improvement. His fever returns as soon as the syrup wears off, and he's asleep most of the time. The dentist's words, 'even with antibiotics, children can succumb to illness' keep coming back. Kazu was never a strong boy, and perhaps the lack of nutritious foods has weakened him even more.

The Yamagiwas, the dentist – so many have lost a child. Can I expect to be spared? Oh God, please give me moral strength and hope.

Thursday, 14 February

One day blurs into another, and time seems to pass so slowly, yet it is already four days since we took Kazu to the dentist. There is still hardly any perceptible change in his condition – when his breathing sounds less laboured, I start becoming hopeful, and then his face reddens again with fever.

Tamiko dropped by in the morning to take Taka for the day – as she has been doing for the last three days. Today, she came with a gift from Irma – the same powdered medicine that gave strength to Yumiko enabling her to enjoy Christmas before she had her relapse.

'Irma was her typical motherly self,' Tamiko reported.

'She wanted to know every detail of Kazu's symptoms.' Tamiko imitated Irma: 'With the antibiotics, he will be better, *ganz bestimmt*, *ganz bestimmt*! Just make sure Eiko gives him lots of liquids. Put this powder in water and make him drink many times a day!'

'When Irma gets excited, she's even bossier, and German words come flying out,' she said with a soft chuckle.

'But Eiko, she really is quite certain that Kazu will get better, and when Irma says so, it's bound to be true.'

Tamiko gave me an encouraging squeeze on the arm. I must be strong and keep up my faith.

Monday, 18 February

Having slept little during the night, I was dozing in the sitting room while Hiro took over to keep an eye on Kazu. I must have had a moment of deep sleep because it took me a while to realize that I was being nudged on the shoulder. And then I heard Hiro's voice saying 'Eiko, wake up, wake up!' right by my ear.

As soon as I regained total consciousness, I jumped out of my chair in panic. I grabbed Hiro's arm, and swallowed hard, preparing myself for the worst.

Hiro looked surprised at my sudden reaction. 'What's the matter? I just came out to tell you that Kazu is asking for you. I was dozing a bit myself when I suddenly heard Kazu calling "Mama, Mama," and when he saw me, he said he's hungry. You better go and take a look.'

I felt as if my legs would give way from relief, but didn't dare believe all was well. I gingerly went into the bedroom, still apprehensive of what to expect. Kazu lay on the bed, his round eyes wide open, with a little smile on his face.

'*Mama, onaka suita,*' he repeated – of course, he had eaten little in the last ten days. I took his little hands into mine, noticing how bony they had become, and planted a gentle kiss on his forehead. The fever had gone, leaving a pleasing softness against my lips.

'Shall we have some *ojiya*, then?' I said, and he beamed an eager smile for some rice gruel.

What a joy it was to see spoonful after spoonful disappear into his mouth, which kept opening as if he were a goldfish! I pray this is the turning point, and tomorrow, I can drop an egg into the gruel to help him recover his strength.

Thursday, 28 February

Tamiko hosted a dinner for us last night to celebrate Kazu's recovery. We took our own rice as everyone's rations are now running low, but despite the limited ingredients, Tamiko managed to whip up a lovely meal of dumplings, vegetables and tofu.

Although still a bit pale and thin, it is hard to believe that Kazu had been so ill only ten days ago. Once the antibiotics kicked in, and helped by Irma's powder no doubt, he quickly perked up, well enough to get out of bed and play with his toys.

It was Taka who was overjoyed by his brother's recovery, wanting to be constantly by Kazu's side. When Kazu got tired and lolled around the bed, Taka would bring him his most precious toy – his multi-coloured boat – as an offering to cheer him up. I hadn't realized that little Taka had been missing his brother so much! On his behalf, too, I haven't stopped saying my prayers of thanks.

Even concern over repatriation, which had loomed large in my mind, had been blown away during Kazu's illness.

But Rokki brought the subject again to the foreground. 'I heard from Daisuke that Li Koran managed to produce papers proving she's Japanese. She's on the repatriation boat that left Shanghai today,' he said.

I hadn't even known that another boat was leaving, and felt relieved our turn hadn't yet come. What would we have done, with a sick Kazu? But it made me realize that there would be plenty of sick people on the boats, and I shuddered to think of the conditions.

'There are fewer and fewer Japanese left in Shanghai now,' Rokki continued. 'You'd think things would get better for the Chinese, having won the war, but the economy is collapsing. The Nationalist officials arriving here from Chunking are grabbing whatever they can get their hands on. At this rate, the Communists will start becoming more popular, and tensions will mount.'

'I can't imagine it's going to be much longer before our repatriation,' Hiro said. 'A good time to leave if things are going to get even more difficult here.'

I looked towards Tamiko. 'I'm totally convinced that we'll be on the same boat,' I said cheerfully, expecting a light-hearted response. Instead, she gave me a strange look, which I took as an admonishment.

'I know, Tamiko, you already told me it wasn't a holiday cruise. There'll be lots of hardships, of course I know. But I want to look on the bright side. We're going back to Japan and we don't know what awaits us, but we'll be together, what more could I want!' I blurted.

Tamiko gave me a sad smile and said, 'Eiko, Rokki's work won't be finished for a while yet, so I don't think we'll be leaving at the same time as you.' I stared at her, unable immediately to accept her words.

'Uncle Uchiyama and Cheeko and Daisuke will be around until everyone is repatriated, so we'll be in good company,' she added. Feeling deflated, I tried to interpret her mysterious expression.

Rokki leaned into the table, his hands firmly planted to sustain his weight, as if about to give a lecture. 'I don't know when it will ever be a good time for me to leave,' he said emphatically.

'Now that the war between China and Japan is over, it's time to think of building bridges. Just think how mutually beneficial China and Japan could be for each other, both economically and culturally! I believe there's much I can do.' Rokki spoke with such intensity that neither Hiro nor I had any words to say.

'It's time for dessert!' Tamiko said, breaking the awkward silence. She had somehow managed to assemble enough ingredients to make a Victoria sponge cake, and the evening ended with very contented boys, including Hiro.

But I feel a dark cloud hanging over me. Tamiko's path and mine seem to be diverging, a prospect that had never crossed my mind.

Monday, 4 March

Another repatriation boat is to leave on the 17th of this month, but once again, our names were not on the list. Knowing now that we will not be going home on the same boat as Tamiko, I'm almost hoping that our turn won't come too soon so I can spend more time with her.

Hiro took the boys out to the baseball field, and I dropped in at Tamiko's, where I found Cheeko seated, deep in conversation. 'I was just telling Tamiko-san that Midori Mao is going back to Japan on the next repatriation boat,' Cheeko said.

With an unusually solemn expression, she added, 'Mao *hsien-sheng* was tried and sentenced last week. He was executed yesterday.'

I had been standing until then, but collapsed onto a seat. My thoughts went straight to Shin-tsu, wondering whether he knew of his father's fate. I felt numb at the magnitude of the tragedy.

Shin-tsu must have been at the forefront of Mr Mao's mind in his last moments – Midori had said Mr Mao was like a man without a core since Shin-tsu's disappearance. And for Shin-tsu, how would he take the news of his father, with whom he clashed over politics? Given Shin-tsu's gentle nature, I could only imagine that those differences would make Mr Mao's death all the more painful for him.

Regaining her composure, Cheeko said, 'Once the trial was over, I think the authorities wanted to get rid of Midori as quickly as possible – not wanting the Japanese wife of a traitor hanging around – and decided to put her on the next boat. We are all shocked at the sentence, although Midori seemed prepared. I wonder if his son's movements affected the trial.'

I let out a sharp cry. Did that mean they knew where Shin-tsu is, and he, too, would be in danger?

Tamiko swiftly tried to ease my fears. 'Eiko, the Nationalists had agents everywhere during the war, and Shin-tsu's political leanings

I'm sure were known to them. It doesn't mean they know what he's doing now, nor that Shin-tsu had anything to do with Mr Mao's sentence.' I gave her a grateful nod.

'Midori is remarkably strong,' Cheeko said. 'Of course she is devastated, but didn't seem surprised by the outcome, and said "Wen-tsu will now find peace." She says she was always a survivor. She even gave me a wicked smile saying, "I worked hard as a cabaret dancer before I met Wen-tsu, and in post-war Japan full of American GIs, I'm sure there'll be plenty of opportunities for my talents!"'

Midori had always been a bit of an enigma to me – her mysterious past, her worldliness, her fluctuating persona. But there was never a doubt over her love for Shin-tsu. My heart goes out to her, and I pray that Shin-tsu and she will be reunited sometime, somewhere in the future.

Sunday, 10 March

I spotted Irma in the Hongkew Market. It wasn't difficult to miss her, a foreign lady with wild grey curls, walking with a duck-like gait among a sea of Chinese people. I rushed over and tapped her shoulder from behind.

'Eiko, Liebling, what a total surprise!' she exclaimed, dropping her basket and giving me a tight hug. 'The Lord has brought us together, I am sure! I have been so busy with refugee work and Quaker things, I fretted that you might be repatriated without a chance to see you. Rokuro mentioned that you were likely to be leaving soon.'

'Oh?' I looked enquiringly at her, wondering when Irma would have seen him.

'Rokuro has become a regular visitor to the Friends' Centre, you know,' Irma said, as if answering my unasked question.

'It's easy for him because he has his special pass to leave the Japanese area to go to his office on the Bund. It's *wunderbar*, how his interest in the Quakers is developing. Always borrowing books, he is! Ever since Keith Leigh visited Tamiko and Rokuro to say goodbye before they were repatriated to England. I miss Joyce and

Keith and little Anna May so much! But they will be back home soon for a well-deserved rest.'

Irma affectionately held one of my arms and smiled into my face, expecting me to share these welcoming developments. But I was simply stunned – all these things happening, without my knowing anything! Why had Tamiko not mentioned seeing Keith, and the news of the Leighs' departure?

Irma, oblivious to my feelings, went on. 'Eiko, the Quakers will be setting up a study group. If it starts before you leave Shanghai, you must come along. In typical Quaker fashion, they're keen to gather all the new faces in Shanghai – people out of camps, or from inland China – to study what went wrong and how reconciliation could be brought about. I shall be leaving for America as soon as my papers come through. And you will be back in Japan soon. But the Friends will be continuing to promote peace in Shanghai. Isn't that *wunderbar!*'

With that, Irma gave me a big hug and a kiss on my cheek, just in case, she said, we didn't see each other again before departure.

Despite the promising picture Irma depicted, I was overcome by uneasiness – a feeling that I was losing Tamiko. I had seen her less than a week ago, but in that short period of time, where had she gone?

Monday, 18 March

Another boat left yesterday, and today, we were informed that it will be our turn next, on the *Unzen-Maru*, scheduled to leave Shanghai on 31 March – news I'd been waiting for all this time. And now that it has come, I feel drained, suddenly awash with sadness to leave this city that is now a part of me, and filled with anxiety over what might await us in Japan.

I think back to the time I first arrived, the excitement to be in a city with a Western flavour that reminded me of London, the joys of being close to Tamiko. Shanghai, the city of Takao and Asako's birth, all the fun of the four children growing up together. And the people I came to know, their faces appearing in my mind's eye, beginning and always ending with Shin-tsu. Once we leave Shanghai, Shin-tsu will become even more distant – will he be safe, will I ever see him again?

I cannot allow myself to wallow. I must get organized. The instructions are to be at the pier at 6 a.m. on the day, with strict restrictions of what we can take with us: one rucksack or suitcase and one carry-bag each, one set of toiletries, one blanket, one duvet, three sets of winter clothing, one set of summer clothing, one overcoat, three pairs of shoes, three pairs of socks, three shirts, one fountain pen, one watch, and one pencil.

The list of prohibited items is far longer – jewellery, gold, silver, artwork, binoculars, photos and documents, medicines, and any type of 'extravagance' unbefitting. Will these items be confiscated to line the pockets of Chinese officials? We know that Japan is in a state of total devastation, with severe shortages of everything. I am going to have to be creative, find ways to take back as many things as possible without being caught.

Friday, 22 March

Chokugetsu-ken turned up on our doorstep, with his usual broad smile. 'Missy, Amah send this,' he said, handing over a bag full of sweets. 'Amah miss boys, she cly evly day,' he added, cocking his head slightly. His own bright expression never wavered, if anything, his sweet smile became wider as he tipped his worker's cap before pedalling away into the throng.

It was only after he left that I realized he knew exactly what was going on, about our repatriation, and had in fact come to say goodbye. He had made it a particularly short encounter to avoid a prolonged farewell. I felt an actual pounding in my heart, bursting from gratitude and sadness.

And then, some instinct made me reach deep into the bag of sweets. Among the crinkling cellophane wrappers, my fingers touched upon a soft felt pouch, and even before I pulled it out, I knew it contained pieces of jewellery I had entrusted to Mona:

Dearest Eiko, I return herewith some things you might be able to take home with you. Larger pieces will be saved for the future. Faithful Chokugetsu-ken keeps abreast of your family needs.

Love, Mona

Thoughtful Mona. Short as her note was, the message was clear: find a way to smuggle items back to Japan; the rest will be available for Tamiko. I closed my eyes and said a silent prayer of thanks.

Monday, 25 March

How quickly the days go by when, apart from shopping for food, cooking and looking after the family, every waking moment is devoted to finding ways to take useful things back to Japan. Pleased with my latest efforts to make string by twining together strands of cotton thread – sewing materials being precious commodities in Japan, apparently – I decided to take a break and go in search of Akira. How could I leave without saying goodbye?

The Chinese YMCA building was bustling with Chinese officials, but not a sign of Akira's English language classes taking place. After walking around the building twice, I was about to give up, when I saw him come out of a back entrance. The sight of him made my heart leap, reminding me of those days, long time ago, at the Holy Trinity Cathedral. How different he looked now, never having regained the weight he lost in the war. But his smile upon seeing me was the same, and I was pleased I came in search of him.'

I'm leaving on the *Unzen-Maru*, in a few days' time,' I said.

'I'm on the boat after you, the *Hakuryu-Maru* that leaves on 8 April. We're almost at the tail end of the repatriation, and with most Japanese gone, my English language classes ended a while ago,' Akira said. He looked away into the distance, and muttered, more to himself than to me, 'How strange, to be leaving China after all these years.'

And then, he faced me squarely, and to my surprise, gave me a deep bow. 'Eiko-san, getting to know you was one of the best things that happened to me in Shanghai. It is your friendship, your open-mindedness and untainted thinking, that has kept me going on many an occasion,' he said. I could feel the blood rise to my cheeks, almost mortified by embarrassment at these unexpected words. Akira was quick to react.

'I'm sorry, I didn't mean to be dramatic,' he said, with his affable chuckle. 'It's just that I've been thinking a lot about my China experience, and had it not been for meeting you, I'm afraid I'd be going away a disheartened man.' He pretended to ignore another blush rising to my cheeks. 'I don't know how much you are aware of it, Eiko-san, but you are a very strong woman.' And he let out a hearty laugh, leaving me in amused confusion.

'Seriously, as you know, I came out to China wanting to make up to the Chinese for all the injustices Japan was imposing on them. But the truth is, I have achieved nothing on that score. No matter how much I thought I was serving the Chinese, I was always part of the Japanese establishment, never able to break away from the conqueror's mentality.'

'But Eiko-san, you don't have that mentality. You have a solid moral compass, and act according to your convictions. This is what I mean about you being so strong. When I am with you, doing what's right seems easy. I will always try to remember what it's like, being with you.' He took my hand and shook it heartily, and I placed my other hand over his, and shook and squeezed as hard as I could.

Akira is the one who taught me of moral convictions, certainly not the other way round. And he is the one who opened my mind, gave me confidence. Yet he believes I am the strong one, giving me a sense of self-worth. What more can I ask for – a friendship gained in Shanghai that will live with me forever.

Thursday, 28 March

I was busy lining our duvets with extra material and sewing in pieces of jewellery – the star sapphire ring that Hiro brought back from Thailand and the gold brooch shaped as flower petals that he gave me for my twenty-third birthday – when Tamiko came by with a gleam in her eyes.

'Eiko, you must take a break from all your packing and sewing today and come with me to the Friends Ambulance Unit Hostel. I want to spend today with you. We won't have any more opportunities before your departure.' She pulled me into an embrace, filling me with love and sadness in equal measure.

I left the boys with Hiro, and Tamiko and I walked north along North Szechuan Road huddled together despite the warm weather. At first glance, the street scenes seemed little different from normal with all the Chinese activities – hawkers shouting their wares, barbers shaving heads, rickshaws and carts fighting for space. But noticeable were the scattered closed storefronts: Japanese businesses no longer in operation. In fact, North Szechuan Road, the centre of Japanese Hongkew, had become only a shadow of its former self. We passed the Uchiyama Bookshop, no longer in the hands of Uncle, and now indistinguishable from other Chinese establishments.

I couldn't help letting out a big sigh. 'Oh Tamiko, everything is changing. It's not the Shanghai I know any more, and maybe that makes it easier to leave,' I said, trying to contain my sadness.

Tamiko pulled me close to her and said, 'But Eiko, these changes are promising! Now that the war is over, our relationship with the Chinese can start anew. There is so much that can be done, you'll see.'

I didn't know what she meant by 'you'll see,' until I arrived at the Quaker gathering. Rokki was already there, seated amongst a group of about twelve people of different nationalities. The organizer, a handsome British middle-aged lady, whose hair was tied neatly in a bun, rose quietly to greet us, and offer us seats.

'Hello, I am Suzanne, recently arrived from inland China to carry on the work of Keith and Joyce Leigh in Shanghai,' she said. 'We were just discussing the blessings that once again Japanese, Chinese, Russian, Americans, English and other nationalities can meet together in friendship for praise and thanksgiving to God.'

Turning back to the group as a whole, Suzanne continued on with the business at hand. 'This is our fourth Thursday Meeting, and I am delighted that we have a few more Japanese participants. It has been greatly rewarding to study together and explore the message and spirit of the Religious Society of Friends – by helping members of different nations to understand one another, by linking them together in relief and mutual service wherever possible.' I was struck by how each of the participants seemed to hang on to Suzanne's every word, with an intenseness that seemed to generate a collective energy.

'One of the most important things for Christians of all nationalities to do in a difficult international situation is to maintain as far as possible full Christian fellowship with Christians of other nations, including former so-called enemy nations or nations with divergent political ideologies. It is incumbent upon Christians to be informed of causes and issues involving a struggle and to face these frankly and prayerfully. Only through deep understanding can we reach peace and reconciliation.'

Rokki was practically off his chair, leaning forward in eagerness, while Tamiko sat quietly beside him, a serenity enveloping her whole being. I could picture them pouring over books, deeply involved in discussions amidst these good people.

As the group broke from their discussion session to a Meeting of Worship, a silence descended upon the room, and I felt the power of a collective spirit, an overwhelming faith from the group that through living life in imitation of Christ, the Kingdom of God would come. I knew then that Tamiko and Rokki had found their calling; that they would devote their lives to the Quaker way.

Humbled as I was from the Meeting, I also knew that I did not belong, that I would never be able to commit myself in pursuit of such great ideals. It was a moment of revelation, that this was where Tamiko and I must part. Just as the Meeting was breaking, I slipped alone into the Shanghai streets, overwhelmed by a sense of loss.

Shortly, however, my footsteps automatically picked up pace and I found myself rushing home to Hiro and the boys. Yes, I will have to pursue a just world in my own little way, and at that moment, the need was to finish packing for our imminent departure.

Epilogue

Tuesday, 9 April 1946, Shukugawa, Japan

I look out the window and sigh at the beauty of a Japanese spring morning, with the soft sun casting a sheen on the new green leaves, and mottled shadows shifting gently on the sandy earth. I am enjoying a quiet moment in the early morning, while the rest of the household is still asleep. It feels so strange to be back in Japan, in this unfamiliar house in Shukugawa. Shanghai now seems a lifetime away, yet it was just over a week ago that we sailed off from the chaotic pier.

*

It was still dark when we were loaded on to the back of an American army truck, along with several other families laden with heavy rucksacks, to be taken to the Whangpoo docks. Thankfully, it was cool enough to wear all our best clothes in layers, as we were desperate to take back as much as possible. By the time we joined the queue to get our luggage inspected, day had broken, casting greyness all around us. The weather seemed to be reflecting our mood, and the gloomy atmosphere was enhanced by the severe expressions of the inspectors, a row of three Chinese military officers, silently going through people's possessions.

I felt my palms getting sweaty as we inched forward, and each time an item from someone's luggage was cast aside to the 'confiscation' pile, my stomach churned. In my own bag, I had packed a small packet of antibiotics, handed to me by a doctor friend of Akira's, at Akria's insistence. He had said we would never be able to obtain it in Japan and I should save it for emergencies.

When it came to our turn, Hiro's rucksack was the first to be opened. I had helped with his packing, and was confident that there was nothing there to cause a problem. But when the inspector stuck in his arm and rummaged around, to my surprise, he pulled out two golf balls! Hiro must have snuck them in at the last minute. The inspector immediately confiscated the balls, and perhaps astounded by the temerity of packing so useless an item, swiftly pulled off Hiro's beautiful camelhair coat. He then made a rudimentary check through the boys' and my luggage and sent us off in disgust.

Hiro was frowning throughout, eyeing the golf balls amongst the pile of confiscated things. As soon as all of us were finished with the inspection, I nudged him to move up the gangplank. Once past the inspection, despite the sombre-faced Chinese soldiers lined up around us as we boarded the ship, I felt my tension ease, leaving me in an odd state of euphoria: the medicine was safe, as were my jewels, and my diary, which had been shoved in the bottom of Taka's rucksack, in amongst his colouring books.

When I first saw the golf balls, I didn't know whether to laugh or cry. Perhaps, if the inspection hadn't ended as it did, I might have cried, after all that effort of packing. But I could see that the inspector, pleased to have taken Hiro's coat, was no longer interested in the rest of us. Hiro's eccentricity had saved the day. How could I not find Hiro's sheer optimism endearing – the very thought that he might be able to play golf in war-devastated Japan!

The euphoria was short lived, however, because once we were on the boat, there was a mad scramble to find space – no easy matter for nearly 5,000 people to fit into the *Unzen-Maru*, a 3,000 tonne cargo ship. The lower decks were arranged into four layers of wooden shelves, each only a little over a metre high, and broken into small cubicles, somewhat like rows of double-decker bunkbeds filling a vast gymnasium.

When we tried to descend one of the ladders, we were told that there were no bunks left. Fortunately, we were relatively early to look for space on the upper deck, and managed to find a cabin for three people. With another family of four, we quickly secured the space, grateful for the relative comfort. In the circumstances having three small beds between the eight of us seemed like luxury.

But there were still Japanese authorities wielding power, and just as we were settling the boys in, we were told to vacate the cabin because it was to be set aside for the sick. The moustachioed man giving orders appeared to be a doctor, and looked apologetic while rushing us out. But much to my disgust, the moment we emptied the cabin, without even waiting for us to be out of sight, he shoved his wife and three children in and quickly closed the door.

By now, there really was no space anywhere, and the only place we could find was the hallway in front of the toilets. So we set ourselves down there, and spent the days and nights in the midst of heavy foot traffic. Even when we were asleep, people would go over our heads, saying, 'excuse me, excuse us.' And the smell was terrible. It only got worse as usage mounted, and I founded myself gagging on several occasions. I worried we'd be exposed to germs: shoes wet from the toilet floors passed by our sleeping mats only inches away.

The one advantage, if you could call it that, of being in such a public space was that we ran into unexpected people. Although the Japanese had been confined in a limited area of Hongkew, we'd been so preoccupied with getting through each day that we hardly kept up with acquaintances. Kazu was very excited when he recognized a boy from the Grosvenor House courtyard rush by with his little hands covering the front of his trousers. 'Ken-chan!' Kazu shouted, and after the boy had relieved himself, he stayed for a while to play.

Apart from the unpleasant experience with the moustachioed man, people on the boat were extremely courteous. Perhaps that was the only way to live through the crowded conditions, but I felt that the shared adversity brought out the best in the Japanese character, a natural orderliness and consideration for others. As we exchanged light bows with the people going in and out of the toi-lets, in a strange way, it gave me hope in the resourcefulness and strength of Japanese people.

It was through one of these civilized encounters that I was made to face a major moral dilemma. Two ladies, appearing deep in conversation, were approaching the toilets when one accidentally kicked my leg. Bowing deeply, she apologized profusely, almost in a state of tears. I looked up surprised, and the other lady quickly said, 'Please excuse us, her 12-year-old son has just been taken ill, a very high fever, and she is beside herself.' I asked what the matter was, and learned that the ship doctor (the real one without a moustache) said it was a bronchial infection, but nothing could be done because he had no medicine.

I immediately thought of the antibiotics in my bag. Should I mention that I have some medicine? I am ashamed to say that I couldn't make up my mind immediately, and simply wished the ladies well. And then I mulled over the matter for the next three hours, distracted from everything else. Even Hiro noticed how quiet I was. 'Are you feeling all right?' he asked, and so I told him.

'We might need the medicine ourselves, remember how desperate we were with Kazu's infection,' he said. Strangely, that response helped me decide to give it away. How desperate the twelve-year-old boy's family must be! Besides, Hiro seemed much less reluctant than I thought he might be.

When I went to collect our meal – gruel and some greens that seemed to have been cooked in seawater, four scoops thrown into the pot in response to my 'four' – I made a detour to find the doctor and handed him the medicine. The elderly doctor looked at me incredulously. '*Oku-san*, are you sure you want to do this. You know how precious it is.' I nodded and quickly turned around before there was any chance of me changing my mind. The doctor, too, was rushing off to the patient, muttering, 'He'll just about survive now with this.' Once I gave it away, I felt happy, and thought that was exactly what Tamiko would have done.

By the third day, the discomfort of living by the toilets, compounded by the meagre rations and lack of sleep, made the journey seem interminable. The boys were flopping over us to get comfortable, and I had to feign sleep, even in the daytime, to keep my wits about me. As I was lolling my head against the wall trying to shift Taka's full weight into a more tolerable position, I heard a voice by my ear and opened my eyes. It was the elderly doctor, who was crouched by my side.

'Oku-san, this really isn't a place for your family to be situated. Please come and join me in our room. It's crowded, but better than here.' So we gratefully collected our belongings and followed him to the other corner of the deck. His was a little private Japanese room, about the size of three *tatami* mats, which already accommodated seven people – a family of three and a collection of adults. It was extremely kind to invite us, because now nobody could stretch their legs, and we all had to sleep in a seated position. But we were scheduled to arrive in Hakata the following day, so anything seemed tolerable till then, and we were immensely grateful.

And finally, we reached Hakata. How happy I was to see land! I could hardly wait to stand up and stretch out. But the doctor, who had gone above deck first, came rushing back to tell us that we would not be able to disembark for another four days. There had been an outbreak of smallpox on an earlier repatriation boat, and now all returnees had to be quarantined for seven full days since leaving Shanghai. Those last days were truly the most trying – knowing we were finally in Japan and yet still stuck on the boat. We were all in a kind of stupor, even the boys, with no energy to talk, let alone complain.

It was only when I set foot on shore that the world around me seemed to come to life again. When we disembarked, there were American MPs all over the place, and some Japanese officials scurrying about to tell us where to go. Our belongings were inspected once again, but thankfully, not as thoroughly as when leaving Shanghai – they seemed interested only in making sure we weren't carrying anything dangerous. Then came the dousing of DDT. They poured the stuff over our heads, covering us in white powder, which had a chemical smell. How unpleasant it was, having our already grimy skin and hair covered with the disinfectant!

To mark the end of the process, we were stamped on our arms. Kazu was first, and then Taka, who, the minute he received the stamp, screamed, '*Bujoku da!*' making the Japanese officials wince in embarrassment towards the American MPs. How could little Taka, not even three years old, know the word 'insult'! Hiro and I couldn't help exchange a quick glance – of hidden pride and satisfaction – at his outburst of indignation. The American MP also seemed to be impressed, and stamped my arm and Hiro's with a noticeably softer touch.

We were then assigned to huts that were like horse stables – our accommodation before getting the train to take us home. The hut had a bare wooden floor, covered by a thin layer of straw. The so-called toilet was just a board set up to provide a makeshift shield. But it was the first time we could sleep with our legs stretched out, and Kazu declared, 'What a fine house this is!'

The highlight of our one-night stay in the 'fine house' was a totally unexpected visit from a man from the Kishimoto Company who brought us some small *onigiri* rice-balls. I thought it was the most delicious thing I'd ever eaten. Hiro, too, looked thoroughly contented for the first time during the journey.

At the same time, he was puzzled that a company man should show up in this port town, so far away from Osaka or Tokyo. 'Head office asked me to check that you were on the *Unzen-Maru*. The company now has a small office in Fukuoka, not far from here, which happens to be my hometown,' the man said.

'With such shortage of goods, Osaka no longer has enough positions to accommodate all former employees returning from the war. Besides, housing is a problem with so many places burned down. The company sent many of us back to our hometowns, with instructions to muster up any kind of business. I sell shoelaces and work-gloves now,' he said, with a soft laugh. 'But I'm grateful to the company to have any job at all.'

When the man left, Hiro seemed unusually shaken. 'The situation in Osaka sounds dire. To think the Kishimoto conglomerate has come down to trading everyday sundries. I worry about Father. And what might I end up doing back home?'

Early evening the following day, we were crammed into an unscheduled special long-distance train to take us back home. There must have been over 2,000 of us dishevelled-looking returnees, all carrying big rucksacks on our backs, scrambling to find space on the train. For us, it was an overnight journey of nearly 400 miles from Hakata, in the North of Kyushu to Osaka, which would take over ten hours. We squeezed into a row by the window, Kazu on my lap and Taka on Hiro's, with luggage crammed by our feet and above our heads in the bulging racks. This last bit of discomfort seemed easy to bear, however, knowing that we would soon be home.

The boys were very excited about the train ride, especially Kazu, who was fascinated to hear that we would be going through a tunnel, to cross the Shimonoseki Straits between the island of Kyushu and Honshu, the main island. He kept on asking, 'Are we under water yet?' and finally, when we were, he pulled down the window and stuck out his hand, exclaiming, 'But Mama, we can't be, because my hands are still dry!'

We dozed on and off throughout the night, lulled by the movement of the train. At every station, a large number of people got off, giving us hope that there would be more space to spread out, but mysteriously, even more people seemed to get on, with even bigger luggage than ours. Someone shouted to a newcomer, 'This is a special train for returnees from abroad.' The newcomer shouted back, 'Train schedules are a mess. We have to take whatever comes.'

The train stopped at Hiroshima station, and perhaps it was my imagination, but the constant din of voices seemed to stop, everyone trying to peer out into the dark in silence to see if the horror we had heard of was true. I was thankful it was night time, making it hard to see – I could only sense that there was barely a shadow of a building.

We arrived in Osaka in the early morning, and changed on to a local train to get us to Shukugawa, a suburb between Osaka and Kobe. The landscape from the window was desolate: so many areas of rubble where houses used to stand. I didn't know what to expect in Shukugawa, never having been here before. The train station was by a river, and to get to Mother and Father's house, we had to walk along the banks, towards the hills.

The cherry trees lining the sandy banks were in full bloom, making it the most beautiful and uplifting scenery I could have imagined.

And finally we arrived back home, to this very fine house, the largest in a Western style compound of three houses, with a swimming pool and tennis court in the middle of the grounds – all belonging to Father Kishimoto. It was almost like a fairy tale, coming back to such luxury after experiencing the worst living conditions. I felt that we were too filthy to cross the threshold.

Mother, who had changed little since I saw her last, leapt to take Kazu in her arms, and then took a good look at Taka. 'He looks like a spirited one!' she laughingly said, making me instantly realize how I had missed her liveliness and sharp wit.

Mother had the Japanese bath ready for us, and after much scrubbing and a good soak I felt transformed and human again. When we were clean and somewhat rested, we descended to the living room, where, it appeared that Mother and Father had gathered many relatives to celebrate our homecoming.

Hiro entered first, and went straight to his father. Father Kishimoto had aged, his hair much greyer and his face gaunter. But he stood erect, looking at us lovingly as Hiro bowed deeply to formally announce our safe return and gratitude for everyone's safety. Father and Mother returned bows and we turned to the others for a further exchange of greetings.

Hiro affectionately patted his brother, Sumio, on the shoulder. How long we had been away! Sumio was no longer the youthful younger brother, but had gained a professorial air, and was now married. Looking serious, he nudged his wife forward to introduce her and their baby boy. Hiro's cousin was there with her husband – she too, now married. And another cousin, who had been a teenager, was now a tall, lanky university student, dressed neatly in his uniform.

For Mother and Father, the presence of Kazu and Taka was the biggest fascination. Mother couldn't get over how big and strong Kazu had become – remembering the weakly baby she so reluctantly sent off to Shanghai with Miyo. And Father seemed genuinely amused by Taka, who rustled about, fingering every little object that caught his fancy in the nicely furnished room.

It was only after we sat down for dinner that the reality of things set in. For a start, the meal on the table was even sparser than our meals in Shanghai after defeat. The rice was not fluffy white as it used to be, but greyish beige, flickered with small dark dots – tiny stones, I hoped, rather than bugs. We had small pieces of dried fish each, and sweet potatoes to fill up our stomachs. 'I'm sorry about the lack of greens,' Mother said. 'We've planted spinach in the flowerbeds, but it will be a while before they're ready for eating. If we still have access to the garden, that is,' she added, making Hiro and I both look up quizzically.

Sumio, looking even more serious, with a deep frown etched between his eyes, said, 'The Occupation forces are going to take over the house. They've already requisitioned the other two houses, and want this one as well. I went over to speak to the SCAP authorities, but didn't get anywhere.'

Mother was getting visibly indignant. 'Sumio, you should tell Hiroshi and Eiko-san about the arrogant interpreter, who wasn't conveying at all what you were saying!' Before Sumio had a chance to open his mouth, Mother herself started explaining the situation.

'Sumio told them that we have all been burned out of our homes, and that, because the other two houses are already taken, three families plus young Ichiro are all crammed into this one house. But what does the interpreter tell the American officer? That the Kishimotos are happy to give up the house to the Occupation and consider it an honour! He didn't even consider that Sumio actually understands some English.'

Even before the news of not being able to stay in this house sunk in, I felt very foolish for having thought that the gathering of relatives was for our homecoming. Everybody actually lived here! For us, having lived in extremely cramped circumstances in Shanghai the last seven months, this large house seemed still a luxury – but a luxury not long to last.

Father, who was silently listening to his wife's outbursts, calmly spoke out. 'Hiroshi and Eiko, as you can see, we are facing a crisis. Housing is short everywhere, and it will be difficult to find places for us to move into. The Supreme Commander of the Allied Occupation Forces can't be totally unreasonable. I think there is still room for negotiation.'

He took a deep breath and turned squarely to me. Peering onto my eyes with deep tenderness, but also with a look of urgency, he said, 'Eiko, I would like to ask you to go and speak to the Allied Forces. I have the greatest confidence that with your English language skills and your grace, you will be the best negotiator on behalf of the Kishimoto family.'

All I could do was nod, overwhelmed by the responsibility, and not a little moved by the trust placed in me. I noticed Hiro, looking proudly towards me.

*

I slept better than I can remember, in a real bed with bright white sheets. How happy I was to open the wardrobe upon waking, and find that Mother had been able to save some of my old clothes and shoes! I have laid out my best blue suit, and will wear medium-heeled shoes, the ones that are sensible, but show a bit of toe. I can't help feeling a tinge of joy at the prospect of sliding my legs into stockings, and powdering my face and colouring my lips.

I feel quite ready to face the Commander of the Eighth Division of the Allied Occupation Forces.

Acknowledgements

My late mother, Rosa Hideko Itoh, was the inspiration for this book. Throughout my childhood, I would hear her say, 'When we were in Shanghai…' and some anecdote would follow, giving me the impression that Shanghai was a fun, fascinating place. It was only when I grew up and learned history that I realized my mother had lived in wartime Shanghai. Life could not have been so rosy, yet to her, the place remained magical. I wanted to find out why, and this novel is the result of my quest.

Apart from the few bare facts of my parents' time in Shanghai, such as when they were there and where they lived, and my mother's anecdotes, which usually involved her sister, Tayeko Yamanouchi, the diary and the diarist are my creations. I consulted innumerable books, both fiction and non-fiction, in the pursuit of authenticity, and am indebted to all the authors. Should there be any mistakes or misrepresentations, they are entirely my own.

I am grateful to a number of individuals who lived in Shanghai at the time for their stories, books, photos and maps: the late Arata Ikeda, author of *Kumoribi no Niji* (the 40-year history of the Shanghai Japanese YMCA), the late Eikichi Itoh, Soya Fayers, Kimiko Koi, the late Miyo Tsukamoto, Yunosuke Tsukamoto, and Tsutako Yamamoto for memories of her father. I am grateful to Koichi Itoh, Sachiko (neé Yamanouchi) Itoh, and Masako (neé Yamanouchi) White for their childhood memories. Sachiko was also my guide during our trip to Shanghai, retracing places that lived on in her memory.

Caroline Natzler, through her course at City Lit and her writing workshops, guided me in my transition from historian to novelist. I am immensely grateful to her and my fellow workshop participants for their invaluable comments from beginning to end.

I was assisted by the staff of: The Friends House Library, which houses the Friends Shanghai Committee Minutes and correspondence; Japan's National Diet Library for the microfiche of the newspaper, *Tairiku Shimpo*; and the Diplomatic Archives of the Ministry of Foreign Affairs of Japan for records relating to the repatriation boats.

Many thanks to my friends who read the manuscript for their feedback and support: Maria Arnett, Janet Bacastow, Sir Hugh Cortazzi, Caroline Goulding, Debby Guthrie, Jun Kanai, Junpei Kato, Baroness Helena Kennedy, Daphne Larkin, Janice Nimura, Tsugumi Ota, Chooi Pearson, Steve Richardson, Stewart White and Momoko Williams. Richard Osterweil was a believer and supporter from the very outset. To him I am eternally grateful.

My thanks also go to Ashley Stokes, my editor at The Literary Consultancy, for his wisdom and understanding, and to Paul Norbury for making publication a reality.

Anna Helsby Furniss and Sophie Helsby helped me keep things in perspective with their daughterly asides, especially Sophie, who remained the same age as the diarist, Eiko, as the book progressed, serving as a helpful yardstick. Last but not least, my profound thanks go to my husband, Tommy Helsby, for living through this project with me and providing all the intellectual and domestic support I could wish for.